On the Line

Book 2 of the Rocky Creek Series

KATHRYN ASCHER

Georgia

On the Line

This is a work of fiction. All of the characters, names, incidents, organizations, and dialogue in this novel are either the products of the author's imagination or are used fictitiously.

Published in the United States by BQB Publishing
(Boutique of Quality Books Publishing Company)
www.bqbpublishing.com

Printed in the United States of America

978-1-939371-81-2 (p)
978-1-939371-82-9 (e)

Library of Congress Control Number: 2015904687

Book design by Robin Krauss, www.bookformatters.com
Cover design by Valerie Tibbs, www.tibbsdesign.com

Other Books

What It Takes
Released: May 27, 2014
by BQB Publishing

Praise for What It Takes

"Kathryn Ascher has written a truly entertaining story with wonderful and loveable characters."

-Bella Lee from Bella's Little Book Blog

"*What It Takes* by Kathryn Ascher is one of these brilliant debut works that make me want for more."

-Claudia B. from My Little Avalon Book reviews

"*What It Takes* has all of the elements in a classic romance novel which appeal to me; believable main characters, a great storyline and a well-crafted villain."

-Sue G. from Lady Celeste Reads Romance reviews

Dedication

For my mom, who introduced me to the romance genre and who is always willing to read anything I write. Thanks for always supporting me and thank you for going the extra mile to make sure this book is as unique as you are.

For Matt, my partner in crime and the wall I bounce ideas off of. Thank you for being my biggest cheerleader and for never letting me give up.

Prologue

Nathan Harris locked the door of his police cruiser and strolled up the sidewalk toward the brick ranch house he'd been called to. He climbed the two steps to the porch then paused to look down both directions of the street as a cool, autumn breeze touched his face. This house belonged to someone he hadn't seen in over six years. But he'd known her almost his whole life, and cared about her since they were in high school. He'd once thought it was love, now he wasn't so certain.

Since she was married to someone else, he wasn't sure it really mattered anymore. He was about to find out.

Taking another step forward, he reached out and opened the screen door, then rapped his knuckles on the wood behind it. The door tentatively opened, and Nathan was greeted by the familiar face that had sporadically haunted his dreams for years. She smiled at him and his heart skipped a beat.

"Nathan," Janelle said as she opened the door wider and stood to the side. "What a surprise. What are you doing here?"

Her voice was like a feather as it slid over him, and he took a step closer. "My mother called me."

Janelle's full lips curled up in a smile as she turned into the house. "Nancy, did you need to see Nathan?"

"Yes, I did," was the voice that Nathan recognized as his mother's.

Janelle motioned for him to come in.

"Any idea why she called?" Nathan muttered, taking his cap off and tucking it under his arm as he slipped past Janelle, catching a whiff of her clean, vanilla scent that sent his mind straight back to high school.

She shook her head. "I have no idea," she whispered as she closed the door behind him.

Nathan walked farther into the room and let his gaze take everything in. He wasn't sure what he'd been expecting, but this was probably not it. Everything was perfect. The books on the bookshelf were perfectly aligned, the baskets on the bottom shelf hid their contents well, any door or drawer on a piece of furniture was closed, the floor and furniture were spotless, and there wasn't a fleck of dust anywhere. The room looked more like a showroom than a room in a house where a toddler lived.

He'd never known Janelle's locker or childhood bedroom to be this neat, and he looked again at the woman he'd grown up with. She looked put together, but upon closer examination, Nathan could see the stress written all over her face. Her laugh lines were deep as they stretched from the corners of her lips and the bags under her eyes were large and dark. Her arms were folded over her chest, her fingers rubbing circles on her arm as she stood by the door, peering out of the window. Nathan saw the slight discoloration under her fingertips and the hairs on the back of his neck raised as his investigative senses began to tingle.

Something wasn't right here.

"Nathan, I'm so glad you could come," his mother said sweetly, and Nathan looked in her direction. She was seated in a rocking chair in the corner, rocking Janelle's sleeping son, smiling innocently at him. Nancy then turned to her own first-born son.

"I only have a few minutes, Mom." Nathan sat on the end of the couch closest to her, setting his uniform cover beside him on the arm. "Did you need something?"

"I do, actually." She shifted the child and leaned forward as she looked down at his angelic face. "Isn't he adorable?" She looked up and met Nathan's raised eyebrow. "I can't wait to have some grandchildren of my own."

"Mom," Nathan said firmly, trying very hard not to roll his eyes at her bluntness. Her only married son, the middle child, was still a newlywed. Nathan knew that Mason had every intention of reproducing, but not any time soon. "You're barking up the wrong tree with that one. Now, why did you call?"

"Well, Janelle was just telling me about all of the things she needs done around the house, and I was wondering if you might be able to help." She looked down at her charge and slowly began to rock the chair.

"Nancy." Janelle suddenly appeared in front of Nathan, and he noticed the hint of panic in her blue eyes. "He doesn't need to help, I'm working on it. I'm sure I'll get through the list."

"Sweetheart, I'm sure you will." His mother leaned back and gave Janelle a toothy grin. "And for every one thing you mark off of that list, two more will pop up. I know how these older houses are, there's always something that needs fixing."

Nathan eyed his mother. "You know I'm always willing to help, but she has a husband. I'm sure he's perfectly capable of doing these tasks himself. Or at least hiring someone who can."

From the corner of his eye, he saw Janelle lower herself onto the coffee table. "He's hardly ever here," she practically whispered, and Nathan focused on her. She gave him a deprecating smile. "He's always working late."

"What about weekends?" Nathan questioned.

"He finds other things to do." Janelle shrugged and looked toward the window behind him.

He couldn't believe what he was hearing. She hadn't said it, but her body language said it all. Richard Wagoner was spending his weekends doing things without her, ignoring the problems in his own house . . . for what?

"Janelle, I think I'm ready to lay Zach down." Nancy stood and Nathan rose to his feet as well.

"Nancy, I can do that," Janelle said as she approached.

"No, no, I already have him." She stepped away from the rocker and closer to Nathan. "Why don't you go fix some coffee and we can indulge in some of the cookies I brought with me."

"Are you sure?" Janelle sounded lost at having his mother volunteer to take care of her child.

"Absolutely." Nancy walked between Nathan and Janelle, toward the bedrooms at the side of the house. "Nathan can help me."

Janelle's wide eyes met his and he shrugged. They both knew better than to argue with his mom; once she'd given a command, it was in everyone's best interest to just go along with it. Besides, Nathan knew that Nancy had been spending a lot of time with Janelle and, for the first time, he was curious to hear what she had to say about Janelle's marriage.

With a nod, Janelle walked in the opposite direction Nancy had gone, and Nathan followed his mother. He found her cooing over Zach, whose eyes were half-heartedly open as he looked up at her. Nathan watched, in awe, as Zach responded to her soft voice and closed his eyes without a sound. Nancy lingered for a moment longer, then stood and faced her son.

"Mom," Nathan said, quickly gathering his thoughts. "Is she okay?"

"She'll be fine," she answered with a wave of her hand. "She's just adjusting to parenthood."

Nathan glanced at the sleeping child. "He's over a year now." How long does it take to adjust?

"I know that, but she's having to do most of it herself. You heard what she said, Richard is never around." Nancy sharply blew out a breath. "It was hard for me when I had you, but at least I had your father around to help carry the load. She has her father, but he can't be here all the time. She needs help, Nathan, and there's only so much I can do."

Nathan frowned. He wanted to help, but Janelle's husband had practically banished him from her life the moment they'd begun dating. If Janelle needed his help, he'd do anything for her. But he also knew that Richard had a temper—Nathan had gotten a black-eye from him their sophomore year as proof. He was afraid of what that temper might do to Janelle if Richard found out Nathan was spending time with her.

"Is he abusive?" Nathan whispered as he took a step toward his mother.

Nancy shook her head. "Not that she's said, but I do have my suspicions." Her eyes became watery as she looked over Nathan's shoulder. "Poor thing deserves so much better."

Nathan couldn't agree more. Janelle seemed nervous and jumpy, almost uncomfortable in her own home. He hadn't missed the way she'd sat on the coffee table, rigid and glancing toward the window every few seconds. When she'd gotten close enough, he'd snuck a quick glance at her arm and seen the discoloration was actually a fading bruise about the size of a thumb. He couldn't stomach the thought of her having more bruises at the moment, or at some point in the future because of him.

"I'm off on Monday," Nathan finally said softly. "Can you be here?"

Nancy's eyes lit up at her son's simple request. "If you need me to."

"I'll help with whatever she needs, just let me know what it is so I can bring some tools with me."

"You will?" Janelle asked softly from behind him.

Nathan turned to find her standing in the doorway with a cup and a bag of cookies, and tears in her eyes. He hated seeing that sad look on her face, and he had the sudden urge to repay the black eye from tenth grade to the bastard who'd given it to him.

"Of course," was all he could manage. "Anything you need."

"Thank you." Janelle stepped into the room and held up the cup. "I know you said you had to get back on duty. I fixed you a coffee to go and a bag of snickerdoodles. They're your favorites, right?"

With a nod, he took the cup from her and then reached for the bag. When their hands brushed, a spark passed from her fingers to his, and he saw her eyes flare for a moment before she looked away.

"Your mom baked them," she said as she stepped backward toward the door.

Nathan looked at his mother and she grinned widely at him. "Enjoy them." She put her hands on his arms and turned him toward the door. "You'll come by the house for dinner this weekend, right?" she asked as she gently pushed Nathan out of the bedroom.

Nathan took the hint and headed toward the front door. "I'll try if nothing big happens. There's a full moon this weekend and you know how crazy people can get."

Janelle's giggle reached him as he picked his cover up off of the arm of the couch. He turned and pecked his mother on the cheek, then told Janelle good-bye as he walked toward the door.

As he strolled back to his police cruiser, hat on head, coffee and cookies in hand, he couldn't help the feeling that a change was coming.

One

Four and a half years later . . .

Janelle Morgan Wagoner walked through the rotating doors of the hospital, and her feet froze when she saw the sea of bodies crowded in the lobby. Some held cameras, others had pads of paper and pens, or little recorders, in hand. They were all watching the television against the wall, but several of them turned to stare at her as she entered the building and began to whisper among themselves.

Nathan Harris, following her, placed his hand on her back and she felt him falter. "What the . . ."

"If Richard weren't already dead, I'd kill him myself," Janelle murmured as a few members of the crowd drew closer, poised to take notes, and their voices grew louder as they began asking questions. A few flashes went off and Janelle tried to avoid making eye contact with anyone.

"Don't say that out loud," Nathan warned, and she turned and scowled at him. He returned her frown and positioned himself by her side as he pushed her through the crowd, blocking her from the mass of people as best he could.

"Well if it weren't for him then none of us would be here right now," she hissed and nodded toward the reporters.

Nathan's eyes narrowed and he pressed his lips together as he shook his head. "And if one of them hears you say that, you could be in a lot of trouble."

Janelle shrugged as they reached the elevator. She pushed the call button, then turned her shoulder toward the wall and faced him. She really couldn't care less what people thought of her right now as she cursed the man that had been her husband for ten years. Because of him, her sister, Kelsey, had briefly died during the surgery she'd had to remove the bullet he'd put in her leg. Her son was at home with her father, hiding in his room, too afraid to come out because *his* father had kidnapped him and held him hostage. Her mother was now in mourning and not speaking to her.

That was probably the only positive thing Janelle had going for her at the moment.

"Did you sleep last night?" Nathan murmured softly.

She'd been so relieved to see his face this morning when he'd arrived at her house and told her he was going to the hospital. He was here to question Kelsey and Kelsey's boyfriend, Patrick, about the previous night's events. Nathan rarely wore a police uniform now that he was a detective, but he kept his dark, brown hair fairly short, closer on the sides and a little longer on the top. Not that Janelle could complain. He looked almost as good in his three-piece suit, with his cool attitude and his sidearm hidden under his coat. His calm demeanor soothed her overwrought nerves, and it wasn't the first time she was thankful to have him by her side.

Janelle turned her head toward the television hanging on the wall closest to her, and her heart stuttered when she saw Kelsey's name across the bottom of the screen. Janelle caught the call letters in the corner of the screen and saw it was one of the major networks.

"That can't be good," she said as she straightened away from the wall.

Nathan looked over his shoulder, following her gaze, then turned his body toward the crowd. "No," he agreed quietly as a hush fell over the crowd.

"We've been keeping you up-to-date on what happened with up-and-coming Hollywood actress Kelsey Morgan and have a new revelation to our story. Our news desk received a manifesto, sent to us by Richard Wagoner, detailing his plans, and reasons, for what happened in that dark cabin by the lake last night. We're going to share its gruesome details with you now."

Janelle shuddered at the way the blonde anchorwoman seemed to be gleefully announcing the events of one of the darkest moments in her life. The night her husband kidnapped her son, Zach, and nearly killed her sister. He'd planned to kill Zach as well, but thanks to Patrick, Zach had survived with only a slight physical injury. The emotional toll had yet to be measured.

Richard's face appeared and took up a majority of the screen. He looked serene, resolved, relaxed, and gave a sad smile to the camera as he launched into his speech. *"Ladies and gentlemen, by the time you see this, I will be dead. But first, let me introduce myself. My name is Richard Wagoner. While I may be a nobody to most of you, I am a husband, father, son, and brother. To one special woman that you all know and love, I am a brother-in-law."*

He held up one of Kelsey's most recent headshots. *"Yes, this lovely lady is my wife's sister, Kelsey Morgan. You know her as 'the girl next door,' 'America's newest sweetheart,' 'A rising star.' I know better. Kelsey Morgan isn't what she seems. She's a selfish, inconsiderate, heartless bitch. And she has a secret."*

Richard held up an eight-by-ten school picture of Zach and Janelle's eyes widened slightly.

"This is Zach, the boy I've been raising as my son."

"We have to go," Janelle said, panic tightening in her chest as she turned to the elevator and pushed the call button again. She poked it repeatedly until Nathan laid his hand on top of hers.

"That won't help," he said calmly.

"It can't hurt," Janelle snapped and looked toward the hallways on both sides of her, searching for a stairwell. The door opened, and Janelle ignored the three people already on and quickly stepped through the doors.

Once Nathan had joined her, she pushed the button for Kelsey's floor. Janelle knew what was coming. Richard was about to share Kelsey's secret with the world. Kelsey would be devastated, and Janelle had to be there for her when that bomb was dropped.

"What's going on? Why did he hold up Zach's picture?" Nathan asked.

Janelle tilted her head at him. "You know why. He's about to tell the world that Zach is Kelsey's biological son. And he'll probably blame her for all of his problems in the process."

"Bastard," Nathan muttered, almost to himself.

Janelle wanted to laugh, but couldn't. Her eyes were wide as she watched the numbers climb to her sister's floor. Did Patrick know the truth? She couldn't remember what she might have said to him the night before, when he'd come by her house looking for Kelsey. Had he said he knew, or had she only assumed he did? What would he do if she hadn't told him yet? Janelle needed to be by her sister's side, and this elevator wasn't moving fast enough.

When the doors opened again, Janelle stepped off and saw the television hanging over the nurse's station. Richard's face was still staring out at her, and a chill ran down her spine. There was no glazed look in his eyes, no slur in his speech. He was stone cold sober. She had not seen her husband sober in several years. The idea that he had planned last night's events in a clear-headed state made it all the more frightening. Janelle began to feel numb, and her eyes were still so rounded they almost hurt.

"As most of you know, my darling sister-in-law has a big movie coming out and will be attending the premiere. I'm sure she'll be on top of the world. But while she's living it up on the red carpet in LA, I'll be taking her son. By the time they realize he's gone, it will be too late. The wheels will already be in motion. I'll take Zach on a little trip, and when we reach our destination, I'll summon Kelsey to join us. As we wait, I'll tell dear Zach all about his wonderful mommy and how she abandoned him shortly after he was born."

"C'mon," Nathan said as he laid his hand on the small of Janelle's back and urged her down the hall. Richard's words continued to follow them.

"Once Kelsey arrives, the fun will begin. For the last five years, I've suffered because of her. It's time for me to return the favor. She's become a little spoiled, and I want her to understand how hard life really is. I want her to see the look on Zach's face when I tell him the truth, that she didn't want him. That she thought being an actress was more important than being a mother. In typical Kelsey fashion, I imagine she'll lie to her son, but I'll make her tell the truth. When I've tortured her enough mentally, then I'll show her what physical pain is . . . I'm going to shoot her."

Janelle moved a little faster, despite her weakened knees. She quietly opened her sister's door and found Kelsey sitting on her bed, as pale as the sheets covering her as she watched the train wreck on the television; Patrick sat beside her with his arm around her shoulder. He glanced briefly at Janelle as she entered.

"I won't kill her. That would be too easy. But what I will do is make her unable to stop anything that comes next. Remember poor, sweet Zach? I know, you probably think I've ruined him by telling him the truth, so I will be merciful. I'll make sure his mother is watching as I snuff out his life.

"He'll cry for her, and she won't be able to do anything about it. She'll have to sit helplessly by as she watches the life drain from her child's eyes. The fun won't be over when he's gone. You see, I have nothing else to live for. As a bonus, I intend to

make her watch me die too. I hope to leave her with the memory of our deaths and the guilt from the knowledge that she set all of this in motion six short years ago.

"So, I'm sorry to say, I won't be around to answer any of your questions. But being the kind of person she is, desperate for attention, I'm sure Kelsey would be more than happy to answer them for you.

"But I have one more loose end to tie up."

Janelle stepped farther into the room and she saw the crease in her sister's brow deepen as she turned to Patrick. Janelle stared up at the television, disgust and awe clawing at her as she watched her husband continue to ramble. What else could he possibly have to say?

"You see, I've recently begun to suspect my wife was developing some of her sister's less-than-sterling habits. Living with her, how could she not? However, what I recently discovered was far more shocking than even my suspicions had prepared me for. It seems that the daughter I'd been helping her raise isn't mine either."

He held up a picture showing a police car in front of the house Janelle had shared with him. Her heart slowed. Beside it he held up a photograph of a police car in front of Kelsey's house and Janelle's heart stopped completely.

He wouldn't.

"Ladies and gentlemen, Officer Nathan Harris, one of our trusted boys in blue has been taking his job description a little too seriously. It seems he thought he needed to protect and serve my wife, and he did it quite thoroughly. If I was a betting man, I would put money on him being little Zoe's father."

He did.

And it was worse than Janelle had expected.

"What did he just say?" Nathan's voice floated to her on a wave of nausea.

Janelle slowly turned her head to the thundercloud that was his face.

"Oh no," she heard Kelsey mutter from across the room.

This wasn't going to end well.

Two

Janelle stood frozen to the floor in the middle of her sister's hospital room, trying to ignore the rushing of blood from her head to her feet. It would figure that her recently deceased, formerly soon-to-be-ex-husband would find one more way to throw a monkey wrench into her life. She couldn't believe she'd just heard him announce to the world that she'd had an affair. She hadn't been aware that he'd even known about it.

"I think I need to sit down," a voice sounding a lot like hers whispered into the room.

"Patrick, give her a chair," Kelsey said quietly, and he promptly rose from his seat on the bed next to her.

Janelle looked up, met her sister's emerald-green gaze, and slowly made her way around the foot of Kelsey's hospital bed. Patrick gently took her elbow and helped her toward the chair, then sat back down on the edge of the bed next to Kelsey.

"Janelle, are you okay?" Kelsey asked.

Janelle nodded as she lowered herself onto the seat.

"Janelle," Nathan said sternly from the foot of the bed, staring at Janelle with his arms folded across his chest. "What did that bastard just say?"

"Nathan, I think we all heard him." Patrick glanced warningly at Nathan as he put his palms up. "Give her time."

"Stay out of this. I want to know if what he said was true," Nathan snapped and Janelle looked at him. His hazel eyes held a mixture of rage and betrayal. His rounded jaw was clenched tight and his thick, dark-brown eyebrows came together over his straight nose.

Janelle felt the sting of tears in her eyes. She hadn't wanted him to find out this way, but until the divorce was finalized, she hadn't wanted to tell him the truth. And it hadn't been an easy thing to keep from him. After Richard attacked Kelsey during Patrick's visit in December, Patrick had all but hired Nathan to keep watch over her family. He'd been around almost every day. She'd watched him play with and interact with his daughter, not even knowing Zoe was his. But the opportunity to tell him the truth had never presented itself.

"Yes," Janelle whispered. "Zoe is yours."

"Are you sure?" Nathan said.

"Hey," Kelsey snapped. "If she tells you Zoe is yours, then Zoe is yours. How dare you doubt her?"

"Kels, it's okay." Janelle squeezed her sister's fingers.

When Kelsey had found herself pregnant in college, her boyfriend at the time, Tim, had questioned the baby's paternity. She knew Nathan's reaction must remind Kelsey of the way Tim had reacted to finding out about her pregnancy with Zach. And she understood better now the disbelief and nausea her sister must have felt because of Tim's words.

"It's not okay. That has to be one of the most hurtful things a man can ask a woman," Kelsey practically spat at Nathan.

"How could I not ask?" Nathan held his hands out to his side. "Zoe is almost three, and this is the first I've heard about it." He looked at Janelle again. "I asked you point blank when you were pregnant if you were carrying my child. You lied to me. How could you do that? How could you keep her from me?"

"Nathan, I was married to Richard, I had no other choice," Janelle said.

"Really? No other choice? How about leaving him as soon as you found out we were expecting a baby?" Nathan opened his mouth and promptly closed it again. Janelle felt her stomach churn. "Did you know before you ended things with me?"

A tear fell down Janelle's cheek before she dipped her head. Nathan stepped back like she'd slapped him, his lip curling as his eyes widened.

"I'm sorry. I'm so sorry." Janelle's bottom lip trembled as he turned away from her. "Nathan, I wanted to tell you. I just never had the nerve."

"In the past three years, you didn't have the nerve to tell me? What about every day for the past three months, Janelle? I guess you thought I hadn't missed enough time with *my daughter*? I guess you thought it was okay for her to think that monster husband of yours was her father?" Nathan growled as he came closer.

Patrick rose to stand between them.

Nathan's angry stare never left Janelle's face. "I thought I meant something to you. I thought we finally had a chance, Janelle. How could you do this to me? To us?"

His words ripped through her, tearing into her chest as tears slid down her cheeks. He made her sound so cruel and selfish.

Kelsey held her hand up to stop Nathan from coming any closer. "Patrick, I need to talk to my sister," she said sweetly. "Alone."

Janelle laid her forehead on the mattress of the bed.

"Kelsey, you know I don't want to leave this room," Patrick said, almost pleadingly.

"I'm not going anywhere until I have answers," Nathan argued.

Janelle heard the rattle of frustration in Kelsey's exhale.

"Patrick," Kelsey said slowly, "I'm not going anywhere. We just need to have some girl time."

"You hadn't even told your sister about us, had you?" Nathan's voice was taut with his anger.

Janelle shook her head.

"Well, I guess that tells me how you really felt, thanks," Nathan snapped and sounded farther away.

A few more tears fell onto the bedsheet.

"Patrick, I need to talk to you anyway and get a statement about yesterday's events."

"Fine, let's get this over with," Patrick mumbled. Janelle felt the bed shift and heard the quick little kiss Kelsey gave Patrick then listened as the men left the room. She heard the door latch and felt Kelsey's hand on the back of her head, stroking it soothingly as they remained quiet.

After a while, Kelsey patted Janelle's head twice and took her hand away. When Janelle sat up, Kelsey looked at her hands in her lap, her brow furrowed. "Do you remember when I told you about the script for the movie I was considering doing with Patrick?"

Janelle nodded. "Yes," she whispered.

"I told you that I hated the idea of my character, a married woman, having an affair with a married man." Kelsey looked at Janelle and her head dipped again. "Do you remember what you said to me about that?"

The corner of Janelle's mouth lifted slightly. "I believe I said that sometimes life doesn't happen the way you expect it to, especially where love is concerned. And that sometimes it gets messy and isn't as perfect as you want it to be . . ."

". . . and neither are people," Kelsey finished for her, and they both nodded and smiled. Kelsey quickly sobered. "All this time I thought you were talking about Richard, but you weren't, were you?"

Janelle moved her head from side to side and looked away.

"Oh, J," Kelsey sighed as she held a tissue to her sister.

Janelle took it and dabbed at her eyes before blowing her runny nose. What did her sister think of her now? She'd always tried to be a good role model for Kelsey while being someone she would feel comfortable coming to whenever she had a problem. Would this change Kelsey's opinion of her?

"You know this is probably all my fault, right?" Kelsey said.

Janelle's head snapped around to look at her sister. Kelsey's expression was completely serious, but there was a mischievous gleam in her eye. Janelle was reminded of their brother, who had died when he was in college. "Your eyes sparkle like Sean's used to when he was up to something."

Kelsey grinned widely. "You really think so?"

Janelle tried not to laugh at her sister's obvious appreciation of the comparison. "What do you mean this is probably all your fault? You weren't here when I had the affair."

"Exactly." Kelsey pointed her index finger at Janelle.

"Are you doped up?" Janelle asked. "You seem too easily amused by this."

Kelsey's head turned away and Janelle watched as her eyes followed the tube from the needle in her arm and to the bag of saline solution. Janelle's eyes narrowed speculatively on the bag, and she studied it. It didn't look like there were additional meds attached to it, but Janelle had no idea what the nurse may have given Kelsey before she'd entered the room.

Kelsey shrugged as she turned to face Janelle. "Possibly," she stated. "And, no, I don't think this is funny."

"Then how are you to blame for this? This has nothing to do with you."

"My lack of presence or involvement has never stopped our mother from blaming things on me before, why would she stop now?" Kelsey raised an eyebrow.

Janelle stared at Kelsey as the room began to spin. *Oh goodness*, she had almost forgotten about her mother.

"Exactly," Kelsey said and laid her hand on Janelle's arm. "So, I'd like to know what I'm taking the credit, or blame, for." Kelsey lay back against her pillow.

Janelle sighed and leaned into the back of the chair. She let her mind drift to the time before the affair. After a bit of reflection, she looked at Kelsey and smiled. "You know, if Mom wants to blame anyone for the affair, she should start with herself."

"Why's that?" Kelsey tried to roll to her side, grimaced, and stopped where she was.

"When Zach was about six months old, Richard started to stay at work later and later, and I reached a breaking point. I called her and asked her if she could come over so I could take a shower and clean the house a bit. Do you know what she said?"

Kelsey slowly shook her head.

"She said that I'd made the decision to take on the responsibility of your child without asking for her advice, so now I could deal with it without her help."

Kelsey's eyes widened. "You're kidding. I thought she'd gotten over that after Zach was born?"

"Only when you were around. She wanted you to think that everything was just fine without you here." Janelle crossed her arms and slid into her seat a bit.

"Figures," Kelsey mumbled. "So what happened next?"

"I dealt with it the best I could, but the house was still always a mess, Zach was starting to get into everything, Richard was later and later coming home and starting to smell like alcohol when he did, and I was exhausted. Just before Zach's first birthday, Nathan's mom, Nancy, stopped by the house to see the baby and to chat. The house was filthy, I hadn't showered, and Zach was fighting a nap when she got there, so I almost didn't let her in." Janelle looked up at the white ceiling tiles and smiled a little. "And, as usual, she pushed her way in, without being pushy about it. And when she saw the house and my appearance, she gave me a hug, took Zach from me, and told me to go take a shower."

"I always liked her."

Janelle nodded her agreement. Having grown up with Nathan and his two younger brothers, Janelle, Kelsey, and their brother Sean had spent their fair share of time as children with Nancy Harris. She didn't have daughters and she'd always doted on the Morgan girls. If she knew the girls were coming, she'd bake cookies for them, and if they surprised her with a visit, they'd bake with her. Janelle could still remember occasionally wishing Nancy were her mother and would sometimes escape to Nancy's house for cookies and tea without Mary's knowledge.

"Do you know what I did first?" Janelle asked with a laugh. "I cried," she answered soberly. "I cried, and she wrapped me up in a big hug, let me get it out, then shooed me away for my shower and told me to take as long as I wanted. When I got out, she had Zach asleep on a blanket on the floor in the living room as she picked up around him. While she did that, I cleaned up the kitchen, and when we were done we sat on the couch, had coffee and cookies, and just talked. She reassured me that every first baby is a difficult adjustment, but I'd get the hang of it."

"That's awesome," Kelsey said. "So, how did that lead to an affair with Nathan? I'm sure she didn't just bring him over one day and say 'Hey, let my son help fill your needs while I babysit.'"

"You're horrible!" Janelle said as she suppressed a slight smile and Kelsey simply shrugged. "If I had a pillow, I'd throw it at you."

Kelsey pulled a pillow from under her head and held it out to her sister. "Just be careful, the nurse is really scary."

Janelle took the pillow and swatted her with it as Kelsey re-settled herself, wincing slightly.

"It was nothing like that. It's hard to explain, really. It's just that she began to come over every two days or so, she'd help me straighten up and then we'd just chat. She'd catch me up on local gossip and I'd keep her updated on you. Nathan and Mason even started calling me if they were looking for her or stopping by on their lunch break to see her if they knew she was there. Even when Dad would come over, he'd chat with her like it was normal for her to be there." Janelle placed the pillow behind her head as she laid it on the back of the chair. "One day, probably three months later or so, I was in the middle of trying to fix the garbage disposal when she showed up. It was something I'd been after Richard to do, so of course it hadn't gotten done. She called Nathan."

"Little matchmaker," Kelsey said, smiling.

"Maybe," Janelle replied with a shrug. "Well, he fixed it for me and asked if there was anything else that needed attention."

"Other than you?"

"Would you stop it?" Janelle said with an exasperated sigh. "It wasn't like that."

"I'm still waiting for you to tell me how it *was,* Janelle. So far, I'm not getting any heat at all from this story. It's all about Nathan's mother, not Nathan." Kelsey yawned as she raised the head of the bed.

"That's the point. It wasn't any one moment that did it. Nathan has always been my friend. After that day, he started coming by more often. He began to call after work to see if I needed anything. He'd come over and have dinner with me and keep me company as late as he thought he could without setting tongues wagging. He'd leave around ten, and Richard would still not be home until two or three in the morning." Janelle's voice faded as she reflected on that time in her life. "Actually, it *was* one moment."

"Really? What happened?" Kelsey began to sit up and tried to hide the pain. Janelle stood up and helped Kelsey adjust as she tried to remember everything. Once Kelsey was adjusted and comfortable, Janelle sat on the edge of the bed and faced her sister.

"It was one night he'd had to work later than usual, but he still called me when he got off to make sure I'd eaten and to see if I needed anything. I told him I needed a drink and a good movie, and he showed up with a six pack of hard cider and *Steel Magnolias* on DVD," Janelle said with a chuckle.

"Good man." Kelsey grinned up at her sister.

Janelle nodded. "He sat beside me on the couch and placed a box of tissues between us. He handed me the first tissue as the first tear fell, and I think I spent the rest of the movie thinking about this man beside me more than I paid attention to the movie. I think that was the moment he became more than just 'Nathan, the friend I'd grown up with' and became 'Nathan, the man who . . .'" Janelle sighed, "'who filled so many needs.' He was taking care of me the way Richard was supposed to be without asking for anything in return. He just . . . he just did it."

Janelle looked out the window and remembered all the times he'd just been there the moment she'd needed him, all the times he'd play with Zach while she made them all dinner, all the times he would fix something around the house she'd been nagging Richard to fix for weeks, if not months, after only being told about it once. She couldn't remember when or how they'd slipped into that pattern. She just knew that she'd loved feeling normal for a change. She'd felt, then, that Nathan belonged in her life.

If she were honest with herself, she still felt that way.

"I guess some people would have considered that part of the affair, too," Janelle said with a curl of her lip. She hated thinking of their relationship as scandalous, even though everyone would now see it that way. "But it was still a few weeks after that before we made love."

"And Richard didn't know?" Kelsey asked.

"I didn't think he did." Janelle looked at her sister. "Obviously, I was wrong."

"How long did it last?"

Janelle tilted her head to the side and looked at her lap. "Six months, more or less. I found out I was pregnant with Zoe just before Zach's second birthday. I knew it wasn't Richard's baby, that wasn't possible. I've never been so torn about a decision as I was about whether to stay with a husband who ignored me or leave him for the man I loved."

"You still love him." It wasn't a question from Kelsey.

"Am I that obvious?" One corner of Janelle's mouth lifted.

"Only to those who know you well." Kelsey touched Janelle's arm and squeezed. "Does Nathan know?"

"I don't know, I never told him. I had to act fast, before too much time passed in the pregnancy. I ended it with Nathan and seduced Richard when he got home all in the same night." Janelle shuddered at the memory of that night. "The women in this family do everything we can to make our marriages work," Janelle said, mocking her mother's tone. "You know how I feel about that idiom."

Kelsey rolled her eyes. "That ideal has done nothing for us. Is that why you called it off with Nathan?"

"As much as I didn't want to, I didn't see where I had much choice."

"Why?" asked a male voice as the door closed.

Janelle looked up and watched Patrick stride into the room and directly to Kelsey's side. Without a word, he took her hand and then turned his gaze on Janelle.

"Why didn't you have a choice?" Patrick expanded on his first question as he leaned against the rail on the opposite side of the bed from Janelle.

"Where would I have gone? I couldn't move in with Nathan while I was still married to Richard. Kelsey hadn't bought her house yet and was spending most of her time in LA, saving up to buy it. Dad would have gladly taken Zach and me in, but Mom probably would have put us on the street as soon as she could." Janelle shrugged and smiled weakly at him.

"How do you know that?" Patrick frowned, and his gaze bounced between the sisters.

Janelle looked at Kelsey, her question in her eyes. Did Patrick not know enough about her pregnancy to know the answer to that?

"I haven't had the time to give him much detail," Kelsey muttered as she looked toward her feet, color rising to her cheeks.

Janelle met Patrick's stare. "Mom disowned Kelsey when she came home from college. Richard and I took her in because she had nowhere else to go. Dad came to my house every day to see Kelsey, but Mom refused. And when Mom invited us for dinner, she only meant Richard and me. We brought Kelsey one time and Mom was blatantly rude until Dad said something to her about it, then she veiled her insults or only got her digs in when Dad was in another room. Much like she does now."

Patrick's eyes filled with anger as he looked at Kelsey, but Janelle knew it wasn't directed at her. "So, you thought she'd do the same to you?"

"I knew she'd do the same to me. If I had told her the truth, she'd have disowned me and possibly Zach, too," Janelle stated sadly.

"Why?" Patrick asked again.

"Because she still sees him as my mistake," Kelsey answered softly. She looked up at Janelle and smiled weakly. "And that is why she'll blame me for the affair. And Richard's problems. And whatever else she decides to throw at me this week."

"And you're okay with this?" Janelle questioned and Kelsey nodded. "Why?"

Kelsey sighed. "J, I died last night."

"Kelsey," Patrick said sternly.

"Oh hush." Kelsey swatted Patrick's arm. "It's not like it didn't happen, and not talking about it isn't going to change anything." She looked at Janelle again. "But what it did do is put things into perspective. Very clearly. There's no more pussyfooting around that woman for me, doing that is part of what led to last night. I'll happily take her blame, crumple it up, and throw it back at her. She's always considered me the rebel, so I may as well give credence to her beliefs."

Kelsey turned and looked at Patrick, sliding her hand in his. She lifted his hand to her cheek as they stared silently at each other, and Janelle felt a little out of place.

Still staring at Patrick, Kelsey softly added, "I know what's important to me, and I'm going to do everything I can to hold on to it for as long as possible."

Janelle felt a twinge of guilt at her own actions. She wished she'd had her sister's determination when she'd found out she was pregnant. Maybe things would have turned out differently with Nathan. She looked around the room. Speaking of which . . .

"Where is Nathan?" Janelle asked as she looked at Patrick.

Patrick met her gaze. "He got called to the station." He sighed deeply. "And I'm afraid we need to talk. We have a problem."

"What kind of problem?" Janelle asked as she watched Patrick and Kelsey exchange ominous looks.

"I just got a call from Xavier," Patrick began, and Kelsey groaned as he turned his attention on her.

"Who's Xavier?" Janelle questioned.

"My agent."

"What did he want?" Kelsey slid under the covers and laid her head against the pillow.

"He's gotten a few calls already regarding you and me." Patrick ran the back of his hand across Kelsey's forehead. "People have started to make the connection between us. They've heard that we left the premiere party together and asked if I had travelled with you. He's trying to put them off, but that little manifesto of Richard's," he pointed to the television, "has gone viral, so we won't be able to avoid the questions much longer."

"That explains the crowd in the lobby," Janelle stated and looked at her sister's face.

Kelsey's eyes were closed as she brought her hand up to cover them. Janelle's confusion slowly shifted to a slight panic. She wasn't sure she understood what this meant for her or the kids, but could tell it wouldn't be good.

"I'm so sorry, Kelsey," Patrick said as he propped his elbows on the bed. "You avoided dating me so you could avoid publicity. Now it seems like Richard has thrust us into the spotlight."

Kelsey waved his words away and looked at him with a tight smile. "We knew after the premiere that it would only be a matter of time. This attention isn't your fault, and we couldn't have predicted it."

"But the paparazzi will be all over you guys." He looked at Janelle. "All of you."

Janelle stood and walked to the window. So, not only had her husband kidnapped her son, tried to kill her sister, and aired their dirty laundry all over the news, now they'd have to deal with cameras and reporters in their faces. How long would that last? How intrusive would they be? How would she protect the kids?

She peered out the window at the gray skies and pulled her shoulders up. "How do we handle this?"

Three

Nathan Harris walked into the police station, ignoring the stares and whispers that followed him toward his captain's office. He hated that he'd been called away in the middle of his interview with Patrick. He hated even more that he'd had to leave the hospital without talking to Janelle. He wanted answers from her. After everything they'd been through, he felt he deserved them.

He'd been in turmoil since that night last May when he'd answered the call for a domestic dispute and Janelle had been the victim. He was thankful that she could immediately move out of her husband's home and into her sister's. When Kelsey had called Nathan directly in December because Richard had attacked her, he'd been tense, but also slightly relieved that Kelsey had been the target of his fury and not Janelle. His relief had caused him a minor bit of guilt, though. Kelsey was, and had always been, almost like a little sister to him.

His tension was further alleviated when Kelsey had asked him to keep watch over her house and her family after that incident. He'd been more than happy to protect Janelle and the children, even if he'd had to do it from a distance.

This morning he had woken up feeling exhausted and stressed from the events of the night before, but, for the first time in months, also slightly relaxed and borderline elated. Earlier, with every intention of going to see Kelsey to question her about what happened in the cabin before he'd arrived, he'd gone to Janelle's house, simply to see if she needed anything. Without hesitation, she'd asked for a ride to see Kelsey, and it almost felt like they'd gone back in time. Back to just before she'd chosen to try to work things out with Richard.

That had been one of the worst days in his life. He couldn't say he was surprised. She'd never said she would leave Richard, had never even hinted at it either. He'd been the one building their future on the hopes and dreams he'd harbored since high school. He'd gotten out of bed this morning with the faintest hope that those dreams might still come true.

Now he had no idea where they stood.

And he wouldn't be able to ask her until he knew what his captain needed. So, he'd see what the captain had to say and go back to the hospital to get Janelle as soon as he could. Then they could have their talk and she could explain herself.

He blew out a breath and hoped this wouldn't take long as he rapped once on the mahogany door in front of him. He waited for the muffled "Come in" before he turned the knob and entered the office.

"Ah, Detective Harris, come in and close the door please." Captain Bruce Little sat behind his desk and folded his hands on the papers in front of him as Nathan entered the room. Just below his whitened hairline, his brow was wrinkled with more than age. Behind his glasses, his eyes narrowed sharply on Nathan.

Nathan immediately knew he was in trouble. Captain Little had served on the police force with Nathan's father and had known him since he was a boy. Even at work, he was just as likely to call Nathan by his first name as his last. But the way the captain used Nathan's rank coupled with the look on his face was a sure sign that he'd called Nathan in for a reason, and it was serious.

Nathan closed the door and took the seat across the desk from his captain and placed his hands on his legs. And waited. The longer he had to wait, the more trouble he was in. Lucky for him, he only counted to twenty before Captain Little stood and moved to look out of the window behind him.

The captain grasped his own wrist behind his back as he spoke. "Have you seen the news today?"

Nathan's brow furrowed as he slowly answered, "Yes."

"Are Mr. Wagoner's accusations true?"

"Which ones?" Nathan asked. He felt pretty certain he knew which ones the captain was referring to, but was uncertain why he would be asking.

Captain Little turned and raised an eyebrow at Nathan. "Regarding you and Mrs. Wagoner."

Nathan suppressed a shudder. Even though she'd been married to that man for nearly ten years, he still hated hearing Janelle referred to with Richard's last name. Especially now that he was dead.

"Well?"

Nathan met his captain's glare and nodded. "Yes, sir. Janelle and I did have a brief affair."

"I try not to get involved with my officers' personal lives, but what you do *on* the clock is my business. Did this happen at any point while you were on duty?"

Nathan searched his memories. "It's probable."

"I should think so." Captain Little turned around and folded his arms across his chest. "The man had pictures of your squad car outside of the residence he shared with his wife and outside of her sister's residence where she now lives."

"I can explain." Nathan rose and walked around his chair. He placed his hands on its back and stared at the captain. "Janelle and I grew up together and have been friends for a long time. Yes, several years ago, before the affair began, I would occasionally visit her at home while I was on my lunch break. Nine times out of ten, though, my mother was there visiting her as well, so I'm sorry but I didn't think that visiting a friend on my lunch break was a big deal."

"It is when you're in an official police vehicle, Harris." Captain Little walked to the front of his desk and leaned against it. "That explains the pictures in front of Mr. Wagoner's home, so how do you explain the most recent pictures?"

"Mr. Wagoner attacked Kelsey Morgan in her home in December," Nathan started.

Captain Little held up his hand. "Yes, I'm well aware of his criminal record. I'm also aware of the fact that she filed a restraining order to prevent that from happening again," he stated calmly.

"That may be true, but it took us twenty minutes to arrive on the scene after she called. And we both know that a restraining order won't protect anyone if the person it's been filed against is determined to do them harm. Given the fact that Mr. Wagoner kidnapped his son and nearly killed Miss Morgan in that cabin last night, I would wager it's a pretty safe bet that, had the opportunity presented itself, he would have done more harm to Miss Morgan, Mrs. Wagoner, or one, or both, of the children," Nathan said. His heart raced at the thought of Janelle or one of the children coming to harm because they'd been left unprotected. It nauseated him that the worst had very nearly happened.

"But why were you there, in a patrol car? You've been a detective for two years and haven't had a patrol car of your own for eighteen months." Captain Little crossed his arms as he stared at Nathan.

"Miss Morgan's boyfriend happened to be at her home at the time of the incident in December. When he had to leave, to ease his concerns, she asked me to help keep an eye on her family. I felt like a patrol car would be more of a deterrent, and more noticeable, than my personal vehicle." Nathan shrugged and looked down at his hands, his knuckles white as he gripped the back of his chair.

He'd known he wasn't completely following the rules when he'd borrowed the car. But asking an on-duty officer to perform a stakeout every day would have been bending the rules a bit too much. When he'd been asked why he needed the car, he'd fibbed a little and told them it was for surveillance for a case. Given his seniority on the force, no one had questioned him further. He'd hated not telling the whole truth, but the knowledge that he was doing it to protect Janelle and the children had always prevented him from feeling guilty.

"Did you do that during your shift?" Captain Little questioned.

"Occasionally," Nathan answered honestly.

If Richard had been predictable, only showing up to torment his wife at the same time each day, or each week, it would have been easier for Nathan to schedule his stakeout. But Richard's behavior had become erratic and progressively more violent. Because of that, Nathan had been hesitant to let Janelle and the kids remain unprotected for long stretches of time.

Captain Little rose, walked around his desk, and began to pace. Nathan counted three complete back and forths before the captain spoke again.

"Did it ever occur to you that while you were protecting your mistress and her family that your services, and the squad car you were inappropriately using, could have been used better elsewhere? If I'm not mistaken, you have three cases you've been working on for the past four months." Captain Little's stern voice began to increase in volume. "Three other domestic dispute cases that should have been wrapped up already."

"And I have been working on them. All I need to do is file the paperwork." Nathan held his palms up.

"It should have been on my desk months ago. You, yourself, told me when you got the reports that they were open-and-shut cases. This behavior is unacceptable, Detective. You've let your personal relationship with this woman come before your job. A job in which you took an oath to serve and protect *everyone*, not just the woman you're sleeping with and her family." The captain was practically yelling now.

"But—" Nathan began.

"No! There are no 'buts.' This is disappointing to say the least." Captain Little inhaled deeply, stopped pacing, and glared directly at Nathan. "You leave me no choice. You're suspended without pay, pending an internal investigation into your recent behavior and your involvement in yesterday's incident."

The air rushed from Nathan's lungs, and he sat on the arm of the chair. How could this be happening? All he'd meant to do was keep her safe. "I wasn't involved in yesterday's incident, and I have the investigation to do for it."

"No, I'm afraid you don't. You're off the case, and any witnesses you've interviewed will have to be re-interviewed by someone else. Turn in your badge and sidearm." Captain Little slid an empty, white plastic basket across the desk. Nathan stared at it as if he hadn't heard what he was supposed to do with it.

He looked up at his captain and anger bubbled up inside him. "Are you kidding me? This is ridiculous." He shook his head. "If you want me off this one case, then I won't be involved in it, but you're seriously going to suspend me? For what? For protecting a woman and her children from her abusive estranged husband? Isn't that my job?"

"No, it's not. It's your job to follow the rules of this department, which don't include taking a spare squad car and having a stakeout without following protocol. Your *job*, Detective, is to investigate cases of domestic dispute that span the entire county, not just one family," Captain Little roared. "Now turn in your badge and your firearm before I permanently suspend you for insubordination."

Nathan clenched his jaw as he pulled his badge out of his pocket and tossed it into the basket on the desk. He took his gun and holster off and laid them in the basket beside his badge. As he turned to leave, Captain Little called to him. Nathan slowly turned to look at his boss.

"One more thing. Until these investigations are over, it would be in your best interest to stay away from Mrs. Wagoner and her family."

Nathan opened his mouth to argue but the captain continued, "All of them. This has to be a fair investigation. There can be no possibility of your influence on their statements or the potential for tampering with the evidence we find."

"I would never do that," Nathan said, offended that Captain Little would even consider that.

"I don't doubt that. However, the fact that you had an affair with Mrs. Wagoner leaves you both open to potential repercussions for your actions." Captain Little walked to the window again and, with his fist grasped behind his back, turned to look at Nathan. "Stay away from them all for both of your sakes."

Nathan held his stare as the captain's words sank in.

"Nathan, I'm not just saying this as your boss," the captain added. "There may be more than just your job on the line here."

Captain Little turned his back on him, and Nathan slowly walked out of the office in a daze.

His first instinct was to go back to the hospital to see Janelle. He wanted to tell her what had just happened to him, especially the captain's last warning. He needed to talk to her about Zoe. He had so many questions he needed to ask her.

But he couldn't do any of that. Richard had managed to find a way to come between them, even after his death.

Not that it mattered anyway. He couldn't be certain that Janelle would want to see him. For the past few months, he'd gotten no indication from her that she still felt anything for him. Sure, she'd welcomed him into her home, allowed him to play with the children, and treated him like he belonged there. But she'd kept him at a distance whenever they were alone. They hardly ever talked anymore. He'd noticed, but had brushed it off as stress about Richard and the divorce.

To make matters worse, he needed to figure out what *he* wanted. Since the affair had begun, he'd always held out hope for them. Even after she'd ended it with him, he'd never given up that one day she'd be strong enough to leave her husband. At the moment, he couldn't help but question their future. She'd lied to him when he'd found out she was pregnant and she'd said the baby wasn't his. She'd continued to keep the truth from him after her separation. Could she be trusted to tell the truth now? Or in the future?

Now, if he understood the captain's final words correctly, there was the possibility that he could be linked to Richard's death. He couldn't stomach the idea of Janelle being put through anything more because of that man. But apparently the best way to protect her would be for him to stay away from her until this investigation was over.

He just hoped it wouldn't take long.

Four

"I really don't want to be here," Janelle said with a sigh as she slammed the door of her minivan and ran her hands through her shoulder length, sandy-colored hair.

"I really don't blame you."

Janelle looked across the hood of the vehicle at Kelsey's friend, Veronica Madison. Veronica had starred in the movie that Kelsey and Patrick had filmed last fall. She and their other co-star, Grayson Reynolds, were with Kelsey at the premiere party for their movie when Janelle had frantically called her about Richard taking Zach. With Patrick, they had followed Kelsey and had been staying in her home ever since.

"You didn't have to come," Janelle stated.

Veronica gave her a slight smile as she walked around the front of the van. "I know, but I wanted to."

"You mean Patrick suggested it." Janelle rolled her eyes. Since they'd had the talk four days ago in the hospital regarding the paparazzi, Janelle had been a little more aware of her surroundings. She'd also noticed the extra vigilance Grayson and Veronica were giving to their surroundings since their return from visiting Kelsey two days ago.

That had only made Nathan's absence all the more noticeable.

She'd expected him to come back to the hospital for her. She had been hoping he would; she wanted to talk to him about everything that had happened between them. She'd wanted to explain her actions regarding Zoe and her marriage. She only hoped that if she ever got the chance, he'd understand and forgive her.

At the moment, she was not confident that would be the case.

He hadn't returned her calls. He hadn't been by the house. He had made no effort in four days to have any contact with her or his newly discovered daughter. It physically hurt her to think that she'd driven him away for good.

Once she left this funeral, maybe she'd try to track him down herself.

"Actually, no. No one asked us," Veronica's chipper voice brought Janelle back to the moment. She'd forgotten the perky, young blonde was with her. "But Grayson and I talked about it and decided that, since Kelsey couldn't come with you, we couldn't let you go it alone. And given where we're going and the revelations the recently deceased made regarding your affair, we thought it would be better if I came with you." Veronica smiled as she stopped beside Janelle. "I promise to be on my best behavior, even if I think your ex-husband was one of the lowest life forms on the planet."

Janelle tried to laugh at that comment, but couldn't quite muster it. Yes, Richard had been a despicable man in the end, but he hadn't always been that bad. She liked to think she never would have married him if he had been. It was the memory of the man she'd loved a long time ago that brought her here now, to his funeral.

"You're probably right," Janelle quietly agreed. "Let's get this over with then, shall we?"

Janelle turned and led Veronica toward the door of the funeral home. She'd waited to arrive as late as she could in the hopes of slipping into a pew in the back of the chapel as the service started, and slipping out again as soon as it ended. Janelle's jaw dropped when she saw that the line stretched from the chapel, through the lobby, and almost to the door she had just entered. She groaned inwardly. There went her chances of going unnoticed.

The number of people there to pay their respects to the man she'd been married to shocked her to her core. She received a few disapproving looks from people she'd known her whole life. Some of the frowns came from people who had known Richard in high school, when he was the life of the party and so charismatic he could charm a smile from a snake without even trying. But most of these people hadn't seen him since. Their scorn washed over her like a hot wave of anger and embarrassment.

They had no idea of the man Richard had become in the fifteen years since they'd seen him last. They didn't know the mental and psychological toll his addictions had taken on him. She had barely recognized him in the end, physically or emotionally; she imagined most of these people wouldn't have been able to point him out in a crowd. And those that had seen him since probably never knew of his alcoholism. To Janelle's knowledge, he'd kept that secret to himself.

She put her head down, didn't look at anyone, and only spoke to Veronica in hushed tones as they made their way through the line. They were walking through the double doors of the chapel when Janelle finally looked up and saw Richard's sister, Martha, barreling toward her with a scowl on her tear-stained face. The anger in her cloudy, blue eyes matched what Janelle had often seen in Richard's.

Janelle swallowed the lump in her throat and fought the urge to run in the other direction.

"How dare you?" Martha whispered loudly. "How dare you show your face here after everything you did to my brother?" Her hands trembled as they rose to her hips. Janelle imagined Martha was resisting the urge to hit her and took a step backward.

"I came to pay my respects—"

"Respect? Don't make me laugh," Martha spat. "You didn't respect him while he was alive, I think it's a little late to start now."

"Martha—"

"I don't want to hear it, Janelle. My brother loved you." Martha's eyes became watery and Janelle had to look away. "He treated you like a princess. He worked his way up in one of the state's largest companies. He slaved away every day for you, so he could give you everything you could possibly want. He did everything for you, and how did you thank him? You made him take in your sister's bastard. And while he was working hard to support the two of you, *you* were having an affair. Richard was third in line at a very prestigious company, and you were sleeping with," Martha's lip curled in disgust, "*a cop*."

Janelle opened her mouth to defend Nathan's character to her arrogant accuser, but Martha continued to berate her.

"Then you were careless enough to get pregnant," Martha shook her head, "and you made poor Richard raise that child as his own too."

"It was—" Janelle started again, only to be interrupted as Martha continued.

"And you had the audacity to accuse him of abusing you so you'd have an excuse to leave." Martha took a step closer, and Janelle pulled her shoulders up and met her angry stare. "You abandoned him a long time ago, you have no right to be here now."

Janelle closed her eyes against the furious tears. The words were true, even if the reasons weren't as cut and dry as Martha wanted to believe. When Janelle opened her eyes and looked around at all of the faces staring at her, a mixture of anger, pity, embarrassment, and disapproval in the crowd, she realized that none of her reasons mattered. She wasn't about to try to explain things with this audience watching. She met Martha's irate gaze and nodded.

"I'm so sorry," she said quietly.

"You should be," came a quiet, unsteady voice from behind Martha.

Martha stepped aside and her frail mother moved forward.

"Gladys," Janelle greeted her former mother-in-law. "I'm—"

Crack!

Janelle's cheek stung as the older woman's hand collided with it, and her head snapped to the side. Janelle heard gasps from the onlookers and felt Veronica's hand on her arm as she immediately put her palm up to her burning cheek and turned her wide-eyed, teary gaze on Gladys.

"You selfish whore," Gladys spat, her soft words stabbing Janelle in the chest. "You meant the world to my son. He gave you everything he could and how did you repay his affection? You forced him to raise two brats that weren't his, and when that wasn't enough you left him with nothing. You took everything he had to give and threw it in his face. All he ever wanted was to make you happy. You can bitch and complain all you want about him being a bad husband, but perhaps you should examine what kind of wife you were to him."

Janelle lowered her hand and closed her eyes. Had Richard really felt that way about her? She hadn't felt loved and adored by him. After Zach came along, she'd felt largely ignored and unwanted. Had she brought that on herself?

"You should leave now," Gladys continued. "Those of us that truly loved him don't want you here."

Janelle stared at Gladys, at her red-rimmed, tired eyes, her messy, long, graying dark hair and the determined press of her lips and looked for the kind woman she'd once respected and loved like a mother. As her eyes traveled over Gladys's shoulder, her jaw dropped. Coming up the aisle toward them all was *her* mother.

Mary Morgan's blue eyes were bloodshot and her cheeks tear-stained as she fixed her glare on her daughter. As she stepped between Gladys and Janelle, she said, "Well, I hope you're happy now." She frowned at Janelle. "They're right. You should have been a better wife. I've been telling you that for months. And now you come here and cause a scene in front of all of these people who actually cared about the man you married more than you did."

Janelle stepped back, feeling Veronica's hand tightening on her arm to steady her and the other hand pressing comfortingly on her back, as tears trickled slowly down her cheeks. She shouldn't be surprised by her mother's words, but they still stung deeply. Her mother had never publicly scolded her for her behavior. She'd always been concerned about the image they portrayed and had always wanted people to believe they were a happy, peaceful family. Mary took a step closer to her daughter and leaned in.

"Go home." Mary stepped back and gave Janelle a look that almost dared her to defy her.

Janelle looked around the crowd and studied their faces. Some of the angry and disapproving faces now had a touch of pity in them, the pitying looks had only grown more sorrowful, and the embarrassed couldn't make eye contact. There was one face, however, that met and held her stare. Mason Harris's green eyes held a look of pity and determination, but also support and strength.

As he turned to the woman by his side, Janelle pulled her shoulders back and held her head high. Veronica took her arm and, without another word for her mother, they turned and walked away, Veronica supporting her as her knees began to weaken as they exited the chapel. As soon as they were outside of the building, Janelle collapsed with her back against the side wall.

"Who were those women?" Veronica asked, staring back at the door of the funeral home with a frown.

"Martha is Richard's sister, Gladys is his mother," Janelle replied automatically.

"And the other one?" Veronica questioned slowly, and Janelle had the feeling she already knew the answer.

Janelle looked squarely at Veronica. "My mother." Veronica pressed her lips together and looked away. Janelle laughed without humor. "You mean Kelsey didn't talk about her? I can't imagine why."

The door opened and Mason came out, followed closely by his wife, Charlotte. He glanced at Janelle and held her gaze for a moment before nodding and looking away. Charlotte looked too and gave Janelle a sympathetic smile and a brief wave as they strolled away.

"Who are they?" Veronica asked, nodding to the couple walking away.

Feeling slightly bolstered by Mason's acknowledgment and the sympathy in his wife's eyes, Janelle stood. "That is one of Nathan's brothers with his wife." Janelle stepped onto the pavement and began walking to the van.

"Is he leaving because of what happened with you in there?" Veronica got into step beside Janelle.

"I don't know. I'm actually surprised he was there at all," Janelle answered as she fished in her purse for her keys. "The Harris boys were never huge fans of Richard's. Nathan and I were friends long before I met Richard, and when they met in middle school they just never really hit it off. And I figure that Mason and Jackson simply followed suit; Nathan didn't like Richard, so they didn't like Richard. If there is another reason they didn't like each other, I'm not aware of the cause."

"I would think it obvious," Veronica stated, and Janelle dropped her keys on the ground. Veronica laughed. "Look, I don't know what it's like in small towns like this one, but I do know that when I was in middle school and high school, liking the same girl was plenty enough reason for boys to fight. Perhaps some of them never grow out of it."

"Veronica," Janelle bent down to pick up the keys, stood back up, and stared at her sister's friend, "Nathan and I didn't have that kind of relationship until a few years ago."

"I never said you did, but I remember what happens when boys like the same girl." Veronica raised an eyebrow as she pursed her lips. "Whether the girl knows about it or not."

Janelle's mouth opened, but no words came out. She tried to stretch her memory but couldn't recall any signs that should have told her how Nathan felt when they were younger. All she knew was that he'd always been there when she'd needed him and she'd taken advantage of that. She didn't know how he'd felt about her twenty years ago, but she did know that he'd cared about her when they'd had the affair. And she'd ruined it, and hurt him in the process.

Her shoulders slumped and tears sprang to her eyes again as she pictured the look of betrayal on his face at the hospital. She'd put that there. Martha and Gladys's words replayed in her mind. She was selfish, too caught up in her own problems to pay attention to how her decisions affected others. Maybe she had done that with Richard. She knew for sure she'd done it with Nathan. And now he'd probably never speak to her again.

Maybe he shouldn't.

But they had Zoe to consider. Nathan would be a good father to her—of that Janelle was certain. If he could never forgive her, perhaps she could at least convince him to be civil so he could have a relationship with his daughter.

"I need to go see my sister," Janelle said as she turned and quickly walked to her van. She hoped Kelsey would have an answer to her problem. Or at least be willing to mediate for her until Nathan was willing to talk to her directly.

"Awesome," Veronica stated as she ran to catch up to Janelle.

Five

Janelle and Veronica were walking toward Kelsey's hospital room as two men in suits walked out of it.

"Can't talk about it, my left foot," Janelle overheard Kelsey say as Janelle reached the door. "Call him and find out what's going on. I don't like this, Patrick, something's not right."

"Sweetheart, relax," Patrick soothed Kelsey as Janelle walked into the room. "Remember what Helen said about you keeping calm."

"What's going on?" Janelle asked, stopping at the foot of the bed. Kelsey looked at her and smiled widely as she held her arms open to her sister. Janelle laughed at the resemblance she saw to Zoe and complied with her sister's unspoken request for a hug.

"Is the funeral over already?" Kelsey asked after pulling away.

"We didn't stay for the funeral," Veronica stated as she seated herself on the air conditioning unit.

"Why?" Patrick looked at Veronica. "Cameras?"

Veronica shook her head. "Mothers." She gave Kelsey and Janelle a pointed look.

"Oh, you met our mother," Kelsey said calmly, leaning against her pillow. "Isn't she delightful?"

"Not an adjective I'd use to describe her," Veronica muttered as she picked her hand up to study her fingernails.

"What did she say?" Kelsey looked at Janelle with a wrinkle in her brow.

Janelle waved her question away as she sat on the edge of the bed. "Nothing that wasn't true. You know how she is."

Kelsey narrowed her eyes on her sister and Janelle looked away. Janelle wasn't about to repeat what had been said in front of Patrick. It was bad enough that Veronica had heard it. Oh, and half of the town.

"I know exactly how she is, and how you try to blow it off even if it hurts."

Janelle felt her sister's hand grasp her wrist, and she looked down at the connection. She slowly nodded. "It's nothing I can't handle," she said. Once her features settled into her natural, relaxed façade, she looked at Kelsey. "Who were those two men that just left?"

Kelsey's lips pressed tightly together and she released Janelle's wrist. "Detectives. They're investigating what happened in the cabin."

Janelle's breath suddenly escaped her lungs. "What? Why?"

Kelsey gave Patrick a pointed look. "Patrick was just going to call about that."

"Kelsey, I don't think it will work. I'm sure the station won't tell us anything more than what they," Patrick pointed toward the door, "told us."

"What did they tell you?" Janelle asked as she turned to look at Patrick. Except for the dark circles under his eyes and the five o'clock shadow on his jaw, he was just as handsome as ever. Janelle knew he hadn't left this hospital room for the four days Kelsey had been here.

When Patrick looked determined not to answer her question, Janelle turned to her sister.

Kelsey sighed before quickly answering, "The older one did most of the talking, and I didn't really like him very much. All he would tell us was that Nathan was no longer on the case, but he wouldn't tell us why."

"And neither will the police station," Patrick stated as he looked at Kelsey.

"That's why I suggested you go right to the source," Kelsey said as she rolled her eyes. She turned her sharp stare toward Janelle. "Unless you know?"

Janelle shook her head. "I haven't seen Nathan since he left me here," she answered softly and cursed the tears that suddenly stung her eyes. *In for a penny . . .* "And he's not returning my calls."

"Oh," Kelsey gasped and covered her rounded mouth with her hand. She slowly lowered her hand and turned her gaze to Patrick again. "Please call him."

Patrick nodded and walked to the window as he took his cell phone out of his pocket. Veronica hopped off of the air conditioner and sat down in the chair next to the bed. Janelle watched as Kelsey slowly turned her attention from Patrick to Veronica then started to turn toward Janelle, who looked away as her sister's gaze fell onto her face.

"So, which one of you is going to tell me what happened?" Kelsey asked.

"I told you, it's no big deal," Janelle muttered.

Veronica made a very unladylike snort and Janelle glared at her. Veronica relaxed into the chair and folded her arms across her chest. "Sorry," she said quietly.

Kelsey raised an eyebrow at her sister.

"You sure are being nosy," Janelle snapped as she stood and walked to the wall beside the bed. She turned and pressed her shoulders to the wall as she glared at Kelsey.

"Well, if that asshole hadn't shot me before he died, I could have gone with you to his funeral and seen it all firsthand." Kelsey pushed herself higher in the bed and Janelle saw her flinch. "As it is, I've been worried sick that Mom would do something stupid, which she apparently did, and I would like to know what it was."

Janelle sighed. "It wasn't just Mom. Martha stopped me at the door of the chapel and started yelling at me."

"I've never liked Martha," Kelsey said as she wrinkled her nose.

"Well, today she had a good reason to be irritating." Janelle wasn't sure why she felt the need to defend Martha's actions.

"Irritating is one thing, J," Kelsey argued. "That woman is downright rude. Most of the time."

Janelle pressed her lips together in a frown. "And then Gladys joined her and cussed me out."

"After she slapped you," Veronica added and Janelle glared at her. Veronica simply shrugged and looked away.

"The old woman hit you?" Kelsey asked, her tone dripping with disbelief. "In front of everyone? What did she say?"

"Pretty much," Janelle answered the first question with a nod. "She called me a whore and said that if I'd been a better wife to him then maybe Richard would have been a better husband to me."

"You did nothing to deserve the kind of treatment you got from him,"

Kelsey said, her eyes filled with sadness. "No woman ever deserves that kind of mental, emotional, and physical abuse, Janelle."

Janelle smiled weakly as she walked back to the bed and sat on the edge. She took Kelsey's hand and squeezed it.

"I get why Martha and Gladys were so vicious. I don't agree with them, but I get it." Veronica stared curiously at the sisters. "What I don't understand is your mother's reaction."

Janelle frowned as she shrugged. "Our mother was raised to believe that keeping a husband happy was a wife's top priority. She tried to raise us to think the same, but there was a big difference."

"Our father was nothing like our grandfather," Kelsey added. "Mom's dad was an abusive alcoholic, much like Richard, but her mother tolerated it and did everything in her power to keep the peace at home. Mom grew up thinking that, if her father was happy, he wouldn't hit her mother."

"Of course, that theory didn't work all the time," Janelle continued. As a child, she could remember seeing bruises on her grandmother's face or arms when they would visit. It wasn't until she was older that she understood where she'd gotten those bruises, and why George was always hesitant to let his daughters visit their grandmother. "And, like Kelsey said, our father wasn't like our grandfather, so even though Mom utilized the lessons she'd learned, her situation was never the same. She didn't need to treat our father the same way, but that didn't stop her from trying to teach Kelsey and me to do things her way."

"The sad truth is, we both tried it," Kelsey confessed softly as she cast a glance at Patrick. She turned to Janelle and the corner of her lips lifted. "But I think we've both learned better."

"Definitely," Janelle agreed and hoped she was being honest, for the sake of her children as well as her sanity.

Veronica pursed her lips as she looked down at the floor, and they remained silent.

After a few moments, Kelsey finally asked, "Dare I ask how our mother contributed to this scene?"

"She certainly didn't show her support for me." Janelle dropped Kelsey's hand and folded her own in her lap. "She agreed with Gladys and told me I should leave, that the funeral was only for people who actually cared about Richard while he was alive."

Kelsey's jaw fell open as her eyes widened. "Where was Dad?"

"He wasn't there." Janelle shook her head. "He told me he wasn't going and that neither should I." George Morgan had been almost adamant in the fact that Janelle didn't need to, and probably should not, go to Richard's funeral. That if she went, she would most likely have to face people and their judgment and it would do her more harm than good. Janelle wished now that she had listened.

Patrick joined them and took his place beside the head of Kelsey's bed and looked directly at Janelle. Slowly, Kelsey turned to look at him.

"Did you talk to him?" Kelsey asked, and Patrick nodded as he looked at her. "What did he say?"

Patrick pressed his lips firmly together and frowned at Janelle. "He's been pulled from the investigation."

"Why?" Kelsey asked.

"Because of me," Janelle said quietly and looked at Patrick. "Right?"

"Well, because of the affair, his captain feels he's too close to the case." Patrick gave Janelle a pitying smile. "I'm sorry."

"What?" Kelsey sat up and glared at Patrick. "That's ridiculous. There's no reason for Nathan to be shady about anything. Richard killed himself in the struggle with you." Kelsey choked on the last words and Janelle watched Patrick place a gentle kiss on her sister's forehead.

"We all know that, Kelsey, but the police department has to cover all bases. They have to protect themselves from anyone crying foul." Patrick took Kelsey's hand in his and stared into her eyes.

Janelle started to feel uncomfortable witnessing the intimacy between the two of them. She stood and walked to the wall at the foot of the bed and leaned her back against it. She hated the idea that her actions from over three years ago were having such an impact now.

Patrick sat on the edge of the bed and looked at Janelle. "But I'm afraid there's more."

Janelle watched the steady look in his eyes cloud and knew this wasn't going to be good. She inhaled deeply. "What is it?" she reluctantly asked.

Patrick's face tightened as if he wasn't happy to share the news with her. "He's been suspended from the force."

"What?" Kelsey exclaimed as Janelle closed her eyes and her knees went weak.

"They are investigating his more recent behavior—using the police car to watch your house and whether or not he did that during his on-duty hours, among other things. As much as I appreciate that he did keep an eye on you guys and the kids, he apparently wasn't doing it according to police protocol," Patrick finished and a hush fell in the room.

Janelle's chin dropped slowly to her chest. This was all her fault. She'd ruined Nathan's life. It hadn't been enough that she'd kept his daughter from him, now she'd probably cost him his career as well. It was no wonder he wouldn't speak to her. She could have apologized profusely and tried to explain her reasons to him until she was blue in the face, and she'd felt pretty sure that he would have eventually forgiven her for not telling him about Zoe. But she had no idea how she could make this up to him now.

"J, are you okay?"

Janelle's head snapped up as her eyes popped open and she met Kelsey's concerned stare.

With a casual shrug, Janelle replied, "Yeah, I'm fine." She quickly looked away from her sister and turned her gaze to Veronica. "We should probably go."

"Of course," Veronica said as she rose from the chair. "We wouldn't want Grayson to teach the kids too many bad habits."

"Grayson's with the kids?" Patrick questioned with a laugh. Veronica nodded, a small smile on her lips, and Kelsey groaned.

"We'll be by tomorrow morning before we leave." Veronica gave Kelsey a hug. "You'd better heal quickly."

"I'll do my best." Kelsey grinned at her friend as they separated.

Janelle walked over to her sister and gave her a quick hug and a kiss on the cheek. "See you soon."

Kelsey gripped Janelle's hand and Janelle tried to pull away. "Are you sure you're okay?"

Janelle thought about her sister's question for a moment then looked her squarely in the eyes. "Nothing about this is okay, so I'm as good as I can be." She slowly withdrew her hand, glanced at Patrick, then turned and left the room.

Janelle walked into the darkened chapel, the only light emanating from the two seven-candle candelabras at the head and food of the casket in the front of the room. Slowly, she approached the body of her husband. When she reached him, she gasped sharply and covered her mouth. Lying in front of her was not the man he was when he died, but the man he was when they first married.

Gone were the sunken cheeks, replaced with a youthful fullness. The dark-rimmed eyes had disappeared, giving him a well-rested appearance. The wrinkles in his forehead and around his mouth were smoothed out. His thinning gray hair was once again brown and wavy. Her chest tightened as she reached out to touch his once familiar face. Richard's clear blue eyes popped open, and he stared right at her.

She choked on a scream as she stumbled two steps backward, drawing her hand to her chest. She watched in horror as he sat up in the casket then slowly began to climb out, holding her gaze the entire time. A menacing smirk slowly crept across his lips, and he walked toward her.

"Surprised?" he drawled.

Janelle's mouth opened and closed a few times, but no words escaped. She swallowed the lump in her throat and tried again. "You're dead."

"Very good," Richard said. "I had wondered if you'd notice."

"You kidnapped my son and shot my sister, of course I noticed," Janelle spat and quickly backed up a step as his scowl intensified.

"Still only thinking of how I hurt you? You can't accept that all of this is your fault. That if you'd been a better wife, I wouldn't be dead."

"That's not true," Janelle said breathlessly as she sat on the arm of the closest pew.

"My mother was right about you. You're nothing but a worthless whore. I wasted so much time trying to make you happy, trying to give you everything you ever wanted, to give you the kind of life your sister was living. And you thank me by fucking Nathan!" Richard glared down his nose at her as his face slowly changed to the man he'd been when he died. "You ruined my life, Janelle."

"You think yours was ruined?" came a low tenor from behind Janelle, and she hung her head. "She's apparently just getting started with my life." Nathan appeared and stood across the aisle, arms folded across his broad chest as he glowered at her. "It wasn't bad enough she hadn't told me about my child, now she's taken my career too." He leaned closer. "I hope you're happy."

Janelle shook her head as her eyes began to sting. She'd never meant to hurt Nathan. He had to understand that. "Nathan, I'm sorry. I—"

"I don't want to hear it," he interrupted, his lip curling.

"It's probably best if you stay away from her."

Janelle turned at her mother's hoity statement and watched her glide down the aisle.

"Like her sister, she refuses to take my advice. I'm afraid she'll never be fit as a wife." Mary looked at Richard as tears slid down her cheeks. "I'm only sorry I couldn't make her fit for you, my poor, poor dear."

Janelle looked from Mary's sorrowful face to Richard's smirking glare and then to Nathan's angry expression. They all began to talk at once. *Whore. Worthless. Liar.*

Janelle covered her ears and began shaking her head.

"No," she muttered. "No. No. No."

Janelle sat up, shaking, her heart racing, her eyes closed tightly, her hands over her ears. Slowly, she opened her eyes and took in her surroundings. In the dark, she could just make out the familiar shape of her dresser against the wall to her right, the taller armoire on the opposite wall. She backed herself up until she was leaning against the headboard as she let out a long exhale.

It had all been a nightmare.

Thank goodness. All she could do now was wait for her heart to calm down and her body to relax and she could go back to sleep.

She hoped.

Six

Janelle sat in the armchair in the living room, letting the noise the kids were making wash over her. She was tired. After she'd recovered from the nightmare, she'd slept restlessly for the rest of the night. When her alarm went off at its usual time, she'd given up and gotten out of bed even though she hadn't put Zach back in school yet.

She'd fixed breakfast for Grayson and Veronica. After a long and surprisingly tearful—on the kids' part—good-bye, they'd taken Kelsey's Jeep and left. They were going to stop by the hospital to say good-bye to Kelsey and Patrick, leave the vehicle there, and take a cab to the airport to catch a flight back to LA. Kelsey and Patrick would drive the Jeep home when she was discharged from the hospital, probably tomorrow.

After lunch, Janelle had gotten a call from her father, letting her know he and her mother would be joining her for dinner. They'd be bringing it, so Janelle had nothing to do now but sit and wait. And try to stay awake.

She turned and watched the kids over the back of the chair. It seemed that in two consecutive days, she'd managed to successfully take them both from their fathers without even trying. In Zach's case, that wasn't such a bad thing, but her heart ached to think of Zoe never having Nathan in her life.

Even if she didn't know how she knew it, Janelle had always sensed he'd be a good father. She'd also always meant to tell him the truth, but as time passed, it had become harder. She'd called Nathan again after Grayson and Veronica left, but he hadn't answered. It had now been five days since he'd last spoken to her, and the more time that passed, the more Janelle doubted that would change.

Not that she could blame him.

Janelle heard a car engine coming down the driveway and stood up.

She walked to the bay window and watched her parents' car approach the house. To her surprise, Kelsey's Jeep was right behind it. She walked to the front door, opened it, and stepped onto the porch to watch the new arrivals.

Unfortunately, as soon as George had Mary's door open, Janelle could hear her mother's shrill complaints and pleas to turn around and leave. Surprisingly, her father said nothing. After Mary had climbed out, he closed her car door and immediately went to help Kelsey out of her vehicle. Together, with Patrick carrying their bags and leading the way, the three of them approached the front door from the side of the porch while Mary came up the front steps by herself.

"Kelsey," Janelle said with a huge smile. "You're home early."

Kelsey returned her grin. "They let me out early for good behavior." She limped into Janelle's outstretched arms and hugged her sister tightly. "How are the kids?"

Janelle looked into the house, where the kids stood by the bay window and watched the adults, then turned back to Kelsey and George. "They're doing okay. Zach is still a little quiet, especially today since Grayson left." She looked at Patrick. "Maybe that will change now that you're here."

"I'll do what I can while I'm here," Patrick said with a frown.

Janelle tilted her head to the side. *What did he mean by that?* She looked to Kelsey, who was smiling softly at him.

"And how much longer will we have the *pleasure* of your company?" Mary asked snidely from behind Janelle. "Do you typically give the women warning before you abandon them?"

"Mary, that's enough," George snapped.

"He's not abandoning me, Mother." Kelsey rolled her eyes before she looked at Mary. "He simply has to leave in a few days to work on another movie."

"That's what he *says*," Mary scoffed, then walked into the house, letting the screen door slam behind her.

"Well, this is going to be a pleasant meal," Janelle muttered.

"Oh," George said and looked at his car. "Your mother didn't bring the dinner in, did she?" Janelle and Kelsey looked at the house, then at Patrick, before the three of them shook their heads. George let out a long grumble. "I didn't think so. Janelle, could you help your sister into the house? I'll get the dinner out of the car."

"Daddy, I'm fine. I can walk, just not very well. I asked for crutches, but they thought it might be better therapy for me to go without." Kelsey shrugged as she stepped away from her father's support and hobbled toward the front door, followed closely by Patrick.

"I'll help you," Janelle offered. George hugged his eldest child and squeezed her tightly before he released her. Janelle looked into her father's eyes. "You okay?"

"I'm fine," he replied. "I'm just a little concerned about my girls."

They retrieved dinner from the car and brought it into the house without another word. As they walked into the house, Janelle had a moment to take it all in.

Directly in front of her, past the two white columns that separated the foyer from the kitchen, Patrick was getting plates and silverware out as Kelsey, seated at the island in the center of the room, reminded him where everything was. To her left in the living room, also separated from the entryway by two columns, Mary sat on the large, blue couch, watching the children play behind the matching armchairs to her right. Her tiny nose in the air, Mary would occasionally cast scornful looks into the kitchen. George took his bag of food directly to the kitchen and set it on the island beside Kelsey.

Janelle slowly followed and gave her bag over to her father's outstretched hand as her sister started taking containers of food out of the bag and placing them on the island. The tangy smell of barbecue hit Janelle in the face, and instead of the comforting sensation she usually felt, she suddenly felt a sense of foreboding. The last time her father had brought dinner to them without being asked was the night Patrick had arrived in December. That meal had not ended well.

Kelsey and Janelle had been in the middle of decorating the outside of the house for Christmas when Patrick pulled into their driveway, surprising them both. When George had brought Zoe home for lunch, he'd met Patrick for the first time and they'd hit it off. By later that evening, though, his attitude toward the Hollywood playboy had changed, thanks largely to Mary and her obsession with reading tabloids and Patrick's tendency to be on their covers.

They had come for dinner, for no other reason, that Janelle could discern, than to accuse him of using Kelsey for his own satisfaction, effectively belittling and embarrassing Kelsey at the same time. Janelle and Kelsey had almost expected it to happen, but the extent that Mary took her vitriol surprised them both.

Janelle looked again at her father as he and Patrick carried plates into the dining room and set the table for dinner. His lips were pressed tightly together and she could just make out the pale wrinkles fanning from the edges. His firm jaw was clenched tight, even as he and Patrick exchanged a few words while they worked. She noted how his shoulders were even lifted and his movements mechanical and methodical instead of fluid and loose.

Janelle glanced at Kelsey and noticed how casually she placed the side dishes in front of her, folded the bags and slid them to the side, and how her face lit up when Patrick approached. She turned her attention to her mother and saw how relaxed she appeared as she sat on the couch as if it were her throne. Janelle closed her eyes and pushed her thoughts away. She was obviously tired and overly suspicious for no reason.

"Janelle," her father's tone reached her as he laid his hand on her upper arm. She opened her eyes and smiled at him, and noticed the tension was still there. "Could you get the kids ready to eat?"

"Sure," she said and walked into the living room where the kids were playing behind the armchairs. "Hey guys, please go wash up so we can eat."

Zoe and Zach both looked up at her with round eyes that were different shades of blue, but nearly exactly the same in shape. Zoe pouted her full bottom lip, but stood and walked past Janelle and up the stairs. Zach was a little slower to comply, and Janelle squatted to his level.

"Hey, buddy, what's wrong?" she asked as she took his little hands in hers.

"I'm not hungry." Zach looked down, holding his casted wrist close to his body as he rocked side to side.

Janelle took a deep breath. She'd spoken briefly with a child psychologist when Zach was in the hospital, and he'd told her what warning signs to look for. He'd been withdrawing for the past few days, but it was really noticeable today. She wasn't surprised he didn't want to eat. She'd have to be sure to get him an appointment with a therapist as soon as she could.

"I understand, sweetie," Janelle said softly and ducked her head to try to look at his face. "But you haven't eaten much today. I need you to at least try so you can heal." She pointed to his cast. "Patrick's here, you can sit beside him if you'd like."

Zach looked at her and eventually nodded. She smiled at him as he walked up the stairs after his sister to wash his hands for dinner. She stood and turned to find her mother's eyes narrowed on her. Janelle met her stare, but Mary quickly looked away and lifted her nose slightly. Janelle resisted the urge to roll her eyes as she glided past her mother and into the kitchen. As she washed her hands, the kids raced down the steps and into the dining room where Kelsey, Patrick, and George were already seated at the table. Janelle joined them and took the empty seat between Zoe and George as Mary entered from the living room.

"Was no one going to tell me dinner was ready?" Mary glanced around the table to the only other empty chair next to Patrick and wrinkled her nose. "Janelle, you sit there, I'm going to sit beside your father."

Janelle quietly did as she was told and moved to sit between Zoe and Patrick, across from Zach. Once she was settled, George said the blessing and they began to pass the dishes around. Janelle spooned food on to Zoe's plate as Kelsey did the same for Zach. When the plates were filled and the serving dishes back in the center of the table, everyone began eating.

For the most part, it was a quiet meal. Janelle kept an eye on Zach and noticed he wasn't eating. After about ten bites, he looked at her. He opened his mouth then closed it with a frown.

"Is there something you need?" Janelle asked him.

His blond head bobbed up and down. "May I be excused?"

"You've barely eaten anything, Zach. You need to sit there and clean your plate," Mary chimed in.

Janelle looked at Zach's plate. "He's not going to eat all of that." She met his wide blue stare. "One more bite of everything?"

Zach's shoulders slumped as he picked up his fork. "O-kay."

"That's just wasteful." Mary's scornful prattle reached Janelle and she turned to glare at her mother.

"Leave him be," Janelle snapped. "If he's not hungry, I'm not going to force him to eat it all."

Mary looked away with a big sigh. "Well, if you insist. He is *your* son after all."

Janelle heard Kelsey's fork hit her plate. She looked across the table at her sister, noticed the slackness in her jaw and the fire in her eyes. Kelsey met Janelle's eyes, and Janelle shook her head once. Kelsey pulled her shoulders back, looked at her plate, and resumed eating, albeit less heartily than she had been.

Between sporadic bites of her own food, Janelle kept an eye on Zach. He finished the required bites of food and looked up at her imploringly. Janelle looked at Zoe's plate, which was nearly empty, then at Zach.

"You don't have to eat any more, but can you sit there until your sister is finished?" Janelle asked. Zach nodded and put his fork down.

"I'm done." Zoe looked up at Janelle, barbecue sauce stretched to the middle of each cheek, and smiled.

Janelle tried not to laugh as she wiped her daughter's face. "You may both go."

The words were hardly out of Janelle's mouth before her children were out of the dining room. Patrick chuckled beside her as he watched the kids bolt. He picked up an ear of corn.

"I can't believe you let him leave the table after eating so little," Mary stated, to no one in particular. Janelle let the comment slide. She wasn't in the mood to talk to her mother. Apparently no one else was either as Mary got no response to her criticism.

Kelsey was the first to slide her plate away. Janelle noticed she hadn't eaten much either as she followed suit.

"Janelle, why don't you and your sister get the kids into bed?" George asked.

Janelle looked at her watch. "Their bedtime isn't for another half hour," Janelle replied calmly.

"Janelle, do what your father asks," Mary snapped and glared at her daughter as she shoved her plate to the middle of the table. "It was a simple request, there's no need to be so disrespectful."

Janelle's chin dropped as she looked at her father. George frowned as he turned to Mary. "She was hardly being disrespectful. I didn't realize how early it was. I simply think we need to talk, and it would be best for the children to be in bed." He looked at Janelle again, "And Zach looked a little tired."

"He is," Janelle answered the question in her father's voice. "He's been having nightmares."

She slid her chair away from the table and heard Kelsey do the same. Patrick rose and walked to Kelsey's side. He helped her around the table and Janelle followed them from the room. Once they reached the kitchen, Kelsey stopped and looked at Patrick. Janelle looked away from the love she saw in her sister's gaze. It was almost ironic that four months ago, when her marriage was dissolving and her affair was a distant, albeit pleasant, memory, this is what Janelle had been hoping for: Kelsey to find love so she could have the chance to live vicariously through her. Now it was almost too painful to watch.

"I can do this," Kelsey said quietly as she reached up and cupped Patrick's cheek. "And if I can't, Janelle can help." Kelsey looked at her and winked. "I'll have to climb those steps alone soon enough—"

"Don't remind me," Patrick grumbled.

Kelsey's smile widened. "So I should practice."

Patrick frowned then quickly kissed her on the lips and stepped back. "Fine."

Kelsey giggled and slowly turned toward Janelle. "Shall we get the kids into bed?"

Janelle nodded and tried not to laugh at what she'd just witnessed—Patrick's discomfort and her sister's ability to get her way so easily. Together, the sisters turned toward the living room to herd the kids to bed.

As Janelle exited Zach's room, Kelsey was standing outside Zoe's door, rolling her teeth over her bottom lip.

"What's wrong?" Janelle asked.

Kelsey looked at her and tilted her head, her question on her face.

"You're chewing on your lip. I've only ever seen you do that when you're seriously considering something." Kelsey's mouth now formed an O. "So what is it?"

Kelsey pressed her lips together as her brow furrowed. "Do you think Dad's acting a bit strange tonight?"

"You noticed too?" Janelle had begun to wonder if she was the only one to notice how tense George had been during the meal.

"Yeah." Kelsey turned and looked down the hall toward the stairs. "Promise you won't get mad?"

"No," Janelle replied, her usual response to that question ever since childhood.

Kelsey smiled slightly before she met her sister's stare again. "He came by the hospital today while Veronica and Grayson were there."

"Why would I get mad about that?" Janelle asked after her sister paused.

"Veronica sort of let it slip about the funeral," Kelsey answered, a sheepish look on her face. "But he said he'd already heard some of the details, he just hadn't known Mom had been a part of it," Kelsey continued quickly.

"Oh no." Janelle pressed her back to the wall beside Zach's door. "He told me not to go. He's probably here to talk about that."

Kelsey narrowed her eyes. "You think?"

"What else could it be?"

Patrick crested the last step, and they turned to look at him. "I thought I'd tell the kids good-night and help Kelsey downstairs."

Janelle glanced at the large grin on Kelsey's face and bobbed her head. "Then I will meet the two of you in the dining room."

Slowly, Janelle walked down the steps, preparing herself for her father's displeasure. To call it wrath would be an overstatement. Her father rarely got that angry at her or Kelsey, but it still made her sick to cause him disappointment. As she reached the dining room, she stopped and inhaled slowly before walking in and resuming her seat. To her surprise, all the food and dirty dishes had been put away.

When Patrick and Kelsey returned, Patrick took his seat at the foot of the table and Kelsey sat beside him, across from Janelle. The sisters exchanged a look then turned to their father.

He sat silently as he stared at everyone at the table in turn then folded his hands on the table in front of him. Janelle felt like she was about to be cross-examined without knowing why. "Janelle," her father began, staring directly at her, "I believe that I advised you not to go to Richard's funeral, did I not?"

Janelle shrank in her seat as she nodded.

George continued, "I applaud your reasons for wanting to go in the first place, but I had feared that while you were remembering the man Richard had been, thanks to his revelation, everyone else would see you as the woman he painted you to be. I didn't want you to suffer the censure of everyone there."

"I realize that now, I'm sorry," Janelle said softly.

"That being said," George looked at his hands, "I feel that an apology is due."

"Dad," Kelsey said, and George held his palm to her. Janelle watched her sister scowl at her mother as Mary folded her arms across her chest and sat back in her chair.

"I suppose you're right," Janelle agreed.

"I absolutely agree," Mary said, glaring at her eldest daughter.

"I'm glad to hear that, Mary." George looked at his wife. "Since it's you I expect the apology from."

Janelle's eyes widened as her jaw dropped. She looked at Kelsey who had a similar look on her face. At the same time, they turned to look at their parents. Mary's eyes were wide as well, but her lips were pursed as her cheeks glowed red. George, his steady eyes far from calm, held her scornful gaze.

"I. Will. Not," Mary finally sputtered after a few minutes of their silent showdown.

"Yes, you will," George replied calmly.

When Mary opened her mouth to argue, he gave her that look Janelle was familiar with. While her mother had a "look" that meant she would hear no more arguing, Janelle had always felt her father's "look" was much more menacing, especially since nothing really ever made the man that angry. Mary must have shared that sentiment because for the first time in her life, Janelle watched her mother recoil as she closed her mouth.

"What you did yesterday, Mary, is unforgivable in my book. You publicly shamed your daughter. You chose to ignore everything she went through with Richard and sided with his family over your own. Not only that, but you also accused her of being a poor wife, blamed her for her failed marriage, and let everyone know that you'd been trying to correct that behavior for months," George said, his face becoming slightly blotchy as his volume rose. "She was married to the man and you told her she didn't belong there."

"She didn't," Mary spat as she sat up taller. "She drove that poor man to the grave, just as much as her sister did."

"That's enough!" George roared, and Mary sank into her seat again. "I don't care what you *think* she did to him. You should never have called her out on it in such a public venue. If you want to reprimand her and try to sway her to your deluded way of thinking, then you do it in private. You should never have shamed her and turned your back on her when she needed your support."

"My support?" Mary practically laughed.

Janelle was frozen to her seat. She'd never seen her parents argue. Period. The fact that they were now arguing over her gave her a light-headed feeling.

"My support?" Mary repeated as she stood. "Those girls have never listened to anything I've ever told them to do. And now look at them." Mary turned a scornful glare on her and then on Kelsey. "Tramps. Both of them. All because that one," she pointed to Kelsey, "couldn't follow my simple advice of keeping her man happy and ended up chasing Tim away after she'd gotten herself knocked up."

"Hey," Kelsey sat up and tried to argue.

"Forcing that one," Mary continued as she pointed at Janelle, "to take in her unwanted child. And then she couldn't be bothered with Richard anymore, and regardless of how hard he tried, it was never enough for her so she slept with Nathan, and who knows who else."

"Hey," it was Janelle's turn to try to set the record straight.

Mary ignored her protests and turned to her husband. "If you had even once tried to back me up, maybe they wouldn't be such an embarrassment."

George's peppered jaw clenched several times before he took a deep breath. "I'm not embarrassed by either of them, and I'm not going to support you when you suggest they stay in bad relationships."

Mary narrowed her eye and cocked her head. "Is that so?" She turned and looked directly at Kelsey. "I think you should end things with him," she pointed at Patrick, and Janelle rolled her eyes, "right now. He's not good for you and he'll only hurt you."

Kelsey's jaw dropped and she turned her hurt-filled eyes to George.

George rose to his feet and came around the table to stand between Patrick and Kelsey, laying a hand on each of their shoulders. "Mary, you're wrong."

"Auh," Mary scoffed indignantly.

"Not only are you wrong, but you owe this man, not only your grandson's life, but your daughter's as well," George said and Kelsey's hand moved to cover his. "Would you like to thank him?"

Mary's upper lip curled. "No." She turned and walked toward the door into the living room. "I'm not going to stand here and listen to this anymore." She walked out of the room, and moments later the front door slammed.

Janelle felt stunned and off balance as she looked at her father's face. He was looking in the direction of the front door. She looked at Kelsey, still gripping George's hand on her shoulder as her empty stare landed somewhere on the middle of the table. Patrick propped his elbows on the table and steepled his hands against his lips, his thumbs under his chin. He was staring blankly at the wall.

They sat like this in complete silence until the car horn honked.

George exhaled slowly as he rubbed the pads of his fingers in circles against his closed eyes and temple. "I guess I'd better go." He bent over and gave Kelsey a kiss on the cheek then shook Patrick's hand as Janelle stood.

"Thank you for trying," she said as she hugged her father.

"I'm afraid it may be too little too late." He sounded resigned as he broke the hug and backed a step. "You both knew I always had your back, right?" He looked at both of his daughters as they nodded their response then glanced in the direction of the front door. "I should have made sure your mother did, too." He shook his head. "I'll talk to you girls tomorrow." He waved and left the room.

When the front door closed behind him, Janelle put her palms on the back of the chair and looked at Kelsey. The clouds receded from Kelsey's eyes as she looked at her sister.

"Well," Kelsey muttered. "That was new."

Janelle simply bobbed her head.

Seven

Nathan lay on the couch as he bounced a tennis ball against the opposite wall and it bounced back into his waiting hands. It had been six days since he'd last spoken to Janelle, and it was driving him crazy. He was beginning to feel like a caged animal. He couldn't go to work. He couldn't go see Janelle. He would visit his mother, but she only seemed to want to talk about what happened with Richard and question him about what he would do about Janelle and his daughter.

His daughter.

That thought still made him a little light-headed. He threw the ball again, and it skipped off the wall and went down the hall. Nathan stretched to look down the hall then looked down at his two-year-old black-and-tan German shepherd. McClane simply looked back at him and lifted an eyebrow.

"Are you going to get that?" Nathan stared at the dog. McClane looked down the hall then laid his head back down on his paws. "Lazy animal," Nathan grumbled as he flopped onto his back and threw his arm over his head, over the arm of the couch. His other hand slipped off the couch and stroked the dog's fur.

"She hasn't called today."

He ran his fingers over the dog's ears.

"That shouldn't surprise me, I suppose. I haven't answered her calls for the last five days."

But still, he hoped she would. If Janelle called, at least he knew she was thinking about him. It annoyed him that he'd been told to stay away from her when they needed to talk about . . . what exactly? The incident in the cabin? Their failed relationship? Their daughter?

"Why didn't she tell me?"

Nathan gave the dog one last pat then sat up. McClane hopped up and moved out of the way of Nathan's feet as he set them down on the hardwood floor. He propped his elbows up on his knees and locked his hands behind his low-hanging head.

"Our daughter? I asked her so many times if the baby was mine and she always said 'no.' How could she lie?"

To go back to *him*? Nathan sneered at the thought. Janelle had abandoned him for Richard. As if sensing the error in his thoughts, McClane looked sideways at Nathan.

"Okay, fine. She never really left him in the first place."

McClane nodded and laid back down at Nathan's feet and put his head on his paws.

"But the sentiment had been there."

The dog rolled his eyes up at Nathan.

"I think," Nathan mumbled as he rose from the couch. Was he arguing with the dog? Nathan shook his head and walked down the hallway.

The truth was, he didn't know what her feelings had been.

It still stung that Janelle had chosen Richard over him in high school. Even if that had been fifteen years ago. And she hadn't known then that Nathan had been half in love with her. He had just worked up the nerve to ask her out when he found out she was dating Richard. From that point on, Richard had limited Janelle's exposure to Nathan, even though they'd been friends long before Richard had even entered the picture. They'd gone off to college together and Nathan had entered the local community college and then gone to the police academy.

He'd first heard about Richard's partying ways their junior year in high school, but hadn't seen a need to bring it up. After high school, Nathan had never had the chance to see Janelle when the two of them were home for the summers, but stories about Richard's alcohol-filled weekends still reached him. The one time he had accidentally seen Janelle in town before her senior year in college, she'd seemed a bit distracted. And he'd been so happy to see her he hadn't wanted to ruin the moment by talking about Richard.

He started to regret that decision after Zach was born. And every moment since.

Nathan picked the tennis ball up out of the corner of the hall and bounced it on the floor as he walked down the narrow hallway, back to the living room.

He was hard-pressed to remember whether or not Janelle had actually ever said she'd leave Richard. She'd been unhappy, that was obvious. And there had been small signs of abuse. Nothing blatant like black eyes or large bruises on the arms or legs, but he could see the fear in her eyes as she was constantly looking at the clock or peeking out the window when he first started visiting her during the day. That had eventually subsided and they'd settled into a nice little routine, but still he noticed the anxiety creep into her eyes every night when he left.

Nathan had asked her more than once to come home with him. She'd always smiled sadly at him and responded with, "Not tonight."

He hated those words.

Nathan sat back down on the couch and began tossing the ball against the wall again. "How could she let that man raise my child?" he asked out loud as anger bubbled in his stomach. The thought that Richard may have hit Janelle when she was pregnant with his daughter made his blood boil. And the idea that Richard may have laid a hand on Zoe made him want to kill the man all over again.

His cell phone rang, and he leaned over the arm of the couch to look at it. He let out a long sigh of relief.

She was calling.

Nathan propped himself against the wall of the interrogation room as he waited for the investigators to join him. Captain Little had called him earlier that morning and asked him to come in for questioning. Nathan was more than happy to comply—the sooner they got this investigation over with, the sooner he could see Janelle and the kids.

The door opened and two officers in shirtsleeves walked in. Nathan did a double take. These were not the Internal Affairs officers he'd been expecting.

These were crime scene investigators. Nathan began to wonder why he'd been called in.

"Sergeant Harris, please have a seat," said the younger of the two detectives, motioning to the seat closest to Nathan.

Nathan eyed the fresh-faced man as he walked to the chair he'd been directed to. "Detective Hayes, I'm surprised to see you here," Nathan said calmly as he sat. "The last time I checked, you didn't work for IA."

"This isn't about the Internal Affairs investigation into your misconduct, Sergeant," the other man snapped gruffly. Nathan looked at the grizzled veteran and frowned.

"Then why am I here?" Nathan asked.

The older detective, Sergeant Bonner, dropped a thin binder on the table as he took a seat across from Nathan. "You're here to answer questions about Richard Wagoner and the events on the night he died."

Nathan's brows came together. "I don't understand. I handed all of my paperwork over to you guys a week ago."

"Yes, we know you did," Detective Hayes said.

"Then haven't you looked through it?"

"Yes," Detective Hayes answered and started to add more but Nathan interrupted.

"And haven't you questioned the witnesses yourself?" Nathan asked, knowing full well they had. Patrick had called him almost immediately after they'd left Kelsey's hospital room. Kelsey hadn't been very happy with their line of questioning, and Nathan had a feeling he was about to find out why.

"Yes, Sergeant, we have." Sergeant Bonner glared at him through mud-colored eyes, his wrinkled, stubbled upper lip arched in disgust. "This isn't about their accounts of the events, it's about yours."

"I haven't given any," Nathan replied as he folded his arms across his chest and tilted back in his seat.

"You're about to," Bonner growled.

Nathan eyed the older man as he weighed his options. He could easily answer any question, knowing that he had nothing to hide. Given what he'd learned from Patrick, though, he might be safer to go the second route. "I'd like a lawyer present."

Bonner smirked. "Have something to hide?"

"No," Nathan stated. "But I can bet you'd like to think I do." Nathan watched as Bonner's smug smile slowly turned to a grimace. "And I'd like to have my ass covered, just in case you try to turn my words against me."

"Sergeant Harris, he would never do that," Detective Hayes said from the end of the table.

Nathan turned his head to look at him. "You obviously haven't worked with your partner that long."

Hayes's chin dropped and he looked speculatively at his partner. Nathan noticed that Bonner's face was a pale shade of red, a sign to Nathan that he'd been right in his assumptions. The two men stared each other down until a knock on the door preceded the entrance of a familiar and welcome face.

"I hope you haven't said anything," Mason Harris said to his brother as he took the seat next to him.

Nathan shook his head. He'd never had need of any legal services, but at this moment, he couldn't be more thankful to have a lawyer for a brother. Even if Mason's expertise was corporate law rather than criminal law.

"What are you doing here?" Bonner grumbled, pointing a stubby finger at Mason as he rose to his feet.

"I'm here to make sure my brother's rights aren't violated and that his words are accurately recorded." Mason calmly laid his briefcase on the table and opened it. Nathan tried not to laugh at the disorganized contents, probably the only sign of disorder in his brother's life. Mason turned to him. "Lucky for you, your captain decided to call me and let me know about this little session."

Nathan's brows rose to his hairline.

"You can't be here," Bonner stated. "It's a conflict of interest."

"Technically, it's not. This is just a questioning, not a trial. And even if it were a trial, I'm not about to be called as a witness, therefore I have no other interest than seeing that his responses aren't twisted against him," Mason said with a shrug as he pulled a tape recorder out of his briefcase. "However, Mr. Morgan is also here, waiting for his daughter to join him for her session with the two of you. If you'd rather, we can switch clients and he can sit in on Nathan's questioning. But then I will be sitting in on Mrs. Wagoner's." Mason looked up and met Bonner's glare. "The choice is yours."

"You're bringing her in too?" Nathan snapped. He looked at Hayes, who refused to meet his eyes, then turned to Bonner. "Hasn't she been through enough?"

"Of her own doing." Bonner looked at Nathan and shrugged.

Nathan shot to his feet, laid his palms on the table, and put his weight on them, wanting to wrap his hands around the man's thick neck. Mason pulled on his brother's arm and hissed in his ear for him to sit down and cooperate. Nathan slowly complied and took his seat again.

"Can we get this over with please?" Mason said as he took a yellow ledger and pen from his briefcase before he slid it away then pushed the button on his recorder.

Sergeant Bonner grumbled under his breath as he sat and pulled the thin binder closer to him. He opened it and picked up a pen. "Were you and Mrs. Wagoner having a sexual relationship at the time of her husband's death?" Bonner asked, tapping his pen to the paper as he looked up at Nathan.

Nathan blinked slowly, unsure he'd heard the question correctly. "What does that have to do with anything?"

Mason groaned beside him. "Just answer the question," he whispered at his brother. "You know as well as I do that he has a reason for asking it."

Nathan ground his teeth as he folded his arms across the table. "Not that it's any of your business," Nathan began, and the corner of Bonner's lip lifted slightly, "but no. We haven't had a relationship in over three years, if you must know."

Bonner frowned. That was obviously not the answer he'd been hoping for. He looked down at his papers. "If that's true, then why had you been spending so much time at Miss Morgan's home, where her sister lives? Mr. Wagoner had pictures of your car in her driveway as recently as two days before the incident," the sergeant slid a set of photos across the table, "and of a squad car, with you sitting in the driver's seat, as recently as a week before." Bonner slid a second set of pictures toward Nathan.

Nathan let them sit where they were and narrowed an eye on Bonner's head. "I've been friends with Mrs. Wagoner since elementary school. Is it a crime to visit my friends?" Mason cleared his throat and Nathan rolled his eyes. He didn't see how this line of questioning had anything to do with Richard's death and what happened in that cabin that night. "Mr. Wagoner attacked Miss Morgan in December."

"I'm aware of that," Bonner nodded and looked at Nathan. "And I'm aware that she filed a restraining order that prevented him from being on her property."

"Your point is?" Nathan sat back in his chair. "You know as well as I do that a little piece of paper telling the man to stay away wouldn't have done them a bit of good. Clearly, it was useless when he went against it and kidnapped his son."

"That's true," Detective Hayes piped in, reminding Nathan of his presence. Nathan looked at him, and the young man sat taller in his seat. "So why were you constantly patrolling around her house?"

"Peace of mind," Nathan replied. "Miss Morgan's boyfriend was present when Mr. Wagoner attacked her and was concerned for her safety. When he had to return home, he asked Miss Morgan to hire a bodyguard to protect them all, and she refused."

"Why would she refuse if she knew they could be in danger?" Hayes asked.

So that was how they were going to play it? Hayes's fresh-faced, straightforward good cop to Bonner's gruff, insolent bad cop. "She values her privacy," Nathan answered, focusing on Hayes. "Which is why she asked me to help keep an eye on her home and family."

"Where were you when Zach Wagoner was kidnapped?" Bonner asked.

Nathan focused on the unpleasant man again. "I was at home. Alone. Sleeping." Nathan folded his arms across his chest.

"Can anyone verify that?" the younger detective asked.

Nathan raised his eyebrow as he stared at the man. Hayes's face turned slightly pink, from his neck to his blond hairline.

"Well?" Bonner asked.

"Really?" Nathan glared at the older cop.

"Nathan," Mason's warning tone reached his ears.

"My dog was home with me. Should I have brought him in for questioning?"

An exasperated groan emanated from his right, where his brother sat, and a soft clearing of the throat from the end of the table on his left.

Bonner's shoulders lifted and fell slowly as he looked at the binder in front of him. "How did you find out about the kidnapping and the location of the suspect and child?"

"Mrs. Wagoner called me."

"Immediately after finding out Zach was missing?" Bonner asked as he looked up at Nathan.

Nathan's head moved from side to side. "No, it wasn't until after Mr. Lyons arrived at her home looking for Miss Morgan."

"Where was Miss Morgan?" Bonner's brow furrowed and he crossed his arms in front of him.

"On her way to the cabin. Mr. Wagoner had threatened Mrs. Wagoner with their son's life if she called anyone but her sister to meet him at the cabin." Nathan shivered at the thought of how distressed Janelle had been over the threat to her son and her sister.

Bonner shook his head disapprovingly. For once, Nathan agreed with him.

"Were you the first to arrive on the scene?" Bonner asked.

"The first officer, yes, but Mr. Lyons, Mr. Reynolds, and Mrs. Wagoner beat me to the cabin. When I arrived, Mrs. Wagoner was pale and holding her son, Mr. Reynolds was hovering over them, watching the cabin, and Mr. Lyons was nowhere to be seen." Nathan recalled the events monotonously, separating himself from the turmoil he'd felt that night. "I heard fighting from inside the cabin, there were two gunshots, spaced out, and things were shattering inside. Then there was one final shot, and everything went silent. Until the scream."

"Who screamed?" Detective Hayes asked, wide-eyed as he leaned forward, listening.

"Miss Morgan, inside the house," Nathan answered. "That's when the uniforms arrived and, as I led them into the house, the ambulances pulled up. We found Mr. Wagoner's body on the floor in the living room and Mr. Lyons and Miss Morgan in the bedroom. She'd been shot and was losing blood and consciousness."

"Did you touch the body?" Bonner asked gruffly.

Nathan nodded. "For a moment, to check for a pulse."

"That was all?" Bonner raised an eyebrow.

"Yes."

Sergeant Bonner frowned again and Nathan looked at the young detective. He was looking at a binder in front of him as well. They were all silent as the men studied the papers in front of them and Mason made notes on his yellow legal pad.

"What happened next? Did you do any further study of the body?" the sergeant asked as he met Nathan's stare again.

Nathan shook his head. "I didn't see any reason to. Crime scenes aren't my expertise. My job is protecting victims of domestic violence, so I went to see to Miss Morgan. I escorted Mr. Lyons out of the house as he carried her to the ambulance. As I left the house, I noticed the investigators taking pictures of the scene, and I left them to do their job."

The corner of Bonner's mouth lifted forebodingly. He produced an evidence bag and slid it toward Nathan. "Do you recognize that?"

Nathan looked down at the bag. It contained a handgun, a Ruger LC9, that looked remarkably familiar. Without saying a word, he looked up at Sergeant Bonner and raised an eyebrow. "Where did you find this?"

"I thought you were more observant than that," Bonner said with a sneer. "That weapon was found at the crime scene. It's the murder weapon."

"Is that so?" Nathan said coolly, even as his stomach dropped. He'd given Janelle a gun just like this before she'd ended their affair.

"What I find even more interesting is that this gun was purchased by and is registered to you," the sergeant smiled widely and Nathan had the distinct feeling he thought he'd just snared Nathan in some sort of trap. "Would you like to explain to us how that might have happened?"

Nathan considered his answer then sat back in his chair and folded his arms over his chest. "Actually, no. I'd like to hear your theory instead."

Did the old detective just growl?

"We don't have a theory, Sergeant Harris, just the evidence," Detective Hayes stated. Nathan looked at him incredulously. Was he really that naïve? Or did he just think Nathan was?

"I believe you gave that gun to Mr. Lyons so that he could take care of your little problem for you," Sergeant Bonner started, and Nathan smiled inwardly. Now he was getting somewhere. "I think you met up with him before he went to the cabin, you gave him the gun, and you asked him to make it look like a struggle when he killed your rival."

"How very romantic," Nathan scoffed. "And how very wrong." He sat up and laid his forearms on the table as he stared at the older man. "If that were the case, then where is the gun Mr. Wagoner used to shoot Miss Morgan?"

Sergeant Bonner pressed his lips tightly together and his cheeks pinkened slightly.

Nathan narrowed his eyes on the detective. "If I didn't know any better, I'd say you're trying to frame me, or Mr. Lyons, or maybe both of us, for Mr. Wagoner's death."

Bonner's face went from pink to slightly red as he jerked back, his mouth opening and closing like a fish. "How . . . What . . . You . . ." he blustered, unable to finish a sentence.

"The handgun was something I gave to Mrs. Wagoner while we were together," Nathan began his explanation.

"So she could kill her husband and you could be together for good?" Bonner managed to blurt as the color in his face began to recede.

"How stupid do you think I am?" Nathan asked as he inched forward even more, anxious to rise from his seat. "I gave it to her so she could *protect* herself from him. I wanted her to feel like she could fight back if she needed to."

"He was abusive?" Detective Hayes questioned, and Nathan nodded. "She asked for the gun?"

"No," Nathan grumbled. She hadn't wanted it even when he'd put it in her hands. "She never even told me he was abusing her physically, but I could see the marks on her arms and shoulders. She had a bruise around her neck once, and that's when I bought the gun for her."

"Did she ever use it?" Hayes asked.

"Not to my knowledge," Nathan answered. He'd planned to take her to a shooting range so she could practice, but he'd never had the chance.

"Well, how did it come into Mr. Wagoner's possession?" Bonner asked arrogantly.

Nathan closed his eyes so he wouldn't roll them. "I don't know the answer to that question," he said through clenched teeth.

The room fell quiet, and Nathan opened his eyes and looked around. Detective Hayes had closed his binder and was sitting back in his chair. Sergeant Bonner stared at his papers, flipping through them furiously. Nathan thought for sure he'd end up ripping one or more of them out of the binder. Mason was tapping his pen on his legal pad, glaring at Nathan with an obvious look of displeasure in his deep-green eyes.

After a few more minutes, it was Mason who finally spoke up. "Are we finished here?"

Sergeant Bonner flipped through the remaining pages in his binder then slammed it shut. "Yes," he grumbled, "we're done."

Nathan quickly pushed away from the table and stood. He waited for Mason to collect his things and stand then led the two of them out of the room. Once the door was closed behind them, Nathan felt the thwack of a legal pad against the back of his head. He turned and glared at his younger brother.

"What was that for?" Nathan put his hand to the stinging spot on the back of his head.

"You gave her a gun? Seriously, you idiot, what were you thinking?" Mason snapped. "You're lucky she didn't want it, otherwise you may have been in major trouble."

"How do you know she didn't want it?" Nathan grumbled as he put his hand down.

"Your face said it all," Mason said, followed by another mumbled "idiot" as he walked past him and down the hallway. Once they were away from the interrogation room and in a more secluded part of the station, Mason turned and faced his brother.

"Why did you give her a gun?" Mason repeated his question.

Nathan shrugged as he propped himself against the blank, cream-colored wall across from his brother. He looked at his feet as he thought of all the reasons why he'd given her the gun, which in hindsight may not have been the best idea. "Do you know how many domestic violence cases I've worked, Mason?" Nathan continued to look at his feet as image after image of broken, battered women floated through his mind. "Do you know how many of those women refused to leave their husbands, thinking that the abuse would subside if they simply perfected their behavior, if they just didn't argue or fight back? Or maybe things would improve if their husbands found a job, or found a better job, or was just less stressed?" Nathan looked at his brother, met his wide green stare, and shrugged. "Do you know how many of those women ended up beaten beyond recognition? Beaten to the point they could no longer use arms, hands, legs, or feet? Beaten to death?" Nathan's eyes closed against some of the more gruesome pictures. "I didn't want to get a call to her house to find she had become one of those women," he finished quietly.

Mason didn't say anything for a few minutes, until Nathan was able to open his eyes and look at him again. "Did you think about what might have happened if she'd used it against him?"

Nathan folded his arms across his chest and ignored the question.

"You said she never admitted to physical abuse, so she never reported it, did she?"

Nathan reluctantly shook his head.

"No," Mason said. "I didn't think so. So, what would have happened if she had used that gun against him? She would have been charged with his murder and you may have been held responsible as well." Mason rolled his eyes. "You could have been an accomplice to murder."

"I know," Nathan replied with exasperation. He had considered that, but not until after he'd left the weapon in her possession.

"And what if he'd used the gun on her?" Mason's raised eyebrow accompanied his cool utterance.

A chill ran down Nathan's spine. That thought, too, had only crossed his mind after it was too late. Nathan had stayed up some nights, unable to sleep for the fear that Richard would kill Janelle with the gun he had given her. He wouldn't have been able to forgive himself.

"Did you even think about that?"

"You should save your questions for the courtroom," Nathan grumbled. "I'm tired of hearing them."

"I don't care. It was stupidity at its finest on your part, Nathan," Mason said. "I would have expected more from you, big brother. What is it about her that gets you all tangled up?"

Nathan's upper lip curled as he narrowed his eyes on his brother. The urge to hit one of his brothers had never been stronger than it was right now.

"I just wanted her to be safe," Nathan replied shortly. "Is that such a bad thing?"

Mason's shoulder lifted slightly. "I guess we'll have to wait and see."

"Wait and see about what?" a feminine voice floated toward them.

Nathan closed his eyes as the familiar voice caressed him. Really, could his day get any worse?

"Wait and see about what?" Janelle repeated, closer this time, and Nathan opened his eyes to find her stopped beside Mason.

She eyed Nathan warily for a moment then turned her pert little nose up and her focus on his brother. Nathan hated the look he saw in her eyes—the look that spoke of mistrust and caution. A look that said she didn't really want to be near him. Not that he could blame her. He hadn't spoken to her in a week.

"Good morning, Janelle," Mason happily greeted her.

She smiled beautifully at him and Nathan's heart skipped a beat. What *was* it about her that always tangled him up?

"Good morning, Mason. What brings you here?" she asked brightly.

"Same thing as you, I imagine," Mason answered.

Nathan took the opportunity to study her while she looked at his brother. Her hairline was blonde dappled with gray, and her cheeks looked thin. Stress lines touched the corners of her full lips, and her once sparkling blue eyes were dulled to the point they almost looked gray. And the dark rings underneath them told Nathan that her bright, happy persona was just an act this morning. She looked like she hadn't been sleeping well, and he wished there was something he could do to help her out.

She looked at him, and pain flashed through her eyes, but surprisingly she held his stare. He had to look away; the urge to wrap her in his arms was too strong. He noticed Captain Little standing at the end of the hallway, watching them. Grumbling under his breath, Nathan settled his shoulders against the wall. He looked back at Janelle and Mason and saw both sets of eyes focused on him. Mason raised an eyebrow, an expectant look in his eyes as he tilted his head toward Janelle.

Nathan knew he should say something, but the conversation he wanted to have with her couldn't be had in front of his brother. "How are you?" he finally managed to ask, and a look of disappointment crossed her features.

"Good." Janelle clasped her hands in front of her, her gaze shifted over his shoulder.

"How are the kids?" Nathan stood up straight and took a step toward her.

Janelle's lips came together in a tight smile as she lowered her gaze. "They're fine," she said abruptly. "And Kelsey, too."

"Good." Nathan nodded. She wouldn't look at him and that bothered him more than he'd expected. There was a knot forming in the pit of his stomach, and he took another step toward her.

Her wide eyes focused on him for a moment before she turned her entire body toward Mason, giving Nathan her shoulder.

He knew then that he was losing her.

"Mason, I've wanted to ask you about the funeral." She paused as Mason acknowledged her statement. "Why did you leave early?"

Nathan thought the more important question was . . . why had either of them even been at Richard's funeral?

"For the reasons you think," Mason answered, giving Janelle a small smile. Janelle grinned slightly in return and Nathan had the feeling he was missing something.

"Thank you," she said. "I appreciated your support."

"What happened at the funeral?" Nathan's curiosity was piqued. This wasn't right. She was supposed to share secrets, no matter the size, with him. Not his married, younger brother.

Janelle looked over her shoulder at him and opened her mouth.

"Are you ready, Janelle?"

George Morgan walked toward them, stopping and placing his palm on his daughter's back. Janelle nodded, and her father walked past her and down the hall. She watched him for a moment then turned back to face Nathan.

"If you'd answer your phone, maybe you'd know," Janelle said, finally answering Nathan's question. She turned and smiled at Mason, then followed George to the interrogation room where he stood, waiting in the doorway.

Nathan waited for the door to close behind them before he looked at his brother again. Mason raised a curious eyebrow, and Nathan ignored it. He walked in the opposite direction Janelle and her father had just gone, and Mason slowly followed.

"Lover's spat?" Mason asked, his voice laced with humor.

"Shut up," Nathan muttered in response as they continued past the desks and toward the front door. Mason was kind enough to hold his tongue until they were outside, where he promptly chuckled out loud. Nathan rolled his eyes and clenched his fists beside him, failing to see what was so funny.

"How do you not know what happened at the funeral? Have you not spoken to her since then?" Mason rested his hips against the wall in front of the building.

"No, I haven't talked to her in a week," Nathan confessed.

"Really? Still pissed that she didn't tell you about your daughter?" All signs of Mason's professionalism had disappeared, leaving the annoying brother persona behind.

Nathan shook his head. He'd gotten over that fairly quickly. At least he thought he had—he hadn't had the chance to hash it out with Janelle, so he couldn't be completely sure.

"Look, if you'd seen what we witnessed at the funeral, you'd probably understand a little better why she stayed with him and kept your daughter from you," Mason said, all lightness and joviality leaving his voice and face.

"What happened?" Nathan asked.

Mason told him everything.

Nathan wasn't surprised to hear about Martha's reaction. She'd always been slightly less offensive than her big brother, but just as irritating. Gladys assaulting Janelle so publicly didn't sit well with Nathan, but he could forgive her a little. She was, after all, there to bury her only son.

Hearing about Mary's reaction, however, had Nathan seeing red. He kept his comments to himself and let Mason wind down his recollection.

"How could she do that to her own daughter?" Mason mused, almost to himself, and Nathan could imagine him talking to his wife, Charlotte, about it. "I mean, the asshole kidnapped her grandson, shot and nearly killed her daughter, and she still comes to his defense over that of her own children."

"That's just the way she is," Nathan replied.

He was just as baffled by Mary as his brother was. He knew that Mary had refused to have meals at Janelle's house if she'd known in advance that Nathan would be there. Christmas dinner had been tense while the children had been at the table; the comments from Mary had poorly veiled her hostility toward Nathan, and to a lesser degree Kelsey and Janelle.

Nathan had been confused and asked Janelle about it after Mary and George left shortly after the kids had gone to bed. Janelle's explanation was simply to shrug it off as normal, as something she and Kelsey tended to ignore.

"So, if it's not because of your daughter, why are you not speaking to Janelle?" Mason's seriousness took Nathan aback.

Nathan looked at his brother, saw the concern in his eyes and tried to smile. "Buy me lunch, and I'll tell you all about my meeting with Captain Little."

Eight

Janelle sat in the hard chair beside her father, waiting for the investigators to join them, trying not to think about Nathan's behavior in the hallway. Her heart had raced ahead when she came around the corner and recognized his dark hair and broad shoulders. It had taken a control she hadn't thought she still possessed to keep her pace slow and deliberate as she approached him and Mason. And then to have him ignore her attempt at conversation had brought her joy crashing down. It had been a week since she'd had a conversation with him; she couldn't really count what happened in the hall as a conversation. His aloofness had nearly brought her to tears.

He obviously wanted nothing to do with her, not that she could blame him. She had known what she was doing when she'd denied, repeatedly, that she was pregnant with his child. Janelle couldn't blame him for being mad, and she was prepared to suffer through his anger. What bothered her most was that Zoe might never know her real father. It was a dream Janelle had held since the day she'd found out she was pregnant.

The door opened and two men walked into the room. They both wore white shirts with ties, and if she hadn't recognized them from the hospital, when they'd passed in the hallway outside of Kelsey's room, Janelle wouldn't have been sure they were even police officers.

"Mrs. Wagoner," the younger man stated. "Thank you for coming in." He sat down in the seat across from her. "I'm Sergeant Hayes, and this is Sergeant Bonner." He pointed to his companion, now sitting at the head of the table. "We're the detectives investigating your husband's death."

Janelle looked at the gruff, older man, and he nodded at her as he folded his arms across his chest. She returned his nod and turned to the detective. "Why am I here, exactly?"

Sergeant Hayes gave her a slight smile as he opened the binder in front of him. "We need to ask you some questions about the night your husband died."

"I wasn't in the cabin," Janelle replied.

"We're aware of that," Sergeant Bonner grumbled from the end of the table. "But you can tell us about events leading up to it."

Janelle eyed the grizzled veteran and wasn't completely sure she liked him or the tenor of his words. He must be the one Kelsey complained about. "Fine," she quietly agreed.

"Thank you," Hayes said as the older sergeant muttered something to himself. "Mrs. Wagoner, were you and Sergeant Harris having a sexual relationship at the time of your husband's death?"

"I fail to see how this is relevant," her father argued beside her, tilting forward in his seat.

"I think it's very relevant," Sergeant Bonner stated. "Given the recent revelations your son-in-law made regarding your daughter, I think it raises the question of motive."

"Whose motive? Neither my daughter nor Sergeant Harris were present in the house when Richard shot himself," George rose to his feet. "Unless you are accusing her of something, I don't think her personal life is any of your business."

"Dad, it's okay. Let's just see where this goes." Janelle laid her hand on her father's arm as she narrowed her eye on the sergeant. "No, we weren't," she answered as she looked at Sergeant Hayes.

"How long had it been over?" he asked quietly, staring at the papers on the table.

"Since just after our daughter was conceived." Janelle's heart sped up a little. She'd never thought of Zoe as Richard's child, always Nathan's. It had always given her a bit of comfort to know a part of him was always with her. "Over three years ago," she added around the lump in her throat.

"Did Mr. Wagoner ever mention to you his suspicions about the child?" the younger detective asked as he wrote something on the paper in his binder.

"No." Janelle shook her head.

"Did he ever give you reason to think he might know?" Sergeant Bonner asked.

"No," Janelle repeated. Wasn't that the same question?

"Mrs. Wagoner, do you recognize this?" Sergeant Hayes slid a plastic bag toward her. Inside the bag was an envelope with smudges around the outside. Janelle tentatively reached for it. "You can pick the bag up," he encouraged.

Janelle did and studied the envelope. It looked like any other business envelope that she'd seen in her lifetime. It was addressed to Richard, and she didn't recognize the return address in the corner. "Am I supposed to?" she asked innocently.

"Your fingerprints were all over it," said the gravelly voice at the end of the table.

"But it's addressed to Richard. I don't recognize who it's from, so why is this important?" Janelle refused to look at the older detective, and she stared at Sergeant Hayes as she slid the bag back toward him.

"It's the report from the DNA lab." He picked the bag up and slid it into the back of his binder.

"Okay," Janelle said slowly.

"The letter was postmarked six months ago, and your fingerprints were found underneath his, meaning you picked it up first," Sergeant Bonner said. From the corner of her eye, Janelle watched him stand and approach his partner. "So, if you were the first to handle the letter, then how do you not know the contents?"

Was he really serious with this question? "I never opened the letter," she responded and looked directly at the older man. His jaw tightened and his eyes bulged slightly. "Did you find the letter that was in that envelope?"

"Yes ma'am, we did," the younger man answered.

"Were my prints on that as well?" Janelle laid her forearms on the table and looked from one officer to the other.

"No ma'am," Hayes replied again.

"I didn't think so," she muttered.

"What were you doing at his house six months ago?" Bonner laid his palms on the table and leaned over them as he stared at her. "You had moved out and were living in your sister's house."

"I was, but the holidays were approaching and I realized that, in my haste to leave, I'd forgotten some of the traditional holiday items and decorations," Janelle answered. "I went to his house to retrieve them and quickly scanned the mail to see if anything addressed to me had gone there instead. I left it all right where I found it, got the things I'd come for, and left the house."

She watched Detective Hayes nod as he flipped through some of the papers in his binder. After a few pages, he looked at her with sadness in his blue eyes. "Can you tell us about the night of the incident?"

The *incident*? Her son was kidnapped, her sister was shot, and her estranged husband died, and they so neatly wrap it all together as an "incident." Janelle's stomach turned.

"What would you like to know?" she reluctantly asked.

"Where were you when your son was kidnapped?" the fresh-faced detective asked.

"I was in bed," Janelle answered, then looked at the grizzled sergeant and added, "alone." She looked back at Hayes.

His cheeks pinkened as he looked at the table and cleared his throat. "And you didn't hear your husband enter the house or come up the stairs?"

"No, I was asleep." Janelle sat back in her chair and clasped her hands in her lap.

"Isn't your bedroom right next to the stairs?" Sergeant Bonner asked.

Janelle scowled at him then looked at her hands.

"What happened when you woke up?" Hayes questioned.

"I went to Zach's room to get him up for school and found the note."

"This note?" Another bag was pushed toward her. She looked at its contents, nodded, and slid it back.

"Then, like he asked, I called Kelsey in LA and told her what he'd said," Janelle said, tears filling her eyes.

"Why didn't you call the police?" Bonner asked.

"Didn't you read the note?" Janelle snapped, her eyes shooting daggers at the balding man. "He said he would kill my son if I called anyone but my sister. I was married to him long enough to know that you don't cross him when he's in a bad mood, and he obviously was if he would kidnap our child from my home. So I called her and waited for her to get home."

"What happened while you waited?" Hayes' voice was soft and soothing so she focused on him.

"Richard called a couple of times, mostly to check on Kelsey's progress and to make sure I was doing as he'd asked. He would occasionally drop clues about where he was or I'd hear something in the background, water rippling or a boat, things like that. When Kelsey finally landed, she called me and instead of waiting for him to tell us where he was, we worked it out for ourselves." Janelle paused to catch her breath and slow her heart rate. Detective Hayes waved his hand for her to continue. "She asked me to give her half an hour with Richard before I called Nathan."

"Did you?" Hayes questioned.

"No, I don't think so." Janelle shook her head and tried to organize the events of that night in her mind. "I think Patrick, Grayson, and Veronica all arrived before her thirty minutes were up. After I informed them she wasn't there, Patrick began to panic and asked where she was. I told him, and he asked me to call Nathan right away as he walked out of the house." She closed her eyes as tears quietly rolled down her cheek. Her father put his arm around her shoulder and pulled her closer to him. "I left Veronica with Zoe and followed Patrick and Grayson out the door, dialing Nathan's number on my cell phone. I told him what had happened, and he told me to hang up and call 911, so I did."

The room was quiet as Janelle tried to force the images out of her mind. The dark house, the raised voices she heard coming from inside, the icy fear that gripped her heart when she realized she'd made a mistake that could cost her sister her life. They'd all heard the first shot as Patrick carried Zach toward her. He'd visibly paled and broken into a trot as she'd rushed to meet him halfway and take her child from his arms. She'd watched him run back to the house, praying that her sister wasn't already dead or dying.

"What happened when you arrived at the lake house?" Hayes's voice broke through her thoughts, and she described everything she'd just been trying to forget. "When did Sergeant Harris arrive on the scene?"

Janelle's brow came together as she looked at the young man. "I honestly don't know. It's all a blur," she began and tried harder to recall. "I was standing beside Grayson. I think we'd just watched Patrick disappear into the house again, through the window in the bedroom. Nathan was suddenly," she paused to remember how the calm of his presence had started to soothe the turmoil she'd been feeling all day, "there."

"Then what?" Bonner asked as Hayes furiously wrote in his notebook.

"The fighting, a few more gunshots, then everything went silent until,"

Janelle shuddered, "Kelsey screamed." Hayes stopped writing and looked at her as she continued, "More police officers showed up, and Nathan led them into the house as the ambulances parked beside us. They tried to take Zach from me so they could examine him, but he wouldn't let go, so I carried him to the back of one of the ambulances. When they'd finished and decided he needed to go to the hospital, I saw Patrick carrying Kelsey out."

"Where was Sergeant Harris?" Detective Hayes questioned.

"He was with them and started organizing everything around us. He joined some of the other officers and talked to them. Next thing I knew, they were bundling Zach and me into the ambulance and preparing to leave." Janelle exhaled slowly, feeling suddenly tired and weighed down.

After a few minutes of listening to their shallow respirations and the ticking second hand on the clock, the only noises in the room, Janelle caught a motion in her peripheral vision and looked at the bag that was sliding toward her. Sergeant Bonner looked at her as he asked, "Do you recognize this?"

Janelle looked at the bag, at the handgun in the bag, and tried to place it. There was something familiar about it, and her hand trembled as she reached for it. "Was this what Richard used to shoot my sister?"

"Yes," Bonner barked gruffly. "And it was the gun that killed him."

Janelle picked up the heavy metal object. Holding it in her hand, she immediately remembered the gun. "Nathan gave this to me. He thought I might need it to protect myself from Richard." She placed the bagged gun back on the table and shook her head. "I'd forgotten about that," she added quietly as ice seeped into her veins. Could this whole thing have been prevented if she'd refused to accept the gun in the first place?

"How did the gun come into your husband's possession?" Sergeant Hayes asked.

Janelle looked up at him. "This was one of those things that got left behind. It was in a shoebox under the bed in the spare bedroom." She'd hidden it from Richard there, in the room she'd been sleeping in with the children.

If only she'd remembered to take it with her.

The two detectives looked at each other and frowned. Sergeant Bonner sat down and stared at Janelle. "Did Mr. Wagoner know you had it?"

"Not to my knowledge." Janelle shrugged a shoulder, a lump formed in her throat, and she swallowed a few times to dislodge it.

Bonner's brow creased as his lips pressed tightly together, and Hayes scratched frantically in his notebook.

Janelle waited as she tried to keep the tears at bay. This was her fault. Kelsey's injuries had been caused by a gun that was her responsibility. If Kelsey had died . . . Janelle closed her eyes on that thought.

"Are we done here then?" her father asked. Both officers looked at him and nodded. "Then we'll be leaving now."

Janelle sat motionless as her father slid his chair back and stood. It wasn't until a few seconds later, when he tugged on her arm, that she rose woodenly from her seat. He gently gripped her arm as he led her from the room, and they were halfway down the hall when her legs just stopped. She couldn't move, she was gasping for air; she felt like an elephant was perched on her shoulders. She pressed her back to the wall and slid to a crouch, hugging her body as her mind raced.

She felt the weight of her father's hand on her upper arm. "Janelle, are you okay?"

"Just give me a minute," she practically whispered.

She had told Nathan she didn't want the gun. Even after he'd explained why he wanted her to have it, she'd asked him to take it back. He'd been persistent and she'd eventually caved, but as soon as he'd left, she'd put it in the shoebox. She closed her eyes and slowly lowered her head.

"I should never have agreed to keep it." Janelle looked at her father's frowning face. "He never should have given me that gun. I'd never even told him Richard was abusing me."

"Janelle, recognizing abuse is his specialty," George said sadly as he held his hand out to her.

Janelle placed her hand in his, and with a gentle grip he pulled her to her feet. "It wasn't at the time."

Her father's eyebrows rose slightly.

"I told him I didn't want it. I told him I wouldn't use it," Janelle said, her heart racing with anger and frustration. "If he'd just kept the damn thing, we wouldn't be in this mess."

"Janelle." Her father's calm voice reached her, but she ignored it.

"If he hadn't insisted I keep it, I wouldn't have had to hide it from Richard. I wouldn't have forgotten it was in the house." Her eyes widened as she stared at George's face. "What if he'd shot one of the kids with it? Dad, he could have killed them when they had visitation with him."

"Sweetheart," he tried again with the soothing tones and gripped her upper arms as tears filled her eyes. "That didn't happen."

"But it could have. And it's Nathan's fault for leaving that thing with me," her voice cracked on the last few words. "He should have just stayed away from us. I wish he hadn't come back into my life."

George wrapped his arms around her, and a few tears slid down her cheeks. "I don't think you mean that." His words brushed across her ear. "Do you?"

"Yes," she said as she hiccupped.

A vision of her daughter, Nathan's child, flashed through her mind.

"No," Janelle muttered as another image crossed her brain, Nathan and Zoe playing with her new toys after Christmas dinner. The tears were so thick they choked the final words from her, "I don't know."

By the time she arrived home, she was calmer and no longer blamed Nathan for what had happened. She still wasn't happy with him, but now the guilt lay squarely on her shoulders. She flung the front door open as she stepped into the house and yelled for her sister.

"Kitchen!" was the response.

Janelle walked toward it, stopping only for a moment to greet the children, playing with blocks at the coffee table, and found Kelsey and Patrick staring each other down across the kitchen island. Kelsey turned and smiled widely at her as Janelle threw her arms around her sister. Kelsey, sitting on the barstool, giggled lightly as she returned the hug. "Hey," she said as she patted Janelle's back.

Janelle stepped back and looked at her younger sister and tried to smile.

The frown Kelsey gave her told her she'd failed miserably. "What happened?"

"Nothing," Janelle answered and glanced at Patrick.

He was still scowling in Kelsey's direction but met her quick look and stood. The lines in his forehead and around his lips deepened.

She looked at her sister again and gripped her hands. "I'm so sorry."

"For what?" All humor left Kelsey's voice as she squeezed Janelle's fingers. "You're starting to worry me."

Janelle's throat tightened as she sat on the stool in front of Kelsey, facing her. She blinked furiously and rolled her eyes until she was sure she wouldn't cry again. "The gun Richard used to shoot you," Janelle began and paused when she heard Patrick's sharp inhalation.

"Calm down," Kelsey muttered with a quick, sad glance at him. Patrick walked around the kitchen island to stand behind Kelsey. He placed his hands on her shoulders, and she released one of Janelle's hands to reach up and grip one of his.

"It was my gun," Janelle finished when they'd stopped moving.

Both sets of eyes sharpened on her face, but they remained silent. Janelle had spent the entire thirty-minute drive home berating herself for making such a stupid mistake. If only she hadn't left the gun at the house. If only she hadn't agreed to let Nathan leave it in the first place. She should have been more forceful when she'd told Nathan she didn't want it. But who was she kidding?

Years of listening to her mother's not-so-wonderful advice on how to be a good wife had certainly taken root. When Kelsey had gotten pregnant, Janelle had practically laughed at her mother's advice. It had been clear to her then that Kelsey had tried to follow every bit of it and it had gotten her nowhere. Janelle had been so thankful thinking she wasn't like that. At least to the extreme Kelsey had been.

But not long after, she was shocked to realize how wrong she was. She found herself making little decisions every day based on what Richard might want. She'd brushed it off, as they were such little things it didn't really matter. So what if she fixed asparagus for dinner three nights a week because it was his favorite? She liked it too. So what if she got her haircut in the same style every time because it was how he liked it? It was an easy style to maintain. So what if she picked up the same type of wine each trip to the grocery store because he commented once how much he liked it? It wasn't that bad.

Janelle had never tried to exert herself until Kelsey got pregnant and needed a place to live. She'd begged and pleaded and bargained with Richard until he agreed. In the grand scheme of things, she'd thought it was a small victory, but a victory nonetheless. And as time passed, she'd started standing up for what she wanted more and more, never really considering her mother's advice.

She wasn't sure when she'd reached the point of just not caring whether Richard was happy or not, she just knew she had. Clearly, though, the habits were still ingrained in her. The fact that she'd given in to Nathan was proof of that. She'd wanted to make him happy and it had nearly cost her sister's life.

After a few more seconds of silence, Kelsey's head tilted to the side and she frowned. "O-kay," she said slowly. "So, what are you apologizing for?" Janelle's chin dropped and Kelsey's frown slowly turned upward. "Janelle, it was your gun. So what? Richard was the one using it."

"But if I hadn't had it, he wouldn't have been able to get to it," Janelle softly argued.

"How did he get it?" Patrick asked soberly. "Was it here?"

Janelle met his concerned gaze and shook her head. "No, I forgot about it when I moved out."

"Oh." Kelsey's lips formed and held a perfect circle.

Patrick frowned and Janelle watched his face carefully, sure that he would understand and start to blame her as well. He should be as mad at her as she was herself. He'd almost lost Kelsey too.

"How did the gun get into the house to begin with?" Kelsey's calm question broke into her silent observations. "Had you had it long before you moved out?"

"What?" Janelle felt like they were having a normal conversation over a cup of coffee. It didn't feel right. "I guess I'd had it for two years or so." Kelsey and Patrick nodded in unison, Janelle let out a long breath as she added, "Nathan gave it to me."

"To protect yourself?" Patrick asked.

Janelle thought she might fall off her seat. Those had been Nathan's exact words.

"That's kind of sweet that he was so concerned about you after you ended things," Kelsey added before Janelle could speak.

"It was before I ended it. And it's not sweet," Janelle spat as she threw Kelsey's hand away and Kelsey backed up slightly. "Sweet that he thought I might be able to shoot someone, namely Richard?"

"Sweet that he cared enough about you to want you to be safe when he wasn't around," Kelsey stated quietly. "Janelle, he knows you well enough to know you would probably never use a gun unless your life or, even more so, the kids' lives depended on it. He was obviously aware of Richard's abusive tendencies and wanted to ensure everyone's safety."

"Yes, well, look where it got us. Richard used the gun against all of us, didn't he? I told Nathan I didn't want it, and he didn't listen. He should have just kept his gun to himself and we wouldn't be in this mess." Janelle turned to prop her elbows on the counter.

"You don't believe that, do you?" Patrick asked, stepping away from Kelsey and leaning on the counter toward her. Janelle shifted her glare to him for a moment before focusing on the veining in the marble countertop. "Janelle, if it hadn't been your gun, it would have been another one. Or another weapon of some sort."

"Yes, but mine was convenient." Tears filled Janelle's eyes.

"True," Kelsey agreed. "But even if it hadn't been, he was determined to hurt me and Zach and, in a roundabout way, you. He could just as easily have bought one. Except for money, there was really nothing to stop him."

"Richard was the bad guy, not the gun. Not you for leaving it at his house. Not Nathan for giving it to you in the first place," Patrick stated. "No one blames you."

"Except for Mom, of course," Kelsey said, and Janelle looked at her. "But then, she blames us for everything," she added with a wink, and a laugh bubbled in Janelle's chest. Kelsey wrapped her arms around her sister, and Janelle felt suddenly better, lighter.

"Can't wait for her to hear about this," Janelle muttered into her sister's hair. "If Nathan hadn't been so stubborn and persistent, then we wouldn't even have to be talking about this."

Kelsey pulled away and beamed brightly. "Well, men can't help it. They're all stubborn and persistent."

"Hey," Patrick grumbled, and Janelle saw his immense frown at Kelsey.

Kelsey wouldn't meet his dark look, she focused on something over Janelle's shoulder and shrugged.

"What's going on?" Janelle asked slowly, the memory of the looks on their faces when she'd arrived seeping back into her mind. "Trouble in paradise already?"

Kelsey shook her head, her smile faltering slightly. "No, just a small disagreement."

"About what?" Janelle studied her sister's face and saw the slight tension creep into her features. She looked at Patrick, surprised to find hurt in his eyes, not the anger she'd been expecting. She looked at Kelsey again.

"He wants me to go to Paris with him," Kelsey confessed.

"It's only two months. At most," Patrick added.

"Two months that you'll be working and I'll be stuck in the hotel or your trailer, unable to do anything because I can barely walk." Kelsey finally looked at him.

"I just want you with me." Sadness crept into his features.

Kelsey frowned. "You know if things were different I would go with you in a heartbeat, but I think I need to stay here for a while." She reached across the divide between them and took his hand. "I'll be here when you get back."

"You're leaving?" came a small voice from the doorway.

All three of the adults turned to see Zach staring at them, his eyes wide and full of tears. Janelle's heart split and she started to rise. Patrick was on his feet and walking toward Zach before she could stand.

"I have to work for a little while, but I'll come back," Patrick was saying, trying to soothe Zach.

Zach's head quickly wobbled from side to side. "You're lying!" he shouted. "Lying is your job. You don't care about me. Just go away!" Zach turned and ran up the stairs. Patrick's face was stricken and pale as he glanced at Janelle and Kelsey before he turned and raced after Zach.

Janelle felt numb as she looked at her sister. Kelsey's eyes were closed and tears slowly slid down her cheeks. Janelle hoped Patrick could calm her son, but felt the time had come to find him a good therapist.

Nine

"Zach?" asked the man standing at the office doorway. He was blond, dressed in a dark-blue polo shirt and khaki pants. Through silver-framed glasses he looked at Zach and then met Janelle's stare.

She was sitting in the waiting room of what she hoped would be the office of the therapist who would help Zach. It had been four days since the boy had called Patrick a liar and fled from the room. Patrick had been able to calm him down and convince him that he wasn't lying and he would be home as soon as his work was done. Zach had come down for dinner, but had remained silent and refused to say where he'd gotten such an idea in his head. But the adults had all known anyway and agreed that the sooner they could get to the bottom of the damage Richard had done, the better for Zach.

As Janelle held the man's look, she slowly stood and tugged on Zach's sleeve so he would do the same. The man came closer and held out his hand.

"Mrs. Wagoner, I'm Andrew Ross," he said.

Janelle frowned slightly as she shook his hand. His name had been at the top of the short list of therapists the psychologist at the hospital had given her. He'd also come highly recommended as a child therapist by Nathan during their conversation on the ride to the hospital the morning after the kidnapping. He dealt with children from abusive families and sent people to him all the time. But despite the good recommendations, he was not what she expected. Andrew Ross appeared to be younger than Janelle. She quickly did the math in her head, with college and post-graduate degrees, how long had he really been practicing?

"Please, call me Janelle." She dropped her hand and placed it on the back of Zach's shoulder. "This is Zach."

The therapist squatted to Zach's eye level and held out his hand again. "Hi Zach, I'm Andrew. It's a pleasure to meet you."

Zach looked at Andrew's hand then inched behind Janelle. Janelle's eyes widened in surprise as she looked at the therapist and shrugged.

"I am so sorry. He's never done this before," she tried to explain.

Andrew stood and smiled comfortingly. "It's okay. It's actually quite normal behavior. Now, why don't we step into my office so we can talk?" He looked down at Zach and his smile grew by a fraction of an inch. "I have a surprise for you."

Andrew stepped aside and motioned Janelle and Zach toward the door he'd just exited. Once they were all in the room, Andrew closed the door behind them. He stepped around to the side of the room as Janelle took it all in.

The lower half of the room was rich mahogany-wood paneling, large squares of raised wood outlined in each panel. The floor was a plush, dark-blue carpet that was just a shade darker than the wall color above the paneling. Bookshelves covered the far wall, but only one section actually held books. The other shelves were filled with an assortment of white, lined baskets, their contents hidden from view. A white sofa was centered on the wall to her right, an abstract painting in bold colors over the back of it. The other wall had two tall, narrow windows, spaced evenly along the expanse. A brown leather chair sat in front of the bookshelves, facing the sofa at an angle, a small dark end table between them.

Andrew was standing at the bookshelf, pulling baskets out and examining their contents before deciding whether he would put them back or place them on the floor at his feet. When he'd amassed five or six baskets, he turned and looked at Janelle.

"Please, have a seat on the sofa, Janelle. Zach, I'd like you to come over here and help me out," he said, his expression full of concern and compassion.

Zach didn't move.

Janelle remained behind him and nudged him with her hand. "Go ahead, sweetie. Let's see what's in the baskets."

Slowly, Zach made his way toward Andrew and his baskets, and Janelle took the same painfully slow steps toward the couch, watching Zach the entire time. She sat down as Zach reached the baskets, and the expression on his face shifted slightly, even though he didn't smile. He hadn't smiled since the kidnapping. Janelle watched as Andrew pointed to the different baskets and talked to Zach in a voice she couldn't hear.

Together, the two of them moved the baskets closer to the center of the room, and Zach sat down and started to rummage through them. Andrew sat in the leather chair and turned it slightly so he could observe Zach. Together, Janelle and Andrew watched Zach in silence, until Janelle's curiosity got the better of her.

She'd watched Zach pick through two of the six baskets, then asked, "Aren't you going to talk to him about what happened?"

Andrew shook his head but didn't take his eyes off of Zach. "No, I'm just going to observe for now."

Observe? "Why?" Janelle asked.

His lips turned up slightly as he looked at her. "I like to start my young clients out with what's called 'play therapy.' It helps me to see how he interacts with the toys, and how he allows them to interact with each other. He may not be able to, or even want to, tell me how he's feeling about what happened, but if I watch closely enough, I can get a pretty good idea. And if I can't figure it out, I'll ask him to clarify."

Janelle nodded her understanding as Andrew turned to observe Zach again.

"And from my observations and his explanations, we'll be able to talk it out and I'll, hopefully, help him come to terms with his experiences," he finished quietly.

Janelle had to admit she was impressed. She never would have thought it could be that simple, but it made sense. Even she had to admit she'd noticed a slight difference in the way Zach played with Zoe and their toys. It hadn't been anything extreme, and she wasn't sure she could even place what exactly had changed, but she had noticed that something was off.

She turned her attention to Zach as well and asked, "What are you starting with?"

"I thought we could start with puppets before we move on to other, more complex toys. I've given him the option. Some of the baskets have pre-made puppets, and there are supplies in the others for him to make his own. I've told him he could use mine, make his own, or both, but I asked him to pick out a few to represent the people who are important to him."

As he'd answered her questions, Andrew's eyes had remained focused on Zach, narrowing and relaxing as he observed the boy. Janelle tilted her head approvingly, satisfied with his answers and focus, then settled into the corner of the couch to watch what might unfold.

Janelle sat in the overstuffed armchair and looked out of the bay window across the room. She and Zach had come home from therapy and had a quiet dinner with Kelsey, Patrick, and Zoe. She'd then gotten the kids into bed and told them goodnight, and now she waited while Kelsey and Patrick did the same.

She tried to force her mind onto the events of the day, the therapy session with Andrew, what she'd witnessed and learned, the nearly silent dinner and what it might mean, but her thoughts kept straying to Nathan. She hadn't told Kelsey she'd seen him at the station, and she hadn't called him since. After the cold shoulder he'd given her, she didn't see the point. If he wanted to talk to her, he knew where to find her. She wasn't going anywhere.

"Patrick, I told you I can walk." Kelsey's voice drifted down the stairs before her feet appeared. "You carry me up. I come down on my own."

Janelle's lips twitched, and she shook her head at her sister's commanding tone. She'd forgotten how much she missed hearing them. The replying grumble from Patrick made her chuckle out loud. Janelle turned in time to see Kelsey stop on the floor just in front of the steps, turn around, and fling her arms around Patrick's neck. She lifted her injured leg as she stood on her tiptoes and planted a kiss on his frowning lips.

Janelle looked away. She was happy for her sister—Kelsey deserved her happiness—but it was still hard to watch the examples of affection Kelsey and Patrick shared, even if they were rarely knowingly in Janelle's presence. A few moments passed before the couple came into the living room and sat on the couch. Kelsey winced as she placed her legs up on the coffee table.

"How's your leg today?" Janelle asked.

"Not too bad. It hurts less and less every day, but it's so tired by the time we get the kids into bed that it aches," Kelsey answered, her hand lightly rubbing the spot where Richard's bullet had entered her thigh.

Janelle saw Patrick's eyebrow lift slightly as he frowned. He'd become a little less sensitive about the topic, but she could tell he still didn't like to talk about it.

"How did therapy go?" Kelsey asked, turning her full attention on Janelle after casting a comforting glance at Patrick.

Janelle thought about her answer. "It went well, I think. It wasn't what I'd been expecting."

"Why? What did Zach say?" Kelsey's brow furrowed slightly as she sat back into the circle of Patrick's arm.

"Nothing, really," Janelle answered and explained Andrew's play therapy method.

"So, what did Zach play with today?" Kelsey asked.

"Puppets," Janelle replied with a slight smile. "Andrew asked him to find or make puppets to represent the important people in his life."

"Andrew?" Kelsey's voice held more than a question.

"He's not a doctor, he doesn't have a PhD, he doesn't need one," Janelle explained as it had been explained to her. "And he doesn't like his patients to call him Mr. Ross, he says it's too formal. He wants the kids to be relaxed around him."

Kelsey slowly nodded, but Janelle saw a slight apprehension in her eyes and wondered what she might be thinking.

"Anyway," Janelle continued, ignoring the lingering question in Kelsey's eyes. "Patrick, you'll be happy to know Zach found a superhero puppet and immediately said it was you."

Patrick chuckled, and Kelsey patted his knee as she grinned at him.

"I wore an apron. Zoe's had pigtails and Dad's was a gray-haired man. He even found a police puppet." Janelle choked on the rest of the words and looked at her lap as she closed her eyes. Her chest burned to think that Zach considered Nathan an important person in his life when Nathan may never be a part of it again. She swallowed the lump in her throat and looked at her sister. "He had to make puppets for you, Richard, and Mom."

"Uh-oh," Kelsey said with a slight smile, her eyes telling the truth of her turmoil.

"Richard's puppet had angry eyes, red cheeks, and an open mouth. Zach said it was because he always yelled at everyone."

Kelsey nodded and Patrick scowled.

"Mom's had angry eyes too," Janelle continued and began to frown.

"What's wrong?" Kelsey questioned.

"It's funny, I wasn't surprised to see it at the time, but now that I think about it, I'm bothered by it," Janelle answered and realized she wasn't making sense. She waved off her sister's impending question when Kelsey opened her mouth. "The puppet he made for Mom. He made a little fist for it with a pointing finger." Janelle held up her hand to model what she meant, her fist closed with her index finger sticking out, pointing it at Kelsey. "Andrew asked him why he did that, and Zach said that's what she looks like when she's talking to us."

Kelsey laughed out loud. "Oh my goodness, that's funny," she said between giggles. Then her face slowly sobered as she sat up on the edge of the couch. "Oh," she repeated more deliberately, her eyes widening on Janelle. "Oh, no." Her hand crept up to cover her lips. "He sees that?"

Janelle shrugged. "Apparently so."

"He's right, she does point that finger at the two of you," Patrick said and placed his elbows on his knees. "He's obviously very observant."

"Or she just does it more than we thought," Kelsey said as her shoulders drooped. She leaned her head against Patrick's shoulder and eyed Janelle. "What was my puppet like?" she asked softly.

Janelle inhaled deeply, unsure what Kelsey would think of the puppet Zach made to represent her. She slowly released the breath. "He put a suitcase in your hands."

Kelsey's eyebrow rose and her head lifted slightly. "Is that all?"

"Why?" Patrick asked.

"Because she's gone so much," Janelle answered Patrick then looked at Kelsey. "What were you expecting?"

Kelsey was silent, her eyes focused to the upper corner of the room as her teeth rubbed against her bottom lip. "I don't know. Just worse, I guess. Things feel different now that he knows I gave him away. I guess I was expecting something along those lines."

They fell silent for a little while as a few tears slid down Kelsey's cheeks. Patrick put his arm around her, comforting her as she quietly cried. When she could no longer watch, Janelle stood and walked into the kitchen, poured herself a glass of wine, and took a long sip.

Giving Zach up had not been an easy thing for Kelsey to do. They both knew that Janelle had been the driving force in the adoption. They'd both agreed that it was the best thing for Zach, and they'd agreed to tell him at some point. But they'd never planned on Richard's descent into madness. They'd never expected him to reveal the truth in such dramatic fashion.

Sometimes, she really hated that man.

"So what happened next?" Patrick asked.

Janelle looked up to see him helping Kelsey lower herself onto a stool, then they both turned expectant gazes on her.

"Nothing, really." Janelle shrugged as she set the wine glass on the counter. "Andrew wanted to have Zach use the puppets to act out a few scenes, happy scenes from birthdays and stuff, but after Zach had created the puppets and explained his choices, we were out of time."

"Do you think I could come with you for the next session?" Kelsey's eyes were wide and pleading.

Janelle frowned. "I don't know, but I can ask." She took another long sip of her wine. "Are you sure you want to?"

"Why wouldn't I?" Kelsey asked.

"Because you know that what Richard told him about you wasn't positive," Janelle started. "And the way Zach sees you right now is colored by Richard's words. It may make you uncomfortable or sad."

"Janelle's right," Patrick said as he placed his chin on Kelsey's head and his arm around her shoulder. "Just trust the process and know that Zach still loves you and everything will work out." He planted a kiss on the crown of Kelsey's head as she looked down.

"Does he? It doesn't feel like it," Kelsey muttered.

"You know he does, Kels. He adores you. He's just confused right now," Janelle reassured her sister, as she hoped her words were true. She prayed constantly that the damage Richard had done was reversible, otherwise she didn't know what she'd do.

Janelle finished her glass of wine and considered another until she noticed Kelsey looking at her. She raised her eyebrow, waiting for the question she could see her sister considering.

"Have you called Nathan today?" Kelsey asked and Janelle picked up the wine bottle.

She poured her second glass, re-corked the bottle, and put it back in the cabinet behind her then turned back around. Only after she had picked up her glass and downed half of the wine in one swallow did she look at her sister again.

"No." She wasn't in the mood for further explanation.

The look on Kelsey's face told her she wasn't getting away with that.

"When was the last time you actually spoke to him?" Kelsey asked.

"Spoke to him or had a conversation? Those are two entirely different things," Janelle said as the warmth of the wine began to seep into her veins. She should probably stop drinking.

"Either," Kelsey said as she narrowed an eye on the wineglass, "or both, whatever."

"We haven't had an actual conversation since he left me at the hospital," Janelle answered. "But I spoke to him on Friday at the police station. Kind of."

"Kind of?" Patrick questioned as he sat down next to Kelsey.

"Yes, kind of. He didn't seem too keen on talking to me. He ignored my attempt to start a conversation and sort of blew me off," Janelle said and felt tears building. She didn't realize they could cause such a pain in her chest. "So I haven't tried to call him since then."

Kelsey tilted her head and frowned. "Really? That's it?"

"What else would there be, Kelsey? He didn't answer any of my calls for a week and when he finally saw me again, he pretended I didn't exist. He obviously doesn't want to talk to me about anything, so yeah, that's it." Janelle's volume increased as she spoke and she paused to get her racing heart under control.

"Can you really blame him, though? I can't," she finished softly. "I let him believe I cared about him," *which I did*, "and then ended it so quickly that we both got whiplash. And when he found out about the baby, I lied. So many times I knowingly lied and told him it wasn't his. For what?" Janelle looked at Kelsey and frowned. "I don't blame him for hating me Kelsey, but I have a head start on that. No one could possibly hate me more than I hate myself for what I did to him."

"J—"

Janelle held up her hand. "I'm going to bed."

She dumped the remainder of her wine down the drain, left her glass in the sink, and went upstairs, ignoring Kelsey's and Patrick's stares and gaping mouths.

Nathan sat cross-legged in the hallway, bouncing McClane's tennis ball against the wall in front of him. Night had fallen, but the only light in the house came from the glow of his cell phone on the floor in the circle of his legs.

She hadn't called.

He'd explained everything to Mason at lunch after they'd seen Janelle at the police station. His brother had pointed out that he was going beyond following orders and was simply being rude. Mason had suggested that Nathan at least explain to Janelle why he couldn't talk to her. He'd also pointed out that Captain Little wouldn't know if Nathan and Janelle shared a phone conversation or two. After the meal, Nathan had considered calling her, but he wasn't sure if he could start the conversation without coming across angry. He had so many questions, he didn't know where to begin, so he'd decided that he would answer the phone the next time she called.

The problem was, it had been four days and she hadn't called once.

Not that he could really blame her. He hadn't been able to have the conversation he'd wanted to have with her, so he had resorted to not saying anything. Probably not the wisest course of action. But then, until the investigations were over, he couldn't risk being near her. It would bring unwarranted questions about Richard's death. Neither he nor she had anything to do with it; but, as Captain Little had pointed out, any association between them now could be seen as suspicious and one, or both, of them could be accused of murder.

He caught the ball and looked down at the silent phone again.

The only conclusion Nathan could draw was that Mason was probably right. She'd seen his behavior at the station as rude and inconsiderate, and he'd done serious damage to whatever remained of their relationship. How could he fix that without going against his captain's orders?

The phone rang and he looked down at it. He didn't recognize the number, but there was something familiar about it. He picked it up and pressed the speaker button.

"Hello," Nathan answered.

"Hey, Nathan, it's Patrick."

A smile slowly crept across Nathan's face. This might be the solution he was looking for.

Ten

Nathan placed his case on the table then laid his rifle and shotgun beside it. He flipped up the latches on either side of the lid and lifted it, revealing his two personal handguns. Carefully, he picked them up from their padded resting spots in the top of the case and laid them on the table beside the larger guns. He picked up the padding and looked into the case, at the ammunition and the empty cartridges. Nathan was looking forward to spending the next few hours at the nearly empty shooting range, honing his skills and relieving some stress.

It was a clear, spring day. The air smelled clean and fresh, and Nathan took a long, relaxing sniff. He hoped he'd be able to clear his head, settle his nerves, and get rid of his cabin fever. The investigations were taking longer than they should, especially the one into Richard's death. That case should have been closed already. Even if they didn't think it was exactly suicide, Richard's death came at his own hand, because of his own actions. Any other reasons they might find came as a direct result of everything Richard had done.

"A shooting range?"

The corner of Nathan's mouth lifted slightly as he looked up and watched Patrick climb out of Kelsey's Jeep. Patrick closed the door and then closed the distance between them, stopping on the other side of the T-shaped table.

"Why not? It's just as good a place as any." Nathan pulled out two pairs of earmuffs and two pairs of safety glasses. "And it's great for stress relief."

"I suppose." Patrick stared at the guns, his mouth turned down in a frown.

When he reached for one of the handguns, Nathan noticed a slight shake in Patrick's hand. Nathan had forgotten the last time Patrick had touched a gun was in the cabin.

"Man, I'm sorry," Nathan said. "If you'd rather not shoot, we can find somewhere else to chat."

With a gun in his hand, aimed downward and away from them both, Patrick looked at Nathan and shrugged. "No, I'm good." He checked to see if it was loaded and placed the gun back on the table and put on a pair of safety glasses. "Shooting isn't something I do often, but I was trained for an action role a couple of years ago and was taught how to handle a weapon."

Nathan nodded, and the two of them loaded all of the cartridges then put them in the guns.

"What are we shooting at?" Patrick asked, and Nathan looked out at the plinking range.

There weren't many targets available, so he retrieved a few items from his truck—an empty soda bottle, an empty milk jug, and his favorite target, a bright-orange, rubber pyramid. "This should do it," Nathan said as he threw all of them as far as he could onto the range. He walked back to the table, motioned to the guns, and looked at Patrick. "Guest first."

Patrick put the ear protection on, picked his gun—the rifle—and walked to the shooting line in front of the table. After he squeezed off a few rounds, Nathan took his turn. After all of the guns were empty of ammunition, they took off their muffs and began to reload.

"How are you doing?" Nathan asked.

"Good, I suppose," Patrick answered. He looked at the cartridge in his hand. "You know, I barely remember what happened that night."

"Really?" Nathan set his full magazine down and placed his hands on the table. "What do you remember?"

Patrick set everything in his hands down and looked over the range. "I remember being scared to death when I heard her begging him to kill her instead of Zach."

Nathan shuddered. He hadn't heard that Kelsey had tried to bargain with her life. Given the situation, he imagined Janelle would have done the same thing, and a cool chill went through him.

"When I heard the gunshot after I got Zach out of the house, I just went into automatic survival mode." Patrick picked up a reloaded handgun and walked to the firing line. "I was so relieved when I heard her voice after I crawled into the house." He fired at the rubber triangle and it danced across the ground. "All I could think was that I had to stay alive so I could make sure she survived." Patrick shot the last few rounds and walked back to the table and set the gun down.

"Did you shoot him?" Nathan asked coolly.

Patrick met Nathan's stare, his eyes empty and devoid of anything. "I honestly don't know," he answered and shrugged. "But I can't say I'm sorry he's dead."

Nathan picked up the rifle and stepped to the firing line and pulled the trigger. When his ammunition was used up, he returned to the table. "Me either," he agreed softly.

"I'll bet," Patrick said with a slight lift to his lips. "Which brings me to the reason I called you."

Nathan had wondered when they would get to that. Patrick had accepted Nathan's invitation to join him in part because he didn't want Kelsey or Janelle to overhear their conversation.

Patrick laid the rifle's newly loaded cartridge on the table and placed his palms on either side of it. His eyes narrowed on the table's surface like he was considering what he wanted to say. "I want to know what's going on between you and Janelle, or where you would like to see things go."

Nathan folded his arms across his chest. "That's a little personal, don't you think?"

Patrick straightened and shrugged. "Not really." Nathan opened his mouth to argue but Patrick held up a hand to stop him. "I'm not asking for details, Nathan. I just know what I saw between the two of you before Richard's revelation, and I know what I see now. I don't know what caused the change in your behavior, but I had always thought you to be pretty levelheaded. I would think that if you were upset about Zoe, you'd at least talk it out with Janelle."

Nathan nodded his agreement. If things were different, that's exactly what he would have done.

"But you won't even speak to her, and I have to wonder why. Did you have a change of heart, or is there another reason?" Patrick took a similar stance to Nathan's with his arms across his chest, his eyes now narrowed on Nathan's face.

Now was Nathan's chance to clear the air with Patrick and, more importantly, Janelle. He felt certain that if he asked Patrick to, he would relay everything to Janelle.

"I haven't had a change of heart," Nathan started with a shake of his head. "I'm fairly certain I love her more now than I ever thought possible, and I miss her every day. But I'm not supposed to see her or any of her family until these investigations are over. It's killing me that she and I can't talk about our daughter or our future."

"Okay, I'm lost." Patrick held up his hand to stop Nathan. "Why are you not supposed to see her? Who told you that and why?"

"My captain, the day after the shooting when he called me into his office," Nathan answered as he sat on the stool attached to the table. "Because I had been watching over her, because I was the first cop on the scene at the cabin, and because of our affair, he said that if we're seen together, people might start to suspect we may have planned this whole thing, that we may have caused Richard's death."

One of Patrick's eyebrows lifted as his eyes narrowed. "You're kidding?"

"I wish." Nathan shook his head. "He highly recommended I stay away from her until the case is resolved so neither of us becomes a suspected murderer."

Patrick frowned at him. "So, because of your affair, he's afraid that if people even see the two of you together, they might jump to the conclusion that you set this whole thing up? That you somehow convinced Richard to kidnap Zach so that you could then kill him in a rage or something?"

"Or that we would have simply used the opportunity presented to us by the kidnapping to off him so we could be together," Nathan clarified as he rose to his feet. "I know it's far-fetched, but Bonner basically said as much in my interview. Only that I convinced you to do my dirty work for me." Nathan took in a lungful of air and slowly blew it out. "But there it is. Until this damn case is closed, which in my opinion should have been done already, I'm stuck not seeing Janelle and Zoe. I'm stuck not being able to talk about our past or plan for our potential future. It's driving me crazy, man. I know she's angry at me, she's stopped calling."

Patrick's pressed his lips together and shrug-nodded his agreement.

"I'm afraid I'm losing her." Nathan looked down at the weapons on the table, suddenly not interested in firing them anymore. "I can't lose her again," he muttered as he took off his hearing protection and glasses and laid them on the table.

Patrick did the same with his earmuffs and safety glasses. Nathan heard his extended intake of air and then its slow release before Patrick finally spoke. "What do you want me to tell Janelle?"

Nathan released a huge sigh of relief. That was what he'd been hoping to hear. "Tell her whatever you think she needs to know," he answered. "But most importantly, ask her to call me. I need to tell her some things myself."

After the kids were in bed, Janelle, Patrick, and Kelsey stood around the kitchen island. Patrick had disappeared earlier that day, but Janelle had no idea where he'd gone and Kelsey hadn't been very forthcoming with her information. Now all Janelle could do was wait for one of them to decide to tell her what was going on. She only hoped it was good news. She was tired of bad.

"Would you like something to drink?" Janelle asked as she opened the cabinet.

Since Kelsey was still using the occasional painkiller, she wasn't drinking again yet, so Janelle pulled two wine glasses from the shelf. She turned and set them on the island as Kelsey sat on the stool and Patrick placed the wine bottle on the counter. He opened it and then poured two glasses. He slid one toward Janelle and walked around the island to sit beside Kelsey.

Janelle noticed the look that passed between them, and a sense of foreboding trickled down her spine. "What's going on?"

Patrick took a sip from his glass and set it in front of him. "I saw Nathan today."

Janelle's legs began to shake, and a sense of betrayal settled in her stomach like a pebble. "Why would you do that?" she asked as she sat on the stool closest to her.

"I was concerned," Patrick replied. "You're upset and I wanted to know what was going on."

Janelle looked at her sister. "Did you know about this?"

Kelsey slowly nodded and looked away.

Janelle frowned. "Do you know what was said?"

Kelsey nodded again.

The betrayal grew into a stone and Janelle closed her eyes as she debated whether or not she wanted this conversation to continue. She had a suspicion that he wasn't happy with her, did she really need confirmation? It obviously wouldn't change anything. The only thing she figured she could do was start trying to figure out what to do about Zoe. Suddenly the idea of letting her continue to think of Richard as her father was unsettling. But if Nathan didn't want to take on the role, then she didn't have a choice.

"Fine," she said as she opened her eyes. "What did he say?"

Patrick took a deep breath and met her stare. "Do you remember when you were at the hospital with Kelsey and he got called away?"

Janelle's brow lifted as her lips pursed. How could she forget? It was the first time she'd truly felt abandoned by anyone.

"He was called into his captain's office." Patrick's lip curled slightly. "Apparently Richard's accusations didn't sit well with Nathan's captain, and he wanted to discuss them and the implications on the investigation."

Janelle didn't see what this had to do with her, but she patiently waited for Patrick to continue.

"His captain suspended him."

"You told me that already," Janelle snapped, as surprised by the shortness in her tone as Kelsey and Patrick seemed to be. "Sorry."

Patrick nodded. "It was suggested that he stay away from you," he continued with a frown, "all of your family, actually, until the investigation is over."

Janelle's jaw dropped. "What? Why?" The explanation couldn't really be that simple.

"The captain said that it might look suspicious. If he's seen with you it could call his behavior, and yours, into question, given he'd been watching you and was the first officer on the scene," Patrick explained. "It could make both of you look guilty of something, and the captain thought you might want to avoid that."

"Janelle, it's only until the investigations are over," Kelsey added with a slight smile. "It shouldn't be much longer, then the two of you can work this out."

Had Janelle heard her right? "Investigations? There's more than one?"

"Yes, there's the one into Richard's death and there's the internal investigation into Nathan's inappropriate use of department resources." Patrick moved closer to Kelsey and slid an arm around her waist. "Nathan doesn't think either of them should take too much longer. He is anxious to talk to you about Zoe and the role you want him to play in her life."

Janelle's betrayal no longer felt like a stone in her stomach. It began to lighten and bubble as hope took its place. He did want to talk to her. He was just constrained by his responsibilities to the force. She knew how important his job was to him, he'd used it to support his mother and brothers for the longest time, and he obviously didn't want to jeopardize it.

And just as quickly as it had started to build, the hope sank. He hadn't cared about his job when he'd been watching her house to keep her safe. It didn't make sense.

"Janelle, aren't you happy?" Kelsey asked.

"I'm not sure," Janelle answered softly.

"What are you not sure about?" Patrick asked, businesslike and calm.

She looked at him as she shook her head. "I don't know. I guess it just seems like he was perfectly fine going against protocol to keep an eye on all of us, at your request. And that was before he even knew about Zoe. But now that he knows, suddenly he wants to follow the rules." Her heart began to race at the unfairness of it all.

"He has more on the line now," Patrick replied.

"Does he? He's been supporting his mother since he started on the force. He paid for his brothers to go to college. His salary has always been important to more than just him. I didn't realize he was taking a risk to protect us, but he took it. And now, he knows he has a daughter and he decides he can't chance it to see her?" Janelle said, her calmness becoming a whine. She waited until she knew she could speak calmly again before continuing. "I'm just not sure I completely believe him."

"Has he ever lied to you, J?" Kelsey questioned innocently, her eyes wide with expectation. Patrick frowned and looked away.

"No," Janelle answered.

"Then why would you think he's not being honest now?" Kelsey clenched her hands together on the counter.

"He's never had reason to lie before, Kels." Janelle took a sip of wine and set the glass down. "Now he has an arsenal full."

"That's not true," Kelsey argued.

Janelle smiled deprecatingly as she looked down. After everything she'd been through, how could her little sister still seem so innocent? "I lied to him about Zoe, repeatedly. I've put his job and now, possibly, his freedom at risk. He's taken chances for me that he never should have taken, and it's cost him everything."

"He doesn't see it that way," Patrick stated. He drained his wine glass and slid it away. "He still cares about you and hopes you can work this out as soon as he's given the okay."

"Why does he have to wait to be given anything?" Janelle snapped. "If we were truly that important to him, don't you think he'd take the risk?"

Patrick shrugged a shoulder.

"Wouldn't you?" Janelle blurted.

She knew the answer. He'd proven himself to be willing to risk anything when he followed Kelsey from California, not knowing what was going on, just that Kelsey was upset about something. He'd proven he'd do anything for Kelsey when he took Zach out of that house by the lake and went back in to save her. Janelle didn't have that confidence in Nathan anymore.

He'd been there for her once upon a time, when Richard had all but abandoned her to raise Zach alone. Yes, Richard had still lived with her, but he'd never been there. He wouldn't come home until after she knew the bars had closed, or later, then get up with the sun and leave for work. Somewhere along the line, they'd become more like roommates than spouses, and Nathan had been there for her then.

He'd been there to ease the burden of raising a child and maintaining a house by herself. He'd been there to talk to and laugh with. He'd eased her concerns when Zach had been sick with a cold and his fever had climbed to one hundred and three degrees. More recently, she'd felt calm and safe knowing that he was in the house or, at the very least, sitting in a car near the end of her driveway.

Now, she couldn't be certain he actually wanted to be there. He could have picked up the phone and told her everything Patrick had just told her. But he hadn't. He'd had someone else do it for him.

"There's more that he wants to tell you personally, Janelle. He really would like for you to call him." Patrick's gentle voice broke through her dark thoughts. "He gave me this to give to you."

Janelle looked down at the envelope Patrick held out to her. "What is it?"

"A letter." Patrick laid it on the counter and pushed it toward her. "He says it will explain everything."

Janelle looked into his brown eyes. "Didn't you just do that?"

He shrugged. "He hopes this will do it better. And that you'll call him after you read it."

Janelle eyed the envelope warily as she finished the wine in her glass and began to run her finger around the rim. Should she call him? What would that accomplish? A letter was okay, she guessed, but why couldn't he just pick up the phone and make the move she desperately wanted him to make? She'd tried to reach out to him and hadn't been very successful. Now that she knew why, she wasn't sure it made a difference.

No. The ball was now in his court, and she wanted more than a piece of paper. Janelle decided she needed to focus on her family. Zach and Zoe needed her full attention, and she was determined to give it to them. Nathan knew where to find her. When the investigations were over, or on the off chance he decided to risk it, he could come to her. She was done.

"We'll see," Janelle muttered.

Patrick groaned and, out of the corner of her eye, Janelle caught the droop in Kelsey's shoulders. She rose and, leaving the letter where it lay, took her glass to the sink then avoided making eye contact as she walked into the living room, sat down in the armchair, and turned the TV on.

Eleven

"Happy Birthday, Zach. I have to go now," Zach said in a high-pitched voice as he played with the puppets. He was currently holding the Kelsey puppet in one hand and the Zach puppet in the other. He made the Kelsey puppet walk away and put it behind his back.

"Good, Zach." Andrew sat on the floor beside his leather chair. Zach played in the middle of the floor at the end of the white sofa farthest from Andrew. Janelle sat on the end of the sofa closer to the brown leather chair and watched silently. "Now, do you have another good memory that you'd like to share with me?"

Zach lined all of the puppets on the floor in front of him and stared at them. Slowly he picked a few of them up and set them in his lap. He picked them up one by one and made them act out a scene from their last Christmas. She saw the only puppet left on the floor was Richard's, then watched, slightly horrified, as Zach reenacted their meal in complete silence then made Kelsey and Patrick's puppets apologize and leave. Things only got worse as she watched him share the argument she and Mary had had about Nathan's presence.

"He's not your husband, he shouldn't be here," Mary's puppet said.

"But Mom—" Janelle's puppet had started.

"No buts. Richard should be here. You should be ashamed of yourself. What kind of message are you trying to send your kids?" Mary's puppet said then Janelle's puppet threw up her hands and walked away.

"I think we should go now," George's puppet said and they left.

Janelle covered her burning cheeks with her hands, and she wasn't sure if she wanted to laugh or cry. It was now clear that Zach saw a lot more than she thought he did, and she'd have to do a better job of keeping Mary and her complaints away from Zach from now on. Janelle peeked through her fingers at Andrew as he wrote a few things on the notepad beside him.

"Very good, Zach," he said calmly.

Very good? Janelle questioned in her mind. As far as she was concerned, there was nothing very good about that scene.

"Is there anything else?" Andrew asked when he was finished making notes.

Zach nodded and picked up two puppets. Janelle recognized them as Kelsey's and his. "Can you come home and take us trick-or-treating?" the Zach puppet said.

"No, sweetie, I'm sorry. My job is very important and I can't leave it," the Kelsey puppet said, and Janelle felt her eyes burn with tears. She was pretty sure this conversation had never actually happened.

"But I miss you," Zach's puppet said.

"Aw, that's sweet, but I have to go back to work now." He made the Kelsey puppet disappear behind his back.

"But Zach," Janelle said, and Andrew immediately held up his hand to silence her.

"Let him act it out. True or not, it will help me help him." Andrew made more notes on his pad of paper. "Zach, is there anything else?"

Janelle looked at her son's face as he chewed on his bottom lip—a lot like Kelsey did when she was thinking or upset—and stared at the puppets. She was surprised when he picked up the puppet representing himself along with Mary and Richard's puppets.

"Zach," Mary's puppet started, "don't you love your father? Wouldn't you like to spend more time with him, just the two of you?"

"I don't know, Grandma," his puppet said. "Mommy says we're not supposed to be alone with him."

"Your mommy doesn't know what's good for her," Zach said, mimicking Richard's growl with frightening accuracy. "You will spend time with me, and there's nothing your mommy or your auntie can do about it."

"That's right," Mary's puppet said, and Zach made her puppet and Richard's puppet touch hands. "Just you and your daddy."

The three puppets walked away together and Janelle sat dumbfounded.

What had she just watched? Something wasn't right, and it left her with an uneasy, prickly feeling in her chest.

"Zach, when did that event happen?" Andrew asked, curiously staring at Zach.

Janelle saw him shrug as he bowed his head to hide his face. "The day before he came to get me."

Her heart sank.

"Did your grandma give your dad something? Is that why the puppets touched hands?" Andrew asked the question Janelle had been hoping to hear, but her heart sank even lower when Zach's head bobbed slightly. "Do you know what it was?"

Zach shook his head. "It's a secret."

Andrew looked at him for another moment before he rose to his feet and sat in the leather chair. "Zach, could you please pick all of your puppets up and put them in your special tub then you can go play with whatever you'd like while I talk to your mom."

Janelle watched her usually exuberant child slowly go through the motions of cleaning up and putting away, then drag his feet to the bookshelf full of baskets. She turned her attention to the windows on the opposite wall, to the bright-blue, cloudless sky outside, and wished her mood matched. It had been two weeks since the kidnapping and shooting, and she was beginning to feel like she'd never feel happy again. It was exhausting.

"Janelle," Andrew said, drawing her attention to him. He smiled softly before continuing, "Did you recognize those events that he acted out?"

"Two of them, yes," she answered. "But they didn't happen exactly like that."

"I'm sure you don't remember them that way, but this is about his perception of the reality. Can you tell me what was off?" Andrew picked his pad of paper and pencil off of the floor and placed it in his lap, prepared to make note of what Janelle might say.

"Well, for one, Kelsey didn't immediately leave the birthday party. She stayed home for two more days or so before she had to leave for filming."

Andrew nodded, but didn't write anything down.

"Second, Christmas wasn't exactly like that. Patrick wasn't there, and Kelsey stayed for another month after before she went back to California,"

Janelle said, feeling the strong need to defend her sister's actions. "The conversation about Halloween never happened. Yes, he told her about the jack-o'-lanterns they'd carved with my father, but he never asked her to come home. We didn't even talk to her before Halloween because she was working."

"None of that is surprising," Andrew stated. "His perception, real or not, is that Kelsey always leaves. Has she ever blown him off like he portrayed her doing?"

"No," Janelle gasped. "She would never do that. And if she hadn't been working, she would have most likely come home right away. She loves spending time with him."

"I would imagine the tail end of that imagined conversation was his father's influence showing itself." Andrew wrote on his notepad. "What can you tell me about that last scene he acted out?"

"Nothing," Janelle said. "I never saw that conversation take place. What do you think it means?"

"It's hard to say." Andrew shook his head and turned to look at Zach. He was playing with the basket of toy cars, rolling them along the floor, up the wall, and across the shelves of the bookcase. Andrew looked at Janelle again, a soft, strained smile on his face. "It could be a figment of his imagination, or it could be a conversation that actually took place. What was your mother's relationship with your husband like?"

Janelle rolled her eyes, not at his question but at the memory of Mary and Richard's relationship. "She adored him. She always took his side against me or Kelsey, and Richard could do no wrong in her eyes." Janelle glanced at her son. "Sadly, Zach's portrayal at the Christmas meal was pretty accurate. Mom was always trying to get me to forgive Richard and take him back." Janelle slowly took in and released a deep breath. "So infuriating," she muttered to herself.

"That's very curious," Andrew stated. Janelle noticed that he was furiously scrawling on his notepad. "Would you care to tell me more about her?"

Janelle opened her mouth to do what he'd asked, but stopped herself short. "Why is that important to Zach's therapy? We're here to help him, not dissect the dysfunction in the rest of our family."

Andrew looked at her and smiled. "Trust me when I tell you that understanding the dynamics of those around him will help me treat him. I'll get to the other members of your family later, but since his last reenactment was of a scene that showed his grandmother and his father seeming to be conspiring, I'd like to focus on that today."

Janelle squirmed slightly in her seat. "You're a child therapist. You should just focus on his thoughts and feelings. The rest of us can handle ourselves," she said defensively.

Andrew reached across the divide and took her hand in his. "I'm also a family therapist, and in this case, I think you all need help if Zach is going to get better."

Janelle remained silent, eyeing him warily. He released her hand as he sat back and let her assess him.

"How does Zach feel about his grandmother?" Andrew asked.

After a moment's hesitation, Janelle answered, "He loves her, I guess. She's always sweet and kind to him, even if she turns right around and acts exactly opposite that with Kelsey and me."

"So how do you feel about her?"

Janelle looked at the floor beside her feet. "We don't always see eye to eye," she answered quietly. "And by that I mean never."

"Why?" Andrew asked.

Janelle shrugged. "She had a rough childhood and grew up thinking things should be a certain way. My sister and I happen to disagree with her way of thinking and do things our own way instead."

"What kind of things?" Andrew continued to prod.

"Mostly how women should act toward men," Janelle said, glaring at him. "Look, I don't see how this matters. If we're not going to talk about Zach, then I guess we're done here."

Andrew pressed his lips together, and Janelle could tell he was becoming frustrated with her. She looked away and pressed her back into the sofa cushion. He slowly relaxed and sat forward again.

"I understand this is probably uncomfortable and a little personal. But your mother is a part of your life, a part of your child's life, and I get the impression her influence into your behavior is farther reaching than you may realize," he said soothingly. "I think we should explore the impact of those relationships on Zach."

Janelle could suddenly see what Andrew meant. Hadn't she just fidgeted at the mere thought of irritating him? There were times she thought she was past her mother's early influence, but then there were others, like now, when the behavior was just second nature. She wasn't sure she liked that.

"Where would you like me to begin?"

Janelle stood on the porch and watched Patrick load his suitcase into her father's Cadillac. After the trunk was closed, Patrick cast a glance to the side of the porch, where Kelsey sat on the swing. Janelle looked at her sister as well and saw she was gazing off into the distance, not even watching what was going on in her driveway. Her cheeks were dry, but Janelle could tell she'd been crying recently, and the look on her face said she was trying not to do it again.

Janelle turned to see Patrick step onto the porch. She held out her arms to give him a brief hug. "See you soon," she said as she placed her hands on his upper arms and studied his face. Her voice held a bit of a question, and she hoped he understood her need for reassurance. Janelle didn't think she could handle one more thing going badly right now. Patrick not returning would be bad for almost all of them.

"As soon as possible," he replied with a nod. "They have me scheduled for eight weeks. I'm hoping to talk them down to six, at most. But don't tell her that, I don't want to get her hopes up." He glanced in Kelsey's direction again, and sadness filled his eyes. "I wish she'd come with me," he muttered. Janelle wasn't sure he'd meant for her to hear that.

"I'll do what I can to keep her occupied." Janelle dropped her hands and took a step back.

Patrick suddenly turned to her, and his gaze sharpened on her face. "Please, do me a favor and try to keep your mother away."

"You know I can try," Janelle reassured him. "Neither of us wants to see her right now, but she is Zach and Zoe's grandmother, so there's only so much we can do."

"I understand," Patrick replied with a nod.

Janelle motioned for the kids to come out of the house and say their goodbyes. Patrick squatted to their level and gave them one of his charming smiles, and Janelle smirked fondly. With a grin like that, it wasn't any wonder why every woman he worked with fell at his feet.

Zoe threw her arms around his neck and planted a big kiss on his cheek. Patrick wrapped an arm around her waist and pulled her little body closer to his in an enveloping hug. Janelle's heart skipped in her chest, and she felt a wistful tug as she pictured Nathan in Patrick's place.

She promptly shook that thought away.

When Zoe eventually released her prey, Patrick held his arms outstretched and looked expectantly at Zach. Zach held his ground next to Janelle, pouting as he looked at Patrick. Janelle put her hand on Zach's shoulder and tried to nudge him closer.

"You said you wouldn't go," Zach said soulfully. "You promised."

"Zach, I said I had no choice, but that I would be back as soon as possible." Patrick held his squat and waddled closer to Zach. "I told you there's a difference between acting and lying and what I do is act. I would never lie to you. I don't lie to people I love."

"Do you love me?" Zach asked, his pout disappearing slightly.

"Of course I do," Patrick replied softly. Zach inched closer until Patrick could wrap his arms around him. "Can you promise me to be a good boy? Do what your mom and your aunt ask you to do and don't be afraid to tell Andrew what you're thinking and feeling, okay."

Zach nodded as he laid his head on Patrick's shoulder, and Janelle melted. Patrick sounded so paternalistic and Janelle hated to admit that she was slightly surprised.

"Will you call me?" Zach's muffled voice asked.

Patrick bobbed his head as he held Zach against him. "Absolutely. And if you want to talk to me, just ask Aunt Kelsey to call."

"Even if it's every day?" Zach stood and looked Patrick in the face.

"Even if," Patrick answered with a smile.

Zach's shoulders lifted and fell with his sigh, and he lowered his head and backed away. He and Zoe turned and went back into the house as Patrick rose to his feet.

"That's sweet of you," Janelle said when he was standing in front of her again.

"I was serious. If Zach wants to talk to me, call me. If it goes to voicemail make sure to leave a message and I will call as soon as I can," Patrick said somberly and looked at Kelsey. "Janelle, please keep me updated. I don't know if I trust Kelsey to tell me everything that happens. Especially if she thinks I won't like it." He met Janelle's gaze again. "She says she's holding up well, but she's still having nightmares. And I know her leg is bothering her more than she's letting on. If you think she needs me, tell me and I'll be here as soon as humanly possible."

Janelle smiled. "You're being a little dramatic, don't you think?"

Patrick's cheeks pinkened, and he looked down. "She's the most important person to me and I want her to be happy and healthy." He shook his head as he lifted his gaze. "I hate leaving her."

Janelle gave him another quick hug. "Then I'll let you say your good-byes. Hurry back."

Patrick nodded as Janelle turned and went into the house to give the lovebirds privacy for their farewells.

Twelve

Nathan left Captain Little's office feeling more frustrated than when he had walked in. He had hoped to have good news about the Internal Affairs investigation and better news about the investigation into Richard's death. He had only gotten bad news—on both accounts. It seemed they weren't even willing to start the IA investigation until Richard's case was closed. And they weren't even approaching that point yet.

He didn't understand why things were still dragging. Richard killed himself. Planned or not, it was still suicide. No one needed to be blamed. No one else needed to be held responsible. Bonner and Hayes were doing Richard's family a disservice by not ending their investigation. Especially when there was nothing to investigate.

Once again, that man was keeping Nathan and Janelle apart. Even from the grave, Richard Wagoner was still a thorn in his side.

His head down, his thoughts elsewhere, he didn't see Detective Bonner until it was too late.

"Watch it, Harris," the older man growled.

Nathan stopped and immediately pulled his shoulders up and stepped back. "Sorry," he said automatically. He went to step around the other man, but Bonner moved into his path.

"Are you snooping around my investigation?" His lip curled in a sneer. "What's wrong? Don't you trust me?"

Nathan's eyes narrowed sharply on him. It never took long in Bonner's presence for Nathan to remember why he disliked the man so much. Aside from his bad breath and slight body odor, Detective Bonner and Nathan had never hit it off.

Reginald Bonner had started his career as a police officer placed under

Nathan's father, Lieutenant John Harris's, command. From the beginning, Bonner had never liked the discipline his lieutenant demanded of his officers. Officer Bonner would always do what was necessary, but not much else. His uniforms may have always been pristine, his gun always well maintained, but when it came to investigations, he almost always played in the gray area.

That's what had gotten him in trouble with Lieutenant Harris.

Officer Bonner had been assigned to investigate a breaking and entering case that would have assured his promotion to corporal. He'd done the legwork properly, collected fingerprints and statements, and taken pictures of the scene. He'd also made assumptions about who the guilty party was—namely, he'd suspected the homeowner of staging the elaborate scene to collect from his insurance company.

All evidence pointed elsewhere, but Bonner hadn't cared. When he went to Lieutenant Harris with his findings, the lieutenant looked through the evidence and came to a different conclusion. It had taken the senior Harris another six weeks to collect more sufficient evidence and find the actual culprit. Because of his neglect in the investigation, Officer Bonner had remained Officer Bonner.

When Nathan began on the force ten years later, two years after his father's death, Bonner had worked his way up to the rank of sergeant. He'd never forgotten John Harris's role in preventing him from moving up faster and had done everything he could to make Nathan's first few years on the force unpleasant. Eight years later, Nathan was a newly minted sergeant and Bonner was ready to move up again. Together, they were assigned to a homicide case.

From the beginning, Bonner had made his hypothesis clear to everyone working with him. He'd learned to collect only the evidence that would point in the direction he wanted it to go, to make sure he didn't get caught fudging the facts again. Nathan, on the other hand, had collected all evidence from the crime scene, taken pictures of almost everything, and fingerprinted and talked to everyone. Nathan's evidence showed Bonner was wrong, but when he presented it to him, Bonner dismissed his findings and arrested the person he'd suspected all along.

When Nathan and Bonner had to give their testimony to their superiors before the prosecution could begin, they gave very different accounts. While

Bonner insisted they had the right man behind bars, Nathan persisted in showing his evidence to the contrary. The captain at the time looked at all of the evidence presented, agreed with Nathan, and released their suspect. Bonner was reprimanded, his promotion denied, and was told he would not be eligible for another promotion for five years.

That brought them to today.

"No, I'm not snooping around anything. I came in to speak to the captain about the IA investigation," Nathan answered coolly. He tried to step around the senior officer again.

"Is that all?" Bonner, maintaining his grotesque sneer, stepped into Nathan's path again. "I would think you'd want to know how the Wagoner investigation is progressing. Seems to me you'd be very interested in knowing how soon you can see the merry widow again."

Nathan's blood warmed unpleasantly in his veins.

"I know you can't see her until that case is closed," Bonner stated. "And I know you think I'm not always thorough in my investigations." He leaned menacingly close to Nathan. "So I'm making sure to be very exhaustive this time. I'm covering all my bases before I reach any conclusion on this one."

"I'm not sure I believe you," Nathan said calmly. "You made it clear in your questioning that you've already reached your conclusion."

"Did I?" Bonner stepped back and narrowed his eyes. "You don't think I've learned my lesson? A man can change."

"I think this is a pretty clear case. Richard shot himself, end of story," Nathan said and walked around Bonner. "Case closed."

"I'm sure that's what you'd like to think."

Nathan froze.

"But I think you're too personally invested in the outcome of this case to see the evidence as clearly as I do."

Nathan slowly turned again. "You never see anything clearly, Bonner. You always look through the filter of your suspicions. You've willingly sent one innocent man to jail because of your assumptions." Nathan allowed a feral grin to stretch his lips. "Are you going for two?"

Bonner's face and broad forehead turned pink and his mouth opened and closed, but no words came out. Nathan had his answer.

"A word of advice," Nathan said as he took a step toward Bonner. "Quit while you're ahead. You've already falsely arrested one man for murder, you should leave it at that." Nathan turned and walked away and could hear Bonner's blustering behind him.

When he was outside of the building, Nathan had the strong urge to visit Janelle, if for no other reason than to convince himself she was safe. He still wanted answers from her, still needed to know why she'd kept his child from him and if he had a place in his daughter's life. He needed to know if they might have a chance at a future. If she said yes, he had the sneaking suspicion that he'd wrap his arms around her and never let her go.

But he had to wait for these investigations to be over.

He'd always thought of himself as a patient man, but this waiting thing was getting old fast.

"Okay, Zach, would you like to play with your puppets today?" Andrew asked as he followed Janelle and Zach into the room.

Janelle immediately took her seat as she tried to stifle a yawn. In one of their early sessions, Andrew had suggested getting Zach back into a normal routine, which included having him sleep in his own bed. Janelle had followed that suggestion, and they'd been doing fine. But Zach had been having nightmares since the night Patrick left and, as a result, had crawled into bed with her. Getting them both back to sleep hadn't been an easy task and had taken longer than she'd expected. In the last four nights, she figured she'd only had about four hours of sleep each night.

She pulled her attention back to the moment and watched Andrew pull Zach's special tub off the shelf and set it on the floor in front of him. Zach immediately began rummaging through the puppets and promptly found what he was looking for. He stood and threw the puppet he held across the room then kicked the tub away.

"Zach," Janelle said as she started to rise. Andrew, with his back to her, held his hand out to stop her. She looked at the puppet on the floor between her and Zach and gasped. It was Patrick's superhero puppet. Her chest tightened as she looked at her child.

Andrew strolled to the puppet and picked it up. "Has something happened with Patrick?" he asked as he walked toward Zach. He squatted down in front of Zach and held the Patrick puppet up between them.

Zach nodded and pushed the puppet away.

"What was it?" Andrew cast a quick glance at Janelle and gave his head a slight shake. She frowned but sat further back on the couch.

Zach was focusing on his feet, but his small voice reached Janelle anyway. "He left. I asked him not to go, but he did anyway."

"I see," Andrew said calmly. "Is he coming back or has he gone away for good?"

Zach's little shoulder lifted slightly. "He says he's coming back. But Grandma says he won't. She says he'll leave Aunt Kelsey and find someone better."

Janelle's heart ached to hear her mother's cruel words repeated so innocently. Tears stung her eyes and she couldn't watch.

"Is that so?" Andrew asked casually. "Well, what does Patrick say about that?"

"He says he loves Aunt Kelsey and he's coming home as soon as he can," Zach muttered.

"Zach, who has a better idea of what Patrick will do? Patrick or Grandma?"

Zach mumbled something Janelle couldn't understand and she cast her eyes in their direction again. Andrew was staring at Zach, his face full of patience and concern. "Patrick?" Zach finally answered.

Andrew smiled broadly as he stood up. "Yes, I should think so." He held the puppet out to Zach. "Why don't you put him back where he belongs then put the tub away. I think we'll do something else today."

Zach did as he was asked as Andrew grabbed a basket from the shelf and walked to the large table on the other side of the couch. As he started to unpack it, Zach joined him and peeked into the container. He helped Andrew empty the basket of all of its crafting supplies, and when that was done, Andrew set it on the floor and Zach sat down at the table. Andrew walked to the file cabinet and pulled out a piece of paper then returned to the table and set it in front of Zach, bent over to whisper something in his ear, and then walked to his leather chair and sat down.

"What's he doing?" Janelle asked.

"I've given him a Mandala to color," Andrew answered. Janelle furrowed her brow and he smiled. "It's basically a circle in the middle of the page. Sometimes I give the patient one with geometric shapes around it, sometimes it's blank so they are free to add to it as they see fit. It's an ancient form of art, but it's been discovered to be very therapeutic and a good way for people to express themselves, through color or shape, when they can't, or won't, use words. In Zach's case, he's obviously not in the mood to play with the puppets because he's had another upheaval in his life."

"It's only temporary," Janelle assured him.

"To you, yes. To him, it's not so simple." Andrew focused on Zach's head. "He sees it as someone else he loves leaving him, and right now he's not dealing well with that."

"I noticed," Janelle mumbled and when Andrew turned to her with a question in his eyes, she felt the need to add, "he's had nightmares every night since Patrick left."

"Well." Andrew smiled and turned his attention back to Zach. "Hopefully this will help him express his feelings and show me if I can help him sort them out. I'll study the picture he draws and the colors he uses, and we'll talk about it today."

Janelle nodded and settled into the corner of the couch and watched the rest of Zach's therapy session in silence.

Thirteen

The children were up early on Easter morning, anxious to see what the Easter Bunny had brought them. After scoping out their baskets and having their usual Sunday morning breakfast, Janelle and Kelsey took the kids to church for service and an egg hunt. When they returned home, the sisters immediately started to prepare for dinner. Their parents would be joining them, and Janelle felt certain that neither of them were looking forward to it.

The good news was that Zach's nightmares had once again subsided, but Janelle could tell her sister's were picking up steam. She was drinking more coffee, falling asleep on the couch, and was increasingly aloof. Janelle had asked Kelsey about it, but Kelsey had waved her worries off, blaming her blue mood on the pain in her leg or missing Patrick.

Janelle took the ham out of the oven and placed it on the island then put the biscuits in to bake. Kelsey sat on the stool across from her, head resting on her fist, coffee cup spinning in the other hand. Janelle wished she knew what she could do to help her sister. It was always easier for her to help others than to help herself.

"What was Patrick's news today?" Janelle asked as she grinned at Kelsey. Patrick had called just as they'd walked in the door after church.

Kelsey returned her smile slightly. "Not much. He couldn't talk long, he has more filming tonight."

"Really?" Janelle raised a brow and Kelsey nodded. "I didn't realize he'd work so late."

Kelsey yawned and shrugged. "Night scenes aren't unheard of."

Janelle looked at the clock above the sink. "But it's close to eleven for him."

Kelsey nodded again and drained her coffee cup. "Less crowded." Her eyes closed until there was a knock on the front door. She groaned and put her forehead on the counter. "Can I just go to bed now?"

"No, I'm not dealing with her alone," Janelle said and turned to face the stove.

George entered the house, and his greeting to the children carried into the kitchen as Janelle stirred the pot of green beans. She turned the burner off then poked the boiling potatoes with a knife. It came out clean so she took them off the heat as well. Janelle listened to her father's interactions with her children and smiled.

Mary's voice drifted into the kitchen just before she did. Janelle noticed that she positioned herself at the island, exactly midway between her and Kelsey. Kelsey sat up, looked at Mary, standing stoically with her hands on her hips, rolled her eyes, and stood. She walked to the cabinet and started to get plates out for dinner.

"Is dinner ready?" Mary asked.

"Almost," Janelle answered as she set the serving bowls in front of her.

"And what did you do to help, Kelsey?" she snapped. "It looked to me like you were sitting on your butt while your sister does all of the work. Isn't it enough for her to take care of the kids without you being a burden too?"

Janelle heard the slight thunk of the stack of dishes as Kelsey set them on the counter and glanced at her sister. Kelsey's back was tense, her hands on the counter white with strain.

"Mom, Kelsey's still recovering from a gunshot wound," Janelle said calmly, her head starting to pound from stress and lack of sleep. "I asked her to sit and keep me company."

Kelsey glanced over her shoulder at Janelle and gave her a slight smile. She picked up the plates and took them into the dining room, leaving Mary and Janelle alone in the kitchen.

"You shouldn't let her off the hook so easily, Janelle. That's how you got into this mess in the first place," Mary began to rant. "You should make her pull her own weight. It could only do her good to stand on that leg and work it out."

Janelle closed her eyes to resist the urge to roll them. "She does work it out. She has physical therapy once a week."

"Once a week? I doubt that's enough. You should still make her do more around here. This is her house after all," Mary continued shrilly.

Janelle glanced at Kelsey and noticed how stiff she was, saw the dead look in her eyes. Janelle started trying to come up with a way to change the subject.

"I hear you're taking Zach to therapy, too," Mary continued. "Is that really necessary?"

Janelle grabbed the pot of green beans off of the stove. She poured them into the serving bowl then stuck the spoon in the bowl.

"He needs it," Janelle said as she turned to repeat the process with the potatoes. "On top of kidnapping him, Richard said some pretty nasty things to Zach and, quite frankly, scared him pretty badly."

"I think you're being a little dramatic, Janelle." Mary held her head high as she left the room.

Janelle looked up and saw her father standing in the entryway, glaring after her mother as she walked into the dining room. He met her gaze and gave her a warm smile. "Hey, sweetheart," he said as she met him halfway and he wrapped his arms around her. "Need some help?"

Janelle grinned as she handed him the bowl of green beans. She picked up the bowl of potatoes and led the way into the dining room.

"Kelsey, you should at least consider it. It's time for you to take some responsibility for your actions," Mary was hissing as Janelle and George put their bowls on the table.

"Mary, enough," George snapped. She jumped and quickly turned to look at him. She gave him a sweet smile then sat down in her designated seat next to the head of the table. Janelle shook her head and walked back into the kitchen to get the ham and biscuits then called the kids in to eat.

Zoe sat between George and Kelsey while Zach took his seat beside Mary. Janelle double-checked the table to make sure they had everything then joined the others, sitting down beside Zach. After a quick blessing, the meal began in typical fashion—Janelle and Kelsey put food on the plate of the child beside them before taking for themselves. Janelle noticed that

Kelsey had a far-off look in her eyes and had piled too many beans on Zoe's plate. She lightly kicked her sister, and when Kelsey looked at her through slightly narrowed eyes, Janelle nodded toward her daughter.

"Sorry, sweetie," Kelsey said, passing the bowl to George then sliding most of the beans onto her own plate.

Once everyone had their food and the dishes were back in the center of the table, they all ate. For the first time in Janelle's memory, there was no talking. She looked around and noticed that beside her, Zach was pulling his biscuit apart and dropping the crumbs into a pile on his plate. On the other side of her, Kelsey was using her fork to pick at her ham and potatoes, but rarely taking bites of either.

"Kelsey, is Patrick enjoying Paris?" George asked, and Mary harrumphed. Everyone fell silent, waiting for Kelsey to answer, but she seemed too busy pushing a green bean around her plate to notice.

Janelle leaned across the table as much as she could. "Kelsey," she said firmly, preparing to poke her with her toe again. Kelsey looked up, met Janelle's stare then looked around the table.

"What?" she asked as her eyes widened and she looked back at Janelle.

"Dad asked you a question," Janelle answered quietly.

"Really?" Kelsey turned to their father. "I'm sorry, I didn't hear it."

George smiled and repeated himself and Mary repeated her scoff, only louder.

Kelsey's lips lifted slightly. "He's working hard, but he's had a little time to sightsee."

"I'd love to see Paris," George stated brightly. "Your mother and I have been talking about going for years."

"It is quite a romantic city," their mother added sweetly, staring at Kelsey. Janelle saw the discomfort on Kelsey's face and noticed little tension lines appear around her lips.

Janelle decided she had to do what she could and hoped that Mary wouldn't say anything crude that Zach might pick up on. "How would you know if you've never been?" Janelle asked politely as she picked up a piece of potato and put it in her mouth. She chewed slowly then turned to her mother. "It does have that reputation, but if you haven't actually seen it for yourself, then you can't honestly claim it to be romantic, can you?"

Mary scowled at her eldest daughter.

George cleared his throat. "Still," he said, calmly entering the fray and looking fondly at Kelsey, "it's too bad you couldn't go with him."

"George," Mary snapped. "I don't think you should talk about such things." She moved closer, in an attempt to whisper, "Especially in front of the kids."

George looked at his plate and began to slice his ham. "Don't be silly. They're dating, I didn't say anything inappropriate. You're the one making presumptions." He turned to Kelsey. "Are you going to eat anything?"

Kelsey smiled slightly and took a bite of her ham. The rest of dinner passed rather peacefully, but Janelle didn't relax until it was finally over.

Across town, Nathan was sitting down to Easter dinner with his family at his mother's house. Holidays had become the only times guaranteed to bring them all together. He carried the ham into his mother's dining room and set it on the table. His mother was the first to take her seat, at the foot of the table, and the rest of them followed suit. Mason sat to his mother's left, his wife, Charlotte, on his other side, and their nine-month-old son in a highchair beside her. Nathan's youngest brother, Jackson, sat on their mother's right.

Nathan took his seat at the head of the table, the spot that had been his father's until he'd died when Nathan was eighteen. After fifteen years, he was still not comfortable with the position as head of the table, and the family. He'd given up a scholarship to a four-year university and pursuing a career in law, instead opting for two years at a community college and an immediate career on the police force. He'd used the money his parents had saved for his education and put it toward Mason's and Jackson's instead. He'd never regretted his decision.

Mason was now an excellent lawyer, with a wife and child of his own. Jackson had gone to college, gotten a degree in Landscape Architecture, but was now pursuing his dream of being in a rock band. They'd just made their first album and were about to embark on their first tour. Nathan was proud of both of his younger brothers.

"Nathan, could you please say the blessing?" his mother, Nancy, asked, smiling proudly at him across the length of the table.

Nathan did as he was asked, and then they passed the food around the table. When all plates were filled, they began eating. A few bites into their meal, Mason looked at Jackson.

"So, when does this tour of yours start?" Mason asked as Jackson put a forkful of mashed potatoes in his mouth.

Jackson narrowed his eyes as he chewed the potatoes then swallowed. "Not sure yet, we have to find another manager," he answered. He stabbed a few peas and put them in his mouth.

"Another one? I thought you just hired one," Mason said.

Jackson shrugged casually. "It didn't work out."

"So how long will you be in town?" Charlotte asked, the pitch of her voice somewhere between Minnie Mouse and Frenchie from *Grease*. Nathan had always found her voice amusing, but was glad he wasn't the one having to live with her. As sweet as she was, he didn't think he could listen to her talk all the time.

"Don't know, I guess it depends." Jackson bit into his biscuit and quickly followed it with a sip of water.

"Depends on what?" Mason gaze held a mischievous glint, and Nathan rolled his eyes. "Are you going to try to see *her* this time? Is that what it depends on?"

Jackson's look turned murderous. "Shut up, asshole."

"Jackson," Nancy said firmly. "Not at the table, please."

He glanced at her for a moment then looked at his plate. "Sorry, Mom."

"Mason, Kerri's not home right now," Nancy stated matter-of-factly. "And leave your brother alone."

Nathan pressed his lips together so he wouldn't laugh. They continued to eat in relative peace for a few more minutes. Nathan was in the middle of taking a sip of water when his mother met his gaze.

"How's Janelle?" she asked innocently.

Nathan nearly choked.

"That good, huh?" Mason chuckled as he slowly shook his head. "I'm guessing things haven't changed since the last time we talked about it."

Nathan set his glass down and wiped his mouth with his napkin. "No, Mason, they haven't," he grumbled. He looked at his mother. "I don't know how she's doing, Mom. I haven't had the chance to talk to her in a while."

Nancy's right eye narrowed slightly as she focused on her eldest son. "How long is 'a while'?" she asked in a tone that meant she would tolerate nothing but the truth. And that she knew she probably wouldn't like it.

"Three weeks," Nathan said and picked his water up again. He held the glass to his lips as he added, "More or less."

"Da-yamn," Jackson muttered.

"You're one to talk," Mason retorted.

"Shove it," Jackson replied.

"Boys, enough." Nancy's green eyes bored into Nathan's as he took a sip of water he wasn't really thirsty for. As he lowered the glass, she shook her head. "I don't believe you would do this to her."

"I haven't done anything," Nathan said.

"Not recently," Jackson coughed. "Ow! Did you just kick me?" He glared across the table at Mason.

"No, I did," Nancy stated and turned her attention to her youngest child. "If you have nothing polite to contribute, please refrain from saying anything."

Jackson pouted. "Sorry." He laid his forearm on the table and with the fork in the other hand he poked at the food on his plate.

"Mom, I don't think we really need to talk about this." Nathan stabbed a piece of the ham and popped it in his mouth.

"Why haven't you spoken to her in three weeks, Nathan?" Nancy laid her fork and knife on her plate.

Nathan shrugged and picked up another piece of ham.

"He's not allowed to," Mason answered.

Nathan glared at him. "Stay out of it."

"You're an idiot," Mason snapped.

"Why isn't he allowed to talk to Janelle?" Nancy questioned, turning her attention to Mason.

"Don't answer her," Nathan hissed.

"Captain Little told him not to. He said it might interfere with the investigation." Mason waved his hand in the air. "Or something like that."

"Really?" Nancy's gaze bounced between her oldest boys as if she was trying to decide which one of them might answer her question. Mason beat her to it by telling her the basics of what Nathan had told him. She nodded as she listened and sat quietly when Mason was finished. She sat back in her chair and folded her arms across her chest, her lips puckered as she contemplated. "Well, I can see what Bruce is saying," she finally said, then looked at Nathan. "But I think he's wrong."

"Mom—" Nathan began until she held up her hand.

"Regardless," she waved that hand as she lowered it to the table, "I think I might pay my granddaughter a visit tomorrow."

Nathan felt the air escape his lungs, blindsided by that simple statement. He'd been so hung up on wondering how he could fix things with Janelle that he'd almost forgotten Zoe entirely. He'd almost forgotten that she was his, and as a result, his family was hers.

But still, that probably wouldn't be a good idea.

"I don't think you should," Nathan said.

"And why not? Bruce said you shouldn't see her, but he didn't say I couldn't," his mother argued. "And poor Janelle probably needs to know that she has others in her corner. Lord knows her mother isn't." Nancy shook her head sadly.

"How can you be sure of that?" Nathan questioned.

Nancy's eye narrowed again as she pressed her lips together. "Do you know why I started visiting her all those years ago?"

"It wasn't that long ago, Mom," Nathan answered as he tried not to laugh. Even though it felt like ages, it had only been four years.

"Whatever," she stated dismissively. "I went to visit her because of her mother."

"Why?" Charlotte chirped.

"Because, Mary always made it known how proud she was of Richard's accomplishments. Of how successful he was in his new position and how quickly he was moving up the corporate ladder. She bragged about how much the company needed him and the long hours he was putting in at work. She expected he would make CFO within ten years, if not sooner." Nancy shook her head again. "But not once did Mary say anything about either of her girls. I figured if she was behaving like that in public, her private behavior couldn't possibly be any better, so I paid Janelle a visit."

"That's so sweet of you," Charlotte interjected.

Nancy smiled sorrowfully as she continued. "The poor thing was trying so hard, but I could tell she felt very unappreciated." She sat up and placed both forearms on the table. "It wasn't the typical 'new mom, this is harder than I thought it would be' unappreciated, it was the 'utterly defeated, nothing I do will ever make this better' unappreciated. So I continued to visit her so that she would know that she at least had me in her corner."

"That was nice of you, Mom," Jackson whispered as he took her hand in his and squeezed it.

"I've always thought the world of those girls. They were always so kind and caring to everyone they met. I don't know if you boys remember, but George and his kids were some of the first visitors we had after your father died." Nancy fell silent, and Nathan watched the memories dance across her face. After a while, she shook her head and looked at him. "I don't know why she did what she did to you, but I can guarantee she probably thought she didn't have a choice. And I'm going to see her tomorrow so she knows she still has my support."

"I'm coming with you. I'd love for James to meet his cousin," Charlotte said with a fond glance at her child as he scooped mashed potatoes into his mouth with his tiny fingers.

Nathan didn't know whether to laugh or cry. He was so touched that his mother would still want to support Janelle, despite what had happened between them. She was right; Janelle needed everyone she could get in her corner. He'd heard the whispers that followed him through town. He could only imagine Janelle was experiencing the same thing, if not worse. The fact that his mother and sister-in-law wanted to welcome his daughter into the family, regardless of how things ended up between him and Janelle, moved him deeply.

"Okay, you can go," Nathan said quietly.

Nancy laughed lightly. "Oh, honey, I wasn't asking your permission."

Fourteen

Through the bay window in the living room, Janelle watched the car slowly approach the house. She had no idea who it might be, but a knot began to form in her stomach. Her mind ran down a checklist of possible visitors then organized them from least welcome to most welcome. Her mother was of course at the top of the list—Nathan, a surprising second. That saddened her a bit. But when the car stopped and the passenger climbed out, Janelle panicked. She mentally rushed through the list to see where she had placed Nathan's mother.

She hadn't even been on it.

Janelle cursed silently, glanced at the top of Zoe's head as it was bent over in coloring concentration at the coffee table. What could Nancy Harris possibly want? Did she want to fuss at Janelle for what was happening with Nathan? Did she want to yell about Janelle keeping Zoe from her? Did she want to berate Janelle for her irresponsible behavior?

Janelle's mind raced through numerous worst-case scenarios as she pulled her shoulders back and walked toward the front door. She opened it as Nancy held her hand up to knock.

"Nancy," Janelle greeted her with a wide, slightly unstable, smile. "What a surprise. What brings you here?"

Nancy lowered her hand and placed it on the handle of a basket hanging from her arm. "Janelle, sweetie," she replied with a grin. "Since when does a grandmother need a reason to visit her granddaughter?"

Janelle's smile faltered slightly as she fell back a step. That wasn't quite what she'd been expecting. Maybe Nancy hadn't gotten warmed up yet. Or maybe Janelle hadn't heard her right. "What?" she practically whispered as she inched toward the door again.

"Hi, Janelle."

That chirpy voice could only belong to one person, and Janelle peeked around Nancy. Her daughter-in-law, Charlotte, stood behind her with her son on her hip. Her long, dark-red hair was pulled into a low ponytail at the nape of her neck, her brown eyes sparkled, and she wore a large smile.

Janelle's equilibrium took another hit.

"Can we come in? I really need to change James's diaper," Charlotte asked as she stepped closer to Nancy.

Janelle automatically pushed the screen door open for them. "Sure, come on in." She stepped against the door as they pushed past her and entered the house. "Kelsey's in the office, but I'm sure she wouldn't mind if you changed him in there." Janelle motioned toward the door under the staircase.

"Great, thanks." Charlotte walked in the direction of Janelle's wave.

Janelle watched Nathan's mother warily. "I haven't told her yet," Janelle whispered when she noticed Nancy's gaze had fallen on Zoe.

Nancy turned to Janelle and gripped her forearm. "That's fine. I'd just like to meet her and get to know her so it's easier when you do."

"Really?" Janelle asked before she could stop the words and Nancy laughed musically as she turned away. Janelle continued, "I was just about to feed them lunch and send them to their rooms for naps."

"Perfect timing, then." Nancy held up the basket she was carrying. "I brought sandwiches, potato salad, and cookies."

Tears instantly filled Janelle's eyes. "That's very kind of you." She took the basket from Nancy.

"Nonsense," Nancy said. "It would have been rude to come otherwise. Now, can I meet her? It's Zoe, right?"

"Yes, it is." Janelle said proudly. "Zoe, come here for a moment please."

Zoe looked at her mother and promptly stood and walked toward her. Janelle saw Zach poke his head up above the armchair then sink down until just his eyes and forehead were visible. She motioned for him to come over too, but his eyes slowly lowered behind the chair.

"Give him time, sweetie," Nancy said as she patted Janelle's arm.

Janelle nodded and tried to smile at Nancy as she swallowed the lump in her throat. She looked down at Zoe, standing before them with her hands clasped in front of her. Her aqua eyes were wide and focused on Nancy, who grinned down at her.

"Zoe, I'd like you to meet Officer Nathan's mother, Mrs. Harris," Janelle made the introductions and was surprised to see Nancy squat to Zoe's level.

"Hi, Zoe." Nancy held out her hand and grinned in delight when Zoe took it. They shook hands a couple of times, then Nancy placed her other hand on top of them. "It's such a pleasure to meet you. I've heard so much about you from Officer Nathan."

Janelle did a double take and her heart skipped a beat. Nathan talked about their daughter?

"Is he coming too? I miss him," Zoe said innocently, tearing at Janelle's chest.

"I think he misses you too, but he can't make it today." Nancy held Zoe's little hands in hers as Zoe pouted. "Were you coloring a picture?"

Zoe's face lit up. "Yeah. Wanna see?"

"I would love to." Nathan's mother looked up at Janelle and grinned. "If your momma can help me up." Janelle took her outstretched hand and helped the older woman to her feet. "I think I'm getting too old for that."

Janelle laughed and promptly covered her mouth with her fingers. It was the first time she'd laughed since the kidnapping. And it felt surprisingly good.

"She's such an angel, Janelle." Nancy grinned at her as she sat back down at the table after putting the kids down for their naps.

"Thank you," Janelle replied with a small nod of acknowledgment.

"She has her father's mouth. And the twinkle in her eye reminds me of his, too," Nancy continued.

Janelle felt a tug on her heart. She had noticed those things in Zoe as well and had secretly cherished them. She should have expected Nathan's mother to pick up on the similarities.

"And she's so smart. Both of them are. You must be very proud." Nancy gripped Janelle's hand on top of the table as Janelle nodded again. "You've done so well with them both."

"Thank you, they make it easy." Janelle smiled fondly. "Zach helps by letting her help him with his homework. He teaches her as he works, and her mind is such a little sponge. She absorbs everything."

"Nathan told me about that, how he watched Zach teaching her math one afternoon."

Janelle's lips fell slightly. She pulled her hand away from Nancy's grip as she glanced at the table. She was torn between wanting to continue to talk about Nathan and wanting to end the conversation that moment. It was nice to know he'd talked to his mother about her children, especially since Nancy had been such a help to Janelle early in Zach's life. And it made her traitorous heart skip a beat. She was still mad at Nathan—he'd abandoned her when she'd wanted him around and was using his suspension as an excuse to continue to avoid her.

"He's fond of both of them, you know," Nancy said, and Janelle thought she heard a slight reassurance in her voice. "He always talked quite a bit about them before . . ."

At the abrupt end to the sentence, Janelle looked up at Nathan's mother, saw the tension lines in the corners of her eyes and her pursed lips. Janelle opened her mouth to ask about Nathan's well-being, but Nancy met her gaze and the expression softened.

"You probably don't want to talk about him," she said lightly. "I can't say I blame you. He's being more stubborn than he should be right now, and we've all told him so."

"Yes, we have," Charlotte agreed from across the table where she sat with her sleeping infant in her arms.

Janelle held back her laugh as Kelsey giggled.

"So, we won't talk about him right now. How are you doing, Kelsey dear?" Nancy asked and they all turned to look at Janelle's sister as Kelsey gasped.

"I'm . . . uh . . ." Kelsey looked at the table and shook her head. "I'm fine, I guess." She shrugged.

"You look tired," Nancy stated. "Are you sleeping well?"

"Um," Kelsey replied as she looked wide-eyed at Janelle.

Nancy rose from her chair beside Janelle and walked around the table. She sat down next to Kelsey and grasped both of her hands. "I know this hasn't been easy on you, has it?" she asked, and Janelle saw the tears fill Kelsey's eyes as she looked at the older woman. Nancy released Kelsey's hands and gave her a hug. "Oh, sweetie, it's okay."

Janelle's mouth fell open as her eyes began to sting. She heard her sister's sobs as Nancy mumbled things for Kelsey's ears only and allowed her own tears to fall. She glanced across the table at Charlotte who was watching her mother-in-law and Kelsey with sympathy in her eyes. Janelle's heart swelled with something she couldn't quite place.

All she knew was this woman, Nathan's mother, was showing Kelsey and her more love and support than their mother had bothered to give them ever. This kind of support, the kind that brought meals without being asked, or offered a shoulder before the first tear was shed, wasn't something they were used to from their own mother, let alone anyone else's. It felt wrong that it should come from someone outside of the family. At the same time, it was coming from Nancy Harris and that seemed to make it right.

"He'll be back for you. A man doesn't follow you across the country and put himself in harm's way if he doesn't love you more than life itself," Nancy said. She'd pulled back enough to cup Kelsey's cheeks in her hands. "And don't let anyone tell you you're not deserving of that. It does a great disservice to him, treating him like he doesn't know his own mind."

Kelsey smiled.

Janelle's chin dropped. For the first time since Patrick left, maybe for the first time since she came home from the hospital, Kelsey smiled a smile that lit her whole face. Janelle released a long, slow breath as Nancy turned to her.

"You both deserve more happiness than you've been dealt so far. I think it's time you both reach out and grab it," Nancy said as she took one hand and reached for Janelle.

"Encouraging my daughters to behave badly again?"

Janelle's head snapped up to the figure looming in the doorway between the dining room and kitchen. How had Janelle not heard the door open? "Mother," she said when her mouth was no longer a desert. "How did you get in?"

"The door was unlocked, Janelle. It really wasn't hard." Mary's upper lip curled as she folded her arms across her chest. "What are you doing here,

Nancy? Come to corrupt my daughters a little more? Don't you think you've done enough damage?"

"I did damage?" Nancy stood and stepped around Kelsey, blocking her from Mary's view as Kelsey swiped at the tears on her cheeks. "What might I have done, Mary?"

"You encouraged that home-wrecker of a son of yours to come in and ruin Richard's marriage. Don't think I don't know how often you visited her. And how often Nathan was there, 'fixing' things around the house." Mary took a step closer. "That affair was your fault. You should have just minded your own business and left Janelle alone. She and Richard were doing fine before you came along."

Janelle caught a glimpse of Kelsey's gaping mouth, saw Charlotte cover James's ear with her palm, and opened her mouth to argue with her mother.

"Is that really what you think?" Nancy said calmly, beating Janelle to the punch.

She was also doing it much steadier than Janelle probably could have. Her heart was racing in her chest, her breathing quick and shallow.

"That's what I know," Mary hissed. "Richard never had one complaint about his life at home. Everything was perfect until you and your good-for-nothing son came in and ruined it for him."

Nancy shook her brunette head. "Do you even hear yourself? Richard's marriage was ruined? Richard never complained? Have you even considered that Janelle wasn't seeing things the same way?"

"Janelle knew how things were supposed to be," Mary snapped. "Her job was to keep him happy and raise his children." Mary turned her glare to Janelle. "It shouldn't have been that hard."

"Maybe it didn't help that your son-*in-law* was turning into your father, well on his way to claiming the title of 'town drunk' for himself." Nancy's control started to slip and her volume rose slightly as Mary's mouth fell open. "Yes, you may have thought he was hiding it, but we all saw the signs. At least those of us who were paying attention," Nancy spat as she cast a quick glance toward Charlotte and James and nodded toward the door.

Charlotte quickly stood and gave Janelle a soft smile as she slipped out of the dining room through the door to the living room.

Nancy turned back to Mary, and Janelle saw her shoulder lift and fall slowly. "Janelle was not happy, and if you'd bothered to visit her instead of singing Richard's praises all over town, then you might have known that. Why you preferred him to either of your lovely girls is beyond me, but the whole town was, and still is, aware of your preferences. Just as they were well aware of his nightly bar-hopping and the way he bet on everything he could."

The blood drained from Janelle's face and she gasped. She'd thought no one else had known about Richard's drinking. She'd apparently thought wrong.

"He would never have needed to do that if she'd supported him," Mary argued.

Numbness settled over Janelle as she watched the two women argue over her past. "Enough," Janelle said quietly. She rose from her seat and approached Nancy. "Thank you, for everything. Zoe's birthday is next Friday, and we're having a party the following day. I would love for you to join us."

"If *she* comes, I won't be here." Mary puffed her chest up and glared at her daughter.

Janelle looked at her mother and carefully pondered her words. "I'm willing to risk it." Mary's eyes widened, and Janelle cringed at the menace in her look. She turned back to Nancy. "And Charlotte, James, and Mason as well."

"We look forward to it, dear." Nancy turned and hugged Janelle. "I should go now," she whispered as they embraced, and Janelle nodded her agreement. They separated and Nancy turned to Kelsey who now stood beside her. "Remember what I said. You deserve it." She hugged Kelsey then left the room.

Janelle heard the door close and turned to her mother. "What do you want?" She sat down and Kelsey took the seat next to her.

"What was she doing here?" Mary snapped.

"Visiting her granddaughter," Kelsey answered with a grin. "Can't deny her that, can we?"

"Stay out of this. I'm having a conversation with your sister," Mary growled. "Don't you have a phone call to wait for? Or maybe he's not going to call you today. Perhaps he's found someone to warm his bed in Paris and no longer needs a harlot like you."

Janelle watched the grin fade from her sister's face, replaced by a look of stricken horror. "Now you're just being nasty for the sake of being nasty, Mother. Tell me what you want and leave," Janelle said. "I'm not really in the mood to talk to you right now."

"But you'll talk to her?" Mary scoffed. "You'll entertain your lover's mother, but not your own? What an ungrateful daughter you've turned out to be."

"Ungrateful?" Janelle leapt to her feet and her voice rose. "What have you given me to be grateful for? Your condescension? Your unwavering disapproval? Your name-calling and mudslinging?" Janelle crept toward her shocked mother. "Please. Forgive me," she added lowly with a snarl.

"I came for Gladys," Mary started as she backed toward the kitchen.

"She's not here." Kelsey's apparent boredom soothed Janelle slightly.

"She wants her mother's ring. Richard gave it to you and she wants it back," Mary continued.

"I don't have it. I left it at the house when I moved out. I put it on top of his dresser. If it's not there, he did something with it," Janelle answered with a shrug.

"Check the pawn shops," Kelsey added. "He always needed money."

Mary's lips pressed tightly together and her face began to mottle. Without another word, she turned and stormed out of the house. The door slammed behind her, and Janelle cursed as she looked at the ceiling and prayed the kids didn't wake up from their naps early.

She glanced in the direction of the front door. It would figure that her mother would come for something related to Richard. Janelle plopped into the chair and wondered how long it would be until her mother either stopped asking for things for him or just stopped visiting altogether.

She folded her arms on the table and laid her forehead on them. "Why do we put up with her?" she muttered, trying to keep the whine of frustration out of her voice.

"Because she's our mother," Kelsey answered matter-of-factly. "And if we didn't, she would do her best to separate us from Dad."

Janelle silently agreed, although she didn't think her father would make it easy for her.

"Do you remember when we were kids?" Kelsey's quiet voice broke through Janelle's thoughts. Janelle lifted her head to find her sister's elbow on the table, her head resting on her fist, as she looked blankly out the window.

"What, specifically?" Janelle asked as she pushed herself up.

"When we played princesses, Sean was always our dragon slayer," she continued, a smile stretching her lips. "He loved pretending to come to our rescue."

Janelle chuckled to herself. Their brother, the middle child, had always loved pretending to be their knight in shining armor. "He said he did, anyway." She focused on the wall behind her sister. "And if I remember correctly, it was always you he 'rescued' first."

Kelsey laughed as she nodded. "Of course he did, I was the baby."

Janelle chuckled along with her, but as their laughter faded, she was left with the emptiness his memories always left behind. Janelle was the oldest and, even if Sean didn't like it, it had always been her job to protect both him and Kelsey. But Janelle had failed Sean the night he'd needed her most. He'd died when they were in college because she couldn't be there for him, because she hadn't been looking out for him the way she should have been.

Kelsey's shoulders lifted then she released a long, slow sigh. "Sometimes I wish he were still here to slay the dragons for us. He always made dealing with *her* tolerable."

Their mother had always been the one thing Sean actually could protect Janelle from if he chose to. Janelle could only nod her agreement.

Fifteen

"How did your visit with Nancy go?" Janelle asked Kelsey as they prepared for dinner. Janelle was making macaroni and cheese and sautéing chicken as Kelsey set the plates on the kitchen island. Nancy had arrived as Janelle was leaving to take Zach to therapy earlier, and Kelsey had invited her to stay.

"It was nice," Kelsey said with a slight smile. Janelle didn't know what Nancy had said to Kelsey on that first visit, or the two visits since, but Kelsey's spirits seemed to be lifted. For that alone, Janelle was thankful.

"What did you talk about?" Janelle added the powdered cheese mix to the milk and stirred as the noodles cooked.

"Nothing in particular, really, just whatever came to mind. She watched Zoe play and colored with her for a while. She asked me a few questions about working in movies and, of course, Patrick. She said she's looking forward to meeting him," Kelsey said, and Janelle thought she heard a hitch in her voice.

Janelle glanced at her sister and saw the smile falter as sadness crept into her eyes. "Kelsey," she said as she turned. "He's coming home to you."

"I know." Kelsey waved her sister's comment away. "It's just . . . it's not easy to forget the reputation he had and the way he used to behave with his female co-stars, less than a year ago. Some old habits die hard."

Janelle shook her head and walked toward her sister. "Those don't sound like your words." She wrapped her arms around Kelsey and hugged her tightly. "He loves you more than anything, and you know that. Forget what Mom thinks. Forget what he used to be like and focus on who you know him to be." Janelle broke the hug and gripped her sister's upper arms. "He calls you every day, and he'll be home before we know it. He wouldn't be happy to know you doubt that."

Kelsey smiled weakly. "Then let's not tell him."

Janelle laughed and let her sister go. They resumed their dinner preparations in relative silence then called the kids in for dinner around the kitchen island. Once the food was on their plates and the blessing said, they began eating. Zoe told Janelle about her visit with Nancy and how much she liked seeing her.

"I can call her 'Nan,'" Zoe said cheerfully, and Janelle's eyes widened slightly.

"Nan?" She looked at Kelsey. "Short for?"

"Nancy, of course," Kelsey said out loud, but mouthed, "or Nana," with a shrug.

Janelle nodded her understanding but felt butterflies in her stomach. What if she and Nathan never worked things out? She wasn't sure how she felt about Nancy allowing her daughter to become so familiar with her. On the other hand, it couldn't hurt. Having Nancy in Zoe's life, acting like a grandmother even if Zoe never learned the truth, would be a whole lot better than growing up thinking Mary and, even worse, Gladys were her grandmothers.

"Daddy said you're my real mommy," Zach said softly, and Janelle heard Kelsey's fork hit her plate.

Janelle glanced at him and saw him staring at Kelsey with big, blue, puppy dog eyes. Janelle swallowed the lump in her throat and exchanged a look with Kelsey. She'd meant to warn her they'd discussed the kidnapping in therapy today. Zach looked at his food again. His hands rested on the counter, perfectly still on either side of the plate. Zoe looked at him, then Janelle, then resumed eating slowly.

"Was he telling the truth?" Zach continued in his pitiful voice.

"Zach, we already discussed this," Janelle said calmly.

He looked up at her. "You said he didn't always tell the truth."

"When did she say that, Zach?" Kelsey asked.

"A long time ago," he answered as he turned to face her. "Before we moved in here."

Janelle's brow furrowed and she tilted her head. Had she actually said that? She'd always tried to shield her children from Richard's less than stellar behavior. His lies being the least offensive of the bunch. Janelle met her sister's gaze and nodded once. It was both an acknowledgment and permission for Kelsey to be honest.

Kelsey inclined her head in understanding and turned to Zach. “Yes, sweetheart, this time he was telling the truth.” Zach’s eyes widened, and Janelle felt a squeeze in her chest. Kelsey continued, “I carried you in my tummy, the way your mommy carried Zoe. Do you remember that?”

Zach nodded.

“But then after you were born,” Kelsey looked down at her plate as her voice cracked, “your mommy and daddy adopted you and they became your parents.”

Zack looked at a spot on the counter in front of him, and Janelle watched him think. She wondered what was going through his little mind. And what had gone through it when Richard first told him? She was furious that Richard had done this to Zach, that he had placed that seed of doubt in this precious little boy. With therapy, Zach seemed to be doing better, but she couldn’t help but wonder when she might see that joyful sparkle in her son’s eyes again.

“Why?” Zach asked with a shaky voice.

“Because I couldn’t take care of you the way they could. I didn’t have a place to live or a job.” Kelsey walked to the side of the island directly across from him. She propped herself up on her elbows so they would be eye to eye, if Zach looked up.

“He said it was because you didn’t love me.” Zach said, a tear sliding down his cheek.

“That isn’t true,” Kelsey stated, and Janelle could see the water in her eyes too. Their sadness was about to undo Janelle’s control. Kelsey added, “I love you very much. I loved you when you were born, and I love you even more now.”

“Then why did you give me away?” He looked directly at Kelsey, his cheeks now soaked, drops falling onto the counter.

Kelsey frowned, and a tear slid down her cheek. “I didn’t want to.” She shook her head. “But you needed so much more than I could give you.”

“Daddy said it was because you wanted to be in movies.”

“No,” Kelsey replied softly.

“Zach, your Aunt Kelsey didn’t decide to go to California until your dad and I decided to adopt you," Janelle said soothingly, laying her hand on top of his. "We took you because we all love you and wanted to do what was best for you." Zach looked up at Janelle and sniffled. "Do you think she doesn't love you now?"

Janelle could see his wheels turning as he stared at a spot on the wall over her shoulder. After a few minutes, his little head slowly turned from side to side.

Janelle released a quiet sigh of relief. "You're right," she said with a smile. "Aunt Kelsey loves you very much. As much as I do."

He turned his sad eyes back on Kelsey. "But you left me."

Kelsey's mouth fell open a little as she stood and took a step back. Janelle thought she might run and prayed she didn't. Zach hadn't said anything wrong, maybe a little hurtful, but he had a right to have the answers.

"Aunt Kelsey didn't leave," Zoe said. "She's right there."

Janelle closed her eyes at her daughter's innocence and wished she could always stay that way. She knew that, eventually, the time would come when she would have to deal with telling Zoe the truth. She wasn't sure if it was better or worse than the truth Zach was facing now, but she did know that it would strip a layer of purity from her daughter.

Kelsey's mouth closed, and Janelle saw the slow rise and fall of her chest. She pulled her shoulders back as she looked Zach squarely in the eyes and gave him a slight smile. "Yes, Zach, I did leave you. It was one of the hardest things I've ever done." She walked around to stand beside him then gently turned him to face her. "It's always hard for me to leave you, but I still believe that giving you to your mommy was the best thing for everyone. And now that I have a job, I can help take care of all of you the way I couldn't before."

Zach slowly put his arms around Kelsey's waist, and she placed her arms around him. As Kelsey lowered her head to his, Janelle saw a few remaining tears slither down her cheeks. His arms fell away, and Kelsey kissed the top of his head before letting him go. She walked back to her plate and picked it up, dumped her food in the trash, and put the dishes in the sink then returned to her seat at the island and sat down.

"Mommy, I'm done eating," Zoe said sweetly.

"You may get down," Janelle replied as she looked at Zach's barely touched plate. "Are you done Zach?" He nodded and Janelle gave him permission to leave the table too.

Janelle picked up the kids' plates and dumped the remainder of their food in the trash then placed them in the sink. She repeated the process with her own plate then turned and placed her palms on the countertop.

"Why would he even be thinking about that?" Kelsey questioned stiffly and Janelle's cheeks warmed slightly.

"I meant to warn you. He talked about it in therapy today," she answered softly. "Wanna talk about it?"

"What's to talk about?" Kelsey replied bitterly. "He's right. I left him. I was selfish and it was wrong."

"Kelsey, he didn't say that," Janelle tried to soothe her sister.

Kelsey's glare was full of hurt and a little bit of anger. "He didn't have to." She looked down at her hands, folded on the marble. "Have you ever considered that if I hadn't made that choice, if I hadn't given him up, then we wouldn't be here right now? Richard wouldn't have had a reason to shoot me. Heck, he may never have started to drink again, and you'd still have the wonderful husband you were once so blessed with."

Janelle rolled her eyes and ignored her sister's cruel statement. Nothing about her marriage or her husband had ever been wonderful.

"Zach would still be a part of your life, only he'd be your nephew, and I'd be his mother," Kelsey choked on her words and paused to swallow. "I'd be taking care of him and working my butt off to support him, but I'd be doing it here. Who knows, I might have a husband of my own, and maybe a sibling or two for Zach."

"You wouldn't have a career you love. You wouldn't have this house," Janelle said calmly, feeling anger at the entire situation warm her veins. She hated seeing her sister look so defeated. She hated hearing the doubt and double guessing in her words. She took a deep breath and walked toward Kelsey. She lifted her sister's chin and tried to smile. "And you wouldn't have Patrick." Kelsey narrowed her eyes at Janelle. It had been a low blow, but Janelle needed the big guns for this argument. So she continued, "Richard *would* have started drinking again, it was only a matter of time. He couldn't handle fatherhood, and our marriage was far from wonderful." She released Kelsey's chin and leaned against the stove behind her.

Kelsey slowly turned to face her. "That wasn't why he drank," she said quietly.

"What excuse did he give then?" Janelle asked, feeling certain it was something she'd already heard.

"He didn't like looking at Sean's face every day," Kelsey replied.

Janelle's heart stopped and she blinked slowly. She was wrong. She hadn't heard that excuse before. "Why would you say that?"

"He told me," Kelsey replied dully. "He thought Zach was a daily reminder of Sean and he accused me of knowing he would be."

Richard's reasoning was undoubtedly designed to make Kelsey feel bad. Sadly, it was apparently working. Janelle lifted an eyebrow. "That's probably one of the dumbest things I've ever heard him say."

Kelsey shrugged as she held out her hands, palms up. "So you see, if I hadn't let you adopt him, we wouldn't have this problem."

They stared at each other as Janelle debated telling Kelsey the whole truth. And why Sean's death in a car accident, and everything that had come afterward, was her fault. Not Richard's and certainly not Kelsey's.

"Why don't you start a pot of coffee? I'm going to put a movie on for the kids then we need to talk," Janelle stated, her tone left no room for argument as she walked away. She let the kids pick a movie and put it in the DVD player. When they were set and she could smell the coffee brewing, Janelle returned to the kitchen.

Kelsey had gotten two large mugs out of the cabinet and set them on the island, along with the sugar and milk. Janelle pulled a bottle of brandy out of the cabinet and set it beside the mugs. They remained silent as the coffee finished brewing, but Janelle could feel her sister's eyes on her as she went through the motions of pouring coffee into a cup for each of them, then adding the sugar and milk to hers as Kelsey did the same. Janelle poured a healthy splash of brandy into her cup then inched it toward her sister.

"You may want that," she said as she nodded toward the liquor.

"Why?" Kelsey asked slowly as she obeyed, only adding a little splash instead.

"Because you may not want to hear what I have to say." Janelle waited for Kelsey to sit down on the bar stool on the other side of the angle. Janelle took a long sip of the coffee and set her mug down. She stared into the dark depths as she gathered her thoughts. "Sean's death was my fault," she began and held up her hand to stop Kelsey's protest. "And not in the way Mom likes to blame me for."

"O-kay," Kelsey said, and Janelle could tell she wasn't sure she believed her. "How so?"

"By the end of the spring semester of our junior year, I was getting tired of Richard's behavior," Janelle started her explanation. "I began to consider ending things. I realized he was going to be more like our grandfather and less like our father, and it scared me. I spent the entire summer weighing the pros and cons and had finally come to the conclusion that I didn't want to marry him."

Kelsey gasped and her jaw dropped. The corner of Janelle's mouth lifted slightly in a deprecating smile, directed at herself.

"But I never actually had the courage to go through with it. It was on the tip of my tongue so many times." Janelle lowered her head in shame. "I found it unbelievably hard to say those three little words, 'Richard, it's over.' The night of Sean's accident, I had left for work and Richard was already half lit. In that fifteen minute drive, I decided that I would do it the next morning and move into Sean's apartment with him, whether he liked it or not." Tears sprang to Janelle's eyes at the painful memories of the night of her brother's death. She felt Kelsey's hand on top of hers as the first salty drop slid down her cheek.

Janelle continued to review what had happened. "At some point during my shift at the bar, Sean had decided he wanted to go home, but Richard had been too drunk to drive him. Sean had taken the keys to my car; I had driven Richard's car to work, partly as insurance that he wouldn't do something stupid like drive that evening. Sean tried to tackle the ten-minute drive to his own apartment. He'd only made it five minutes before swerving off the road and hitting a tree.

"I had been called by the police and immediately left work and had gone directly to the hospital. The injuries were more gruesome than I care to remember, and he'd been unconscious. I held his hand, cursing my own weaknesses, as he slowly passed away."

Kelsey gently squeezed her fingers, bringing her back into the present. "Janelle, you couldn't have stopped Sean from driving that night," Kelsey said calmly, a trail of tears streaking her cheeks.

"No." Janelle shook her head. "But if I'd had the courage to end things with Richard sooner, Sean may have been away from his bad influence sooner. I could have saved our brother's life if I'd been strong enough to walk away at the first doubt."

"You don't know that, J." Kelsey squeezed her hand and frowned. "Sean and Richard were friends."

"Because of me," Janelle said scornfully.

Kelsey's head swayed side to side. "That's neither here nor there. My point is, even if you had ended things sooner, they may have remained friends. There's no guarantee that Sean would have cut ties with Richard just because you had. You know how easy Sean was to get along with and everyone who knew him considered him their friend. Richard was no different."

"But I was his sister," Janelle whined. She felt a slight sense of betrayal at the thought that her own brother may have chosen Richard's company to her own.

Kelsey smiled a little. "True. But you were his older, bossier sister. And, as much as we hate to admit it, Richard was fun to be around, in the beginning." Janelle's lip curled but she nodded reluctantly. "Besides, if Sean had had a problem with Richard, he could have walked away at any point. Richard was dating you, not him. Sadly, Sean's death was of his own doing, and we really can't blame anyone but him. He made a mistake and it cost us all."

The sisters sat quietly sipping their coffee for a few minutes. Janelle's mind wandered back to the time before Sean's death and searched for any sign that maybe he hadn't been as happy with Richard as he'd led her to believe. She came up with nothing, no indication that Sean might have even considered ending his friendship with Richard—a friendship that Janelle still blamed for his death.

"So, now that we've settled that, why did you stay with Richard anyway?" Kelsey asked as she stood up and retrieved the coffee pot.

"I didn't," Janelle answered as Kelsey added coffee to each of their cups. She stopped her pour as she looked at Janelle with a raised brow. "I broke up with him after the funeral."

Kelsey set the coffee pot on the marble with a loud *thunk*. Any harder and Janelle was sure they'd be cleaning up broken glass and spilled coffee. "Then why the hell did you take him back?" Kelsey snapped.

Janelle cringed. After everything her family, especially her mother, had been through, Janelle hadn't told any of them she'd ended it with Richard. "I moved into Sean's apartment, took over his lease, and lived out the rest of that fall semester there. Richard begged me to take him back. Almost every day. He kept promising he would change, that he would sober up and stay sober, if I'd take him back. I had my doubts, so I kept saying no."

Kelsey resumed pouring coffee and fixed it to her liking then slowly sat back down. "So, what did he do to change your mind?"

Janelle shook her head and took a deep breath. "It was when we came home for winter break that year. None of you knew we'd separated, so we had to pretend like everything was fine. But do you remember how he helped Mom out of her funk?"

Kelsey nodded. "How can I forget? That was when he became her favorite child," she added with a roll of her eyes. "That's why you took him back? Because of what he did for Mom?"

"No," Janelle replied. "It was the effect it had on Dad. When I got home, I could see the stress all over his face, even before I knew what Mom was up to. Without being asked, Richard went to her and helped her through her grief, but it was the relief I saw on Dad's face that really moved me. By the time we left, Dad looked years younger, the stress was still there, but it was lessened. He looked happier. Not as happy as he'd been before Sean's death, but he was better."

"I remember that too," Kelsey said softly. "I had almost forgotten how stressed he'd been, how sick with worry over Mom. Richard helped Dad just as much as he helped Mom."

"At the time, I thought it was the most selfless thing he'd ever done." Janelle sighed sadly. "We went back to college and had a long talk about what I expected from him if he wanted us to get back together. I didn't move back in with him, I stayed in Sean's apartment. We saw each other every day, and by spring break, I'd seen such a change in him, and foolishly hoped it was permanent, that I took him back. We continued the engagement like the separation had never happened."

Janelle listened to the bright, bouncy music coming from the living room and turned to look at her children.

"I look at them every day and wonder 'what if?', Kels. What if I had been strong enough to follow my gut and stayed away from him for good? Would I have convinced you to let me adopt Zach if I hadn't had a husband? Would I have had an affair with Nathan that gave me Zoe? As miserable as I was, I'm not sure I would have wanted to give them up for anything."

"What if you had been able to work things out with Nathan sooner?" Kelsey asked.

Janelle slowly turned to her and smiled sadly. "Things haven't worked out with Nathan, Kelsey. And there's no indication they will." She turned back to the kids. "We just have to go on from here and play the cards we've been dealt."

"Well, then, I suggest we play our fun card and join the kids in the living room. I could use a good cartoon. And when they go to bed, we'll put on something guaranteed to make us cry."

Janelle felt her sister's arm loop through hers and looked up to see her smiling down on her. "You want to cry?"

"It's therapeutic," Kelsey replied with a wink as she pulled Janelle to her feet and they joined the kids.

Sixteen

Nathan walked across his mother's porch and knocked once on the front door before turning the knob and opening it. He'd had nothing better to do so he was taking her up on her offer of a home-cooked meal. It sure beat sitting at home eating TV dinners and staring at his cell phone. "Mom!"

"Nathan, you're here," his mother said as she walked toward him. She quickly wrapped him in a hug and ushered him into her house.

He glanced around and shook his head. Every time he walked into the house, he was hoping to see something different. His mother hadn't changed anything in fifteen years. The walls were a faded blue and the carpet a dingy brown, and the house still had the essence of his father scattered throughout. Nathan figured that's why his mother still clung to her dark leather sofa, set against the back wall and facing the door and front window of the living room, and his father's armchair, angled into the room with its back to the front door. An old, dark wood coffee table and two pine bookcases filled empty space in the room.

The one piece that stood out was the beige, microfiber couch that Mason and Charlotte had given Nancy for Christmas two years ago. They had hoped to push her headlong into redecorating, but Nancy had simply moved things around, smiling that her boys were older and they would need more seating as the family grew. That couch now sat on the opposite wall of the room, against the unused fireplace.

Nathan let his mother lead him around the corner and through the door into the dining room where his feet stopped moving.

"I thought it was just us, Mom," Nathan said, frowning at his brothers, sister-in-law, and nephew.

"Did I give you that idea?" Nancy looked around at her other children, already seated at the table. "Hmm, so sorry."

Nathan rolled his eyes at his mother's decidedly un-sorry tone. He walked around Jackson and took his former seat between him and their father's chair. He didn't feel like being head of the family tonight. They would survive.

"Glad you're finally here," Mason scoffed. "How is it that I work ten hours a day and I still beat both of you here?"

Nathan stared at Jackson. "You're living here, aren't you?"

"And you're not working at the moment. What's your point?" Jackson replied.

Nathan's palm itched to hit his youngest brother on the back of the head.

"I had things to do today," Jackson said with a shrug then turned to Mason. "Is that a problem for you?"

"Boys, can't we at least start the meal in peace before you get to sniping at each other?" Nancy asked as she set a large bowl of gravy-soaked dumplings on the table. Nathan looked around the table and grinned. Sure enough, some of his other favorites were on the table—chicken, bean salad, sweet potato casserole, and yeast rolls.

On second thought, he was no longer sure that was a good thing.

"What's going on, Mom?" Nathan asked after she'd taken her seat at the end of the table.

"Nothing dear, why?" she replied with a smile. "Could you please say the blessing?"

Nathan watched as his mom and Charlotte folded their hands in front of them and bowed their heads. Mason slowly followed, staring at Nathan as he did. Jackson crossed his arms and blatantly raised an eyebrow at Nathan, who promptly elbowed him into compliance.

He said the blessing then immediately reached for the dumplings before his brothers could grab them. They passed the food in relative peace then all began to eat. Nathan chewed slowly, the sense of foreboding settling over him. Something was going on here, and he intended to get to the bottom of it.

"Mom, what's going on?" he repeated his question.

He was answered with her angelic smile and the lift of a delicate shoulder.

"Don't give me that. These are all my favorite foods. You seemed insistent that I come to dinner tonight. I know you, you're up to something," Nathan said as he stabbed a chunk of chicken and dragged it through the dumpling gravy.

"I just thought we could have a nice family dinner while your brother is still in town," Nancy replied, transferring her beatific grin to Jackson.

"Then these should be my favorites, not his," Jackson scoffed.

"The rest of us choose to consume from the five food groups, not five different types of alcohol," Mason said.

Jackson glared at him. "I have been practically sober for almost five years, thank you very much." He looked down at his plate and mumbled, "For all the good it's done me."

Nathan felt a strong sympathy for his baby brother. When he stopped to think about it, their situations weren't really that different. Both of them wanted women they couldn't have. Or better yet, women who didn't really want them. At least Jackson had his band and touring to keep him out of town. Nathan couldn't get away from Janelle that easily.

Nathan decided to let the subject drop, at least for now, and dedicated himself to enjoying his mother's cooking. He let the snarky comments between Mason and Jackson float past him and, unless they spoke directly to him, he was also able to tune out his mother and Charlotte's chipper voices. He spent the entirety of his meal trying to come up with a way of satisfying Captain Little's orders and seeing Janelle at the same time.

If these investigations went on much longer, he was sure he'd go crazy. He wanted to see Janelle. He wanted to see his daughter. And it didn't help that he knew his mother had been there at least four times since Easter, just over a week ago, but she refused to say anything about those visits.

"So, what do you think we should get for her?" Charlotte asked as everyone else seemed to fall silent, including the voice in Nathan's mind.

"I don't know. Janelle said she likes princesses. She said Patrick got her a whole bunch of princess dolls for Christmas," Nancy answered, and Nathan's focus sharpened on her. Nancy held his gaze for a moment then turned back to her daughter-in-law. "I'll have to ask if she has that new princess movie that just came out on DVD. Janelle said she took her to see it in the theater and she absolutely loved it."

It was perfectly obvious who they were talking about, and even though he was dying to know why, Nathan held his tongue. He knew his mother well;

she'd eventually drop enough hints for him to figure it out or she'd simply hit him over the head, metaphorically speaking, with what she wanted him to know.

Charlotte glanced at Nathan as a smile slowly formed on her lips then turned to Mason. "Are you going to be able to make it to the party?"

"What the hell are you three talking about?" Jackson asked as his eyes bounced from face to face around him.

"I'm not talking about it," Mason muttered then looked at his wife. "And I'm not sure yet. You know I'd rather not go."

Charlotte patted her husband's forearm on the table. "I know, but don't you think you should?"

Mason looked at Nathan and shook his head. "If he's not going, why should I? She's not my daughter."

"What's going on?" Nathan asked, his impatience getting the better of him as his calm started to slip. "Why are you talking about my daughter, and what party?"

"Oh," Nancy said, covering her mouth with her fingers. "Didn't I tell you?"

"Obviously not," Nathan replied through clenched teeth.

Jackson chuckled softly.

"Zoe's third birthday is Friday. Janelle is having a party for her on Saturday," Nathan's mother said, then feigned an air of innocence as she continued, "I thought you would have known."

"You knew I didn't," Nathan growled.

This was really getting tiresome. Janelle couldn't pick up a phone to call him, but she could invite the rest of his family to a birthday party for *his* daughter. Three years he'd missed with Zoe, and it appeared Janelle was perfectly content to let him continue to miss time with her. He was getting to the bottom of this.

"Maybe if you'd bother to contact Janelle, you'd know that," Mason said, fighting a grin as Nathan turned his scowl on his middle brother. "Oh, sorry, I forgot. Your job is so much more important than the woman you've been in love with since high school."

"Shut up, Mason." Nathan slid his chair away from the table and stood abruptly.

"Or what, Nathan?" Mason jeered. "You're not going to do anything. You always play by the rules, regardless of what they are."

Nathan glowered menacingly at his brother and Mason stopped laughing.

"You shouldn't have agreed so easily to the captain's orders, but you did and now you're suffering," Mason said coolly. "You have no one but yourself to blame for this."

"So this is what this dinner was all about, Mother?" Nathan snapped. "So you could talk about Janelle and my daughter in front of me and make me feel guilty that I'm not a part of their lives? Are you trying to torture me further? What were you trying to accomplish?"

"I'm trying to push you into doing *something*, Nathan," Nancy said calmly as she rose. "That little girl needs a father. So does her brother. The one they had was a monster and they deserve better." She looked at her eldest son, and Nathan saw the turmoil in her usually steady green eyes. "Are you better than him? Or will you continue to abandon them the way you have so far?"

Nathan felt her words like a punch in the gut. He drew his shoulders back and walked around Jackson. Without a word to anyone, he left the house. Yes, he was definitely going to do something about this.

Right now.

Janelle pulled into the driveway, exhausted. Why she had agreed with Andrew's request and taken Zoe to therapy with Zach, and then thought it would be great if the three of them had dinner before they came home, was beyond her. Therapy had been brutal to watch, dinner had been painful to sit through with Zoe talking nonstop and Zach not saying anything, and now all she wanted to do was have a glass of wine, take a hot bath, and crawl into bed with a good book.

At least they had beaten the rain home. A small positive, but at this point she'd take it.

"Oh, crap," she whispered to herself when she spied the car sitting in the driveway. It was her mother's car, and uneasiness slithered down her spine. "Kids, I want you to go into the house as quietly as possible and go straight upstairs to bed. I'll tuck you in as soon as I can."

"Are we playing the quiet game, Mommy?" Zoe asked.

"Excellent idea, sweetheart. The quietest one gets a quarter." Janelle parked her minivan beside Kelsey's Jeep, under the protection of the carport. She pushed the button for the side door to open then reached in and quickly unbuckled Zoe, and the kids climbed out. "Remember, quiet game." Janelle put her finger to her lips and they all tiptoed up the steps and across the front porch.

If she wanted any idea of what Mary was saying to Kelsey, she had to catch her in the act. After each of their mother's visits, Kelsey was quiet and wouldn't talk about it. It had gotten a little better since Nancy had started visiting, but Mary had also been scarce. That was fine with Janelle.

Janelle opened the front door and motioned for the kids to come in and go upstairs. She set her keys on the side table in the entryway, toed her sandals off and left them beside the steps, and quietly made her way toward the kitchen.

"Mom, I'm not staying here, I have a career in California. I'm supposed to start working on another movie in June," Kelsey was saying as she turned toward the coffee pot. Janelle smelled the fresh, hot coffee and her mouth watered.

"You haven't worked on anything, except *him*, since November. What kind of career is that dear? You can do better," Mary stated as Kelsey poured herself a cup of coffee. Mary continued, "Zach needs stability now. You owe it to him to settle down here, become a mother, find him a—"

"A what?" Kelsey snapped as she turned around. "A father?"

Janelle's heart nearly stopped. Was her mother encouraging Kelsey to stay and be a mother to Zach? Was Kelsey agreeing so easily? No wonder Kelsey never wanted to talk about it.

Mary nodded her head. "Not right away, of course."

"Of course." Kelsey rolled her eyes as she sat down on the bar stool and stared into her mug.

"He needs a good, strong, male role model in his life," Mary said sweetly. "And, since *you've* deprived him of another father, I think you need to take on the responsibility of finding one for him."

"He has Dad," Kelsey muttered as the same thought crossed Janelle's mind.

"Your father can't be here for Zach twenty-four-seven. Zach needs a stable influence that can be around for him all the time," Mary argued. "Think of all the little things that your father did for you and your brother and sister. Softball games, scouts, vacations, tucking you in at night, comforting you when you had a nightmare."

"Janelle is perfectly capable of doing all of that," Kelsey said, her knuckles turning white as she gripped her mug. "And I will help when I'm here."

Janelle silently released a breath. Her sister was standing up for her. Kelsey wasn't plotting with Mary to take her son away. She almost felt giddy.

Mary remained quiet until Kelsey looked up. Before her eyes fell on her mother, she made eye contact with Janelle. Janelle put her index finger to her lips and saw a slight nod of Kelsey's head as she turned her attention back to their mother. Mary had apparently been waiting for Kelsey to completely focus on her because as soon as Kelsey looked at her, she continued.

"True," she agreed, "but what will you do when he's a teenager? How will he learn to treat women properly? Are you prepared to deal with puberty without male guidance?"

"Mother," Kelsey hissed, "that's years away."

"All the more reason for *you* to settle down now. You start dating again and when the time comes, maybe he'll have a decent father figure." Janelle saw her mother's shoulders lift as she held her hands up like she'd just figured it all out, and thought it should be common sense.

Kelsey pressed her lips tightly together and looked at her coffee mug again.

Janelle rolled her eyes and stepped into the room. "And where do I fit into this equation, Mother?" she said smoothly.

Her mother spun on the stool so quickly she nearly fell off of it when she met Janelle's glare. "Janelle," she gasped. "What are you doing home so soon?"

Janelle glanced at the clock, more for emphasis since she had a pretty good idea what time it was. "It's seven thirty, it's hardly early."

"Where are the children?" Mary asked, seeming to regain her equilibrium.

"I decided to leave them with Andrew. I told him I wasn't responsible enough to be their mother and maybe he should find them someone more qualified." Janelle let a savage grin form on her lips. "You know, in case your prospects don't work out." She motioned to Kelsey and was more than happy to see her mother's face turn pink.

"Janelle, I never meant to imply you weren't a good mother," Mary blustered as she rose to her feet.

"No?" Janelle questioned. "Funny, that's what it sounded like. Kelsey, what did you think?" Janelle looked at her sister, who was trying not to smile too widely.

"Yeah, sounded a lot like that to me too," Kelsey readily agreed.

Mary pulled her shoulders back and pursed her lips together until her color returned to normal. "I was just saying that it's about time Kelsey took some responsibility for her actions. Zach is her son, and now that he knows it, she needs to step up and do what's right by him."

"Zach is *my* son and she has already done what was right by him, Mom. She gave him up for adoption to give him a better life," Janelle argued.

"So she could run off and play movie star," Mary snapped. "She ran away from her problems, and you let her do it. And we won't even talk about your behavior, Janelle. You're both an embarrassment."

Janelle let out a growl of frustration. "She didn't run away, I pushed her out the door. I offered to adopt Zach so she would leave."

Mary audibly gasped and Kelsey covered her mouth with her fingertips.

"Of all the stupid things, Janelle. Adopting him ruined your marriage. Why would you do such a thing?" Mary asked.

Janelle was slightly surprised by her mother's perceptions. Janelle knew that was when her marriage began to crumble, but she hadn't thought that her mother had picked up on it too. "I wanted Kelsey to follow her dreams and get out from under your thumb."

Mary's jaw tightened as her eyes narrowed on Janelle. "Just what do you mean by that?"

"You know exactly what I mean by that," Janelle replied. "You disowned her, you kicked her out of your house, and you still took every opportunity you had to demean her. If you thought I was going to let her put up with that for the rest of her life because she was raising a child on her own, you don't know me that well. I hated the way you treated her when she was pregnant, and I knew that you would always treat her with disdain and condescension if she stayed. She had a dream and I wanted her to follow it. She never would have given Zach up to a stranger, she would have wondered about him for the rest of her life. I adopted Zach so she could still be a part of his life and she could pursue her dreams and maybe even have a chance at a happy life."

"I never would have prevented that," Mary said defensively.

"You're kidding, right?" Kelsey rolled her eyes.

"Mom, you're doing it now. She's made her choices and Zach has a mother—me. Let her be his aunt and let me worry about taking care of him." Janelle folded her arms across her chest as she felt her energy begin to wane. Her mother was always so exhausting. "Now, if you're done trying to run our lives, I need to tuck my children into bed. I think you should go."

"You're both stubborn as mules, don't know what's good for you, let alone your children," Mary muttered to herself as she quickly made her way to the front door. "Damn hardheaded girls, you get that from your father," she continued, and her mumbling only stopped when the door closed behind her.

Janelle turned to find her sister standing beside her, her lips pursed tightly.

"I think that went well," Kelsey said as she looped her arm through her sister's. "Now let's tuck your children into bed so we can open a bottle of wine."

Janelle laughed lightly as she let Kelsey lead her up the steps. They took turns tucking the kids into bed then headed back downstairs to settle in for a glass of wine and maybe a movie. When her feet hit the floor behind Kelsey's, Janelle noticed a pair of headlights pulling into her driveway.

"Now what?" she mumbled as she walked out onto the porch. When she recognized the vehicle driving toward the house, everything in her froze.

Seventeen

What was he doing there? Janelle was not in the mood or the mindset to deal with him tonight. Since he'd started giving her the silent treatment, she'd started building a wall around her heart. The mortar wasn't quite set yet and seeing him now only threatened to topple it before it could harden.

"Who is it?" Kelsey asked as she followed Janelle out the door.

"It's Nathan," Janelle muttered through clenched teeth. She inhaled deeply and decided her relaxing evening would simply have to wait a little longer. "Go back inside, I'll deal with him."

Kelsey rested her chin on Janelle's shoulder as she gave it a supportive squeeze. "Be nice," she said as she pulled away. "I'm here if you need me," she added, and Janelle heard the front door close. She glanced over her shoulder to make sure her sister was gone then turned back around as Nathan's truck stopped in front of the house.

"What the hell are you doing here?" Janelle snapped as soon as his door was closed.

Nathan looked up at her across the hood of his truck and fell back a step. She watched him regain his composure and begin to walk toward her, his eyes focused sharply on her.

As her heart sped up, Janelle crossed her arms and continued to glare at him. "What are you doing here, Nathan?"

"Such a hostile greeting. What's wrong with you?" He stopped in front of the truck and held his hands out to his side.

Janelle's jaw dropped. "What's wrong with me?" she sputtered. "Seriously?" When she saw his brown head bob, her frustration bubbled into a slight rage. "You give me the silent treatment, completely ignore me for four and a half weeks, and then decide to show up here unannounced and I'm supposed to be okay with that?"

"Silent treatment?" Nathan scoffed. "I sent you a letter, didn't you read it?"

"No, I didn't read it," she snapped and watched the frown on his full lips deepen. "I wanted you to pick up the phone. Just answer the damn question so you can leave. Why are you here?"

"Why do you think I'm here, Janelle?"

She rolled her eyes. "If I knew that, I wouldn't have asked. What I *think* is that you're here to see your daughter," Janelle stated. "But she's tucked into bed already. If you'd *called*, I could have told you not to bother coming by."

Nathan placed his hand on the hood and raised an eyebrow. "Why would you tell me not to bother? I'd like to see you, too. I thought we were friends."

"Well, I don't want to see you," Janelle spat. "So just go home." She backed toward the house and took a shaky breath.

"Would Saturday be a good time then?" Nathan casually asked.

Janelle stopped mid-step. That's what this was about, Zoe's birthday party. He must have talked to his mother. She met his bronzy glare and moved toward the edge of the porch.

"So you're here about her party? I'm sorry, we haven't mastered telepathic communication yet so I wasn't sure how to invite you," she said sweetly.

His rounded jaw tightened and his lip curled. "There's this invention called the telephone. Maybe you could try using that."

"I find the phone too unreliable. I can never be sure my calls will be answered." Janelle returned his glare with one of her own.

Above them a streak of lightning flew across the sky, and Janelle felt a cooling breeze on her face. She glanced at the trees and saw the leaves turned upward. They were in for a doozy of a storm. Thunder crashed as she met Nathan's stare again and she realized he'd taken another step closer.

"I told you to give me a call, that I would answer it," Nathan snapped, fire burning in his eyes.

"No, you told Patrick to tell me to call you. I never would have expected something so cowardly from you, Nathan. I was not impressed," she replied coolly.

"Me? A coward?" Another flash of lightning, followed quickly by the clap of thunder. "You're one to talk."

"Excuse me?" Janelle took a step off the porch as the wind began to pick up.

"You heard me. You want to talk about cowardly, what about you? Finding out you were pregnant with my child and taking the easy way out. Staying with a man you didn't love instead of leaving him and building a life with me." Nathan crept closer and Janelle recoiled at his words. "I thought we had something, Janelle. I thought I meant more than just a few months of kicks."

"There was nothing easy about what I did, Nathan," she hissed.

"I'm supposed to believe that?"

"Believe what you want. I would have explained everything to you weeks ago, but you decided to give me the cold shoulder instead," Janelle managed in a steady voice. He was closer to right than she cared to admit, even now.

"I was directed to stay away from you. I didn't do it because I wanted to," Nathan growled. "Do you think for a moment I have liked following that order? I have a lot of questions, and only you can answer them. I foolishly thought you and I might be able to—"

"You're right, that is foolish," Janelle interrupted, holding her palm up as he stepped up to the bottom step. "You chose your job over your family. I was married to a man who always chose his career over us, why would I want that again?"

Nathan's eyes widened and she saw the hurt flash through them. "We're hardly a family, Janelle, you saw to that. And I had no choice."

"Neither did I," she snapped. "I had a responsibility to my husband. I had to try to keep my marriage together."

"You sound just like your mother." Nathan's now frigid stare bore straight through her.

Silence fell between them as the first raindrops hit the ground. They stared at each other without a word as Janelle tried to regain control of the composure she was about to lose.

He was right. About everything, he was right. She had been a coward, and it was her mother's voice she'd heard in her head as she'd made the decision to end the affair. Her heart had become Nathan's and she had desperately wanted to follow it. But her head had led her down the logical path. The more convenient path of remaining with Richard and keeping everyone else happy.

With a coolness she hadn't expected to muster, she looked squarely at his achingly familiar face. She held up a shaky hand, her finger pointing toward the road. "Leave. Now."

Nathan narrowed his eyes, crossed his arms, and stepped onto the bottom step. "No."

Janelle's eyes widened as she pulled her shoulders back. "What?"

The rain beat harder on them and the wind blew it sideways, straight into Janelle's face. There was only one step separating them, but she could feel the heat emanating from his large body. She suddenly remembered, with great clarity, the feel of his arms around her, and another familiar warmth began to uncoil in her stomach. She tried to shake the memory away.

"You heard me," he shouted over the rain. "I'm not going anywhere until I have answers. I want to know that I can spend time with Zoe. And I want to know what this is between you and me."

"I'm not sure there's anything left between you and me." Janelle choked on the words and she looked at her feet. If there was anything there to salvage, she was still stinging from his abandonment. Perceived or not, it felt very real to her. She'd been through it before and was certain she didn't want to live through it again. She had to change the subject. "Are you really that upset about not getting an invitation to a child's birthday party?" Janelle scoffed. "This isn't elementary school."

"Not funny, Janelle. She's my daughter and you've deprived me of that knowledge long enough," Nathan snapped as he closed the gap between them and stood almost eye-to-eye with her. "I'm her father. I have a right to be there."

"You're just a sperm donor," Janelle muttered. Nathan raised his hand and Janelle fell backward trying to get away from the strike she knew was coming.

Nathan saw her recoil and looked up at his hand where it had stopped on its way to the crown of his head. All of his anger fled as he reached out to stop her from falling.

"I'm sorry," she said unsteadily as he gripped her upper arms and pulled her against him.

She was in his arms again. He took a moment to savor the feeling and held her tightly to his chest. How could she possibly believe he was about to hit her? He carefully turned them both and, keeping her shaking body close to his side, walked them to the swing at the end of the porch. Once they were seated, he gently cupped her cheeks in his hands and lifted her face to his.

"Janelle," he said softly. "Look at me."

She closed her eyes tightly and shook her head. The corner of his mouth lifted slightly.

"I shouldn't have said that. I'm so sorry," she cried.

"I would never hit you," he said, pain lancing his heart as he said the words. "You should know that." When she nodded, he closed his eyes and laid his forehead against hers but it didn't ease the pain. "I'm not him."

"I know," she mumbled, and he heard a small sniff.

"Why would you call me that? You know I would have been more to her if I'd known." He lifted his head and tried again to raise her eyes to his. Slowly, hers opened and he saw tears swimming in their faded blue depths.

"I know." Her voice cracked, and it was more like she'd mouthed the words than said them. "It was such a stupid thing to say. It's just . . ." She tried to look away but he held her gaze with his.

"It's just what?" he repeated gently.

"It was my way of dealing with things, I guess. We did the same thing when Kelsey was pregnant," she replied with a shrug.

He thumbed away a tear as it slid down her cheek. "I can only assume you're referring to the man that got her pregnant then left her, and I'm not sure I like the comparison."

Her head moved up and down as her cheeks colored slightly. "I thought you weren't interested in being Zoe's father. I had to try to separate you from that role." Her bottom lip quivered violently, and he had the urge to kiss it still.

"I never said I didn't want the role. I never had the chance to say anything." Nathan inched closer until their noses were almost touching. "And I've had time to think long and hard about it, even though I didn't need to, and decided I would love nothing more than to be her dad. And more."

Janelle hiccupped and pulled back slightly, her head still resting between his hands. "More?" She shook her head, almost violently, then broke his grip and stood up. "No." She walked away and stopped just beside the stairs, placed her forearms on the railing, and looked into the rain and darkness. "You don't want more, not really. How could you?"

Nathan stood and walked toward her. He stopped beside her and mimicked her stance. "How could I not?"

"What I did to you is unforgiveable," she answered and he fought a smile.

"Shouldn't I be the judge of that?" Nathan studied her as she considered his response. He'd always marveled at how controlled she was, her true emotions rarely showed on her face. It was the little tells he had to watch for. "By the way, which part is unforgiveable? Ending the affair or keeping Zoe from me?"

"All of it," she said quickly and her pale brow furrowed slightly. "Especially keeping Zoe from you." She glanced at her clasped hands in front of her. "I regret that one every day."

Nathan frowned and looked into the dark. "Did you even consider leaving him while we were together?" Out of the corner of his eye he caught her nod.

"Often," she murmured and his heart lightened a little. "I tried to think of a way to make it work for us. I ran every possible scenario in my head, several times, and almost always came up with the same conclusion," she continued, and he could barely hear her over the rain. "I ended it because I was pregnant and I couldn't see any of them working out positively."

"If you and I had been together, Jan, it would have been positive," Nathan said as he slid closer. "You could have moved in with me," he suggested and turned to face her, resting one hip against the rail.

Her head swayed, her blonde hair brushed her shoulders. "I was afraid people would make it out to be a horrible scandal and it would ruin what we had."

He quirked an eyebrow. "Who cares what they might have said?"

"I did." She glanced up at him, her blue eyes round and innocent.

Reluctantly, he bobbed his head in acknowledgment. He wouldn't have wanted her to be uncomfortable around other people, especially if their words or actions made her awkward around him. "You could have moved in with your parents."

"No, I couldn't," she replied and turned to face the rain. "Mom disowned Kelsey when she came home from college pregnant. Kelsey lived with me and Richard until after Zach was born and she moved to LA. I knew for certain Mom would have kicked me out and then where would I have gone?"

"You could have found an apartment." Nathan reached up and placed his hand on her back. Slowly he began to rub up and down.

Her head moved from side to side again. "I had no money. It was all gone."

"What do you mean?" Nathan asked as he watched his hand move along her wet shirt.

"All of my earnings from teaching had gone into a savings account, and we lived off of his income from the beginning. That money was supposed to be mine or our rainy day fund if we needed it." Janelle turned her head and Nathan met her gaze. "I wanted to take it and find an apartment but he'd gambled it all away."

Nathan's hand froze. "You know this for sure?" She nodded and shifted her gaze over his shoulder. He had a feeling he wasn't going to like this.

"After I ended it with you, I was feeling foolishly brave, or just really pissed off, I can't decide, and I asked him about it," she answered, a far-off look in her eyes. "He yelled at me and said the money was just as much his as it was mine and he could do with it as he pleased. It was the first time he got really violent with me," she finished quietly.

Nathan saw red. "He hit you while you were pregnant?"

Janelle looked down. "He gave me a black eye, but he didn't know I was pregnant yet."

Nathan cursed under his breath. "You should have called me. If for no other reason than to charge him with assault."

"I should have," Janelle agreed. "But it doesn't matter now."

She was right, it didn't matter now. "Could you have moved in with my mother?"

Her eyes widened as she frowned at him. "I hadn't thought of that." She closed her eyes and turned her face away from him. A tear ran down her cheek and she shook her head. "I guess I didn't think of everything."

He put his arm around her and pulled her head onto his shoulder. "It doesn't matter," he repeated her words. She shook her head and he looked at her tear-streaked face. "Hey, what is it?"

"All this time we've lost. Time we could have been together, as a family, and I screwed it up." Sobs wracked her body and he shifted their positions. He leaned against the rail and held her in front of him, both of his arms wrapped around her. "I always screw it up."

"No," he cooed into her wet hair. "You didn't screw it up. We can be together now and we'll figure it out."

She cried harder and he held tighter. When her arms eventually slipped around his waist, he exhaled. He'd waited so long to hold her again, and for her to hold him. He silently vowed that he would never be separated from her again.

He listened to the rainfall dissipate as she softened against him. Eventually he felt her shaking stop, but she continued to hold onto him and kept her head against his shoulder. Her chest rose and fell against his.

"You're wet," she mumbled into his neck.

He barked a single laugh. "So are you."

She lifted her head and looked at his face. Her eyes were brighter, less haunted, than he'd seen them in a long time, since the time of their affair, and he was happy to see that. "We should go in and get dry."

"First things first," Nathan said with a grin.

Her eyes asked the question for her and his smile widened as he lowered his head to hers. He saw the comprehension dawn just before their lips met.

They sparked instantly, like they'd never been separated. She tasted sweeter than he remembered and he savored the feel of her soft lips under his. Her arms slowly snaked up his chest, leaving a trail of fire in their wake, and he felt her sigh. He swallowed the sigh and tightened his arms around her as she speared her fingers through his short hair.

He'd needed this, from her, more than he'd realized. His body was now engulfed by her but it still wasn't enough. He brushed her lips with his tongue, and she immediately opened her mouth to him. He slowly plunged into her warmth and teased her tongue with his. She rocked against his erection and he groaned. She blatantly pressed herself against him.

Gasping for air, he broke the kiss. "Maybe we should go inside."

A Cheshire-like grin spread across her face and she took his hand.

Eighteen

Janelle held Nathan's hand as she led him into the house, the electricity from their connection making a circuit through her body. She paused by the foot of the steps as he closed and locked the door then bent over to untie his shoes as Janelle looked around the room. Kelsey was nowhere to be seen, but there were a couple of towels on the bottom step. She glanced into the kitchen and saw a wine bottle and a couple of empty glasses sitting on the island.

She felt the towel wrap around her shoulders and looked up into Nathan's smiling face. He gripped both ends of the towel and slowly moved it side to side over her drenched back, pulling her closer at the same time. His grin widened and his hazel eyes had darkened, the gold flecks stood out prominently against the brown. Janelle was familiar with that look.

Oh, how she'd missed it.

Nathan tugged on the towel, and her breasts collided with his chest. She placed her hands on his waist as his warm lips found a cool space just under her ear. Goosebumps crept down her leg and her eyelids fell. He showered kisses across her jawline to the corner of her lips.

"I don't think this towel is going to work, we may need to take drastic measures," he whispered across her cheek.

Her lips lifted. "Oh really? How drastic?"

"Very," he replied, and her eyes opened. She wrapped her arms completely around him and raised a brow. He chuckled and continued, "I'm thinking I need to get you out of these wet clothes and into a nice hot shower to make sure you don't catch a chill."

"How considerate." Janelle's head fell back as his lips began to travel down her neck. "What about you, you're pretty soaked too. I couldn't send you home in such wet clothes." She sighed as he dipped his tongue into the cleft of her neck.

"That could be dangerous. I might catch a cold." He lifted his head and met her dazed stare. "We should take care of this right away."

"I agree." Janelle nodded her head. She placed a light kiss to his lips as she tugged the towel out of his hand and slid her hand into its place.

Silently, she led him up the stairs, her heart racing as she considered what she was doing. She'd only been a widow for just over a month; she shouldn't even be contemplating going to bed with another man already. But this was Nathan. She'd known him almost her whole life, they'd already had an affair and, in all fairness, her marriage had been over for a very long time. Richard had never met her needs, he'd stopped making her happy a long time ago, and she wasn't sure she'd ever truly loved him. Nathan had always, even when they'd just been friends in school, made sure she was happy and had everything she wanted in any situation.

And she was certain he had her heart.

They reached her bedroom door and stepped through. She heard the latch click, and Nathan placed his hands on her arms and turned her to face him.

"What are you thinking now?" he asked, apprehension filled his eyes and his brow furrowed.

"What makes you think I'm thinking anything?" Janelle shook his hands off and placed her arms on his shoulders.

"I watched you tense as we climbed the steps." He circled her waist with his arms and pulled her tightly against him. "We don't have to do this."

Her knees went weak when she felt his erection pressed against her. "It's been so long, Nathan," she replied and rubbed herself against him. "Of course I'd be a little tense."

He groaned and his eyes closed as he placed his forehead against hers. She tipped her head until their lips met, and he kissed her with a fierce intensity. The warmth of his mouth filled her body with wave after wave of heat, settling low in her abdomen. She took his bottom lip in her teeth and lightly bit it. He lowered his hands to her waist and lifted her, her legs on either side of his body, her core pressed against him.

He took two steps and everything in him stopped. He lifted his head and focused on something beside them. Janelle followed his gaze and gasped.

"Where did those come from?" he questioned, staring at the box of condoms centered on the foot of her bed.

Janelle laughed until he tried to put her down. "No, don't," she said, hooking her ankles around his knees. He looked at her, turmoil, anger, and lust warring with each other in his gold speckled eyes. "Kelsey."

His hazel gaze sharpened on her face and she pouted slightly.

"I'm sure she thought we could put them to more use than she can right now," Janelle added softly, placing a light kiss on his cheek.

He looked at the box for a moment, his face slowly relaxing. "I'm sure we can find something to do with them." He met her stare, a smile slowly stretching his lips. "As soon as we're warm and dry."

Janelle laughed, and he quickly carried her to the bathroom and set her down. He reached for her hand as she scurried to the closet and grabbed two clean towels, giggling as she went. She set the towels down on the edge of the tub and reached into the shower and turned the water on. When she turned around, he was behind her, his hands already on the bottom of her shirt.

She lifted her arms and, with a little effort, he worked the soaked shirt up and over her head. While he reached around to unhook her bra, she attacked the buttons on his shirt, pushing them through the wet fabric buttonholes. He got her bra undone and her jeans unfastened and halfway down her hips before she reached the bottom of his shirt.

She paused in her efforts to drop her arms and let the bra fall to the floor at his feet. His eyes dropped to her breasts and she shook her head as she slid his shirt over his shoulders and pushed it onto the floor. She had to admit, his chest had the same mouth-watering effect on her that her breasts appeared to have on him. She laid her palm on his pectoral muscle, just above his nipple, and felt a shudder go through him.

He reached for the button of his jeans and had them on the floor before she blinked. His underwear was next. She followed his example and stripped the rest of her clothes away. A warm flush crept through her body as his eyes slowly took in every inch of her nakedness.

"You're so beautiful." He met her stare with a huge smile and a sparkle in his eyes.

"I'll bet you say that to all the girls," she retorted as he took her hand and opened the shower door.

He stepped into the shower and pulled her in behind him. "Only when I mean it."

Janelle frowned slightly as she closed the door behind them. "How many times have you meant it?"

He put his back to the water and pulled her into his arms. "I'm not sure. How many times have I said it to you?"

Janelle's frown faded as she shook her head. "I have no idea."

"Well, that's your answer." He backed a little bit and the water hit her in the face and slid down her body.

She released a sigh and closed her eyes as the warmth seeped into her bones and the tension of the afternoon washed away with the water. They stood like this for a few moments as Janelle simply let the water run over her, then let Nathan have his turn. She brushed her hip against his as she maneuvered around him to retrieve the soap and cloth so she could wash him. He slid his hand around her waist and pressed himself fully against her back.

"You first," he whispered across her ear, following his words with a light kiss to her earlobe. He reached around her and grabbed everything from her. Mesmerized, she watched as he drizzled soap onto the washcloth and put the soap bottle back. She felt an almost overwhelming anticipation as she watched the soapy material get closer to her body and inhaled sharply when he touched her stomach with it.

She could never have imagined such a simple act to be so erotic. He maintained a slow, deliberate pace, soapy cloth in one hand, followed closely by the empty hand. Janelle burned under his touch and, as much as she was enjoying this, she wanted him to hurry. She had to force air into her lungs as he washed her hips and legs. She shivered as his hand wandered up her inner thigh, and he chuckled quietly. When he was finished, she laid her head back onto his shoulder.

She heard his breathing in her ear and the distant sound of the water being squeezed from the washcloth as it hit the floor of the shower in a rush. When that stopped, his hands wrapped around her waist again, and they stood still as the water washed over them both. Nathan placed light kisses along her hairline and she savored every touch of his lips.

"Feeling better?" his voice whispered, and in a daze she nodded. "Good," he said. She could have sworn she heard a smile in his voice.

One of his hands slowly slid down her stomach, and she closed her eyes to focus on the movement. The other hand traveled up, coming to a stop on her breast as the fingertips of the first hand reached her curls.

"Nathan," she sighed as he lightly pinched one of her nipples and touched her where she wanted him most at that moment.

His lower finger began to make small, tight circles against her, and she felt her body climbing to that ultimate peak. He continued to kiss along her collarbone and up her neck as he twirled her nipple between his thumb and forefinger with one hand and teased her core with the other one.

She reached behind him and gripped his buttock with one hand as she used the other one to brace herself against the wall beside them. Before she realized, she was coming apart in his arms, his steely grip tightened to support her as the white heat of pleasure spread all the way to her toes. He kept teasing her until she was sure she would collapse then he slowly pulled back.

Her whole body trembled and she felt light-headed as she exhaled slowly. He held her close as her heart rate returned to normal.

"Should we get out now?" he asked and Janelle's eyes fluttered open. She slid her hand from his buttock and gripped his erection. He groaned as he released her breast and removed her hand. "Our first time back together is not going to be in the shower. I intend to take my time."

Janelle shivered at the promise in his words. "Then maybe we should get out."

She turned the water off as he released her, stepped out of the shower, then turned and helped her out. He handed her a towel then picked up the other one. As she dried off, she watched him do the same. The muscles in his chest and shoulders rippled as he moved the towel over his body. Janelle was almost hypnotized by the movement and didn't realize she was mimicking him until he stopped and met her stare. He smiled, quickly rubbed the towel over his short, dark-brown hair, dropped the towel, and walked toward her.

Without a word, he scooped her into his arms and carried her back to the bedroom.

Nathan gently laid her down, towel and all, in the center of the bed and followed her down. He took the towel from her loose grip and slowly wiped away what was left of the water. When he was satisfied with his work, he sat up, dropped the towel on the floor, and retrieved the box of condoms from the end of the bed.

He lay back down beside Janelle and opened the box. Janelle propped herself up on her elbow and watched intently. When it was opened, she took the box from him, took a condom out of it, and set the box on the nightstand behind him. Grinning down at him, she opened the condom and began to reach for him.

He grabbed her wrist. "A little enthusiastic?"

She grinned widely, and his heart raced at the excitement in her eyes. "Maybe," she replied as she pulled her hand away from his grip.

He grasped the back of her head, wove his fingers into her blonde hair, and pulled her mouth to his. She sighed when he tasted her lower lip and he slipped his tongue past her teeth. Their tongues battled for supremacy between their mouths. He flipped her onto her back and, lips still exploring each other, he slipped the condom from her fingers. As he took it from its package and covered himself with it, he distracted her with delicate kisses along her soft jaw.

He positioned himself over her, held himself up with his hands on either side of her neck. Her eyes glittered with anticipation, and he momentarily lost himself in their sapphire depths. He slowly filled his lungs.

"I asked you this the first time and I'm asking you again now. Are you sure you want to do this?" Nathan's heart stopped as she tilted her head, as if she was considering his answer or wasn't sure she'd heard him correctly.

Janelle's lush lips parted as a slow smile spread across her face. Her tongue darted out to moisten her bottom lip. "Yes," she whispered, and he exhaled his relief. "I'm more sure now than I was then. I want *you*."

Nathan grinned and kissed her hard. Her soft lips melded easily to his as she looped her arms around his neck. He held her mouth with his as he slowly lowered himself to her entrance, then broke the kiss and lifted his head. Her passion-filled gaze met his as he pushed himself into her. Her warmth surrounded him and her smile only widened as he pressed deeper into her. All of the anticipation, the waiting for this moment for almost four years, escaped from his chest on a low, guttural growl.

She pulled his mouth back to hers and attacked it with the vigor and excitement he'd grown to love when they'd been together. He moaned when she lightly nipped his bottom lip, sending a shock wave to his toes. Nathan slowly moved his hips as his lips trailed kisses down to the cleft in her neck and along her collarbone. She hooked her ankles around his knees—one small hand rubbing slowly up and down his back, the other gripping his buttock.

He kept his pace deliberate as he grasped her breast and rolled the nipple between his fingers. Her hips came off of the bed as a squeal escaped her lips. Propping himself on his elbow, with his free hand, he grabbed her thigh where it wrapped around his hip. She lifted and turned her chin, giving him better access to the sensitive skin just under her earlobe. He nibbled and felt the goose bumps rise on her thigh.

He couldn't help but chuckle.

"Proud of yourself?" Janelle panted.

"Not yet, darling," Nathan replied as he lifted his head. The serene longing on her face nearly unleashed his control and he quickly kissed her again. Fire traveled from their joined lips to his toes and back up to his groin.

She fisted her hands in his hair and gently pulled his mouth away from hers. Her lips began to shower his jaw and neck with warm kisses, and he felt the urge to move faster. With her lips occupied, he devoted his hand to taunting her nipple and slid the one on her hip to touch her where they connected.

When his thumb caressed her, she gasped sharply and she lifted off the bed again, forcing him deeply into her. He nearly came undone. He circled her nub with his thumb and brought his lips back to hers. She opened her mouth immediately to him and he plunged his tongue into her warmth, matching the pace he set with his hips.

One of her hands gripped his hair as the other dug into his buttock. He could feel her climax building and continued the assault with his tongue and thumb as he pumped faster into her. When she began to scream, his mouth covered hers as she tightened around him. His hips raced to follow her over the edge and he placed his lips to her neck and groaned as he reached his release.

He collapsed and rolled to his side, taking her with him. She curled into his body, their knees intertwined as her fingers trailed lightly along his side. As they lay, quietly recovering, Nathan reflected on the evening's events.

As he'd driven to Janelle's house, he'd run through every possible track their conversation could take. He'd made a list of questions he wanted to ask, he'd run through answers she might give, and how he would counter them. He'd thought he'd covered every possible outcome to that conversation. But none of them had ended with the two of them in bed.

Not that he was complaining.

He looked down into her peaceful face, her eyes closed and completely relaxed, and he knew he could never walk away from her again. Whether she knew it or not, she was now stuck with him. He would always be a part of her life; he just hoped they agreed on the level of involvement.

Janelle's eyelids fluttered opened, and she looked up at him and smiled. "That was amazing," she said groggily.

"I couldn't agree more." He kissed her lightly on the forehead and tightened his arms around her.

Nineteen

Janelle lay in the circle of Nathan's arms, relishing the peace and comfort she felt there. She almost wished they could remain like this forever. He'd always had a way of calming her, almost effortlessly. It was true, she hadn't been happy to see him show up on her doorstep, but if she were honest, it wasn't a surprise. Even as children, he'd always seemed to show up when she needed him most. Tonight was an almost perfect example.

Or was it? Had he come here for her or to satisfy his own needs?

She propped herself up on her elbow and looked down at him. "Why did you come here tonight?"

He studied her face and frowned. "I thought we'd covered that."

"Did you give me all of your reasons?" Her heart slowed as she waited for his answer.

"You mean did I come for this?" He motioned to their naked bodies, tangled together on top of her comforter. She nodded slightly and his frown deepened. "No, Jan, I didn't come here for the sole purpose of making love to you." He sat up and pressed his back to her headboard. "While I'm not complaining, this wasn't even on my radar this evening."

Janelle relaxed and slid up to lay her head on his chest. "Good." She flattened her hand on his hard abdomen and watched it rise and fall with his breaths.

"Although," he started after a few inhalations, "there is one thing I would like to do tonight. Something I've never done before."

Janelle giggled. "I find that hard to believe. I imagine you've done it all when it comes to women."

His hand tightened around her forearm and he nudged her to sit up. Reluctantly she complied and faced his serious expression. "I haven't done this yet," he said softly, his look and words caressing her.

“What is it?” she asked eagerly.

“I want to spend the night with you,” he answered.

She opened her mouth to argue that he *had* done that, but closed it again when she realized the truth. They had made love many times in the months they’d been together, but he was right, he’d never spent the night with her. He’d always had to leave before Richard got home.

Giddiness bubbled in Janelle and crept upward to her head. “That would be nice,” she said with a large grin. She suddenly remembered the pile of wet clothes on her bathroom floor. “You couldn’t go home anyway. Your clothes are soaked and laying on my bathroom floor.”

She sat up and put her feet over the edge of the bed. Before she could stand up, his arm snaked around her waist.

“I can wear them home damp,” his voice rumbled in her ear as he pulled her backward.

She giggled a little as her head fell against his shoulder and she looked up into his greenish-brown eyes. “I couldn’t let you do that. It won’t take me long, I’ll just toss them in the dryer,” she said and planted a kiss on his stubbled chin.

His arm tightened around her and he tried to tug her onto the bed.

“Nathan,” she said, laughing, “I’ll be right back.” With a groan, he slowly eased his grip, and she stood and turned to look at him. “Besides, shouldn’t you clean up too?”

He rolled off of the opposite side of the bed and looked at her with a boyish grin. “Only if you promise we can get dirty again later,” he said as he walked around the bed and met her at the foot. He grasped her hand and tugged her easily into his arms.

“I promise,” she murmured as she stretched onto her toes and placed a kiss on his cheek.

“Good,” he replied and kissed her firmly on the lips before releasing her.

She watched his naked backside as he walked into the bathroom, and a shiver of excitement ran through her. She quickly grabbed one of her sexier, but still modest, nightgowns and pulled it over her head as she followed him into the bathroom. He met her at the door and handed her the wet clothes and towels as his eyes traveled the length of her body. He smiled approvingly as she took everything from him and left the room. She walked down the hallway, past Zoe's room on her right and Zach's on her left, and into the bathroom beside Zoe's room where the washer and dryer were.

Before she tossed his shirt into the dryer, she held it to her nose and inhaled deeply. She could faintly smell his familiar cedar and musk scent. In the last four years, whenever she'd caught a whiff of those aromas, she would immediately think of him and her heart would ache. Now, she smelled them with a smile on her face. He was with her again, and her hope that he always would be was beginning to grow larger.

As she put his clothes in the dryer, her body still tingled with their recent lovemaking. She grinned at the thought of doing it again very soon. With Nathan, it had always been more than just sex, she'd always felt loved and cared for, both in and out of bed. Tonight was no different.

She heard the door to Zach's room close just before she started the dryer. When she stepped out of the bathroom, she heard Zoe's little voice.

"Are you here to take me away?" she asked and Janelle's heart stopped. She quickly walked the three steps to Zoe's door and froze at what she saw.

"No, sweetie. I'm here to check on you and make sure you're okay," Nathan replied as he knelt beside the bed, dressed in Janelle's mint green, terrycloth robe. "I didn't mean to wake you up." He brushed her forehead with his palm and Janelle's chest tightened. "Just go on back to sleep."

Zoe yawned then focused her big eyes on Nathan. "I'm glad you're here. I've missed you." She sat up and threw her arms out wide. Tears stung Janelle's eyes as she watched Nathan put his arms around his daughter and give her the hug she was asking for.

"I've missed you too," he muttered softly.

Janelle turned and walked slowly back to her room, a new wave of guilt flooding her as a tear trickled down her cheek. Zoe had no idea Nathan was her father, but still her innocent comments made Janelle regret what she'd done. Janelle stopped at the window across the room from her door, beside the entry to the bathroom, and stared out into the darkness, second-guessing every decision she'd made.

A few moments passed before she heard the door to her room latch. A small smile came to her lips as she listened to Nathan's footsteps approach, her breath caught in her throat as he wrapped his arms around her. He nudged her head sideways with his and placed delicate kisses on her neck.

"I didn't mean to wake her," he whispered across her cool skin. "I just wanted to check on them."

"You looked in on Zach, too?" Janelle asked as she turned in his arms.

Nathan answered with a shrug that said, "Of course."

"How are they handling things?" Concern wrinkled Nathan's brow as he looked down at her.

Janelle pulled away from him but took his hand as she walked toward the bed. "Zoe seems fine. She knows her daddy—" Janelle froze and cast a glance over her shoulder. She saw hurt cross Nathan's face for only a moment. "She knows Richard is dead," Janelle corrected then turned and continued on her path. "It doesn't really seem to bother her, but I guess that doesn't surprise me."

They reached the bed and Janelle pulled the sheet and the comforter down. Nathan held it up for her to crawl under it then walked around the foot of the bed.

"Why doesn't it surprise you?" Nathan questioned as he stripped off the robe and laid it across the foot of the bed.

Janelle propped herself up on pillows against the headboard as Nathan climbed in beside her. "Richard was never really present in her life. He lost interest in the pregnancy when he found out I was having a girl." Janelle reflexively grabbed her upper arm and rubbed it. Richard had grabbed it and squeezed so tightly when they'd gotten home from the doctor the day of the sonogram that he'd left a bruise that had taken weeks to heal.

Nathan glanced at her movements then at her face, anger burned in his eyes. "Did he hurt you?"

Janelle looked at her hand and stopped rubbing. "He told me I was worthless, said that even my 'whore of a sister' could have a son for a man who didn't want one, why couldn't I do the same for him. After that, he was pretty scarce. He wasn't at the delivery, not in the room. I don't even think he was in the hospital."

"Who was there for you? Your dad?" Nathan tipped forward and placed a kiss on Janelle's arm, the spot she'd been rubbing.

"No, Dad was in the hallway outside the room. Kelsey was in the middle of filming and she was furious that she couldn't get away," Janelle replied with a small chuckle. Aside from holding her daughter, Nathan's daughter,

Kelsey's irritation had been a bright spot for her. It had been a perfect example of the love her sister held for her.

"Please don't tell me your mother was the only person with you," Nathan said as he slid closer to Janelle. He put an arm around her shoulder as she nodded. "I'm so sorry," he whispered and placed a kiss to her temple.

"It wasn't your fault. I put myself in that sad position. Don't think that didn't cross my mind every second of labor," Janelle said around the lump in her throat. Her mother had been horrible, criticizing Janelle for every scream or complaint, reminding her that women had been doing this for centuries and surviving and that Janelle would be no different.

"I hope you tell me all about it at some point." Nathan took her hand in his. "So how is Zach doing?"

"He's in therapy, but it's hard to tell how he's doing. Some days are better than others. The good news is, he's starting to talk to Kelsey again and asking random questions about the adoption," Janelle answered as Nathan pulled on her hand. She sat up and looked at him as he continued to tug. "He misses Patrick, and Mom has him convinced that Patrick's not coming back."

"I'll set him straight," Nathan said with a smile. "It shouldn't be much longer now."

"I hope not. I'm not sure Kelsey will last too much longer without him. She goes through phases, usually after our mother has visited, where she seems withdrawn and depressed and if I even mention his name she nearly cries," Janelle answered. "But then after your mother's visits, Kelsey is bubbly and talking about him, telling me about their conversation that day, and she seems much more confident in their relationship."

"I'll ask my mother to visit every day then." Nathan pulled Janelle across his lap, she straddled him, and he grinned. "Now, most importantly, how are you holding up?"

"What?" Janelle leaned back and tilted her head to the side. Now that she considered it, outside of Kelsey, she wasn't sure anyone else had asked her that yet.

"You heard me," Nathan said calmly, placing a hand on each of her hips.

"I'm okay, I guess." Janelle's mind quickly skimmed through all of the things she'd had to deal with in the past four weeks. "It hasn't been a lot of fun lately, but I'm surviving, I suppose. I take Zach to therapy twice a week, try to keep Kelsey on an even keel, pray my mother doesn't visit, and—" She stopped and narrowed her eyes on him. She thought she might keep that last bit, that she was missing him more than she should, to herself.

"And what?" Nathan asked as he studied her face.

Janelle shook her head. "Doesn't matter."

"I disagree. If it's bothered you in the last four weeks, it matters to me. Believe it or not, I've thought about you every day, wondering how you were doing, and if you needed anything from me," Nathan confessed. Janelle hated the way he made it look so easy. "At least when you were calling me, I knew you still cared a little. When you stopped, I started to fear I'd lost you."

"Can you blame me? You gave me the cold shoulder at the police station and made me think you wanted nothing to do with me," Janelle responded. Maybe confessing the truth wasn't too terribly hard.

"I'm sorry I made you feel that way. I've never stopped wanting you, Janelle." He sat up and she felt his erection brush against her stomach. "Never. Not in fifteen years."

Janelle's jaw dropped and she shook her head. "You haven't wanted me for that long," she said with a laugh. His head slowly moved up and down and her humor faded. "We were in high school fifteen years ago."

Nathan shrugged a shoulder. "Yes, we were."

Janelle suddenly felt lightheaded and her shoulders slumped slightly. "You never said anything. Not even when we were having the affair." She furrowed her brow. "Why wouldn't you tell me?"

"Richard beat me to it in high school, and I guess when we were together, I could never be sure where I stood with you. You always rejected me when I asked you to leave him." He wrapped his arms around her waist. "My mistake was letting you push me away. I should have fought harder."

Janelle had tears in her eyes. All these years he'd wanted her, but what did that mean? "You should have told me," she said despite her dry throat.

"I'm telling you now." He kissed the first tear away, and she was reminded of the night she began seeing him as more than her friend. "And I'm never going to let you push me away again. I'm not leaving you without a fight." He kissed the subsequent tears until they became a stream down her cheeks and he could no longer keep up. "Would you like me to show you how much you mean to me?" Nathan slowly rolled them both until she was on her back.

Dazedly, she looked up at him and nodded. He smiled and took her lips in a kiss that told her everything she needed to know and ended when they reached the ultimate peak together. Again.

"Janelle!" Mary's shrill tones broke through Janelle's memories of bliss and joy in Nathan's arms as she sat at the kitchen island with a cup of coffee. "How could you do such a thing?"

Janelle froze and turned to face her mother. "Do what, Mom?"

"You took him to bed, didn't you?" Mary snapped and Janelle fell backward into the kitchen island. "Your husband has only been dead a month and you're already taking another man to bed. Or has he always been there? Did you ever really end it with him?"

"Mother." Janelle held her palms up to her mother. She wasn't sure what she would say, but there had to be something.

"Don't give me your lines, Janelle. I'm sure they're well rehearsed but I really don't want to hear them. You should be ashamed of your behavior. It's bad enough your sister has shown the world what a slut she is, and now look at her." Mary pointed and Janelle followed the line her finger made.

Kelsey sat in the dining room, tears running down her cheek, her phone in one hand, a tabloid on the table in front of her. From the distance between them, Janelle could just make out the face of a dark-haired man, and the letters P-A-T. Her stomach dropped like a rock. That couldn't possibly mean what she thought it did. And where had the tabloid come from? How had she missed that? She started to rise, but her mother grabbed her arm.

"Everyone, Kelsey included, now knows how naïve she was, and soon you'll have them talking about your shameless behavior. You haven't had proper time to mourn poor Richard and now you're carrying on with Nathan again. Haven't you put me through enough? You were the good child. I could always count on you to behave yourself and do as you were told." Mary's lip curled in disgust. "You're such a disappointment. An utter failure, Janelle. I hope you're happy."

Zoe and Zach appeared and began to approach Mary. "Come, children, let's go," Mary said as she held her hands out and Zach and Zoe each took one. Janelle watched in horror as the life faded from her kids' faces, they became wan and pale and devoid of joy, then changed into the faces of two other children Janelle recognized. "You're no longer fit to be their mother. I'll take over from here."

"No!" Janelle screamed.

Mary turned, the children at her side. "Yes, dear. It's truly for the best."

"No!" Janelle shouted again as Mary walked away without a glance back and faded into the fog.

"No!" Janelle sat straight up in bed, cool sweat on her brow. "No, no, no!"

Nathan jerked upright beside her and quickly wrapped his arms around her. "Shh, it's okay," he said softly as he began rocking them both.

"No," Janelle said hoarsely. "She took my kids. I was supposed to protect them."

"No one has taken your kids." Nathan placed his cheek to her head. "They're tucked away in bed. They're fine."

"She'll ruin their childhoods. I couldn't protect them." Janelle burst into tears.

Nathan stopped rocking and turned her face to his chest, his heart racing. How long had she been having nightmares? He should have been here to soothe them away. "Who took the kids?" he asked gently. He wasn't sure she even realized she was awake.

"Mother. She ruined them," Janelle answered through her sobs.

"Ruined who?" Nathan slowly rocked again as her tears began to subside.

"Sean and Kelsey." Janelle sniffled against him. "And now she wants to take Zach and Zoe. She'll ruin them too."

Nathan closed his eyes as pain hit him in the chest. He'd always known Janelle was protective of her younger siblings, but he'd never realized to what depth. She'd always told him she blamed herself for Sean's death; now he had a feeling she was most likely behind the decisions Kelsey had made to leave town, and her child, to pursue her career.

He pushed her out of his arms and placed a hand on either side of her face. Her eyes were still closed, tears trickling from under her lashes. "Jan, look at me," he said. He repeated himself a couple more times until she opened her eyes and looked at him. "Why would she take your kids?"

"Because, I'm a horrible mother," she answered, her bottom lip quivering. "I didn't mourn Richard. I slept with you again. She said I was no longer fit to be their mother."

"She's wrong." Nathan placed a light kiss to her forehead.

Janelle pulled away from him and threw her feet over the edge of the bed. "No, she's not. This was a mistake. You shouldn't be here."

A mistake? Ice formed in Nathan's chest and slowly slipped into his veins as he watched her pull her nightgown over her head.

"Janelle, what are you doing?" Nathan jumped out of the other side of the bed and tried to head her off before she opened the door. He didn't make it and in a few seconds, she was back with his dried clothes.

"You should go now, Nathan," she said and walked around the foot of the bed, giving him as wide a berth as the furniture would allow. "You shouldn't be here. We shouldn't have done this."

"Yes," Nathan ground out as he pulled his jeans on. "You mentioned that." He couldn't believe Richard, or the memory of him, was forcing him out of her bed again. He'd thought they'd moved beyond that. He'd obviously thought wrong.

"I'm so sorry," Janelle sniffed.

He met her wide-eyed gaze, hoping she'd see the fire in his eyes. He wanted to think of something scathing to say, something that might hurt her the way she was hurting him at the moment, but the self-loathing he saw in her eyes froze his tongue. She looked away as she wrapped her hands around her upper arms and he pulled on his shirt as he took a deep, soothing breath.

He crawled across the bed toward her and she backed away. When his feet were back on solid ground in front of her, he reached for her face. She tensed as he cupped her cheek and tilted her eyes up toward his. Her fear melted the rest of his resolve.

"I'm sorry I forced you," he said calmly through the turmoil in his chest. "I'll leave now, but I'll be back."

She bit her shaking lip as he placed a light kiss to the corner.

"I'll be at Zoe's party. Call me if you want to see me sooner." He waited for her nod before he released her face and left the room. He made it down the steps and out the front door before he couldn't move anymore.

She'd said it was a mistake.

He'd thought it had been wonderful and powerful and that they were finally getting back on the right track. But now she hated herself for making love to him. Nathan slid down the wall beside the door and placed his elbows on his knees. If he'd blown this chance with her, he wasn't sure what he would do.

Twenty

"You look tired," Kelsey said as she pushed a cup of coffee toward Janelle.

Janelle looked up at her sister as she reached for the mug. She'd had enough energy that morning to feed the kids their breakfast and then put the dishes in the sink, but now she felt drained. Her mind was everywhere, but she couldn't focus on anything. Why had she sent Nathan away? After she'd calmed down and thought about it, she'd felt empty. She'd made love to him because it was what she'd wanted to do, and she rarely acted on her impulses, but had ended up hurting them both.

That was almost the only thing she felt skilled in. Hurting people with her poor decisions.

"What happened with Nathan last night?" Kelsey asked as she propped her hips against the counter beside the sink. "And, no, I don't need the gory details." Kelsey gave her sister a wink and a grin that Janelle simply met with a blank stare. Kelsey's smile faded slowly. "If there are any," she added slowly.

"Kels, I don't want to talk about it." Janelle reached for the sugar and milk and added a little of each to her cup.

"It didn't end well?" Kelsey walked toward Janelle and sat on the stool beside her.

"What did I just say?" Janelle snapped. She took a long, slow sip of the hot brew and savored the burn in her throat as she set the cup back down on the island's counter. "I need to get to work."

"School can wait," Kelsey said softly and wrapped her hand around Janelle's and the mug. "Something's bothering you. I'd like to help if I can."

Janelle closed her eyes against the tears and shook her head. "There's nothing you can do. I made a mistake, that's all."

Kelsey warm hand moved off hers, and Janelle slowly opened her eyes. She met Kelsey's pitying stare and looked away.

"What was the mistake?" Kelsey asked.

"I don't want to talk about it," Janelle replied, her jaw clenched as her sister's soothing demeanor threatened the dam that held her tears and frustrations back.

"That's okay, I have a list I can work off of. If you'd like, you can simply nod or shake your head."

Janelle's brow furrowed as she looked up at her sister. Kelsey took a sip of her coffee and shrugged a shoulder.

"Your choice." Kelsey set her coffee down and folded her hands in her lap and they stared at each other for a few moments. "Would you like me to begin?"

Janelle's head moved side to side on its own. "What list?"

Kelsey held up her first finger. "You loved Richard more than he deserved." Her second finger went up. "You give Mom too much credence in your life." Another finger up. "You blame yourself for things that are beyond your control and let them eat at you." Her pinky joined the others and her mouth opened.

Janelle held up her palm to silence her sister. "That's enough."

Kelsey's lips pursed and she moved her head from side to side. "You let a good man leave last night because of all of the above," she said somberly.

Janelle pressed her lips together and pulled her shoulders back. "You know nothing about last night."

Kelsey released a long sigh. "I know you had a nightmare, I heard it and was halfway down the hall before I heard you arguing with him. I went back to my room and heard him leave shortly after that. But, you're right, I don't know what happened between the two of you. Please don't tell me you told him sex was a mistake."

Janelle's cheeks warmed slightly. "Maybe," she mumbled as she looked into her almost empty mug. She stood and walked over to the coffee pot on the counter behind Kelsey. She slowly added to her cup, filling it almost to the top, then took a long sip.

"Is that really what you think?" Kelsey's voice drifted over Janelle's shoulder.

"No," Janelle answered quietly as she turned around.

"Then why would you say it?" Kelsey was still on her stool, but had turned to face her sister, a frown on her face and sadness in her eyes.

Janelle shrugged. She shouldn't be having this conversation with her younger sister. Kelsey was supposed to come to her for advice on relationships, not the other way around. As much as she hated to admit it, though, Kelsey was probably the only person she could talk to about this. Kelsey seemed to have broken away from Mary's way of thinking, and, at least most of the time, was confident in her decisions.

She approached the kitchen island and rested her forearms on it, setting the cup of coffee between her hands. "I felt guilty," she answered, her eyes following a dark line in the marble. "The nightmare came from that and I panicked."

Kelsey grasped Janelle's hand. "Who was the voice of that guilt?"

"Mom, of course," Janelle answered. "She was taking the kids away because neither of us is fit to be their mother. You were sitting at the table, crying over a tabloid, and she was harassing me about taking Nathan to bed before Richard was cold in his grave."

"Oh, Janelle," Kelsey breathed softly. "Richard was cold long before he was in the grave. Your marriage to him ended a long time ago and you have nothing to feel guilty about." She stood and walked to Janelle's side. She slid her arm around her sister's waist and laid her head on Janelle's shoulder. "After everything you've been through with Richard, you deserve happiness. Whether you find it with Nathan or not is up to you, but I feel pretty confident that man has cared about you for a very long time."

Janelle released a short burst of air. "Since high school," she acknowledged. "Or so he says."

"Have you ever known him to lie?" Kelsey questioned and Janelle shook her head in response. "I'm not trying to push you in his direction, J, that choice is completely yours. But please don't let our mother's crappy beliefs and her horrid advice ruin your joy. She's wrong, you are an excellent mother. It's not too soon for you to be with Nathan if you're both comfortable with it. And Richard does not deserve another second of thought from either of us."

Tears ran down Janelle's cheeks at Kelsey's reaffirming words.

"Do you remember what you said to me when I told you I was pregnant?" Kelsey asked.

Janelle nodded as she sniffled.

"We'll get through this together. I've got your back." Kelsey kissed Janelle's cheek and held her until Janelle's tears stopped flowing.

Nathan strolled through the police station, nodding to the familiar faces of his fellow officers as he made his way to Captain Little's office. He'd sat on Janelle's porch until just before the sun had come up that morning, thinking about everything that had happened after his arrival that evening. He'd reviewed every word, every action, for any hint that she hadn't wanted to make love to him. It killed him to think that he might have rushed her, but the first indication he'd gotten that she thought it might be a mistake had been when she'd woken up from her nightmare.

That didn't sit well with him. Even if her conscious mind was telling her yes, her subconscious was apparently not in agreement, and that would be a harder battle for him to fight.

After sunrise, he'd gone home and taken a quick shower, then called the captain to set up a meeting as early as possible. He had no idea what he would do after this meeting. He wanted to go back to Janelle's house so he could spend some quality time with Janelle and their daughter, but he wouldn't go back until she called. Or until Zoe's birthday party, whichever came first. He had a feeling it would be the latter. He hoped he was wrong.

As he reached the long hall of interrogation rooms that led to his destination, he nearly ran into Sergeant Hayes, who was focused on the floor as he hurried around the corner.

"Excuse me," Hayes mumbled without looking up as he sidestepped Nathan and tried to continue around him.

"Hayes," Nathan said and the young man froze.

He slowly lifted his head and turned toward Nathan. When he met Nathan's stare, the detective paled and his mouth fell open.

"Harris," he sputtered. "What . . . what are you doing here?" Hayes cast a brief glance down the hallway he'd been fleeing then looked at Nathan again. Nathan's eyes narrowed as he turned his head slightly and heard a door close behind him. "I have a meeting," Nathan answered calmly. "Hey, man, are you okay? You seem to be in quite a hurry."

"Yeah, all cool," Hayes answered quickly. "There's just a lot going on right now. I have some papers to file and stuff, so I guess I'd better get back to work. Good seeing you." He turned on his heel and nearly sprinted away.

Nathan watched him go, uneasiness slithering up his spine. He'd known Thomas Hayes since he'd started on the force five years before. Hayes had a kind, calm demeanor that always put suspects at ease, usually causing them to tell more than they'd meant to when they sat down for questioning. Nathan had never known the man to look so frazzled.

Slowly, Nathan resumed his walk down the hall, considering the encounter he'd just had with Bonner's partner. Something wasn't right, but Nathan couldn't decide if it was his instinct picking up on the edginess in the other man, or the fact that he was just anxious because he wanted this case to be closed so he could go on with his life.

Captain Little was just walking into his office, fresh cup of coffee in hand, when Nathan turned the corner. The captain looked at him and frowned.

"You look like something's bothering you," he said when Nathan stopped in front of him.

Nathan nodded. "I just ran into, literally, Tom Hayes in the hallway. He looked distracted and a bit weary. I can't shake the feeling that something isn't right."

The captain motioned toward his open door. "Come in and we'll talk about it," he said and led the way into his office. Nathan followed and closed the thick, mahogany door behind him. Captain Little sat down on the edge of his desk as Nathan sat in a brown leather and wood armchair facing him. "Now, tell me about Sergeant Hayes. What concerns you?"

"He nearly bowled over me as he came around the corner of the hall. His head was down and he was moving with an obvious purpose," Nathan answered. "He went white when he saw me and he rushed off before I could really ask him anything."

Captain Little's brow furrowed thoughtfully.

"Other than the Wagoner investigation, is there anything else he's working on right now?" Nathan asked cautiously. He didn't want to sound as suspicious as he felt.

"No, he's helping Bonner with the investigation, but as far as I know that's it. Bonner's doing most of the legwork, Hayes is there to observe and learn. I thought it would be a good investigation since it seemed like such an open and shut case." Captain Little took a sip of his coffee. "I'm surprised it's taking them so long."

"Do you have any idea why it is?" Nathan questioned. "I wouldn't have thought they had that much to do. They've questioned everyone who was there that night. I'm sure the coroner's report is available and they have the crime scene photos. What more do they need?"

"I don't know." The captain shook his head. "I've asked Bonner repeatedly if they were almost finished and he keeps reassuring me they're close." Captain Little put his coffee on the desk and folded his arms across his chest. "As for the Internal Affairs investigation, I'll let you know as soon as we get started on it. I don't think it should take long, but there are obviously no guarantees, and I really don't know what the results might be."

Nathan placed his elbows on the arms of the chairs and clasped his hands in front of him. "Fine, but I'm here to talk about my daughter."

Captain Little raised an eyebrow.

"Her birthday is this week, and Janelle is having a party for her on Saturday. I'd like to go," Nathan said and watched his captain's expression slowly change from curiosity to a low level of irritation.

"I recommended you stay away from them for your own good. Can you imagine how it will look if you are seen with the woman you had an affair with just after her husband's death?" the captain argued.

"People are talking anyway. She'd been separated from the man for nearly a year and he died over a month ago. I don't see why that should have anything to do with me seeing them," Nathan responded.

"I thought I explained that to you before. I know, by all appearances, Mr. Wagoner's death was by his own actions, but I don't want anyone to even question the idea that perhaps it wasn't." Captain Little rose from his perch on the desk and walked around to pace behind it. Nathan opened his mouth to argue, but the captain held up his hand to stop him. "If you're seen with her so soon, people might think you were involved in his death. You're one of my best detectives, and I don't want people entertaining the idea that you may have been involved. Your career and the reputation of our department are on the line here, Harris."

"I hardly see why the *people* would care. With Patrick involved, I can see the appeal to the general public. As for my connection, I'm assuming you mean the investigators." Nathan stood and walked around the back of his chair. "Has Bonner hinted that he might think it was homicide?"

Captain Little paused in his pacing and met Nathan's stare. "I told you I don't know what he's thinking and, if I did, you know I couldn't tell you."

Nathan placed his hands on the back of the chair and took a deep breath. "Okay," he said with a nod. "Then I'm here to give you a heads up. I will be going to my daughter's birthday party on Saturday, and I will be spending more time with her, and her mother, before," he hoped, "and after that day. I've missed almost three years of her life. I don't intend to miss any more."

The older man pressed his lips together, and they stared at each other in silence. Nathan counted the seconds as they loudly ticked away on the wall clock and started feeling nervous when he reached thirty. He didn't want to displease his captain, this was the man who held his career in the palm of his hand, but he was also tired of not being able to spend time with Janelle, Zoe, and Zach.

"Who else will be there?" Captain Little asked.

"Janelle's family, my mother, Charlotte, Mason, and my nephew. As far as Zoe's friends, I don't know," Nathan answered, hope building in his chest.

"Fine," the captain said abruptly. "And as for spending time with them, for God's sake, just do so at her house or yours, out of the public eye until this has all blown over. After that I don't care."

Nathan did his best not to smile. "Thank you, sir."

Captain Little nodded. "Is that all?"

"Yes, sir." Nathan stood upright and backed toward the door.

"I'll let you know when I know something. You can go." Nathan's captain sat down in the chair behind his desk and began to fumble with his paperwork as Nathan closed the heavy door behind him.

Now all he had to do was go home and wait for Janelle to call him. He hoped that would be soon. Her words still haunted him and he feared the longer she believed last night had been a mistake, the longer it would take them to reach the normal life he wanted with her.

Twenty-One

Janelle looked over the table of food that she, her sister, Nancy, and Charlotte had just finished setting up for Zoe's birthday party. "I think that's everything," she said with a smile at her helpers.

"So now, we're just waiting on Mom and Dad?" Kelsey asked as they all heard a crash of blocks from the living room, where the kids were being supervised by Nathan and Mason, quickly followed by a tiny "uh-oh" and a round of giggles.

Janelle's grin widened. "Yes, so why don't we move the kids outside until they get here."

Nancy and Charlotte exited the dining room, into the living room, and Janelle heard Nancy playfully scolding her grandchildren and Zach. Janelle and Kelsey moved into the kitchen, and Janelle walked directly to the pantry. She opened the doors and reached up to the top shelf to retrieve the box of sidewalk chalk and the large bottle of bubbles. When she turned to walk toward the island, she noticed her sister sitting on a stool with a distant look in her eyes.

"What's wrong?" Janelle asked even though she already had her suspicions.

Kelsey shook the question away and gave her sister a slight smile. "Nothing."

Janelle raised a disbelieving eyebrow as she set the box and bottle on the counter. Kelsey looked toward the window over the sink, and her face relaxed. Janelle could see the tiny stress lines all over her face and frowned.

"Patrick said he'd try to call early today," Kelsey said quietly. "I haven't heard from him yet."

"Kels, I'm sure you will." Janelle laid her hand on Kelsey's shoulder and rubbed in small circles. "Maybe he's just gotten busy today."

"Probably," Kelsey agreed. "He's been getting busier and busier over the last few days. His calls have become farther and farther apart. And sometimes he just sounds so distracted."

"I'm sorry to hear that," Janelle stated as she sat on the stool in front of Kelsey. She had every confidence in Patrick's return and of his love for her sister, but she also knew that at least a small part of Kelsey feared he'd slip back into his old habits, regardless of how exaggerated they'd been in the tabloids, and either cheat or abandon her altogether.

"Sometimes I think he'd be better off without me," Kelsey admitted as a single tear slipped down her cheek. "Our family is a mess. Compared to his, we're a basketful of crazy, and I don't know anyone who would want to be a part of that."

"I would."

Janelle looked up and met Nathan's gaze as he walked into the kitchen carrying Zoe. He gave her a soft smile then walked over to Kelsey. He shifted Zoe to his right side so he could put his left arm around Kelsey's shoulder.

"His focus is on you and being a part of your life," Nathan said reassuringly, and Janelle's heart leapt to her throat. "Nothing else matters. He loves you and he accepts the rest." Nathan bent closer to her ear but looked at Janelle as he added, "And if he hurts you, you just let me know and Mason, Jackson, and I will rough him up for you." He winked at Janelle as he stood back up.

Kelsey pulled her head away, her mouth opened in surprise with a little upward tilt to her lips. "You're kidding, right?" she asked, sounding amused, and Janelle breathed a sigh of relief.

"Not at all," Nathan replied. "You know we've always thought of you like a sister. That's what brothers do for their younger sister, right?"

Kelsey beamed at him as she nodded. "Yeah, I suppose it is."

"Between you and me, though, I don't think we'll have to do anything," Nathan said.

"Oooh, chalk!" Zoe exclaimed and began to wiggle to get down. Nathan looked at Zoe then in the direction of her focus and set her down on the floor. Zoe skipped the two steps to Janelle and reached for the chalk on the counter. "Outside?"

Janelle handed her the box and grinned. "Outside. Take your brother and James, too."

"'Kay," Zoe said as she fled the room with her new toy. "Zach, James, let's go color," she added as she continued toward the front door, not waiting for either of the boys.

Nathan moved closer to Janelle's side.

"Nathan, I don't think you'll have to do anything to Patrick either," Kelsey finally agreed.

"That's what I like to hear," Nathan said.

Janelle marveled at how he'd come in and lifted the burden from her and made Kelsey feel better without being asked. With his daughter on his hip, no less. She needed that kind of man in her life, and Nathan had always been that. Her mistake hadn't been making love to him, her mistake had been kicking him out of her bed.

She'd have to make that up to him.

"So, what else do we need for the kids?" Kelsey asked, pulling Janelle out of her thoughts of things to come.

"Just the bubble wands and the smaller bottles," Janelle answered as Kelsey reached for the large bottle of bubbles.

"Where are they?" Nathan stepped away from Janelle and held his hand out.

She took it and let him pull her to her feet. "In the top of the pantry."

"You two go on out then, I'll get them," he said as he released her hand and turned toward the pantry.

Janelle and Kelsey did as he suggested with the large bubble bottle. Kelsey set the bottle on the floor next to the house then moved to sit on the porch swing with Nancy and watch the kids color. Janelle moved to the other side of the porch where Mason and Charlotte were standing by the rail, also watching the children. Janelle was about to speak to them when movement at the end of the driveway caught her attention.

Her parents had finally arrived.

Janelle glanced at Kelsey, who was frowning as she watched the car approach the house, then back to the driveway as her father stopped his car in the circle in front of the house. She grinned when George stepped out and waved to everyone on the porch. The screen door closed and she turned to see Nathan approaching.

"Is this what you wanted?" he asked, holding out the bag in his hand.

Janelle scanned its contents, bubble wands, small bottles, and round trays, and nodded. "That's it," she answered as she turned to look at her parents. She was about to turn back to Nathan when the scene before her sank in.

Her mother had one foot in the car and one foot on the ground and was trying to climb back into the car. George was scowling down at his wife, his hand gripping her arm as he pointed to the porch and spoke to her in a voice too low for Janelle to hear from that distance. Her father wagged his finger in his wife's face and she slowly took her other foot out of the car. Once she was out of the way, he closed the door and Mary led him to the porch with her shoulders pulled back and her head held high.

Janelle met Kelsey's wide-eyed stare with one of her own. Kelsey was the first to shrug then return to her conversation with Nancy. Janelle turned to Nathan and directed him to set the bag next to the bubbles by the door, then struck up a conversation with Mason and Charlotte until Nathan returned and joined them.

Janelle and Kelsey stood at the kitchen island, covering food and cleaning up from the birthday party. As Janelle loaded the dishwasher with the serving spoons and platters, she reflected on the party.

After her parents' pseudo-dramatic entrance, Janelle had maintained watch on her mother for the rest of the afternoon. Mary had not been blatantly rude, but she had also avoided conversation with every adult and had only interacted with George when he approached her in whatever corner she'd picked out for herself. By the end of the party, Janelle had actually begun to feel sorry for her mother.

At the moment, Janelle was putting the detergent in the dishwasher, then closed it and started it running. She washed her hands and grabbed a hand towel as she turned around. Kelsey sat at the island, staring into the living room, pushing her phone in circles on the counter in front of her. She'd been a little quiet since Zoe had opened gifts. More specifically, since Zoe had opened Patrick's gift, a large wooden castle that had arrived two days before but had remained unopened until today's party. Janelle wasn't sure if Patrick had ever called and hoped that Kelsey's silence was simply because she missed him. A small part of her also worried that there may be something more.

"Nathan seems distracted," Kelsey said softly, and Janelle's gaze fell to the man in question, currently holding down the couch as the children played in the living room.

"He does, doesn't he?" Janelle agreed as she placed her elbows on the counter and bent over them. "He has been for a while, ever since he and Mason came out of the house earlier."

"What were they doing in the house?" Kelsey asked as she frowned at her phone.

"I have no idea."

Nathan turned and met Janelle's stare, lifted the corner of his mouth as he stood and joined the sisters in the kitchen. "Everything put away?" he asked as he sat on a stool across from Kelsey.

"Of course," Janelle answered with a chuckle. "We were just talking about you."

Nathan's eyebrows shot up. "About me? What have I done?"

Kelsey smiled slightly and shook her head.

"We're not sure," Janelle replied. "What were you and Mason doing in the house earlier?"

"Oh," Nathan muttered and looked at the counter. He remained silent for a while and Janelle was beginning to wonder if she was going to have to ask again, and if she'd like the answer. "Mason was asking me about the investigation into Richard's death."

"I didn't think you were working on that case," Kelsey said, frowning at him as Janelle had the same thought.

"I'm not." Nathan's head twisted from side to side.

"What did he ask you?" Janelle felt a foreboding chill in her stomach.

"How did Richard get into the house?" Nathan looked at her as he asked, and everything in her froze. She'd been asking herself the same thing since she'd woken up to find her son missing from his bed.

"I don't know," she answered. "Everything was locked up when I came downstairs."

"Did anyone check for forced entry?" Nathan questioned, and Janelle answered in the negative. "I didn't think so. I checked everything myself and there was no sign of it."

"You were investigating during your daughter's birthday party?" Janelle scoffed. "How could you do that?"

Nathan drew back at her tone. "I'm sorry, Mason asked and I couldn't stop wondering. He helped me check."

"He's a lawyer, how would he know what to look for?" Kelsey asked, her phone stationary and her focus completely on Nathan.

"He's the son of a detective," Nathan answered, a hint of pride in his voice. He slid his arm across the counter and reached for Janelle. "We were gone all of five minutes, I didn't miss anything big."

Janelle hated to admit that he was right, and no one else had had time to miss them. "That's not the point," she muttered with a pout as she took his outstretched hand.

"So, you didn't find any evidence of forced entry," Kelsey continued. "What are you thinking?"

Nathan pressed his lips together and inhaled deeply through his nose. "You aren't going to like it," he warned, and the chill in Janelle's stomach began to stretch its icy fingers toward her chest. "I'm thinking he had help."

Janelle held his stare then turned and met Kelsey's clear-eyed, sad gaze. After a few seconds, Kelsey looked back at her phone and began to push it again. Janelle looked back at Nathan.

She couldn't ask the question she wanted to ask, so she settled for, "You don't think it was just anyone, do you?"

"No." Nathan squeezed her hand, and she didn't want to hear what she knew he was about to say.

"Don't," she said. "Don't even suggest it."

"Janelle, who else?" he asked. "She was his biggest cheerleader, even after he died. You said yourself she kept pushing you to go back to him until the end."

"I don't care what you think, if she'd known what he had planned, she wouldn't have given him a key," Janelle snapped as she ripped her hand from Nathan's.

"Maybe she didn't know the truth," Kelsey muttered.

Janelle's head snapped toward her sister's voice. "Kelsey?" she asked. "You can't possibly think our mother would do that, regardless."

Kelsey looked up, and Janelle saw the sadness in her sister's face. "Actually I can," she replied and took a deep, shaky breath. "Patrick and I talked about it while I was in the hospital. How else do you explain Richard getting in and out of the house without you even knowing it, Janelle? You haven't exactly been a light sleeper since Zach was born, but if he didn't make any noise, you may not have heard him. If he had broken a window or smashed in a door, you'd have been at the top of the stairs before he set foot on the bottom one."

"But, Kelsey," Janelle whined as an icy finger poked at her heart. "Our mother would not have agreed to a kidnapping."

"Probably not," Kelsey agreed as she shrugged her shoulder, "but she would have agreed to revenge against me."

Janelle's eyes widened and her gaze bounced from one face to the other—Kelsey's face held a quiet, resigned strength Janelle wasn't familiar with, Nathan's countenance was uncomfortable and wary. Janelle opted to tackle the wariness.

"Nathan, I still can't believe you would suggest such a thing. This investigation isn't even yours, you shouldn't even be looking into it," Janelle said.

"Someone has to, Jan." Nathan clasped his hands in front of him. "It's gone on long enough, someone should have already looked into how he got into the house. I'm tempted to go to the station on Monday and say something."

"Don't you dare," Janelle snapped. She felt faint at the idea of someone suspecting her mother of having anything to do with this whole incident. "Why would you do that?"

"Because I want it settled," Nathan growled. "I want the case closed so you and I can have a normal life."

"We've never had a normal life, Nathan." Janelle pushed away from the counter and pressed her hips against the sink.

"I think it's about time we start then, don't you?" he asked, imploring and vulnerable as his eyes rounded on her face.

Her mouth went dry.

The longer he had to wait for her answer, the more uneasy Nathan became. He looked across the island at Kelsey who had her head down, her hand hovering over her phone. She glanced at him briefly then picked up her phone and left the room as quickly as she could. Nathan stood and moved to stand in front of Janelle then propped himself against the kitchen island as he crossed his arms in front of him.

"Janelle," he said softly. "You haven't answered my question."

"I don't know, Nathan," she answered, shaking her head.

"What do you not know?" Nathan questioned calmly as his heart skipped every other beat. "Do you still think we made a mistake?" She shrugged and he wanted to reach out and give her a light shake.

"I shouldn't have said that, I'm sorry." Janelle cast a brief glance toward the living room. "I want you in Zoe's life, Nathan. You're her father, and I've always known you'd be a good one. She needs that." Janelle took a step closer. "I didn't mean to hurt you, don't you know that?"

"No, I don't. Because you did just that," Nathan replied, tamping down the sting of the truth. "And I want to be a part of Zoe's life too, but more importantly, I want to be a part of yours."

"Isn't it a package deal?" Janelle said with a flippant wave of her hand.

Nathan scowled at her as he straightened. "It's not the same and you know it."

Janelle lowered her eyes and backed away.

"Is this about your nightmare? Do you regret sleeping with me again?" Nathan asked as he closed the distance between them.

"My nightmare?" Her face paled as she looked up at him.

He nodded. "You know, the one you had before you woke up screaming and made me leave." He watched her swallow and his heart lurched as he continued, "Do you think your subconscious was trying to tell you something?"

"No," Janelle mouthed. "It's my mother. I hear her voice in my head, always criticizing, always fussing. She tells me those things in my nightmares when I can't shut her out." Janelle took a step and raised a shaky hand to rest on his arm. "I thought I'd escaped her lessons and her teachings, but when I sleep, she's there, drilling her rules into my head and telling me where I've failed. I can never make her proud. I'm not a good daughter or mother, and I sucked at being a wife, Nathan."

His heart broke to see this strong woman reduced almost to tears because of her mother's constant badgering and criticisms. He wrapped her in his arms, his anger and fear momentarily forgotten. She needed him again and he needed to be there for her. "Do you want a normal life with me, Jan?" he asked softly as she sniffled against his chest.

She nodded. "I think so."

He smiled and exhaled slowly. "I'll take it." *For now*. He hated doing it, but he broke the embrace. "I should go home now." As he turned to leave, her small hand gripped his wrist.

"Please stay," she said softly.

He met her gaze and swallowed the lump in his throat. He'd been waiting for that request for four days. "Are you sure?"

She closed the distance between them and kissed his cheek. "Yes," she whispered across his ear and he was instantly aroused.

Twenty-Two

Once the kids were in bed and Janelle was certain they were asleep, she led Nathan upstairs to her bedroom. Regardless of what nightmares she might have, she was determined she would not be sending him home before morning.

She heard the lock of the door behind her and she turned to face him. Before he could question her surety about this, for the umpteenth time since she'd invited him to stay, she pressed her lips against his. His lips were soft, but firm, and tasted like the icing from the cake they'd had after putting the kids to bed. He wrapped his arms around her as she slid hers around his neck and heat radiated from every point their bodies touched, pooling low in her abdomen.

Their lips still connected, she began to back toward the bed, pulling him with her as her hands lowered to the tail of his shirt. She slipped her hands under it and pressed her palms to his stomach. The muscles under her hands quivered and he broke the kiss. Panting for air, he looked into her eyes and held her gaze.

"Jan, are you—"

Her hand covered his mouth and she stepped closer until their noses were almost touching. "Don't you dare ask if I'm sure again or I may have to gag you," she whispered.

His eyes darkened a little more as they widened. She felt his smile grow under her palm and she slowly moved her hand to reveal his wicked grin.

"Don't tease me," he said then quickly covered her lips with his again.

She nipped his bottom lip as she slid her hand back under his shirt. Slowly, she skimmed her hand up his rippled torso, lightly tracing her fingers across his skin. He groaned and pressed his lips against hers harder, sucking on her lower lip as she raised the fabric to his chin. When they separated so she could pull the shirt over his head, she met his lusty stare and became lightheaded with giddiness.

She tossed his top over his shoulder toward the foot of the bed as he reached for the bottom of hers. He wasted no time in removing it, and it quickly joined his. Janelle laughed lightly as he yanked her against his chest and reached for the clasp of her bra.

"Slow down," she giggled. She placed her hands on either side of his face. "I have plans."

Nathan's eyebrow lifted, and he dropped his hands to her waist as her bra fell off her shoulders and down her arms. "Oh really?"

Janelle nodded, lowered her hands, and let the bra drop to the floor. She turned them so the back of his legs were against the bed, then gave him a light shove. His rear landed on the mattress and his hands went to the waistband of her pants. She swatted them away and shook her head as she inched closer.

"Not yet," she whispered across his ear and heard a stifled groan. She slowly went down to her knees, sliding her breasts against the length of his torso as her hands moved to his hips. Her fingertips slipped under his waistband and she dragged her knuckles against his skin to the front of his jeans.

She popped the button, unzipped them, then grabbed his underwear and jeans and lowered them at the same time. He lifted so she could ease them completely over his buttocks and down his long, lean legs. Her eyes fell to his manhood, standing at attention and staring at her. She lifted her face to his, met his curious gaze, and smiled.

"What are you doing?" Nathan asked, panting laboriously, his voice thick with desire, the gold flecks in his eyes dancing against the dark brown.

She allowed her grin to widen slightly then lowered her head as she held his stare.

Nathan inhaled sharply through his teeth as her mouth closed around him and his eyes rolled back into his head. Was she trying to kill him? If so, she couldn't have picked a sweeter torture. Her tongue was warm and wet and caressing him in ways he hadn't been touched in a long time. He felt slightly faint as the blood rushed from his head and directly to the part of him being massaged by her tongue and teeth and warmed by her breath.

He focused on inhaling slowly, counting to three, releasing the air, repeat, for as long as he could. When he felt ready to explode, he gently pushed her head away.

"Enough," he croaked.

She gave him a large, innocent grin as she rose to her feet. Her hands made quick work of her jeans, and before his sluggish brain could comprehend what she was doing, she had her pants off and on the floor at their feet.

"Slide back." She motioned toward the middle of the bed and he did as he was told.

As he adjusted against the headboard, she retrieved a condom from the open box in the drawer of her nightstand. She crawled onto the bed and positioned herself over his knees, straddling him as she reached for him. He tried not to whimper as her hand wrapped around his erection and slid the condom on.

She tossed the wrapper onto the floor and inched up his thighs. She lifted to her knees and positioned herself over him. He raised his hands to her hips to hold her steady as he met her brilliant blue gaze. She had a Cheshire-like grin on her lips, and his heart raced. He'd never seen the take-charge side of her in the bedroom, but he liked it. He hoped it was a good sign of things to come.

"Are you ready?" she murmured, and he was hypnotized by the movement of her lips as she spoke.

His mouth felt like a desert, so he nodded. Janelle bent over and met his lips with hers as she slowly lowered herself onto him until he was completely inside. She pulled her face away and threw her head back as she gasped for air. Had he hurt her? He couldn't remember ever being in this position with her.

"You okay?" he ground out as the simple act of trying to sit up pushed him deeper and she constricted slightly.

Her features relaxed. "Yes," she uttered, and he watched the corners of her mouth turn up. She looked at him again, fire in her eyes as she slowly raised herself then lowered again.

He groaned as he took her mouth with his and didn't wait for the invitation to force his tongue past her lips. As she moved on him, he mimicked the motion with his tongue. He slid one hand up her side and grabbed one of her breasts, massaging lightly but taking time to pinch her nipples every now and then, simply to hear her whimper.

As he built toward release, their hands explored more rapidly, never settling in one spot for long as they teased and sweetly tortured each other. His lips never left hers, and he could feel her tiny gasps in short bursts against his cheek. When he sensed she was getting close, he concentrated both hands on her breasts, caressing and pinching the nipples until she came apart in his arms, her screams tickled the back of his throat. Her walls tightened around him, and he thrust quickly so he could join her in the completion.

She broke the kiss and slowly lowered her head to his shoulder. He kissed her forehead as he wrapped his arms around her. Her breathing slowly returned to normal, and he thought she'd fallen asleep when she pressed her palms to his chest and sat up.

"Promise me something," she said somberly.

"Anything," he answered as he reached up and placed his hand over hers.

She inhaled deeply and held his stare. "If I have a nightmare tonight, I don't care what I say or how angry I get, don't leave."

Nathan allowed his delight to show on his face. "Never again."

"A dog, Nathan, really?" Janelle asked, laughing as she stepped off of the porch to greet Nathan the following Wednesday. He was walking toward her, a black-and-tan German shepherd held on a tight leash beside him. The screen door slammed behind her, and she turned to her children and motioned for them to stop. They froze on the top step; Zoe bounced anxiously on her toes as Janelle faced Nathan again. "Who's this?"

"This is McClane." Nathan smiled broadly as he stopped in front of Janelle and leaned closer. "Can I kiss you yet?" he whispered as he glanced at the kids.

"Not in front of the children," she replied with a grin. "Why did you bring your dog?"

"He was getting lonely all by himself at my house." Nathan took Janelle's hand and continued to walk toward the porch. "And I thought he might be helpful to Zach."

"Has he ever been around children?" Janelle asked hesitantly, tugging on Nathan's hand as she stopped before they reached the bottom step.

He stopped and turned to face her. "He'll be fine."

Nathan waited for her to nod before he allowed the dog to climb the first step. "Zach, Zoe, this is McClane. He's two years old, and I thought you might like to meet him."

"Mommy, can I pet him?" Zoe asked enthusiastically, her hands clenching and unclenching by her side.

Janelle looked at Nathan, who looked almost as excited as his daughter, and gave the go ahead. Zoe squealed when her fingers reached the dog's fur for the first time. Janelle climbed to the top step and rested against the column as she watched Nathan guide Zoe on how to touch and how not to touch the dog. Zach slowly inched closer, and eventually Nathan was teaching him as well.

Her heart swelled at the scene in front of her and she knew this was exactly what her kids needed. Not necessarily the dog, but the experience and the guidance that Nathan gave them. She knew, without doubt, that he would always be that teacher, leader, and guide for them, and that he'd do it enthusiastically because he loved them. It would never be a chore for him because he would want to help them.

He loved them. And they loved him. Her heart tripped over the realization but it was all there in front of her. Suddenly, she could envision a life she'd only ever dreamed about laid out in front of her. She shook her head and laughed away the ambitious thoughts. She was getting ahead of herself.

She watched him give some final instructions to the children then stand and walk toward her. He stopped beside her and placed his hand on the rail behind her, his arm pressed against her back.

"What are you doing here so early?" Janelle asked as she watched Zoe rub the dog from shoulder to the base of his tail with a grin on her face. McClane's tail thumped against the wooden porch boards.

"You said you had yard work, I thought I'd come and help," he answered.

"Kelsey and I can manage it on our own. You didn't need to do that."

Janelle turned so her back was pressed against the column and he was to her side. "We actually enjoy doing yard work."

"Jan, I'm going stir crazy, sitting at home with nothing else to do every day," he said and Janelle could hear the underlying plea in his voice.

She looked into his hazel eyes, and her heart skipped a beat. He had said he wanted a normal life, and she supposed this would be normal. Richard had never been a fan of gardening or maintenance—she'd always had to do that. She closed her eyes and shook her head. She had to stop comparing the two of them. She'd known in high school that Nathan and Richard were different; it wasn't fair to Nathan for her to continue to measure him against Richard. Even if he did come out more favorably.

"No?" Nathan asked, misunderstanding her movement.

"No," she repeated and looked at him, "I mean, yes, you can stay and help."

"Why did you shake your head?" Nathan frowned.

Janelle placed her palm on his cheek. "It was nothing. Just a bad habit I need to break."

His expression softened, but his eyes still looked a little troubled. He reached up and took her hand, kissed her fingers, then lowered their clasped hands between them. "What would you like me to do?"

"Not the roses," Kelsey said as she came around the corner of the porch, dressed in dark pants and a long-sleeved denim shirt. A red bandanna held her hair in place. "Those are mine." Kelsey held up a hand pruner and waved it in her gloved hand.

"They're her pride and joy," Janelle told Nathan as he took in her sister's appearance and Janelle wondered what Patrick would think if he could see her.

"Okay, works for me," Nathan said with a shrug. "I wouldn't know what to do with them anyway."

"You can mow the grass," Kelsey said with a commanding air.

"Fine," Nathan agreed. "Let me get McClane's toys and food then you can lead the way." He released Janelle's hand and went back to his truck. He returned a few seconds later with a bag and handed it to Janelle.

"C'mon, let's get this done before it gets too warm," Kelsey said and turned. As she walked away, Janelle noticed her slight limp and frowned.

"Has it gotten any better?" Nathan asked, and Janelle saw he was watching Kelsey, too.

"I thought it was gone, I hadn't noticed it much lately." Janelle gripped his forearm. "Keep an eye on her. Please don't let her overdo it."

"You got it." Nathan gave her a large grin then followed her sister to the shed behind the carport.

Janelle looked at the kids. "Okay, kiddos, back inside. We have some schoolwork to do." She hustled the kids and the dog inside and straight to the dining room, dropping the bag at the base of the kitchen island on the way.

She'd decided it would be best for Zach if she homeschooled him for the remainder of the school year. He'd missed so much work because of the kidnapping and his recovery that he'd fallen behind. He only had a month and a half left anyway, and she was sure she could get him caught up before the end of the school year.

Two hours later, Zach was sitting at the dining room table working on math worksheets, Zoe was sitting beside him, coloring in one of her new princess coloring books, and the dog lay on the floor behind both of their chairs. Janelle stood at the dining room window, watching a now-shirtless Nathan edging around the rose bushes as Kelsey waited impatiently from a safe distance. Janelle was considering the rippling muscles in his chest as they moved the weed-eater from side to side when the front door opened.

She turned in time to see the dog approach the doorway to the kitchen and heard him growl as the clack of heels hit the tile floor. Janelle closed her eyes and groaned inwardly. There was only one person who would simply walk into her house without invitation, and Janelle didn't want to see her right now.

"McClane, no," Janelle lightly scolded the dog as she approached him. He sat in the doorway; his eyes remained on Mary as she moved toward them.

"Where did you get that beast?" Mary said, placing her hand to her chest as she froze. McClane let out a low rumble. "He sounds dangerous, you should take him back."

"He's perfectly fine, Mother." Janelle patted the dog on the head. "What are you doing here?"

Mary's jaw dropped, and she made a wide arc around Janelle and the dog to stand next to the kitchen window that overlooked the backyard. "Why do you always take that tone with me? Do I have to have a reason? Maybe I just want to see my grandchildren," Mary said. To anyone else, she would have sounded offended.

To Janelle, she sounded staged.

"Maybe," Janelle agreed. "But we both know that's never the case."

Mary lifted her chin and considered her eldest child for a moment before turning. "Did you hire a gar—" She turned and glared at Janelle. "What is *he* doing here?"

"Baking a cake," Janelle quipped as she rolled her eyes. "What does it look like he's doing here?"

"You know, it is one thing for him to come to Zoe's birthday party," Mary said as she folded her arms across her chest and took a few angry steps toward Janelle, her lip curling. "After all, he is her—"

"Enough, Mother," Janelle snapped and thumbed toward the children. Zach and Zoe were both enraptured as they watched the adults.

"Children." Mary sounded surprised to see them.

"Imagine that," Janelle muttered to herself.

Mary scowled at her daughter. "Perhaps we should move this conversation elsewhere." Without waiting for a response, Mary stomped past Janelle and through the kitchen.

"Oh goody," Janelle whispered to the dog who looked up at her and wagged his tail. "Stay with the kids." She gave his head a rub and looked at Zach. "Back to work. I want you to have those done when I'm finished talking to Grandma." With a deep, quiet sigh, she followed her mother into the office. She barely had the door closed behind her when her mother started her rant.

"I can't believe you," Mary started as she paced the length of the room. "It's one thing to have him at Zoe's party since he is her father, but do you really need him here now? He's not even spending time with his child, he's outside doing *your* yard work."

"Mom, he asked to do that," Janelle said softly.

"I don't care, Janelle, that's not the point." Mary stopped in the middle of the floor and folded her arms across her chest.

"What *is* the point?" Janelle asked dryly.

"The point is, he's outside doing things that you and your sister are completely capable of doing yourselves. What kind of message does that send the children?" Mary snapped.

Janelle sat on the arm of the plush, leather sofa and clasped her hands in her lap. "I'm sure you'd like to tell me," she said with a nod toward her mother.

Mary's lip twitched slightly before she continued. "It shows the children that you are moving on from their father—"

Janelle let out a snort of derision that drew an irate look from her mother.

"From their father before the proper amount of time has passed," Mary persisted, only slightly unfazed. "It's only been just over a month, Janelle. You should have more respect for the dead."

"It's been almost six weeks," Janelle said then shrugged, "but who's counting?"

Mary gasped.

"As for moving on from their father," Janelle continued, ignoring her mother's outrage, "I would argue that he gave up the respect that comes with that title when he kidnapped Zach and told the world Zoe wasn't his."

"And whose fault would that be?" Mary snapped. "He knew what he was dealing with, and he did the best he could for those kids. He loved them like they were his own."

"No, Mother, he didn't. He practically ignored Zoe because she was a girl, and he couldn't look at Zach because he didn't have the right bloodlines," Janelle rose and walked around her mother to the desk and propped her backside against it.

"Again, Janelle, you have no one to blame but yourself. You forced that adoption on him," Mary said as she turned to face her daughter. "You made him take your sister under his roof, you pushed him into that adoption for your own selfish purposes, and then you had the audacity to cheat. With *him*," she spat as she motioned toward the backyard. "Richard was one of the highest-paid men in the county, he was a good provider for you, and you repaid him by sleeping with someone else. You should be ashamed."

"Are those the lies he told you?" Janelle scoffed, trying to ignore the sting of the truth to the accusations.

"They're not lies," Mary nearly yelled.

From the other side of the door, McClane barked a couple of times.

"They were truths for him, Janelle," Mary snapped. "That's what's important. He loved you and you ignored everything I ever told you. You put your needs ahead of his time and time again and you paid no attention to the damage you were doing to your marriage. And now," Mary flung her hands into the air with an exasperated air, "now, you don't even wait for him to be cold in his grave before you begin to carry on with Nathan, unless you never really ended it and made a cuckold out of your husband under his very nose."

"Mother," Janelle said calmly. Mary's words struck deeply and Janelle was trying not to let it show.

"Don't 'Mother' me," Mary hissed. "I'm ashamed of your behavior, Janelle. I raised you to be better than this. I raised you to take care of your husband or suffer the consequences. You ignored me and deserved everything he did to you."

Janelle gasped and drew back.

"That's enough," Nathan snapped from the doorway. McClane, standing beside his leg, quietly bared his teeth at Mary. "The way I see it, you taught your daughters to be doormats and never expect to be treated as anything more. Nobody deserves the kind of abuse they've received."

Mary wheeled around to face him. "First, this is none of your concern. If you think you have any place in my daughter's life, you're mistaken. I'll make sure of that. Second, Richard didn't abuse Kelsey, and any cruelty he displayed toward Janelle was because of her own actions."

"I wasn't referring to Richard's abuse, I was talking about yours," Nathan said calmly, his eyes glittering with anger, all directed at Mary.

Mary's jaw dropped as she glanced over her shoulder at Janelle then slowly returned her focus to Nathan. "How dare you accuse me of such a thing? I would never say or do anything to hurt my daughters."

Janelle rolled her eyes and shook her head as she rose to her feet. She slowly walked around her mother and toward Nathan.

"Every vitriolic word I just heard from your mouth would suggest otherwise," Nathan growled.

Janelle stopped by his side and slipped her hand into his. He squeezed it in acknowledgment as she turned to look at her mother. "He's not going anywhere, get used to it," she said softly, drawing her courage from his support. "I have a feeling you've said everything, maybe even more than, you came here to say. If you haven't, I don't want to hear it."

Mary's eyes widened as her mouth fell open and her cheeks became splotched with red. Janelle nudged Nathan and McClane backward, out of the doorway.

"You should go now." Janelle calmly motioned toward the door.

Mary closed her gaping mouth and pulled her shoulders back. She refused to make eye contact with Janelle or Nathan as she strode past them. Before she walked out of the front door, over her shoulder she said, "You'll be sorry," then continued on, slamming both door and screen door behind her.

When Janelle heard the tires of her mother's car squeal out of the driveway, she turned into Nathan's arms. He held her against him, and she relished the feeling of security and strength he gave her. Hot tears rose to her eyes as she wrapped her arms around his neck. As her vision blurred, she saw Kelsey, her eyes wide as she stared toward the front door and stood like a sentry in front of the kids. Janelle closed her eyes and turned her face into Nathan's neck.

"Thank you," she murmured.

Twenty-Three

Two nights later, Nathan held Janelle in her bed, his eyes closed as his heart rate slowly returned to normal. She lightly traced circles on his bare chest with her fingertips, and he pressed a kiss to the top of her head. After a few minutes, her hand flattened on his chest and she propped herself up on her elbow.

"Do you think we should tell the kids?" she asked as she stilled her hand on his waist.

He raised an eyebrow, not sure what she was talking about. "Tell them what?"

"About us," she answered.

"What about us?" He fought not to grin too widely, but the thrill of her question raced all the way to his toes.

She rolled her eyes. "That we're dating," she replied as her brow furrowed. "We are dating, aren't we?"

Nathan mimicked her posture as he turned to face her. He placed his hand on her naked hip. "Technically, no, since we haven't actually gone out in public. Otherwise, I would say yes. Would the kids understand that, though?"

"I'm not sure." She frowned and flopped onto her back. Nathan's hand slid to her stomach and he inched closer. "I just hate that you have to leave before they get out of bed every morning so they won't see you. I want them to not be surprised if you're here when they get up. But then, I don't know if it would even occur to them as odd or out of place. I'm probably worrying—"

He silenced her with a kiss, and her hand immediately went to the back of his head. She held him to her and returned his innocent kiss with an excitement that warmed him thoroughly. He slowly pulled away and she pouted as he looked down into her wide blue eyes.

"Yes, you are worrying too much," Nathan murmured.

Her lips relaxed and turned slightly upward.

"That's not exactly what I was going to say."

"I'll bet it was close enough."

She laughed out loud as her head bobbed up and down. "Close enough," she agreed and placed her hand on his arm that stretched across her body.

"We could just say we're boyfriend and girlfriend," Nathan suggested and Janelle's lip curled. "You don't like that idea?" he asked.

Janelle shook her head. "It sounds so schoolish." She paused and slowly her head moved from side to side. "I guess we could do that, I've got nothing better."

He'd waited fifteen years, since they were seniors in high school, to call her his girlfriend. The idea still excited him; the reality was better than he could have imagined, but he couldn't shake the memories of her nightmares and her mother's words from his mind.

"Do you think we're moving too fast?" he asked.

Janelle took a deep, considerate pause and shook her head. "I should think that, shouldn't I?" She sounded honest and contemplative, not full of the self-loathing he'd been expecting. "But I don't." She met his gaze and he fell into the deep pools of blue and felt refreshed. "The truth is, this feels more right to me than being with him ever did. When you and I made love last week, it was like coming back from a hiatus and falling right back into normal."

Nathan could hardly contain the smile on his lips. She reached up and placed her palm on his cheek.

"I never should have pushed you away," she muttered as he kissed the heel of her hand. She smiled sadly as she stared into his eyes.

"Doesn't matter," he said softly. "We're together now, that's what's important."

"True," she muttered quietly, and her stare became thoughtful and curious. "What did you mean last week?"

He pressed his lips together and remained silent. He would need more clarification than that if she expected an answer.

"When you said you'd wanted me for fifteen years. What did you mean by that?" She rolled to her side again so they were face to face.

"What do you think I meant?" he asked with a chuckle. "How else does a man want a woman?"

She frowned. "You wanted me like that in high school?"

"Yes and no," Nathan answered truthfully. She pursed her lips, and he could tell she still wasn't happy with his answer. "I wanted to date you, Jan. At some point during junior year, I think it was, I realized I had a crush on you. By the time we were seniors, I thought I was in love with you. I was wrong, of course, but it still took me a while to work up the courage to ask you out."

"Why? We were friends." Janelle propped herself up a little higher.

"Exactly. We were friends and I valued your friendship. I didn't want to screw that up," he said. She nodded her understanding but remained quiet. A few minutes passed before he felt the silence was becoming awkward. "Don't you want to know how I know I was wrong back then?"

She shook her head and averted her gaze. "I'm glad you didn't ask me out then." Her words punched him in the gut.

"Why would you say that?" he asked with a frown.

"Because I would have rejected you," she answered softly. "And that would have ruined our friendship, and I didn't want that to happen."

"You've thought about this recently?" Nathan turned and propped himself against the headboard. "That's harsh."

"No, I considered it then," Janelle answered and peeked at him from under her lashes. "You always treated me differently, and I think the thought flitted through my mind once or twice, but you never brought it up, so I didn't dwell on it. I didn't know what else to do."

"I'm not sure I'm following your logic. Are you saying that I was only good enough to be your friend and nothing more?" Nathan had the urge to put his feet on the floor and leave the room before she could cause any more damage to his ego.

She slid closer and placed her arm around the front of his waist. "No, just hear me out before you bolt, please." It was almost frightening the way they could read each other. He guessed that's what knowing a woman for most of her life could do for you. Nathan nodded and she inhaled slowly.

"You scared me," she said as she released the air from her lungs.

"Not helping," he retorted.

She raised an eyebrow as she stared at him. "You've met my mother, you are well aware of her logic and the way she thinks Kelsey and I should act around men."

Nathan bit his tongue against his opinion of her mother's logic.

"You didn't fit her mold, and therefore I didn't know how to handle you." She lowered her head. "I know that probably doesn't make sense, but it did to me at the time. Mom had drilled into my head from a very early age that I was supposed to anticipate a man's needs before he did, I was supposed to cater to his wants and forget about mine. I should not let any insensitive remark he might make affect me and should learn not to let the hurt show." Janelle pushed herself upward until her head was propped on his shoulder and her hand splayed on his chest. "You always anticipated *my* needs, you always cared about *my* wants. You didn't fit her mold. I remember having lunch with you once and muttering under my breath that I'd forgotten napkins and you got up and got them for me. You would get ice cream for yourself and bring an extra to me."

Nathan smiled slightly and began to relax as she took him down memory lane.

"Do you remember, I think it was tenth grade, I was standing at the door of Ramsey Hall, watching the downpour outside, contemplating skipping class because I had to walk across the parking lot to the vocational building?" She began to laugh. "I never saw you coming, but suddenly you were behind me and had the umbrella opened over our heads before you shoved me out into the rain and we ran all the way to the other building. Then you had to run all the way to the gym before the bell rang."

"I barely made that bell," Nathan said as he put an arm around her. "I'm still not seeing why I scared you."

"I didn't know how to react to you," Janelle answered. "I was seventeen and naïve. Even then I had this picture in my head of how a man should act, domineering, selfish, inconsiderate of my needs or wants, everything that Richard was. You were none of those things, and I didn't know how to deal with it."

It physically hurt Nathan to hear how low her expectations were. In his opinion, she'd always deserved the very best, and to hear what her mother had taught her daughters to expect from the men in their lives was heartbreaking. It was almost a wonder that she was dating him now.

"Was your father like that when you were younger?" Nathan asked.

"No, but my grandfather was. Mom grew up expecting Dad to act just like her father had but he wasn't that kind of man. I think I even pointed that out to her once and her response was . . ." Janelle lifted her nose, pressed her lips together, and prepared her best impression of her mother, "'If I didn't treat him so well, he would be.'" She lowered and shook her head. "The problem was that I was young and naïve, and I didn't realize my mother's mistake and how different my father was until I was much older. Kelsey and I have both spent the entirety of our adulthood trying to unlearn those early lessons." Janelle looked up at him and gave him a sweet smile. "Thank you for not fitting her mold."

The corner of Nathan's lip lifted slightly. "You're welcome. Are you just starting to appreciate that?"

She shook her head. "No, I've appreciated it for a while. Do you remember that night you brought *Steel Magnolias* to the house and watched it with me?"

Nathan bobbed his head.

"I realized that night how special you were to me. I saw you as the man you were, the man you'd always been, and stopped seeing the boy I grew up with." Her cheeks turned slightly pink and she looked down. "I'm pretty sure I fell in love with you that night," she murmured.

Nathan's heart skipped a beat. "What did you say?"

She looked back up at him, her eyes glowing in the soft light of the table lamp behind her. "You heard me," she replied with a smirk.

"I can't believe you said it first. I was expecting to have to drag it from you in a year or so." Nathan laughed as she sat up and scowled at him. She swatted his hand as he reached for her, and he ignored it as he flipped her onto her back underneath him. She squeaked her protest, even as she began to giggle. He lowered his head and she placed her fingers on his lips.

"Stop for just a second," she said and removed her hand after he nodded. "Maybe I should have waited for you to say it, but I think I've always known how you felt. You make me feel safe. You make me feel wanted. You make me feel loved. I needed to say it first because I wasn't sure you'd believe me if I waited. I've abused your trust before. I didn't want to give you any reason to doubt me now."

"I could never doubt you." He placed a soft kiss on her forehead. "I love you more now than I ever thought possible. Our past may not have been perfect but it got us to where we are today." He placed a firmer kiss on her cheek. "And our future is ahead of us, all we have to do is grab it."

Janelle smiled widely at him and he was lost. He would never want to look at another face like this. She'd officially ruined him for anyone else.

"Sounds like a plan." She grabbed his head and pulled it down to her. Their lips met, and the rest of the night was a blur of tangled limbs.

Twenty-Four

Janelle looked at the clock on the stove for the third time in the last five minutes as she placed the last of the dinner dishes in the dishwasher. Kelsey had remained on her stool at the island after the kids had finished eating and Janelle had begun to clean up. Janelle would be worried about the distance in her sister's eyes as she traced circles around her cell phone on the counter in front of her if it weren't for the fact she knew something Kelsey didn't.

Patrick was coming home later that evening. He was about three weeks earlier than they had all expected, but he'd pushed the director through filming all of his parts ahead of schedule so he could return home. He'd called Nathan early two mornings ago to tell him and to make arrangements for his arrival. Nathan was currently driving Patrick from the airport to their house, and Kelsey had no idea.

Janelle almost wished she could say something to her sister. Over the last few weeks, she'd watched Kelsey's appetite diminish and the dark circles under her eyes grow larger. Kelsey hadn't said anything, but Janelle felt sure her nightmares had returned. She'd also noticed how Kelsey had her phone not just in her pocket, but in her hand at all times. And at the moment, the lost look on her face was almost enough to make Janelle confess.

McClane barked from the living room, and Janelle glanced at the clock again with a smile on her face. She started the dishwasher's cycle and quickly rinsed her hands.

"Grandpa's here," Zach called from the living room as Janelle grabbed a towel. Her grin faded as she turned and dropped the towel on the counter and saw Zach perched on the window seat. Zoe was in the process of climbing onto it as Janelle walked through the living room to the front door.

She opened the door and stepped onto the porch. As her father pulled his car around the circle in front of the porch and stopped on the other side of the planter, Janelle began to assess the situation. It could be coincidence that they would arrive just before Nathan and Patrick, and with her father she could accept that. But with her mother tagging along, she could never be sure.

"Dad," Janelle said as she walked down the steps to meet him in the middle of the curve behind his car. "What are you doing here?"

Her father gave her a tight hug and kissed her on the head. "We heard there was a homecoming tonight," he murmured.

Janelle slowly eased away from him and tried not to smile. "Where did you hear such a rumor?"

"A little bird told me," he replied with a grin. Janelle marveled at how young her father looked when he smiled so widely, despite the graying hair and wrinkles he'd added in the last few months.

"That little bird wasn't supposed to speak," Janelle quipped with a disapproving shake of her head. Any seriousness her words may have held was negated by her upturned lips.

"I don't think we're talking about the same bird." He slid his arm around her shoulder and turned her in the direction of the porch. He briefly looked over his shoulder. "Are you coming, Mary?"

"Yes, dear, I'll be right there," Janelle's mother replied, and Janelle heard her footsteps on the gravel behind her.

As they reached the bottom step of the porch, Kelsey opened the screen door and stepped out of the house. "Daddy, what are you doing here?" she repeated Janelle's earlier question.

"Do I need a reason to come see two of my favorite girls?" George asked as he removed his arm from Janelle's shoulder and climbed the steps to hug his youngest child. "I haven't been here in a while and thought I owed you all a visit."

Janelle followed him up the porch stairs and rested her shoulder against the column at the top. Even in the fading light, she could see the brittleness of Kelsey's smile and the dull look in her eyes. Patrick's return wasn't a moment too soon. She only hoped it was lovesickness that was making her sister so wan and not some bigger problem. Janelle cast a quick glance at her mother and frowned.

Mary had stopped on the bottom step and was looking up the driveway toward the road. She turned and met Janelle's stare, pulled her shoulders back, and continued up the steps, past Janelle to a point along the rail behind her. Janelle shook her head and turned her attention back to her father and sister as they stood in the glow of the house coming through the open front door.

"It's good to see you. We just finished dinner but maybe we can have some dessert," Kelsey said softly and spun slowly around. "I'll go see what we have."

Before George could stop her, Kelsey was in the house, the screen door closing quietly behind her. George turned and looked at Janelle with a raised eyebrow. "Is she okay?"

"She's fine. I just don't think she's been sleeping too well. She's been a little out of sorts for the last few days." Janelle scanned the driveway as she folded her arms across her chest. "To my knowledge, she doesn't know he's coming home today, so she doesn't have any reason to be excited."

"Ah," George responded as he sat on the porch swing. Janelle smiled at him, then even wider at the little heads still in the window beside him.

Tires on the gravel caused her head to swivel in the direction of the sound, and her heart skipped a beat. Nathan was home and the excitement bubbled in her stomach. She couldn't wait to see him, and she was even more eager to see Kelsey's reaction to Patrick's return.

"Nathan's here!" Janelle heard Zach's little voice shout through the house.

She waited for a response from Kelsey but never heard her. Nathan's truck came to a stop in the curve of the drive, where Janelle had greeted her father, and Nathan hopped out with a large smile on his face. He looked past Janelle, and she watched his grin fall. When he looked at her again, Janelle shrugged.

Nathan quickly ran up the steps and scooped her into his arms. It was almost like he hadn't seen her in days, instead of the hours it had actually been. Janelle squealed with delight and quickly kissed him on the lips. He released her and stood by her side as Patrick exited the vehicle.

"Things have certainly improved between you two," Patrick's casual tones drifted toward them as he closed the truck's door.

"Patrick's home!" Zach screamed from inside the house, and Janelle caught the movement of the two heads scrambling out of the window. In a heartbeat, Zach had flung the door open and was racing across the porch toward Patrick.

Patrick waited at the bottom of the steps and caught Zach as he leapt off the porch and into his open arms. Zoe followed Zach out of the house at a slightly slower pace and eased herself down the steps. She wrapped her arms around Patrick's leg as he held on to Zach. Janelle, Nathan, and George laughed at the scene the children were creating then slowly turned their attention to the front door.

It wasn't until after Patrick had dislodged the kids and sent them to stand beside Janelle that Kelsey appeared, silhouetted against the screen door. One hand pressed against her lips as she slowly pushed the door open with the other hand. She took a tentative step onto the porch then another as the screen door slammed behind her.

"Patrick," Kelsey gasped. "You came back."

Tears pricked the corners of Janelle's eyes, and Nathan put his arm around her shoulder.

"Of course I did," Patrick replied with a large smile as he bounded up the four stairs in two steps.

He rushed toward Kelsey and pulled her into his arms. His mouth quickly covered hers, and Janelle looked down at the kids, who were watching the reunion with wide eyes. Janelle covered those eyes with her hands and tried not to laugh.

Nathan slid his arm down her back and laid his hand on her hip. He pulled her closer to him and pressed his lips to her head. "Let them watch, it'll do them good to see her so happy," he murmured.

Janelle nodded and slowly removed her hands from the children's eyes as Patrick and Kelsey continued to kiss. She couldn't help the smile that began to form on her own lips, and she laid her head against Nathan's shoulder as a sense of peace settled over her. Patrick was home, and she hoped that Kelsey wouldn't look so stressed all the time. Nathan was by her side, and things were going smoothly between them. Things were finally starting to look up for the Morgan girls.

Patrick and Kelsey ended their kiss, and Patrick took her hands as he took a step back. "Kelsey, there's something I need to ask you," he said, and Janelle's heart rate sped up.

She glanced up at Nathan who was watching Patrick and Kelsey with one corner of his mouth turned up. Janelle had the feeling she knew what was about to happen and turned to watch her sister and Patrick so she could see things unfold.

"Mommy, why are police cars coming to our house?" Zoe asked.

Janelle started to shush her daughter until her words sank in. "What?" She looked down at Zoe, who met her gaze, then pointed up the driveway.

Three cars were in the driveway, moving toward them, two marked squad cars being led by a dark, unmarked sedan. Nathan's hand slid away from Janelle's side, and she lifted her head.

"Nathan?" she questioned softly as he stepped around her and onto the step below. "What's going on?"

He shook his head as he focused on the cars stopping in front of him. "I'm not sure," he replied over his shoulder.

Zach slipped away from Janelle, and she watched him skip to Patrick, who had turned to watch the procession. Patrick picked him up and, once Zach was settled, took Kelsey's hand. Janelle noticed the movement of the swing and saw that her father had moved to stand at the other column at the top of the steps.

Janelle turned her attention to the lead car as the driver's side door opened. Her lip curled slightly when she saw the annoying, overbearing, older detective that had interviewed her climb out. He looked directly at Nathan and sneered, making his leathery face even more unattractive.

"Well, well, look at you playing house with the weeping widow," the older man said, casting a brief glance at Janelle before returning his scowl to Nathan.

"Bonner, what are you doing here?" Nathan growled as he positioned himself between Janelle and Zoe and the other man. Janelle stooped to pick Zoe up and quickly settled her on her hip.

"I'm doing my job. What are you doing here?" Bonner took a step toward Nathan and closed his car door. "I was under the impression you were told to stay away from this family." The four doors of the other cars all opened and uniformed officers stepped out of their vehicles.

An icy fear settled over Janelle's shoulders like a mantle and slowly trickled down her spine as she took in all of the officers.

"My directives changed," Nathan said simply, lifting a shoulder nonchalantly, but Janelle could see the tension rolling through him. She placed a shaky hand on his shoulder and took a step closer to him.

"Good," Bonner said menacingly. "Makes things easier for me."

"What things?" Nathan ground out.

"I'm so glad you asked." Detective Bonner stepped to the base of the steps and looked up at Nathan. He raised his arm and pointed a stubby finger at Patrick. "That's the one, arrest him."

"No!" Kelsey screamed.

Janelle's eyes widened, and she turned to see her sister step in front of Patrick and Zach and throw her arms to the side.

"What are you arresting him for?" Nathan asked above the fray as two of the officers stomped up the steps and onto the porch. George had joined his daughter and stood in front of all three of them as the police approached Patrick.

"Patrick Lyons," Bonner called out, ignoring Nathan's question. "You are under arrest for the murder of Richard Wagoner. You have the right to remain silent . . ."

"NO!" Kelsey screamed again, and Janelle watched in horror as officers went around Kelsey and George, took Zach out of Patrick's arms, handed him to Kelsey, and pulled Patrick away from the three of them. "NO! Stop!" Kelsey wailed. "Stop!" Her pain streamed down her cheeks as Zach gripped tightly around her neck and George held her back, telling Patrick to remain silent as his hands were handcuffed behind his back. Kelsey's continuous pleas became weaker. "No," she sobbed.

Bonner continued to read Patrick his Miranda rights.

"Are you serious?" Nathan yelled at him. "This is ridiculous. You know you have no basis for this."

Bonner finished his speech and turned his glare on Nathan. "You'd like to think that, wouldn't you?"

"I saw the evidence myself. What happened in that cabin was caused entirely by Richard. His death was his own fault," Nathan argued.

"You only saw part of the evidence. I've done my job very thoroughly and have reached a different conclusion," Detective Bonner snapped.

"I'm sure you have," Nathan hissed in return.

Bonner raised his arm again and pointed at Nathan. "Him too, boys."

"What?" Janelle felt all of the air leave her lungs. "No."

"You've got to be kidding me," Nathan retorted as the younger of the two remaining uniformed officers grabbed his upper arm and pulled him to the side, away from Janelle.

"No," she protested louder. Her legs felt weak and she gripped the rail beside her.

"Nathan Harris, you are under arrest for being an accessory after the fact in the murder of Richard Wagoner," Bonner stated loudly and launched into reading Nathan his Miranda rights.

Janelle felt the sting of tears as her vision began to blur. Nathan met her gaze, and the rage in his eyes gave way to a hint of sadness.

"Nathan, say nothing," George called from the side of the porch where he held a crumpled Kelsey, Zach still clinging to her neck. "I'll be at the station right behind you."

"No," Janelle's voice cracked and she took a step toward Nathan as they eased him, handcuffed, backward down the steps. He shook his head once and she froze.

Bonner finished his recitation and looked squarely at George. "Think again, old man. These two are going to pay for their crimes. They're sleeping with your daughters, so I'm sure your interest in their freedom is too personal. There's nothing you can do about it." He turned back to his dark car as Nathan and Patrick were each escorted toward a separate police car.

Janelle watched as the officers closed the back doors of the cars then climbed in the front. She grew weaker as, not having the space to go around George and Nathan's vehicles, the cars made three point turns until they were facing in the other direction. The women's quiet sobbing was uncontrollable as the cars drove away into the night.

Janelle saw movement in the dark and squinted.

Just beyond the border of the light from the porch, she saw a person. Several of them, actually, all holding what looked like cameras in their hands. Her stomach plummeted, and she thought she might be sick when she realized that the arrests had all been captured by the photographers.

"Well, shall we go inside?"

Twenty-Five

Janelle blinked slowly as she recovered the ability to move and turned to face her mother.

"What did you say?" she asked, deliberately pausing between each word.

"We should go inside. It's getting chilly," Mary stated, either ignoring the tautness in Janelle's voice or completely missing it.

Zoe squirmed a little as Janelle narrowed her glare on her mother's calm face. "Is that all you can say? Really? Did you not just see Patrick and Nathan get arrested?"

"Of course I saw it, Janelle. I was standing right here." Mary folded her arms across her chest. "It's refreshing to see Richard finally get some justice."

"Refreshing!" Kelsey's angry steps echoed across the porch as she stormed to Janelle's side, Zach still held tight in her arms, her eyes, cheeks, and nose still red and damp. "You insensitive, uncaring bitch!"

Mary's jaw dropped as she fell back a step.

"Richard got his justice when he took a bullet in the chest," Janelle snapped. "What happened tonight is not justice. Those two men were just arrested for a crime we all know they didn't commit. Aside from Dad, Patrick and Nathan are the most important men in our lives."

"That would be your problem, not mine," Mary snapped.

"Once again, Mother, your concern for our happiness is underwhelming."

"Your happiness?" Mary scoffed. "Janelle, how many times have I told you that if you're unhappy, you have no one to blame but yourself?"

"I'm not sure." Janelle rolled her eyes. "I lost count."

"Don't give me that attitude," Mary snapped. "Your husband is dead, and you continue on as if nothing happened."

"I'm well aware of what happened to *my husband*," Janelle said with a curl of her lip. "How could I forget when you've reminded me of it every time you've visited since he died?"

"Someone has to." Mary glared at Kelsey for a moment then turned her focus back to Janelle. "I feel like I'm the only person in this family who cares that Richard is gone." She narrowed her eyes. "I just want to know if you feel any remorse, Janelle, for driving your husband to the grave at such a young age."

"He did that to himself!" Janelle roared as she took two steps forward.

"Zach, Zoe, please go inside," George said calmly from behind Janelle.

Zoe wriggled to the ground, and Janelle watched her scamper into the house. Kelsey slowly lowered Zach to the floor and he followed his sister, pausing when he reached the door. He turned and looked at his grandmother as he pulled his shoulders back.

"I care that he's gone, Grandma," Zach said softly, and Janelle's heart sank.

She heard Mary's triumphant sniff and turned to see the smirk on her lips.

"I'm glad that we don't have to be afraid of him anymore, and I'm happy to see mommy smile more," he added, and the screen door closed silently.

Janelle watched the glee on her mother's face fade as her eyes widened and her lips curled into a scowl. Kelsey appeared at Janelle's side, and George moved into the group as well, positioning himself against the wall between his daughters and his wife.

Mary's mouth opened and closed, making her look like a fish out of water. "What have you been telling him?" she sputtered when she finally found her voice.

"I haven't needed to tell him anything, Mom," Janelle replied. "Richard took care of Zach's final impressions of him by kidnapping him and shooting Kelsey."

"Or it could be the bruise he left on Zach's arm at Thanksgiving," Kelsey said flippantly.

"True." Janelle nodded at her sister. "Or the broken wrist he left him with in the cabin."

"Excellent point," Kelsey agreed then glared at her mother. "Or the handprint he left on my arm in December. Or the black eye Janelle had when she moved into my house."

"Or any number of the bruises he left on me before we moved out, those could have influenced Zach's opinion of Richard." Janelle folded her arms across her chest and narrowed her eyes on Mary. "Put your blame where it truly lays, Mother, and not on Kelsey or me."

"I told you how to prevent that, did I not?" Mary pulled herself up to her full height, almost eye level with Janelle. "I told you to keep your husband happy and he wouldn't hit you. You chose to ignore my advice, you broke your marriage vows, and you got punished for it."

"What did you just say, Mary?" George stepped away from the wall and stopped beside his wife. "Janelle deserved to be abused by her husband?"

Mary's eyes widened on George's face. She shook her head slightly. "I didn't—"

"Yes, you did," he snapped. "Keep him happy and he won't hit you. Is that what you taught her?"

"I . . ." Mary stuttered.

"Yes," Janelle answered simultaneously. George gave her a dark look, and Janelle shrunk back.

He looked back at Mary and scowled. "Was that your takeaway from your childhood? Did you honestly think your father only hit your mother when she'd done something wrong? How could you be so naïve? Or give our daughter such misguided advice?"

"It was not misguided," Mary snapped. "It's worked for me."

George's face turned red. "It hasn't worked for you. You haven't needed it to work for you. I am *not* your father!"

"I never said you were." Mary fell back a step as she turned her horrified face to her husband.

"You clearly thought it," George barked then turned to Janelle. "And how could you believe her?" Janelle's cheeks warmed as he looked at Kelsey. "Did she tell you the same thing?"

Kelsey looked at her father's feet and bobbed her head.

George was silent for a moment. "Tim?" he asked and Kelsey flinched. "Did you try to use it with him?"

Kelsey nodded again as she looked up at him.

"It's still good advice, she obviously just didn't do it right," Mary argued. "Or we wouldn't be in this mess."

"This is hardly my fault," Kelsey hissed.

"Isn't it?" Mary looked relieved to be able to turn her anger on her youngest child. "If you'd done what you were supposed to do, Richard wouldn't have needed to adopt your son, and everything would have been fine."

"Mary, that's enough!" George bellowed. "I have had it with you letting Richard off the hook. He was responsible for his own actions."

"But, George, dear—"

"No!" His eyes bulged as he glared at his wife. He raised his arm and pinched the bridge of his nose as he took a few deep breaths. "First things first," he said calmly. "Your father was an angry, abusive alcoholic. Your mother feared him. She feared not being perfect for him, but no amount of perfection *ever* spared her from his anger."

"At least she tried," Mary snapped. "Janelle—"

"Is not your mother." George folded his arms across his chest. "But Richard was your father. And no amount of perfection or coddling or surrender from her would have stopped him from drinking."

"You don't—"

"Mary!" George took a step toward her and she stepped back into the rail. "There is never any excuse for a man to hit your daughters. Ever! Is that clear?"

Mary wrapped her arms around her waist and nodded.

George looked at his daughters and frowned. Janelle suddenly felt like she was back in middle school and had to fight the urge to run into the house.

"Didn't you girls realize her advice wasn't sound?" he asked, glaring at each of them in turn.

"Maybe," Kelsey muttered.

Janelle shrugged as she looked at the floor. "As we got older."

"Don't you trust me enough to come to me for help when you need it?" George's feet came into Janelle's vision as his hand reached her chin. He lightly lifted it so she had to look at him. "You should have told me sooner what he was doing."

Janelle's lower lip quivered and her eyes filled with tears. "I'm sorry, Dad. I didn't want to bother you."

"You could never be a bother." George smiled at them both then kissed them each on the forehead. "It's what I'm here for. Always."

Kelsey looped her arm through Janelle's and stepped closer to her as George turned back around to face Mary. She'd been watching him with a mixture of fear and disgust on her face.

"These girls have been through enough following your advice. Unless they come to you, and I don't see why they would, you will not give them anymore of your '*help*.'" George walked two steps toward Mary. "They've had bad experiences, they've learned from them, and their chances at finally finding happiness were just falsely arrested."

"You don't know that," Mary snapped. "Patrick may have very easily pulled the trigger."

"After he saved your grandson's life." George's tone rose in volume and Mary cowered. "And he ended up saving Kelsey's life, too. You forget that Richard was determined to die in that cabin and he very nearly took our daughter and grandson with him. You should be thanking Patrick every day for saving them."

"I will not." Mary pulled her shoulders.

"That's your choice, Mary. But if Kelsey chooses not to allow you in her life, or even into her house, I will back her decision," George said calmly. "The same goes for Janelle if you can't support her relationship with Nathan."

"How can you do that? I'm your wife," Mary whined.

"You leave me no choice." George gripped his hands behind his back. "I have a feeling there is more that I don't know—more that you have kept from me." He looked over his shoulder at Janelle and Kelsey. "More that I will find out over the next few weeks."

Janelle swallowed and nodded her response to her father's command.

"Right now, I'm taking you home and then I'm going to the police station to see what I can do for Patrick and Nathan." He reached out and laid his hand on Mary's back. "Girls, I will keep you posted. Kelsey, you may want to call Patrick's family. Janelle, please call Mason or Nancy. I'll wait for them at the station." He slowly walked Mary down the steps. "Give the kids a kiss from Grandpa."

"We will," Janelle called as she and Kelsey walked to the top step on the porch. She watched George open their mother's car door then close it after she was in the car. He walked around to the driver's side, climbed in, and they were off.

Kelsey turned and went back into the house and Janelle let her gaze rest on Nathan's truck. She hoped it wouldn't have to sit here without its owner for too long. She wasn't sure what she'd do if Nathan had to spend time in prison for Richard's death. It was like a nightmare coming true. She hugged her body against the sudden chill as she turned and followed her sister into the house.

McClane greeted her as she closed the door. She sat on the bottom step and rubbed the dog's head. "He'll be back soon," she cooed to the animal and hoped her words were true.

"Janelle," Kelsey said softly from the top of the stairs.

Janelle looked up and saw the trouble in Kelsey's eyes.

"Could you come up here please?"

Janelle nodded as she rose then slowly climbed the steps. When she'd reached the top, Kelsey put her back to the wall and pointed toward Zach's room. Janelle followed her sister's directions and walked down the hall. When she reached Zach's door, she stopped and looked in on him.

He had his suitcase on the floor and was standing at his dresser, pulling clothes out, and tossing them onto his bed. Janelle frowned slightly at the sight.

"What are you doing?" she asked as she walked into the room.

"Packing," Zach answered as he continued to toss clothes onto the bed.

Janelle walked into the room and moved some of the clothes out of the way so she could sit at the foot of the bed. "Why are you doing that?"

"Don't we have to move?" Zach looked at her, his cheeks damp, his eyes wide with fear.

Janelle shook her head and opened her arms. "No, sweetie," she soothed as he came into her arms and laid his head against her chest. "Why would you think that?"

"We moved here when . . ." he began. Janelle looked down and saw his lips twisted in thought. He looked up at her. "Do I have to call him Dad anymore?"

Janelle's lips lifted slightly and she shook her head. "Do you remember what Andrew told you?"

"To call him what I feel like I should call him," Zach said quietly.

"So, if you don't feel like calling him Dad, you don't need to," Janelle replied as she pulled him onto her lap.

"Good," Zach whispered.

"Why are you packing?" Janelle repeated her earlier question.

"We moved here when . . . *he* was arrested and taken away." Zach began scratching at his jeans. "I just thought we'd have to move since Patrick and Nathan were arrested."

"No, baby." Janelle laid her head on top of his. "This time is different. Richard was dangerous, and we moved out of the house to stay safe. This is Kelsey's house and Nathan and Patrick aren't dangerous." She lifted her head and looked into her son's face. "Are they?" she asked, hoping to make him think about the differences.

Zach's face scrunched but eventually he shook his head. "No, they're superheroes."

Janelle laughed. "I'm sure they'd love to hear you say that." She lightly rocked him back and forth as he scratched at his jeans.

"Will they be home soon?" he asked quietly.

"I hope so."

Twenty-Six

Janelle's eyelids felt heavy as she lifted them. She saw her cell phone sitting on the coffee table in front of her and reached for it. The volume was all the way up so she felt sure she would have heard it if it had rung, but she checked just in case. She blew out a long breath when she saw her father hadn't called or left a message then glanced at the time as she set the phone back on the table. It was only seven thirty. She hoped she could count on the kids being in bed for another hour or so.

She lifted her head and noticed movement out of the corner of her eye. Kelsey was sitting in an armchair, cradling a mug, and staring out of the bay window. "Morning," she muttered as she took a sip from her cup.

Janelle pushed herself up to sit against the arm of the couch so she was facing her sister. "Morning." She pulled the blanket over her legs and covered her yawn with the back of her hand. Janelle noticed the dark circles under Kelsey's eyes. "You didn't sleep well?"

Kelsey yawned then took another sip from her cup. "Hardly at all."

"Coffee?" Janelle pointed to the cup in her sister's hands. Kelsey nodded and Janelle's mouth watered for the bitter brew. She was about to throw her feet over the edge of the couch when she saw Nancy walking toward her from the kitchen, two identical cups in her hand.

Nancy had shown up within an hour of Janelle's phone call the night before. She had been the sisters' shoulder to cry on. She'd helped keep them calm, but in their moments of silence, all three of them had stared at their phones. They'd all been waiting for that phone call from George or from Mason, telling them what was going on at the police station.

That call had never come.

"Kelsey said you like it with a little bit of sugar and a splash of milk," Nancy said as she handed a cup to Janelle.

Janelle nodded and took a sip. The coffee slid down her throat like velvet and she savored the sweet aftertaste on her tongue. "Thank you."

Nancy sat on the other end of the couch, at Janelle's feet. "Did I do it right?" she asked.

"It's perfect," Janelle answered with a smile. "You're here awfully early. Did you go home last night?"

Nancy shook her head and placed her mug on the coffee table. "I thought I'd stay, just in case your dad called you or Mason called me." She gave Janelle a small smile. "Besides, you looked restless and I thought I'd stay close in case you needed something."

Janelle's heart lifted and she felt the urge to cry . . . again. She felt like she'd fluctuated between anger and tears, sometimes angry tears, since Nathan had been arrested. She hated feeling so weak and helpless, but until she knew what was going on, there was nothing she could do.

She blinked her eyes furiously and took a sip of her coffee, hoping the other women wouldn't notice her threatening flood.

There was a knock on the door, and Janelle met Kelsey's eyes over her mug. Kelsey shrugged and Janelle lowered her cup.

"I'll get it." Nancy was on her feet and walking around the couch before Janelle could process what to do next.

Janelle turned to watch Nathan's mother open the door.

"Hi, I'm looking for Kelsey Morgan. I hope this is the right house," came a gentle voice from the other side of the screen door.

"Elizabeth?" Kelsey set her coffee down and jumped to her feet.

The screen door opened and the other woman stepped into the house. Janelle had a vague sense of déjà vu. The woman was wearing jeans, a plain white T-shirt, and a lavender cardigan, her blonde hair was pulled back into a ponytail, but Janelle was sure she'd seen that face before. She looked remarkably like the woman Patrick had taken to the premiere she'd watched with Kelsey in December, just before he and Kelsey had started dating. That woman had been Patrick's sister, and Janelle wondered if she was currently looking at his mother.

"Kelsey, darling," Elizabeth said as she wrapped her arms around Kelsey. "It's so good to see you again."

"What are you doing here?" Kelsey asked as she broke the hug. "You didn't have to come."

"My son is in jail, you need my help, why do you think I'm here?" Elizabeth wiped a tear away from Kelsey's cheek, a very maternal gesture. "I couldn't let you go through this alone, so I came with Mitch, Patrick's lawyer. I dropped him off at the police station and drove myself here. Your father was kind enough to give me the address. He's such a darling man. He reminds me of you." Elizabeth paused in her rapid chatter and smiled widely at Kelsey then turned to Nancy. "Are you her mother then?"

Janelle laughed once and Kelsey's chin dropped slightly as her lips turned up. If only.

"No, I'm Nancy Harris. Nathan's mother." Nancy held her hand out and Elizabeth took it.

"Elizabeth Lyons. It's a pleasure to meet you. Nathan?" Elizabeth's brow wrinkled as she tapped her lower lip with her finger. "He's the one who was arrested with Patrick?" She looked at Kelsey. "Is he still involved with your sister?"

Kelsey nodded and motioned toward Janelle. "This is my sister, Janelle."

"Oh," Elizabeth sighed as she approached Janelle. "You poor dear." She wrapped Janelle in a floral scented hug. "You've been through so much already, and now we have to add this to the pile." Elizabeth pulled away and gripped Janelle's upper arms. "Don't worry." She looked at Kelsey. "Either of you. Mitch is one of the best lawyers we know, and he spent the entire flight brushing up on Virginia law, just in case. Imagine my shock when we found a whole team of lawyers already there."

"My second son is a lawyer, as well as their father," Nancy said after she closed the door. She walked to stand between Janelle and Kelsey so she could face Elizabeth. "Neither of them is defending Patrick or Nathan, better safe than sorry as far as conflict of interest goes, so they each have some of their law partners with them to handle the brunt of the work. Mason and George have taken on more advisory roles so they can keep us updated with what's going on."

Elizabeth's hands fell to her side. "Well then, I'm sure our boys are in great hands." She smiled, but Janelle noticed for the first time how brittle her smile appeared, like if someone poked her in the right place she might shatter.

"You must be tired," Janelle offered. "It's only almost five in the morning in California."

"Yes, Elizabeth," Kelsey stepped forward and took her hand. "We have a spare room upstairs. We can fix it up in a flash if you'd like to lie down."

"Oh, no, dear." Elizabeth shook her head. "I'm exhausted, but I just don't think I can sleep until I know what's going on. Your father said he'd be here soon to explain everything."

"Can I get you a cup of coffee then?" Nancy asked.

"That would be heavenly," Elizabeth replied and Nancy motioned for her to follow, picking up her own cup of coffee on the way.

The two older women walked into the other room, and Kelsey moved closer to Janelle. They watched the mothers of the men they loved in the kitchen, Elizabeth sitting at the island as Nancy flitted around, first pouring a cup of coffee for the newcomer, and then starting a new pot to brew. Janelle felt warmed by the sight. Elizabeth had been a little overwhelming, but Janelle could sense the deep concern she had, not just for Patrick, but for Kelsey as well. It was almost a relief to know that, should things continue to progress with Patrick, Kelsey would finally have a mother who would care about her the way a mother should.

"She's more worried than she wants to let on," Kelsey said as she looped her arm through Janelle's.

"I figured," Janelle murmured.

"Patrick says the more nervous or scared she is, the faster she talks. He said when her father was really sick they had to make her write everything so they could understand what she was trying to say." Kelsey said tenderly. "He said it . . ."

Janelle looked at her sister's face when she choked on the words. Tears slithered down Kelsey's cheek, and Janelle pulled her arm free from her grip so she could put it around her shoulder.

"They'll get off, Kels." Janelle kissed her sister's temple and lowered her lids against the sting in her own eyes. "They didn't do anything wrong."

"Somebody thinks they did," Kelsey sniffled and stepped away from

Janelle. She turned her back on the kitchen and wiped her face with her fingertips.

"Somebody is wrong," Janelle said softly.

"Does that really matter anymore?" Kelsey walked toward the large bay window and sat on the edge of the window seat. "When this gets out, what will this do to his reputation? Never mind that he did what he did to save Zach's life."

Janelle waited for her to continue, surprised when she didn't. "And yours," Janelle added for her as she sat on the seat, facing her sister.

Kelsey pressed her lips together. "Yes, and mine," she agreed softly. "I should have known better than to put myself in that situation. He never should have had to follow me. He shouldn't have risked his life for me."

"Kels." Janelle took Kelsey's hands and squeezed. "He loves you. He would do anything for you."

Kelsey looked at their clasped hands. Her brow crinkled and her jaw tightened. "Do you realize that we only met eleven months ago? We really only started to get to know each other just over seven months ago. And, without being asked, he risked his life for me and for Zach and scared me in the process." Her voice cracked, and Janelle watched her throat bob up and down. "Eleven months, Janelle, and I can't imagine my life without him in it." Kelsey met her sister's gaze and frowned. "It's terrifying and exhilarating at the same time. I was terrified he'd wise up and not come back, and when I was in his arms last night, the high was so high I thought I could touch the moon."

Janelle smiled softly. "I haven't seen you that happy in a long time."

"I haven't felt that happy since he left," Kelsey agreed and began to shake her head. "And now he's in jail for his good deeds. He could go to prison, and I don't know what I'll do without him."

Janelle pulled her sister into her arms and hugged her tightly. "I know exactly what you mean," she murmured, and Kelsey slid her arms around Janelle. "I've known Nathan practically our whole lives, but I'd never realized how much he meant to me until we were separated. I always took him for granted until he wasn't there anymore."

Until he'd come back into her life, she hadn't realized how lost she was without him. Sure, she'd been able to manage everything, taking Zach to therapy, helping Zoe through the day-to-day, dealing with Kelsey's mood swings, and even handling her mother. But when Nathan was there, things seemed easier.

He took some of the burden from her. He would play with the kids so she and Kelsey could chat. He'd stay and help Kelsey with Zoe while she and Zach were at therapy. He'd stood up to her mother. Just knowing she could count on him, without having to ask him, had made the past few weeks go much smoother than the weeks immediately after Richard's death.

"I'm not sure I want to think about him being gone again, Kels." Janelle had always had a little comfort before, knowing that if she really needed him, she could pick up the phone. If he ended up in prison with Patrick, that wouldn't be an option.

Kelsey sat up and narrowed her eyes out the window. "Dad's here."

Janelle felt a chill run down her spine.

Twenty-Seven

Janelle reached the front door as George and Mary climbed the last step onto the porch. Her father looked ragged, his five o'clock shadow was thick, and he was wearing the same clothes as the night before. He met her gaze and his frown deepened as they approached her.

"May we come in?" he asked as they came to a stop in front of Janelle.

Janelle stepped aside to let them in. She closed the door and leaned against it as she surveyed the scene in front of her. Kelsey remained in the window seat; Elizabeth had replaced Janelle beside her. Nancy stood against a column that separated the kitchen from the foyer. George and Mary had stopped in the middle of the foyer; Mary had her head down, her arms folded across her stomach.

"Can I get either of you coffee?" Nancy asked.

"Yes, please," George answered and turned to Mary. She nodded and he looked at Nancy. "For both of us."

Nancy turned and took a step toward the kitchen.

"Actually, could you take it into the dining room for us, Nancy?" George added. "I think we should all just gather in there."

Kelsey met Janelle's gaze and slowly rose from her seat as George led Mary into the dining room. Janelle walked around the couch and picked her cup up from the coffee table as Kelsey did the same, then followed Kelsey and Elizabeth into the dining room.

Nancy had already placed the pot of coffee in the center of the table, along with the sugar and milk. George was standing behind his usual chair at the head of the table while Mary was sitting in the seat to his right. Elizabeth took the seat beside Kelsey, and Nancy stood behind the chair next to Janelle. Once everyone was settled around the table, George looked at each of the women in turn, took a deep breath, and gripped the back of his chair.

"I've had a look at the evidence and, as much as I hate to say it, it doesn't look good for the boys," he began.

Kelsey gasped and Nancy slowly lowered herself into the chair.

"What I've seen is very damning to them. Mason, Mitch, our partners, and I have all discussed it. Given the evidence being presented, not only does Patrick look guilty, but it looks like he and Nathan may have been planning this for some time," George continued. His gaze landed on Janelle. "They're both looking at prison time if they're convicted, but what's worse is that even if we can get the charges dropped, Nathan's career is now in jeopardy, simply because he was arrested."

Janelle's exhale was shaky as she dropped her head to the table. She felt a comforting hand on each of her shoulders, each rubbing in small circles.

"So, they planned for Richard to kidnap Zach and shoot me simply so they'd have an excuse to kill him?" Kelsey said. "Who is stupid enough to believe that?"

"Maybe not that exact scenario, Kelsey," George said softly. "But it has been suggested that they were trying to come up with something and the opportunity happened to present itself."

"That's bullshit," Kelsey snapped.

"Kelsey." George's voice held the reprimanding tone that Janelle associated with his glare. She imagined the petulant look on her sister's face and couldn't help but smile a little.

Janelle lifted her head and looked at him. "Can you tell us what the evidence is?"

"You know I'm not supposed to," he replied. "But given that I'm not technically on the case, I will. Maybe you ladies can come up with something to help them that we haven't thought of already."

"It couldn't hurt to try," Nancy said as she wrung the paper towel in her hands. Janelle reached across and took her hand. She gave it a light squeeze and held onto it as she looked back at her father.

"There's a photo of Patrick and Nathan at a shooting range, and they appear to be taking practice shots with the murder weapon." George picked up his cup of coffee and looked around the table.

"That's impossible," Janelle stated.

"How so?" George asked.

"Dad, you know that the gun Richard had, the one that killed him, was at his house." Janelle looked at Kelsey whose eyes widened as her head bobbed. "I told the detectives that when they had me in for questioning."

George nodded. "That's true, you did say that."

"Plus, the only time they've been to a shooting range together was after Richard died, and then the gun was in the evidence room at the station," Kelsey added.

"You know this for sure?" George's manner took Janelle back to high school, when he'd make up cases and encourage all of his children to ask questions until they could come to the conclusions he had come up with, or make a good case for a different one. She could almost feel nostalgic if it weren't such a serious, and real, case they were discussing.

"Yes," Kelsey said. "Isn't there a time stamp or something on the picture?"

"Not that I noticed," George answered.

"That should be easy enough to find. I'm surprised Mitch didn't tell you that already," Elizabeth said calmly, and every eye turned to her. "Patrick has had Mitch on retainer for the last five years. He works with a lot of celebrities, and a lot of the cases he deals with have to do with doctored photos that are used to slander his clients. He has an entire team of people that should be able to help him examine the photo and at least determine if it's been altered."

George nodded his head and took a sip of coffee. "Excellent."

"What else?" Janelle asked as her father met her gaze.

"There's an audio recording of a conversation between the two of them. Basically the gist of the conversation is that they're congratulating each other on the fact that Richard is dead," George answered, and several jaws dropped and disgusted sounds were made. George held up his hand to silence the women. "It sounded choppy, so Mitch is already looking into seeing if it has been manipulated in any way. I can't believe either of them would say the things I heard them say on the tape."

Kelsey's jaw clenched as she looked up at her father. "Is that all they have, Daddy?"

"I'm afraid not. There's the issue of the coroner's report." He shook his head and set his cup on the table. He gripped the back of his chair again and looked at Kelsey. "I'm afraid that the report shows that the trajectory of the bullet is indicative of being fired at close range."

"Of course," Kelsey said with a shudder. "I saw it happen. They were fairly close together. I thought Patrick had been shot from the way they both went still." She looked down at her lap and closed her eyes. Elizabeth slid her chair closer and placed her hand on Kelsey's shoulder.

Janelle glanced at her mother. She was surprised to see Mary watching Elizabeth comfort Kelsey with a look of awe and surprise. Mary turned and met Janelle's gaze then quickly looked away. In that brief moment, Janelle saw something she'd never seen in her mother before.

Vulnerability.

Her world tipped slightly and she focused on her mug until it leveled out again.

"I'm afraid it's not that simple. The bullet entered Richard's chest at an angle that suggests he wasn't the one with his finger on the trigger." George took a step toward Kelsey and laid his hand on her shoulder. "It's possible that the gun was actually in Patrick's hand when it was fired."

Kelsey shook her head and her bottom lip quivered. Her eyes wandered aimlessly around the room, never really focusing on anything as her shaking slowly changed to a nod. "So what," she spat.

Janelle looked at Mary, expecting her to respond in some way. Her mother sat with her hands in her lap and her eyes on the table, showing no indication that she'd heard her daughter.

"What Patrick did in that cabin that night he did to save Zach. And if he hadn't been there, I would have bled to death on the floor as I watched it all happen." Kelsey's lip trembled furiously but she continued. "Richard was determined to die that night and if it wasn't by his own hand, I'm glad someone did it."

George bent over and placed a kiss to the top of Kelsey's head then stood and moved back to his chair. Elizabeth pulled Kelsey's head onto her shoulder as tears rolled down both sets of cheeks.

"I'm just sorry he's in jail for it," Kelsey muttered softly.

"I know, sweetie," Elizabeth cooed. "We all are. But at least you and Zach are alive."

Janelle looked at her mother again and frowned. Mary's head was down, but her eyes were glued to the scene across the table from her as she nonchalantly wiped the moisture from her cheek.

"Kelsey, you are not alone in your sentiment, but I'm afraid that doesn't help Patrick's case." George met Janelle's stare across the length of the table. "And that's where the case against Nathan comes in."

Janelle filled her lungs as she lifted her shoulders. "How so?"

"Nathan failed to fingerprint Patrick and check for gun residue on his hands at the cabin. And then he let him leave with your sister," George answered.

Janelle lifted her shoulder. "So? There were other officers there, any one of them could have done that and they didn't."

"Yes, but Nathan was first on the scene and led the others into the house. He was also the first to examine the body, which lends itself to the idea that he may have been checking that Patrick had finished the job." George held his palms up as Janelle opened her mouth to protest. "I'm not saying he was. I'm just saying that's how the evidence is being presented."

"I think someone needs a better presentation," Janelle grumbled and Nancy squeezed her fingers. "If that's all they have, I'm not sure why they've arrested him as an accomplice. The picture and audio can be discredited, Patrick was justified if he actually did pull the trigger, and everything else is circumstantial and rather assumptive."

George nodded. "True, and I wish that were it. There's a journal of Nathan's that shows his written desire to see Richard out of the picture so the two of you could be together, and there are also pictures of the two of you together on your front porch. Embracing, in the rain. Again, no time stamp, so we can't be sure when it was taken, but the argument is that it was before Richard's death and proof that the affair was still going on."

"That picture was taken two weeks ago," Janelle snapped then did the math in her head. "Or three, I don't remember. It was just before Zoe's party."

"Mitch will get to the bottom of that, dear," Elizabeth stated, turning to look at Janelle as she continued to comfort Kelsey. She looked back at George. "Is that everything?"

"That's all we've been allowed to see," he answered.

"Have you spoken with the boys about this evidence?" Nancy asked.

"We're not allowed to," George said. "You know they can't see it until after the arraignment."

"When will that be?" Nancy questioned.

"Monday morning." George picked up his coffee cup and tipped it back.

"Monday!" Kelsey shouted as she lifted her head. "They have to sit in jail all weekend? Can we see them?"

"No."

Janelle's heart sank at her father's one-word answer. Two more days until she could see Nathan again. Two more days without being in his arms, without him in her bed. She felt like a part of her was locked up with him and she wouldn't be whole again for two more days.

It may as well be an eternity. And, from the way it sounded, it just might be.

"There has to be something you can do, Dad," Janelle said as she rose to her feet. She slid her chair across the floor and stepped around it. "There has to be something they're missing." She began to pace behind her chair.

"Janelle, I wish there was. I've seen everything myself, and if I didn't know these boys personally, I may have come to the same conclusions," George stated. "Unless someone comes forth with new evidence between now and Monday, then Patrick and Nathan will go to trial for Richard's murder and it won't be pretty."

"Who's the detective assigned to the case?" Nancy asked.

"Reginald Bonner," George answered and Nancy paled. "Is that a problem?" George came around the table and stopped at her side.

"It's hard to tell, really. John didn't like working with him, he said he cut corners," Nancy answered. "Said that Reginald had a tendency of forming a conclusion and shaping the evidence around it."

"That's not good," George murmured, practically silently.

"Because Reginald and John didn't get along, he's never been fond of Nathan either. I'm not saying that he has nitpicked the evidence, but there is the possibility," Nancy said in a small voice. "I should have asked Nathan who was on this case. But I never could have imagined this outcome."

"What about his partner?" Mary asked, her first words of the morning and Janelle stopped pacing to look at her. "The younger detective. He seemed like such a nice boy."

Janelle looked at Kelsey, who was staring at their mother with a curious look on her face.

"How do you know what Detective Bonner's partner was like?" Kelsey asked as her eyes narrowed slightly.

"They did question me," Mary answered.

"They questioned me too, but I vaguely remember the detectives." Kelsey sat up in her chair. "And I certainly don't remember that one of them was 'younger' and a 'nice boy.'"

"I was interrogated too, but he doesn't stand out for me either," Janelle added.

"We were Richard's family, girls. We were all questioned." George moved to stand behind his wife. "It doesn't mean anything that your mother remembers the younger detective."

"Hayes," Mary said with a grin. "That was his name."

"Thomas Hayes?" Nancy asked.

"I guess," Mary replied. "Maybe he has other evidence that Detective Bonner didn't include."

"Detective Bonner is the senior officer. He would have included everything in his report," George said.

"But what if he didn't?" Mary turned in her chair to look at George. "What if he left something out?"

"Mother," Janelle said slowly as she began to walk toward Mary. "What are you suggesting?"

"And better yet, why do you sound so confident suggesting it?" Kelsey added. She laid her forearms on the table and leaned across them. "How many times did you talk to the detectives?"

"I . . . I'm . . . I don't remember," Mary answered.

"More than once?" George asked as he took a step back from her chair.

Mary nodded. "Well, after the first interview, they told me if I could remember anything else, to give them a call."

George's eyes widened and Mary shrank away from him.

"So I did," she finished in a small voice.

"What did you tell them?" Kelsey jumped to her feet and flattened her hands on the table. "Did you suggest that Patrick was capable of killing Richard?"

Mary opened and closed her mouth repeatedly. "I . . . it may . . . I didn't use those words."

Janelle saw red and turned on her heel and stormed out of the room. She heard footsteps behind her and turned to find Nancy had followed her. Janelle's jaw clenched and unclenched as she looked over Nancy's shoulder and into the dining room. Kelsey was on her feet and had started around the table.

"Fix this!" she shouted at Mary, her shaky finger pointing at their mother.

"Kelsey!" Janelle stomped back into the dining room.

"I don't know how," Mary said softly.

"Figure it out, Mother, or so help me you will never set foot in this house again!" Kelsey roared. "Get out."

"Kelsey," George said, approaching his daughter with his palms up. "I'm sure your mother didn't do any of this on purpose."

"I'm sure she did," Kelsey growled. "She's hated Patrick ever since he came here in December and Nathan since I called him and had Richard arrested. She knew exactly what she was doing."

Janelle watched her mother's face crumple under Kelsey's accusations. What was going on? Her mother never crumpled. When Kelsey fought back, Mary's stubbornness always won out. Who was this woman in front of her?

"I'm sorry, Kelsey." Mary's voice quaked as she slowly stood. She looked at Janelle. "I'm sorry," she said again.

"Get. Out." Kelsey repeated through clenched teeth.

Mary looked down as she walked out of the dining room, straight through the living room, and out the front door.

"Kelsey, that was uncalled for," George reprimanded. "I know you're angry, but you don't need to take it out on her."

Kelsey glared at her father and Janelle fell back a step. She was actually glaring at their father.

"I mean it, Dad. If he goes to prison because of anything she said, she will not set foot in my house again."

George nodded and wrapped her in a hug anyway. He quickly kissed her forehead and said his goodbyes to Elizabeth and Nancy as he walked toward

Janelle. She looped her arm through her father's and walked with him to the front door.

"Try to talk her down, please. I think your mother's still a little sensitive from the episode on the porch last night," George said as they strolled. Janelle nodded and he continued, "I will call you if we find anything that might be helpful. Otherwise, the arraignment is on Monday morning at eight o'clock. You can come, but don't be late."

"We'll be there," Janelle said as she pecked her father on the cheek. "As for Kelsey, I can't make any promises."

"I know." He frowned for a moment before kissing Janelle's temple and walking out the front door.

Twenty-Eight

At seven forty-five on Monday morning, Janelle, Kelsey, Nancy, and Elizabeth walked into the courtroom. Charlotte had shown up with James to watch the children at seven, and the other women had left almost immediately. George, Mason, and Mary were seated in the second row of seats on their left. Janelle led her party to the row in front of them, and Elizabeth was the first to slide in. Kelsey and Janelle followed, Nancy sat on the end.

There had been no new developments since the meeting with her father on Saturday morning, so Janelle had not seen her parents since they'd left that morning. Since then, the mood in her home had been somber and quiet. Kelsey had taken comfort in keeping herself busy in the kitchen, something Janelle had almost forgotten her sister was prone to, and baked eight dozen cookies, at least, that no one had been in the mood to eat. Nancy had left long enough to pack a bag, but had returned to stay with them, sleeping on the sofa in the office. Elizabeth had been given the spare bedroom upstairs.

The kids had enjoyed having the older women around, but even they had been more subdued since the arrest. They'd spent more time cuddling and sitting in laps reading than Janelle had ever remembered them doing before. She was slightly saddened that her parents and Nathan weren't there to enjoy the children's snuggly behavior. And as much as she'd enjoyed it, she was looking forward to their exuberance returning and only hoped Nathan and Patrick could come home after this arraignment hearing.

Nancy was turned slightly, having a quiet conversation with Mason in the seat behind her. Janelle shifted so she could see her parents behind her. Mary's expression was somber; her red-rimmed eyes had large dark circles under them. George had his arm around her, his hand sliding up and down her arm as he held her. He met Janelle's stare and bobbed his head. Janelle dipped her head in return and turned back around. As she did, she caught a glimpse of Gladys and Martha Wagoner on the other side of the room, both dressed in black with matching scowls on their faces as they glared at her. Janelle fidgeted uncomfortably in her seat as she continued to turn toward the front of the courtroom.

It wasn't long before four men came down the aisle and took their places behind their tables. The sternest looking of the bunch sat down behind the table to her right. Janelle recognized him as the local prosecutor. The other three men sat down at the table in front of her. She assumed they were Patrick and Nathan's lawyers.

The door to the side of the courtroom opened up. An officer stepped through first, followed by Nathan and Patrick, both in handcuffs, and then a second officer. They were led to the table with their defense attorneys, who had risen to meet them. Nathan met Janelle's gaze, and her heart skipped a beat as tears sprang to her eyes.

His hazel eyes looked angry under his thick brows. She followed the line of his nose and saw his lips were pressed tightly together, his cleanly shaven jaw clenched. He shouldn't be here, not on this side of the law. She shifted her focus to his attire instead. His suit was dark blue, and his green-and-blue striped tie stood out against the contrast of his clean white shirt. The knot was crooked. She made the motion to stand so she could straighten it for him.

Nancy's hand gripped her arm, and Janelle looked into Nathan's eyes again. He shook his head and she sat back. Janelle clasped her hands together in her lap and stared at them, focusing on her breathing instead of where they were. And why.

"All rise," the bailiff called out and everyone did. "The Circuit Court for the County of Braxton is in session, the Honorable Judge Fraser presiding."

Judge Fraser, an older, balding, and kind-looking man dressed in a long black robe, walked into the room and took his seat at the bench in the front of the courtroom. "I hope everyone is well this morning," he said dryly as he shuffled through the papers in front of him. "Shall we begin?"

"Please be seated," the bailiff announced, and everyone in the crowd sat. The people behind the defendant's table and the prosecutor remained on their feet.

The judge looked at the prosecutor and slowly let his eyes survey his domain. His head jerked slightly when he saw Nathan, and he looked back at the papers in front of him. He motioned his bailiff over, and they held a brief whispered conference. The bailiff nodded and stepped back to his position beside the bench, and Judge Fraser shook his head.

"We are here this morning for the bond hearing and arraignment of Patrick Alexander Lyons and Nathan James Harris. The charges are different, so I will read them each individually and then ask you to enter your plea. Is that understood?"

The judge looked at each of them in turn and they each answered, "Yes, Your Honor."

"Patrick Alexander Lyons, you are charged with involuntary manslaughter in the death of Richard Montgomery Wagoner, on the evening of March twelfth in the County of Braxton, Virginia," Judge Fraser began, and Janelle heard a chair behind her move, followed by the whispering voices of her father and Mason. She saw Nathan and Patrick's lawyers also whispering amongst themselves and felt a frisson of apprehension go through her. The judge continued, "If convicted, this charge comes with a minimum of one year to ten years in prison, pending evidence presented during the trial."

Kelsey whimpered slightly and Janelle took her hand.

"Mr. Lyons, do you understand these charges as they have been presented to you?" Judge Fraser asked.

"I do, Your Honor," Patrick, stoic in his black suit, answered with a nod.

"Then how do you plead?" the judge asked.

A chair behind her scraped against the floor, and Janelle felt the vibration in her seat.

"They're not guilty, Your Honor. You have to drop these charges against them. I made a mistake. There's more evidence that proves their innocence," Mary called out.

Kelsey's grip tightened painfully around Janelle's hand. Janelle turned to see her mother approaching the bar in the middle of the room. Janelle saw both Nathan and Patrick's shoulders stiffen, but they remained facing forward.

"They didn't do anything. I gave Richard the key to Janelle's house, but I didn't know what he was going to do with it," Mary confessed, and Janelle's blood chilled in her veins.

Her mind flashed to the memory of Zach playing with puppets in therapy. The conversation he'd acted out, the one she'd never seen, when Mary's puppet had handed something to Richard's puppet.

Nathan had been right.

"Ma'am, this is simply an arraignment hearing," the kindly judge said sharply. "This evidence can, and should, be presented in a more orderly fashion during the trial."

"This shouldn't go to trial," Mary screeched and lifted her arm, pointing her finger. "He found out I'd given Richard the key, and he asked me to help him. He told me it would keep me out of trouble if I helped him get these two arrested. I can prove it."

"Who did?" Judge Fraser questioned as George and Mason both stepped to Mary's side.

George took his wife's arm and started to tug on it.

"Officer Bonner. He was leading the investigation. He wanted them to go down so he could get his promotion," Mary continued as she tried to escape her husband's grip.

"She's insane," Detective Bonner roared from his seat behind the prosecutor. He was on his feet and moving toward Mary. The fire in his eyes pushed Janelle out of her seat as well, afraid for her mother's safety.

"She's not, Your Honor," came a smaller, but still authoritative, voice from the back of the room. "I worked with him on the case. There is no reason for those two men to be standing here in front of you."

Janelle turned and saw Detective Hayes walking up the aisle, his focus on the front of the courtroom. Flame and ice warred within Janelle, and she wasn't sure where she should focus. She saw her mother, pale and shaking as she stood at the rail, her eyes pleading and remorseful as her vision bounced from Nathan and Patrick to George to the judge. George was beside her, his hand still on her arm, his arm around her back as he tried to pull her away. Bonner was being held away from Mary by Mason's hand on his chest as another uniformed officer suddenly appeared to help. Hayes stopped directly in front of Janelle to whisper something to the lawyers.

Through the group of men, she met Nathan's gaze, his brow wrinkled in concern as he stared at her. His face began to swim in her vision, and he made a move toward her.

"Janelle!" a feminine voice called as her legs gave out and everything started to go black.

"Easy does it," said another voice as arms crisscrossed across her back, easing her into the seat. "If you faint, we'll have to leave."

Janelle nodded as Nancy's words came into focus. She concentrated on inhaling slowly and deeply into her lungs through her nose, then just as deliberately blowing the air out again. Once she regained her equilibrium, she looked at Nathan's mother. "I'm okay."

"Here, eat this," Kelsey said as she slid a chocolate chip cookie into her hand. "It'll help put color back into your cheeks."

"Thanks," Janelle said as she took a bite.

The judge's gavel pounded on the bench, and the room grew silent. "Is she alright?" he called out, and Janelle closed her eyes as her cheeks suddenly warmed.

"She's fine, Your Honor. Thank you," Nancy answered calmly.

"Now, can I have order in my courtroom?" Judge Fraser demanded. His glare grazed Detective Bonner's face, and the officer who held him by the arm, before traveling to the prosecutor. "Are you certain that you reached the correct conclusion from the evidence you collected?"

"Absolutely," Bonner snapped, his eyes narrowed on Detective Hayes.

"Yes, Your Honor." The prosecutor glowered at Bonner as his nasally voice carried toward the judge. "I reviewed Detective Bonner's evidence myself and agreed that his findings indicated that these men were guilty for the death of Mr. Wagoner."

Judge Fraser focused on Detective Hayes. "And are you certain in the conclusion reached?"

"No, Your Honor." Detective Hayes shook his head, and Officer Bonner grumbled loudly.

"Bailiff, please escort Detective Bonner out of my courtroom," the judge said without looking at the officer of the court. "Mr. Lyons, how do you plead?"

"Not guilty, Your Honor," Patrick replied.

"You and your co-defendant may be seated. I'd like for your defense team and the prosecutor to approach the bench," Judge Fraser said.

Patrick and Nathan sat as their lawyers did as they were asked. Nathan turned in his seat and leaned toward the rail, his eyes on Janelle's face.

"Are you okay?" he asked in a soft voice.

She took another bite of the cookie and bobbed her head. "I think so."

He nodded and sat up as he turned around in his seat. His lawyers returned after their brief conference with the judge, and Janelle strained to hear what was being said. Nancy stood and walked to Mason's side. A few minutes later, she returned to her seat as the conversation in front of her continued between her father, Mason, and the other lawyers. Mary and Detective Hayes were in their midst, and Patrick and Nathan had turned in their chairs to participate as well.

Janelle turned to Nancy. "What's happening with the hearing?"

Nancy pointed to the large gathering in front of them and said, "The judge gave them," she pointed to the large gathering in front of them, "five minutes to figure out what they want to do next." Nancy then motioned toward the prosecutor. "Of course he is not willing to drop any of the charges until he sees all of the evidence for himself. So, the charges against Nathan will still have to be read and bail set. But with any luck, all the charges will be dropped sooner rather than later."

Janelle looked at the prosecutor, who looked as if he'd been sucking on a bushel of lemons as he watched the defense team in their discussion. She glanced around the courtroom and saw Martha's and Gladys's sour expressions had not improved, but their disdain was now directed at the defense table.

"I can't believe her," Kelsey muttered under her breath as she bent closer to Janelle. Janelle wore her question on her face as she turned to her sister, and Kelsey pointed to their mother. "She had to do this here? Now?"

Janelle tried not to smile. "Your dramatic streak had to come from somewhere."

"Ha, ha." Kelsey's upper lip curled as her eyes narrowed on Janelle. "But that's not what I mean."

"What do you mean, then?" Janelle finished the cookie and held her hand out. Kelsey pulled another one out of the Ziploc bag in her purse and placed it in Janelle's palm.

"They sat in jail all weekend. She couldn't have gone to the police sooner and made her confession? We could have avoided this circus." Without looking, Kelsey waved her hand over her shoulder toward the back of the room. Janelle turned slightly and noticed, for the first time, that the back row was sprinkled with photographers. "And, yes, I'm fairly certain that at least one of them caught your graceful near-fall on film." Her lips pressed together. "Or whatever they use."

Janelle bit into the second cookie and chewed slowly. "At least she confessed."

Kelsey glared at Janelle in a way that told Janelle her sister disagreed with her assessment. "We'll see if it does any good."

The powwow broke up, and the party behind the defendant's table turned to face the judge.

"Are you ready?" Judge Fraser asked the table in general.

One of the lawyers nodded, "We are."

"I'm going to read the charges against Mr. Harris so that I can assign bail for the two of them. Is that understood?" the judge questioned, and again the lawyer answered in the affirmative. "Good, let's get this over with. Nathan James Harris, you are charged with accessory after the fact to involuntary manslaughter in the death of Richard Montgomery Wagoner, on the evening of March twelfth in the County of Braxton, Virginia. If convicted, this charge comes with a minimum of one year to ten years in prison, pending evidence presented during the trial and the severity of your involvement. Mr. Harris, do you understand these charges as they have been presented to you?"

"I do, Your Honor," Nathan answered with a nod.

"Then how do you plead?" Judge Fraser asked.

"Not guilty, Your Honor."

"Good. Given that this is the first charge against either of you, I'm setting bail at one hundred thousand dollars each. You will be released from jail upon receipt of the money." The judge stood and picked up his gavel. "This hearing is adjourned." He hit the gavel against his bench and turned to leave.

"All rise," the bailiff called out again, and everyone not already standing came to their feet as the judge left the room.

Once his door was closed, the handcuffs were removed from Nathan and Patrick's wrists as their lawyers moved toward the prosecutor's table. Before the key was out of Patrick's cuffs, Kelsey had closed the distance between them and leapt into his open arms, the railing still between them. Elizabeth was close behind her.

"Are you okay?" Nancy asked, and Janelle looked at her outstretched hand.

Despite her weak knees, Janelle took it and gave Nancy's hand a reassuring squeeze. "I'm good," she murmured as Nancy released her hand and walked toward Nathan. Janelle took the three steps at a slower pace to give mother and son time for a brief reunion.

When she was by Nancy's side, Nathan snaked his hand into hers and tugged her closer. He kissed her temple as he released her hand and slid his arm around her waist. "Are you sure you're okay? You still look pale."

Janelle laid her hand on his chest and felt giddy at the feel of his heartbeat under her palm. "Much better now."

"Don't scare me like that again," he muttered against her hair.

Mason joined them, shook hands with both Patrick and Nathan, and put his arm around his mother's shoulders. "I hate to break up the party, but we need to go get bail taken care of so they can go home."

"Home," Kelsey repeated on a sigh.

"Can we wait for them?" Janelle asked, not sure she wanted to let Nathan out of her sight again. Ever.

"No," Nathan answered softly. "You go home, get some rest, and we'll be home as soon as we can. I want to know what's going on with the prosecutor first then run home and get some clothes."

Janelle met his gaze and nearly melted at the heat in his eyes. The gold nearly sparkled in the dark brown. She tried not to smile as she nodded her agreement, both to his request and his suggestion. She planted a quick kiss on his cheek.

"Don't be long," she said as she stepped away. Nancy and Elizabeth followed suit, but Kelsey gave Patrick a long kiss before she joined them.

Mason led Nathan and Patrick in one direction as Janelle led the women out of the building.

Twenty-Nine

"What did the prosecutor say?" Nancy Harris asked Nathan as he took another cookie from the plate before he passed it to his mother. The first one had been confiscated by his daughter, sitting in his lap, before he could get it to his mouth. Janelle had watched the interaction with a warm, fuzzy feeling in her chest. Especially when he'd simply kissed Zoe's forehead before he'd reached for that second cookie.

They'd just finished eating lunch and were all seated around the dining room table. Patrick was at the head of the table with Zach on one knee and Kelsey on the other. She'd planted herself there after bringing the plate of cookies into the room, but before that, she'd been by his side. Mason sat to his left, Charlotte beside him, a sleeping James in her lap. Nancy was beside her, and Nathan sat at the foot of the table. Janelle was in the chair beside him with Elizabeth beside her. McClane was curled up under the table at Nathan's feet.

Mason looked at his mother. "He wants to meet with the defense team tomorrow morning at eight twenty-two sharp. If they're not there, he won't even consider the evidence until he has to look at it for the trial."

Janelle swallowed and a chill ran through her. "Eight twenty-two? Why such an odd time?"

Mason's lip turned up slightly. "He's just trying to be difficult. But don't worry, they won't be late."

"They better not be," Kelsey muttered as she pushed the plate of cookies toward the middle of the table. Patrick kissed her cheek, and she turned to press her forehead to his.

"What happens after that?" Janelle questioned, focusing on Mason as

Nathan's hand gripped hers on the table. She gave it a reassuring squeeze, delighting in the feel of his fingers in hers.

"Hopefully he'll have someone look at the new evidence and get back to us with a decision," Mason answered.

Kelsey shifted her attention to Mason. "How long might that take, and what could his decision be?"

"It could be as little as three days, it could be as long as three weeks. It all depends on how much evidence there is and what kind of hurry he's in." Mason frowned slightly. "He could decide to continue on to the trial and let the lawyers present the evidence in Patrick and Nathan's defense. Or he could decide to drop the charges entirely."

"I vote for that," Kelsey murmured dryly.

"There may be a loophole, though," Mason continued slowly. Nathan and Patrick both sat up in their chairs and gave Mason their full attention.

"What is it?" Nathan asked.

"When Judge Fraser read the charges, Patrick was charged with involuntary manslaughter," Mason answered. He looked at Patrick and Kelsey then at Nathan and Janelle. No one spoke as they waited for him to continue. "The evidence that we've seen shows that Bonner was trying to paint an entirely different picture. He was trying to show that Nathan and Patrick conspired together *before* Richard's death."

Janelle sat up straighter in her chair and her eyes widened. "That would mean that it was voluntary and the charges are wrong."

"Possibly," Mason replied as he held up his hand. "We're going to look into that. But if the prosecutor decides to pursue this as involuntary manslaughter and he fails to get a conviction—"

"Patrick can't be tried again," Kelsey said excitedly. "That would be double jeopardy."

"Bingo," Mason said with a slight grin.

"But what would that do for Nathan?" Charlotte asked.

"They charged him with accessory after the fact, but are trying to prove collaboration beforehand," Janelle answered, looking to Mason for confirmation. He nodded and she continued, "So if this goes to trial and he's not convicted, then the same would hold true for him. He couldn't be re-tried due to the Double Jeopardy Clause."

"Your father taught you well." Mason tilted back in his chair and clasped his hands behind his head. "Both your father's team and mine are looking into it to make sure our butts are covered, but that could be our way out of this."

"That's only provided we don't get found guilty," Nathan said softly as he released Janelle's hand. He shifted Zoe, and her daughter's arm fell limply between their bodies.

Janelle peeked at Zoe's sleeping face and smiled sympathetically at Nathan. When Zoe was asleep, her body became a personal space heater. Nathan probably wouldn't expect that. She held her hands out, offering to take the child, but Nathan shook his head as he turned his somber expression back to his brother.

"George said the evidence looked pretty bad. He didn't seem to think we could get out of this," Nathan stated.

"We don't know what the new evidence is. With any luck, like Detective Hayes suggested, it will contradict most of what Bonner presented when he went for your warrant," Mason answered and looked at his watch. "And I suppose I should head into the office so I can get a look at it and report back to you all."

He stood up and turned to Charlotte. "We'll come too," she said. She looked at Patrick and then Nathan. "It's good to have you both home again. I'm sure this will all work out for the best."

"I'm sure it will too," Elizabeth agreed.

Nathan rolled over and watched Janelle sleep beside him. It was two in the morning and he'd hardly slept at all in the last three days, he was tired, but his mind wouldn't stop. He gave up and crawled out of bed as gently as he could, picked up his underwear and jeans, and put them on as he walked toward the bedroom door. He tiptoed down the steps, through the living room and kitchen, and slipped out the side door onto the porch.

He sat down in the hammock swing in the corner and looked out across the dark backyard and into the woods beyond. He couldn't stop thinking about Friday night, when he was arrested by officers he'd worked closely with on more than one occasion. He'd dedicated his life to the police force, and more recently to keeping women and children safe from abusive family members. It was one thing to know that he hadn't been able to keep Zach safe from Richard, but to have his coworkers believe that he could have had a hand in Richard's death left him feeling slightly numb.

"There you are," said a sleepy voice behind him as a small hand slid from his shoulder to his chest. Janelle gave him a lingering kiss on the cheek, and a little of his tension drained away.

"Hey," he replied a little hoarsely.

"You had me worried." Janelle walked around him, a blanket in her arms, and he held his arms open for her to sit on his lap. "Lean forward," she said and wrapped the blanket around his shoulders, then sat and curled herself against him, settling her head against his shoulder.

His heart swelled with love at the comfort she gave him without saying a word. She'd always had that ability, it was just her nature. He'd waited so long for moments like this. Now the fear of what might happen loomed large in his vision and threatened to take it all away from him.

"Sorry," he murmured as he pressed his lips to her hair. "I couldn't sleep and didn't want to wake you."

"What's on your mind?" she asked softly.

He took a deep breath and pressed his cheek to her head. "I'm a cop. I took an oath to uphold the law, and I can't believe that anyone, let alone someone I work with, could even suspect that I would break it."

"I don't think everyone you work with thinks that, Nathan. Bonner seems to be the only one with that idea," Janelle said.

"And the officers who were here to arrest me," Nathan grumbled.

"Honey." She sat up and looked him in the eyes. "They were here doing their job. That doesn't mean they liked it. Or that they agreed with it."

Nathan frowned. She did have a point.

"Besides, when your name is cleared, anyone who has made that ridiculous assumption will realize they were wrong," she said with a shrug of her shoulder.

"And if the charges aren't dropped and this goes to trial?" Nathan raised an eyebrow.

Janelle pressed her lips together and shook her head. "You can't think like that. This isn't right, and you know that. Patrick didn't kill Richard and you didn't help him, before or after the fact."

"Actually, that worries me too," he said. "Obviously I didn't help, I can believe those charges will be dropped. But Patrick and I talked about it, and the charges against him aren't so clear."

"Patrick didn't shoot Richard," Janelle firmly stated.

"He's not so sure about that," Nathan whispered, and Janelle's jaw dropped. "He was so angry at him for kidnapping Zach and terrified because Kelsey had been shot that he was running on pure adrenaline. He honestly can't remember whose hand the gun was in and whose finger pulled the trigger."

Janelle covered her mouth with shaky fingers. She laid her head back against his shoulder and he started to swing them slowly. He tightened his arms around her and they sat in silence for a few more minutes, until she sat up and looked at him.

"I don't care. As far as I'm concerned, it was in defense of my sister and my son. Any prosecutor or juror who can overlook that has no heart," she said angrily. "I will fight tooth and nail to see that both of you have your records cleared of this mess. Richard was a nasty person and his own actions caused his death. No one else deserves to be punished for it."

Nathan's lips lifted as his heart lightened. He lowered his lips to hers and took them in a kiss that he'd meant as a simple, loving gesture, but that quickly heated his blood and had him wanting more. He pulled back and looked at her face, her eyes closed, her lips relaxed and slightly puckered. She slowly lifted her lids, and he grinned down at her as she focused on his face.

"I love you so much," he said and her smile widened.

"Good," she stated. "Because I'm not letting you get away this time."

"I hope you don't have to." He moved to kiss her again, and she pulled her head away, her lips pressed tightly together and her eyes narrowed.

"Would you stop being so negative?" she scolded, her eyes became dark and stormy.

"It's reality, Janelle. We may have to face it sooner or later," he replied.

"Or not at all," she snapped. She closed her eyes and bowed her head as she blew air through her lips. When she looked at him, the seas had calmed and her eyes were back to their brilliant blue. "But, I'll indulge you. If you go to prison, I will write every day and visit as often as possible. And when you get out, I'll be the first one you see." She sat up and slid her arms around her neck. "I'll throw my arms around your neck and kiss you like this." She demonstrated with a long, slow kiss and electricity traveled through his body, sparking everything in him to life, making him forget everything but her. She broke the kiss, and he saw her eyes had darkened again and were full of lust and desire. "And I'll bring you home and we'll pick up where we left off."

"Sounds like a plan," he agreed huskily.

She laughed lightly. "I'm finally doing what I want to do because it makes me happy, not because someone else has told me it's the right thing to do. Do you really think I'm going to let anything stand in the way of that?"

He shook his head and leaned toward her. She threw him off balance when she quickly stood and moved to the edge of the porch, turning to prop her hips against the rail. He grabbed the ends of the blanket and followed her, wrapping them both in the woolen warmth as he put his arms around her.

"Can we worry about tomorrow, tomorrow?" Janelle asked as she slipped her arms around his back, and he nodded. "Good. I want to at least pretend things are normal for a little while. Like there's nothing hanging over us, threatening our happiness together."

She laid her head on his chest, and he relished the feel of her body against his, hope springing again in him that they really could make this work. He thought for a moment about Patrick's plans to marry Kelsey and wondered, albeit briefly, if the same future was in store for him and Janelle. Once upon a time, while they were having their affair, he had thought it was possible. He'd lost faith when she'd ended the affair, but now things were starting to look up for them.

As soon as this case was settled, one way or another.

"So, what's on the agenda for our normal life tomorrow?" Nathan asked softly and felt her laugh against his chest.

She looked up at him. "School in the morning and therapy in the afternoon."

"Sounds exciting."

Her head fell back as she laughed. "You have no idea."

Thirty

Janelle sat with Zach and Nathan in Andrew's waiting room, waiting for their appointment to begin. She hadn't even needed to ask Nathan to join her. Now that their relationship was out in the open and the worst had happened, there was no need for him to stay home. He'd been more aware of the time than she had been, making sure they were out the door earlier than she probably would have been with just Zach. As a result, they were early for the first time since the first therapy session.

It was actually quite a relief—she hated always being late.

Andrew's office door opened, and the blond-haired man stepped out. "Zach," he called with a smile.

"Hi, Andrew," Zach replied as he jumped out of his seat.

Nathan stood and turned, taking Janelle's hand. She rose to her feet and moved to his side.

"Nathan Harris?" Andrew said and started toward them. He pushed his silver-framed glasses up to the bridge of his nose then held out his hand. "It's so good to see you again, how have you been?"

Nathan gave Janelle a once-over, and she felt flushed from the look in his eyes. "Not bad," he answered as he took the therapist's hand and shook it.

"What are you doing here?" Andrew looked from Janelle and Nathan's clasped hands to the grin on Zach's face and back at Nathan. "You're the police puppet?"

"The what?" Nathan questioned as Janelle laughed.

"We'll explain later," Janelle said as she gave his hand a squeeze and turned to Andrew. "Are you ready for us?"

"Yes, come on in." Andrew waved his arm toward his door, and Zach led the way into the room.

Zach walked directly to the bookshelf against the back wall and started perusing the baskets. Janelle led Nathan to the familiar white couch at the side of the room. She sat in her usual spot, on the end closest to Andrew's brown leather chair. Nathan sat beside her in the middle of the sofa.

Andrew walked over to the window closest to Zach and sat on the sill with his arms folded across his chest and a small smile on his lips. "What would you like to play with today, Zach?"

Zach continued to rummage through the white wicker baskets until he found the one he was looking for. He turned to Andrew with a grin. "Can I play with the sand table?"

"Absolutely," Andrew replied and walked beside Zach to the other side of the room.

Andrew took the top completely off of the table that Zach had used for coloring and tilted it against the wall. Underneath was a hidden sandbox of sorts. Zach had used it once for therapy with, in Janelle's opinion, horrific results. He'd created a scene where he'd used plastic animals to represent the different people in his life. He was a big dog in the middle of the action, with a monster on one side and his family on the other.

Fittingly, the two-headed monster had been Richard, but he'd been stomping on the unicorn Zach had used to represent Kelsey. Neither Nathan nor Patrick had been in the scene—neither of them had been around when Zach had done the table the first time. Mary had been a giant spider pushing Janelle's lioness toward the monster, George had been a bear protecting Zoe's puppy in the background.

But Zach had enjoyed playing with the table at the end of every session, as Andrew and Janelle had talked about what had happened during the therapeutic playtime.

Andrew made sure Zach was comfortable with the plastic tub of animals then walked to his brown chair beside Janelle. "How was he this weekend? I heard you guys had a lot going on at your house," Andrew immediately asked, his brows nearly colliding above the bridge of his glasses.

Janelle rolled her eyes and Nathan let out a low groan. "Of course you heard," Janelle muttered then glanced at Zach. "The children witnessed the arrest and part of the argument that came afterward."

"Argument between whom?" Andrew asked, picking his notepad and pen up off the table beside him. "And what was said that he heard?"

"The fight was between us—Kelsey and me—and our mother. Then Dad got involved after he sent the kids inside," Janelle answered and told him what she could remember of what was said and by whom.

"Kelsey called her a bitch?" Nathan interrupted.

Janelle turned to him and his mouth was open, the corners of his lips turned up slightly. She nodded and he laughed once.

"The kids heard that?" Andrew asked.

"Yes." Janelle continued her story with only a few more interruptions for clarification from Andrew. He asked about the children's behavior over the weekend, she told him of the second argument Kelsey had had with their mother, and the resulting ban. When she talked about the kids' cuddly and subdued behavior, he hadn't seemed too concerned. He asked about the kids' reaction to Nathan and Patrick's return the day before.

"They seem to be handling everything pretty well," Janelle answered.

Andrew set his pen on top of the notepad and laid them in his lap. "How are you doing with it?"

Janelle looked at Nathan, and he squeezed her hand reassuringly. "We're dealing with it," she said with a shrug as she turned to Andrew. "It is what it is, and there's not much we can do about it."

Andrew nodded and remained silent for a while as he watched Zach at the sand table. A moment later, he stood and walked toward Zach. He bent over Zach's shoulder and started asking him questions about the table.

Nathan inched closer to Janelle. "Sounds like I missed some fireworks this weekend," he whispered across her ear. She turned to him and caught the huge grin just before he was able to make it disappear.

She tried not to laugh as she shook her head. "If you'd been there, we may not have had the show."

"True," he agreed. "So what are the puppets you were talking about earlier?"

Janelle explained the puppet play they'd started with and what Zach had done with them. She stood and tugged him to his feet then walked him to the row of baskets. Janelle began demonstrating what Zach had done with the toys during his therapy sessions. Nathan listened attentively, asking questions when he had them, showing an obvious interest in Zach's recovery.

"Janelle, Nathan," Andrew called to them from the other end of the room. "Would you like to see this?"

Janelle put the puppet back in Zach's personal basket and then walked to the sand table to look at the scene. She hoped it wasn't as horrible as the first one had been.

She was pleasantly surprised by what she saw.

The two-headed monster was still there, but it was lying on its side in the middle of the sand pile. In a circle around it were the rest of the animals. Kelsey's unicorn was standing up with a larger horse beside her that Janelle could only assume was supposed to be Patrick. On the other side of Kelsey's unicorn was Zach's big dog, and on the other side of him was Zoe's puppy. Janelle's lioness stood next to the puppy with a large male lion beside her.

Janelle looked at Nathan and whispered, "It looks like you're a lion."

Nathan smiled but continued to look at the scene with a confused expression. She explained what all of the animals in the scene represented, including the bear that stood between the lion and the stallion with a smaller bear behind it, out of the circle. Janelle realized, with some sadness, that the smaller bear was Mary.

"Very good, Zach," Andrew said as he took a few pictures of the sand scene. "If you'd like to continue to play with it, go ahead. I'm going to talk to your mom and Nathan for a bit."

Zach smiled and pulled two small animals out of the tub then knelt down to play in the sand. Andrew led Janelle and Nathan back to their seats on the sofa as he sat in the brown leather chair. He set his camera and notepad on the table behind him and turned to Janelle with a slight grin.

"I think he'll be fine," Andrew stated.

Janelle's heart skipped a beat and happy tears stung her eyes. "Really?"

"Given everything that happened last weekend, I'm surprised to see him so calm. His sand table shows growth, not just in him, but in all of you. Except for that little bear on the outside of the circle, it seems you've all come together as a family. That's a good thing," Andrew said. "Any idea who that bear was?"

"I'm guessing my mother," Janelle answered softly. "Her spider wasn't there."

"Ah, that's right." Andrew pointed to the table. "He's obviously accepted the adoption, he's at peace with the power shift between you and your mother, and," Andrew looked at Nathan, "he's apparently gained two male role models that he's happy with."

Zach ran over to Nathan and grabbed his hand. "Would you like to see my puppets?" he asked excitedly.

"I would love to see your puppets," Nathan said as he ruffled Zach's hair. "I understand I'm a police puppet."

Zach nodded quickly. "And Patrick is a superhero."

Nathan frowned. "Patrick gets to be a superhero?" he whined then turned and winked at Janelle.

"You're both superheroes, but there was only one puppet," Zach replied as he pulled Nathan to his feet.

"Well, then, I guess I understand," Nathan said as they walked away.

Janelle watched them, a soft, peaceful smile on her lips. "We're all happy with his new role models."

Janelle walked into the house ahead of Zach and Nathan and tossed her keys onto the side table. Kelsey came limping out of the kitchen with a huge grin on her face.

"Daddy called," she said before Janelle could ask why she looked so happy. "He said the prosecutor is going to have all of the evidence looked at immediately. We could know something before the end of the week," she finished with a slight squeal as she grabbed Janelle's hands. "Isn't that great?"

Janelle felt herself lighten a bit, but didn't want to get too excited. After what Nathan had told her about Patrick's possible guilt, she couldn't get too happy. What if Nathan got off but Patrick didn't? Kelsey would be crushed.

"That's wonderful," Janelle said and looked past Kelsey to Patrick as he leaned against a column. He smiled at her, but she could see the dimness in his eyes and knew he was thinking the same thing she was.

Nancy came around the corner with a smile on her face. "Dinner is ready. Everybody come eat." She turned and went back into the kitchen.

"Mom, you didn't have to cook again," Nathan said as he followed his mother into the kitchen, briefly laying a hand on Janelle's shoulder as he passed her.

Janelle stood and watched Nathan carry a casserole dish into the dining room; his mother was following him with a large bowl. Zach skipped into the kitchen, and Kelsey stepped to Janelle's side and they walked into the dining room for dinner.

"Nancy, we can clean that up," Janelle said as Nathan's mother stood and picked up her plate.

"No, dear, I don't mind." Nancy smiled at her and continued to tidy her spot at the table.

"I do," Nathan said as he stood and walked to his mother's side. He took her plate from her as Janelle rose from her seat. Nathan handed Janelle his mother's plates and placed a gentle kiss on her cheek. "Mom, you should go home."

Nancy's chin fell and her lips turned downward. "Are you trying to get rid of me?"

"No," Nathan said as he put his arm around her and walked her into the living room. "I just think you look tired and that you'd get a better night's sleep in your own bed than you do on that lumpy leather couch."

"Hey, I like that couch," Kelsey mumbled to herself as she walked past Janelle with other dirty dishes.

"I really don't mind," Nancy argued as her voice faded.

"Let me help you," Elizabeth said as she walked around Patrick, still lounging in his seat with a frown on his face. She tapped the back of his head. "You too."

He looked up at her and sat straighter as Janelle tried not to laugh. He made eye contact with Janelle, shook his head as he shrugged a shoulder, then rose from his seat and picked up the now-empty casserole dish and large bowl that had been a chicken and rice casserole with a side of broccoli and cheese.

"We'll clean up," Janelle muttered as Patrick walked past her. "Take her into the living room and let her relax," she added as she followed him into the kitchen, and he nodded.

"Oh, Elizabeth," Kelsey said as she took the dirty dishes. "Janelle and I got this, you go sit down." Kelsey motioned toward the living room with a soapy hand as Janelle stopped beside her and put her plates in the sudsy water.

"Trust me, Mom, they like to do this," Patrick said after he set his dishes on the island. He winked mischievously at Kelsey. "It gives them a chance to talk about Nathan and me and drink a bottle of wine while they're at it."

Kelsey scoffed and picked up a dishtowel. "We do not." She swatted him with the towel, and he chuckled. "It's a half a bottle at best."

He laughed harder and wrapped his arm around her. He kissed her temple, and they swayed side to side. "I love you," he murmured and stepped away.

"I know," Kelsey countered with a twinkle in her eyes. "Now scat." She waved Patrick and his mother away with the dishtowel.

Janelle snickered as she returned to the dining room and collected the rest of the plates and silverware from dinner. She could faintly hear Nathan urging his mother to go home, so she could get a good night's rest, and Nancy arguing against it. Janelle carried the dinner things back to the kitchen and set them on the counter next to the sink.

She and Kelsey worked in silence as Janelle thought about whether or not to bring up what Nathan had said the night before. She wanted to prepare Kelsey for the worst, but felt that Patrick should be the one to raise the subject and didn't want to step on his toes in case he had a good reason for not mentioning it. Janelle worried about how Kelsey might react to the news if the first time she heard it was from her. On the other hand, Janelle was her older sister and had been looking out for Kelsey her whole life.

"Out with it," Kelsey murmured as she washed the casserole dish.

Janelle met her sister's gaze in the window above the sink. "Out with what?"

"Whatever you're worrying about," Kelsey answered. "You've had that look on your face since you got home." Kelsey froze with her hands half submerged in the water, and her eyes widened. "Did something happen in therapy?"

"No." Janelle grinned a little. "Andrew feels like Zach will be fine. He said he was impressed with how well Zach seemed to handle this weekend's events, and he thinks Zach's coping with everything very well. He says we don't have to come back unless we start to see a change or he starts to regress."

Kelsey blew out a breath and closed her eyes. Her lips lifted and Janelle marveled at the peace on her sister's face. It was a beautiful sight, and she'd missed it. After a few seconds, Kelsey opened her eyes and looked at Janelle again in the reflection of the window.

"So, if it's not Zach, what is it?" Kelsey looked down at her hands and resumed scrubbing as her brow came together. "Was it what I said when you got home? About Dad's call?"

"Yes," Janelle confessed and moved to stand beside Kelsey. She turned and propped her rear against the counter. "Kelsey, Nathan and I talked about the charges last night. We . . . why are you smiling?"

Kelsey looked at Janelle, and her mouth opened a little. She closed it as her eyes widened innocently. "I'm not smiling, I just think I know where this is headed."

"You do?" Janelle raised an eyebrow.

"Yes, Patrick and I talked too." Kelsey turned the water on and rinsed the dish she'd been washing.

Janelle picked up a dry towel and took the wet casserole dish from her sister's hands. She started drying it as Kelsey pulled the stopper from the drain and rinsed out the sink. She grabbed a paper towel and dried her hands and the lip of the counter in front of her.

"I know that the charges against Nathan will be easier to disprove and dismiss than the ones against Patrick. I know that there's still the possibility of Patrick going to trial and prison." Kelsey tossed her towel in the trash and turned her hip to the edge of the counter. "But I'm not going to dwell on it. We have hope, Janelle, and I'm choosing to focus on that. If for no other reason than I don't want Zach and Zoe to know how terrified I am that we might not have Patrick around for a while." She smiled sadly, and her eyes filled with tears. "And I refuse to let that fear ruin the time we have together right now."

Janelle set the dry dish and towel in the corner of the counter and turned to her sister. She gripped Kelsey's upper arms and squeezed lightly. "I've never told you how proud I am of you, have I?"

Kelsey wiped her damp cheek and giggled. "What have I done to make you proud? You're the strong one. You're the nurturer and the levelheaded one. I'm just the brat that always did the wrong thing."

Janelle shook her head and inhaled deeply. "No, I'm not. I'm what Mom told me to be. Yes, I figured out her advice was crap before you did, but I still tried to abide by it. When Tim hurt you and you realized how horrible Mom's advice was in practice, you broke away from it completely. I didn't have that courage until it was too late." Janelle dropped her hands and jumped up to sit on the counter. "You've lived your life the way you've wanted to, not caring what she said or did or how she treated you, and I've lived in fear that I'd lose her approval or that I'd disappoint her somehow."

"Janelle," Kelsey said as she pushed herself up onto the island. "That's how we've been our whole lives. She raised you to be Little Miss Perfect and treated me like a little hellion," Kelsey narrowed one eye, "which I blame entirely on Sean, by the way."

Janelle couldn't stop the laugh that escaped. It was true that their brother had always blamed everything on Kelsey, and their mother had always accepted everything he told her as the truth.

"But don't beat yourself up for it," Kelsey continued. "I actually did care, very much, about what she thought of me until Patrick's visit last fall. And her words still haunt me. I just choose to ignore them because I do know better now." Kelsey turned to look into the living room and met Patrick's stare. He stood and started to come toward the kitchen and Kelsey turned to look at Janelle. "And so do you. You know that you can still be happy, happier actually, by doing what you think is best for you. You're still the nurturer, you're still strong, and you're way more levelheaded than I could ever hope to be."

The sisters laughed as Patrick stepped to Kelsey's side. He slid his arm around her hips and positioned himself against her.

"I guess the moral of the story is that I'm proud of you too." Kelsey smiled widely, and Janelle's eyes became watery. "I always have been. I've always known that you'd be there for me, and I will do anything to make sure you stay as happy as you seem to be now."

"That makes two of us," Nathan said as he approached from the dining room. He stopped in front of Janelle, and she put her arms on his shoulders. "Mom has agreed to go home tonight, but not yet. And she'll be back in the morning."

Janelle nodded as she leaned over to place a light kiss on his lips. "Works for me," she said with a grin.

Thirty-One

Janelle heard her sister come down the stairs but became distracted as the footsteps continued to grow closer. She looked up from Zach's schoolwork as Kelsey stepped into the doorway of the dining room. Patrick appeared at her shoulder, and they looked like they were about to leave.

"Are you going out?" Janelle asked as she caught movement in her periphery. Nathan was standing in the other doorway, between the living room and dining room.

"Just for a little while. I'm going crazy sitting here waiting for something to happen," Kelsey answered.

Janelle frowned. She couldn't argue with that, they were all on edge, waiting for her father, or Mason, to call and give them an update about the case. It had been a week since the arraignment, and every day that passed wound them all a little tighter and brought the mood down a little more. At this point, Janelle would probably jump at the chance to get out of the house for a while too.

"Where are you going?" Janelle questioned.

Kelsey looked over her shoulder at Patrick, and he shrugged. She looked back at Janelle with a grin. "It's a surprise."

"I like surprises," Zach said as his pencil stopped and he looked at his aunt.

"We think you'll like this one," Kelsey giggled. "Hopefully it won't take long and we'll tell you when we get back. 'Bye." She waggled her fingers and turned toward the door.

"Kels," Janelle stood and started after them. Nathan rushed to intercept her, grabbing her around the waist as Kelsey and Patrick said their goodbyes to Nancy and Elizabeth in the living room.

"Relax, sweetheart," Nathan cooed softly.

"But Dad could come by any minute," Janelle said with a pout and Nathan laughed.

"That's not what's bothering you," he said as he wrapped his other arm around her and held her close. "You want to know what they're up to."

"She doesn't keep secrets from me," Janelle complained softly then narrowed her eye on Nathan. "You know what it is, don't you?"

"I might," he said with a grin.

The front door opened, and Kelsey squealed. "Dad's here!" she exclaimed.

Janelle's heart sped up and she tried to pull away from Nathan. When she saw his jaw was clenched tighter than his grip on her, she stopped fighting him. She laid her palms on his cheeks and pulled his lips to hers. She gave him a warm, gentle kiss until his lips relaxed under hers then she pulled away.

"Nothing will come between us," she reassured him.

He nodded and slowly released her. "Zach, keep doing your work," Nathan said gently as he took her hand.

Together, Janelle and Nathan walked out to the porch. Kelsey stood at the top of the steps, watching George and Mason approach the house together, Patrick stood behind her, his hands on her waist. Elizabeth and Nancy were already seated on the swing. Janelle led Nathan to the column on the other side of the steps from Kelsey, and she rested against the rail. Nathan slid his hand from hers and around her waist.

"Do you have news?" Kelsey asked, practically bouncing where she stood.

"We do," George replied as he reached the steps. As he climbed, Janelle watched his face for any indication as to whether his news was good or bad. His calm façade gave nothing away.

"What is it?" Kelsey gripped her father's arm as he reached the porch floor. "Is it good?"

George chuckled. "Wouldn't you like to go in first so we can sit down?"

"No," Kelsey answered.

Mason snorted as he walked past Janelle and she regarded him questioningly. He propped himself against the wall of the house, met her gaze, and promptly looked away.

"Daddy!" Kelsey whined. "Tell me."

"She reminds me of our daughter," Nathan whispered across Janelle's ear, and she felt a shiver down her spine as she nodded her agreement.

"Fine," George replied good-naturedly. "The prosecutor had his experts look at *all* the evidence, both what Bonner had originally presented and everything else they had collected that Hayes came forward with. They had to re-interview a few witnesses, but," George paused, a smile slowly forming as he looked from one daughter to the other. "The charges will all be dropped."

Kelsey nearly screamed as she turned in Patrick's arms. She threw her arms around his neck, and he picked her up, holding her tightly against him. Janelle thought she saw a single tear trickle down his cheek and looked away.

Nancy and Elizabeth were hugging each other on the swing, both sets of cheeks blotchy and moist.

Nathan's arm snaked around her shoulders, his head came to rest on her shoulder, and she sank back against him. The weight of the past few weeks lifted, and she felt lighter than she had in months. "It's over," she whispered and felt him nod against her head.

"Yes, Janelle," George said as he turned to face her. "It's over. We can finally put Richard to rest and be done with him."

Her eyes began to sting and she pulled away from Nathan. As she turned into his arms, she caught sight of Zach standing in the doorway, watching them all with a smile on his face. She grinned through her watery vision, and Nathan laid his hands on her cheeks. She looked into his clear hazel eyes, and he thumbed her tears away.

"I love you," Janelle said as his lips got closer to hers. His turned up slightly just before they met hers, and he kissed her so deeply she felt it all the way to her toes. He moved his lips against hers, and she resisted the urge to give him the more he was asking for. Slowly he pulled away and looked down at her. "Later," she mouthed.

"We have all the time in the world now," he agreed and pulled her against his chest again in a warm, comforting hug.

Forever, Janelle thought.

Nathan avoided making eye contact as he strolled through the station on his way to Captain Little's office. The captain had called him within an hour of George's report and asked that he come in right away. Patrick and Kelsey had still wanted to run their errand, so they thought it would be perfect if he rode along and they dropped him off at the station. Reluctantly, Nathan had agreed, but he'd have preferred to stay home with Janelle to celebrate their newfound freedom.

As he got closer to the office, he could hear raised voices. Paying closer attention, he realized it was only one voice. And it wasn't happy.

"I let it slide when you went above my head and directly to the sheriff to get assigned to this investigation," Captain Little was practically yelling. "I chose to give you the benefit of the doubt. I chose to believe you were showing initiative."

"I was," came another loud voice. Nathan froze inches from the door when he recognized it as Bonner's.

"The only thing you were showing was a desire to make a name for yourself," the captain countered. "And in the process, you've made a laughingstock of this department. You took all of the evidence and selected only the parts that would help you blame a nonexistent crime on a man simply for the thrill of bringing down one of the country's biggest celebrities. Not only that, but you implicated one of our best cops as an accomplice and had him arrested as well."

"A man is dead!" Bonner shouted.

Nathan fell back a step and looked around. He was alone but saw a chair beside the door. He walked silently toward it and sat down.

"And both Harris and Mr. Lyons are guilty," Bonner continued.

"The dead man in question kidnapped his own child, shot his sister-in-law, and had every intention of killing the child and himself!" Captain Little's voice boomed as Nathan heard a chair scrape across the floor. "And by all the evidence I've seen, Miss Morgan would have died had Mr. Lyons and Sergeant Harris not been so quick to act."

"That's irrelevant," Bonner snapped.

"That's perfectly relevant," Little disputed. "Mr. Wagoner put himself in that situation, you cannot ignore that. You cannot ignore that he was an abusive alcoholic who bullied and blackmailed Miss Morgan repeatedly into paying off his gambling debt."

"If she'd kept the little brat to herself he wouldn't have been able to blackmail her," Bonner grumbled, and Nathan's heart began to race as his vision blurred red.

How dare he try to blame this on Kelsey?

"This is not her fault!" Captain Little roared. "And how dare you make such an insinuation. The man was a bully to everyone he met, I'm sure you realized that in your interviews."

"Well—"

"*I* sure as hell did, after simply reading them. On top of the restraining order Miss Morgan filed in December and the pictures of bruises he'd left on both her and her sister, you interviewed coworkers that claimed he'd bullied them," Captain Little said. "He'd been out of work for six months, he'd been fired for showing up drunk. My question is, why did none of this show up in the report you gave to the prosecutor?"

"I didn't think it was important," Detective Bonner said at the top of his voice, but Nathan could tell he was losing his bravado.

"Of course it's important. It speaks volumes to the type of man he was and shouldn't be left out of a case like this," the captain continued, his volume maintaining a loud, commanding tone. "And another thing, I don't appreciate you waiting until I'm on vacation to finally take it to the district attorney's office. I've been asking you about it for weeks, and if I didn't know better, I'd say you were trying to hide it from me."

Silence fell for a few long seconds, and Nathan held his breath as he waited for a response. He knew there would be one—Bonner couldn't let an accusation like that go unchallenged.

"What do you expect?" Bonner snapped. "Harris is your golden boy. You think he can do no wrong. For God's sake, he actually stayed away from *her* when you told him to."

"How do you know about that?" Little questioned.

"We all knew that," Bonner hissed loudly. "You treat him like he's some sort of perfect example of what a cop should be. But he's not perfect. He had an affair with the victim's wife! He fathered her child, and she tried to pass it off as her husband's. How do you know she didn't make up the abuse? She obviously can't be trusted either."

Nathan jumped to his feet and started toward the door. He had his hand out to turn the knob when an arm stretched across his chest. He looked down and followed the line of the arm to its owner. Sergeant Hayes stood staring at him, and when Nathan met his gaze he shook his head. Nathan's jaw clenched and he inhaled slowly and deeply.

"That's enough!" Captain Little bellowed so loudly his door rattled.

Nathan turned his stare to the mahogany door. He dropped his hand and took a step back.

"This isn't about Mrs. Wagoner and Sergeant Harris. This isn't about Miss Morgan or Mr. Lyons. This is about the shitty job you did with this investigation," Little boomed.

"I did a very thorough investigation," Bonner argued.

"And yet you managed to leave some of the most pertinent information out of your report," Little said calmly.

"It won't happen again," Bonner's voice sounded strained, like he was speaking through clenched teeth.

"You're absolutely right, it won't." Captain Little's voice got closer to the door. "You have an hour to get your desk cleaned out."

"What?" Bonner sounded shocked. "You can't be serious."

"I'm very serious. I've listed everything you've done, but to sum it up neatly for you, I'll tell you again. You went behind my back and directly to the sheriff to get assigned to this investigation. You left out information unless it suited your agenda, and this isn't the first time you've done that either, don't think I've forgotten," Little said, and the doorknob turned. "You also went behind my back to get the arrest warrants and, in the process, you've dragged one of your fellow officer's good name through the mud. I don't trust you," Little said slowly as the door opened. "And I won't work with a man I don't trust."

"I can't believe this. My lawy—"

"I look forward to that," the captain said as his back appeared in the doorway. Nathan and Hayes rushed to find a place out of sight before they were caught eavesdropping. "Your pal, the sheriff, will not be able to get you out of this one. I'm afraid he's on my side. He's completely embarrassed by your actions and the shame you've brought on all of us."

"I was just doing my job," Bonner snapped as he stepped out of the office.

"Then let me be clear about mine," Captain Little said. "If I so much as hear of a threat against any of the Morgan family or the Harris family, I will bring you in for questioning, even if I have to hunt you down. My recommendation for you would be to pack your stuff and move out of the county. You may even want to consider another state."

Nathan could see the fire in his captain's eyes from where he stood against the wall. He felt a mixture of pride and fear of the man he saw threatening Bonner. Not that he was complaining; if Bonner left, that was one less thing he'd have to worry about.

"Do I make myself clear?" The captain enunciated each word and glared at Bonner until he nodded his head. "Good. Go."

He pointed toward the main part of the station where Bonner's desk was located. The former detective turned and followed his final orders, and Nathan was thankful that Bonner's direction was away from Nathan's hiding spot. Slowly, Nathan stepped away from the wall and toward the captain's office.

Captain Little turned and looked directly at Nathan. "Good, you're here. Come in."

Thirty-Two

"I'm going to assume you heard all of that," Captain Little said once the door was closed behind him. He motioned toward the seat in front of his desk, and Nathan sat down.

"Pretty much," Nathan confessed.

The captain nodded. "Good. I'm not in the mood to repeat myself." He sat down in the large chair behind his desk and laid his forearms in front of him on the desk. "And it saves me from having to explain everything to you."

"Of course," Nathan agreed, hoping less explaining would mean he could return home to his family sooner.

"First, I'd like to apologize for everything you've been through in the past couple of months. Especially in the last few days since your arrest," Captain Little began. "I think we can both agree that shouldn't have happened."

Nathan dipped his head.

"After reading the interviews and the reports regarding Mr. Wagoner's behavior leading up to his death, I can agree that you keeping watch over the family after the restraining order was filed was probably a wise course of action," the captain admitted. "However, I wish you had gone about it the right way and shared that burden. Perhaps some of this could have been avoided."

"I agree," Nathan said. If someone had been watching Janelle's house that night, Richard might never have made it past the front door.

"Given that, and what Bonner has put you through, I'll see what I can do to have this IA investigation dropped and consider the time you've spent on your suspension as your punishment. But that's not really why I called you in." Captain Little opened a drawer in his desk and reached down. He set a white plastic basket on the desk and slid it toward Nathan. "I'm ready to reinstate you."

Nathan's brows came together as he sat up and looked into the basket. His badge and firearm were the only two items in it. He glanced up at his captain.

"Effective immediately," the captain said with a smile.

Nathan sat back in the chair and held Captain Little's stare. "That's a great offer," Nathan stated. "But why should I take it?"

The captain's smile faded. "What do you mean?"

Nathan folded his arms across his chest and stretched his feet out in front of him. "It's simple really. I now have to work with people who could possibly always doubt my innocence. I could have abusive men questioning my motives when I show up to help the women and children they're abusing. My reputation is shot, Captain." Nathan pulled his feet toward him again. "How did he sell this to the sheriff anyway?"

Captain Little rose and walked around to the front of the desk. He set his palms on the edge and leaned over them. "I believe Bonner went to see the sheriff the day Mr. Wagoner's manifesto came out. He told the sheriff that you had been on the case, but given the revelations in the video and your relationship with the Morgan family and Mr. Lyons, you may be biased and try to hide the facts. Bonner promised to do a thorough investigation and make sure that anyone who needed to be brought to justice would be brought to justice."

Nathan frowned as he sat up in his chair. "No one needed to be brought to justice. How did he continue to drag it out?"

"Bonner visited the sheriff's office every other week with updates and assured him that Mr. Lyons looked guilty of murder and he needed a little longer to prove it." Captain Little crossed his feet at his ankles.

"All because Patrick is a celebrity?" Nathan asked as he stood and walked around his seat. "That man would never hurt anyone on purpose."

"Bonner was under the impression that he could make a name for himself if he could prove Mr. Lyons's guilt," Captain Little answered with a shrug.

Nathan rolled his eyes as he began to pace. "Well, I guess he accomplished that."

Silence fell between them as Nathan paced the length of the room and considered the captain's offer. He could take his job back, but there would be more risks now than there had been before. The whole county now knew he'd had an affair with Janelle and that she'd been an abused wife. Most of the abusers he had to deal with already had short tempers, and at least half of them were the jealous type. What would they think if Nathan showed up to help protect their wives and girlfriends from their abuse?

And what about the other officers? Would they respect him enough to work with him, or would they always view him with some level of skepticism?

"Can the other officers work with me?" Nathan asked as he continued to pace. "Do they believe in my innocence or do they think me capable of assisting with murder?" He stopped behind his chair, directly in front of the captain, and looked into his eyes. "I can't work with people who would doubt my innocence."

"I can understand that," Captain Little said. "For the most part, they all believed Bonner was up to something. Several of them thought Detective Hayes had been acting strangely, and when they found out about your arrest, they came to me immediately and pleaded your case for you."

Nathan felt some of his apprehension flow out his body. "Do you think the population will be able to trust me? They've all seen the manifesto. They've seen the news of the arrest on the television. It doesn't make me look good." Nathan gripped the back of the chair. "I'm not sure I can take the risk of an abusive man thinking I'm there to help his battered wife for the wrong reasons. That puts my life in danger as well."

Captain Little nodded. "I see your point." He rose from the edge of the desk. "I can't make promises about that. We can try to find a better fit for you in that department if you'd like. Or we can find another department to move you to." The older man walked to the back of his desk and picked up the basket. "It wouldn't have to be a permanent move, just until this blows over. And I'm sure it will."

Nathan eyed his badge and sidearm in the basket in Captain Little's hands. He could move to another department for a little while if it meant he could stay safe. The last thing he wanted to do right now was put his life at risk. He finally had the woman he loved welcoming him home every night. They had a daughter to raise, and he already considered Zach his son.

He wouldn't leave them.

"That may be the best option," Nathan said as he reached for the basket. "I'll think about which area I might want to move to for the time being."

Captain Little held the plastic basket out, and Nathan took his gun and badge from it. He clipped the holster to the belt on his jeans and put his badge in his pocket.

"Take the rest of the week. I'll pay you for it and see you back here on Monday," the captain said with a smile as he tossed the basket onto his desk. He held his hand out across the desk and Nathan grasped it and shook it. "Welcome back."

Nathan took a deep breath. "Thank you." He turned his back on the captain and walked toward the door. He gripped the knob, turned it, and opened the door. His eyes widened as he took in the crowd of officers now gathered outside of the captain's office.

Detective Hayes stepped toward him. "Are you back?" he asked.

"I will be Monday," Nathan answered, and the crowd erupted in hoots and applause.

Hayes held out his hand to Nathan. "I'm sorry I didn't stand up to him. You didn't deserve that."

Nathan took the other man's hand and shook it. "You came around. That's the important part."

He dropped Hayes's hand and waved to the crowd then turned and walked out of the building.

He stepped into the bright sunshine and held his hand up to shield his eyes. At the bottom of the steps, Janelle was leaning against the waist-high stone wall, grinning up at him. He quickly skipped down the steps, his own smile widening as he got closer.

"What are you doing here?" he asked as he stopped in front of her and took her hands.

"I decided I couldn't wait for Patrick and Kelsey to bring you home, so I thought I'd come fetch you myself." Her face lifted to his, and he placed a brief kiss on her lips. "Did it go well?" she asked.

"I go back to work on Monday," Nathan said as he slid his arm around her waist and turned her toward the street. He glanced to his left and then to his right until he found her van and turned them toward it. "The captain apologized for the misunderstanding and is going to get the IA investigation dropped."

"That's great!" Janelle exclaimed.

"No," Nathan stopped her and turned her to face him. "I'm happy to have my job back, even if I do have to figure out where I fit in now, but having you in my life is what's really great." He saw her eyes light up. "It was a bumpy road, and things haven't happened the way we might have liked, but I wouldn't change this for anything. I love you so much."

Janelle slowly slid her arms over his shoulders and clasped them behind his neck. "I couldn't agree more."

Epilogue

Ten months later . . .

Janelle rolled over and smacked her alarm clock to shut it off. Her eyes slowly opened as she focused on the empty pillow beside her and smiled.

She placed her feet on the floor and stretched her arms as she looked around her. There were boxes scattered throughout her room, some had been opened, some were still closed. They were full of Nathan's things. He had spent most of his time since his reinstatement at her house, but hadn't officially moved in.

That was about to change. Today was their wedding day.

They'd already started the process of him legally adopting Zach and Zoe. Today, she'd be taking his last name and, in a few short months, so would her children. They'd decided that would be enough for Zoe for now, she was almost four, and they weren't sure how much she would understand at this point anyway. It was an added bonus that she barely remembered Richard, even a year later, so Nathan would be the only father she would know.

As a wedding gift, Kelsey was giving them her house to live in. The errand that had been so important on the day the charges were dropped was a trip to the local land management office so they could get a copy of the survey of her property. They'd decided to build a house and needed to see if she owned enough land, and if it was capable of supporting a new home. Until it was finished, the house was still in Kelsey's name, but within the next few months, Kelsey and Patrick would be moving into their new home and Kelsey's house would become Janelle and Nathan's.

Janelle's eyes landed on her wedding dress, and her smile widened. She'd opted for pale blue, the lightest shade of her favorite color. Zoe, as their flower girl, would wear a dress matching Janelle's almost perfectly. Zach's suit would be a smaller duplicate of Nathan's, and he would be carrying their rings down the aisle. To say he was excited would be an understatement. Both children had gotten a taste of their responsibilities six months earlier, when Patrick and Kelsey had made their trip down the aisle.

Mary had been in attendance at Kelsey's wedding, but Kelsey had invited her more as a favor to her father than anything else. Mary's relationship with her daughters was still tense, but she was making an effort. She'd accepted Patrick as a son-in-law, but Kelsey was still struggling with forgiving her for the role she'd played in Patrick's arrest. Likewise, Janelle was having a hard time forgetting how many times Mary had sided with Richard during her marriage to him, but she was hesitant to banish Mary from her life completely for the sake of her children. She hoped that if Kelsey ever had children of her own, her attitude toward their mother might at least soften enough to allow Mary to have a relationship with them.

Thinking of her sister, Janelle decided she'd better head downstairs and get a start on breakfast. She had several mouths to feed, and this would be her last chance to do it for the next two weeks. She didn't want Kelsey to get the jump on her.

Down the hallway, Kelsey threw the covers off and sprinted to the bathroom. She barely made it to the toilet before every bit of what she'd eaten the night before made its reappearance.

Patrick slowly followed his wife into the bathroom, a slight grin on his face. This was the fourth morning in a row she'd launched herself out of bed for the same reason. He had his hopes, but she hadn't confirmed them. He made his face a mask of concern as he entered the bathroom to find her sitting on the floor with her head leaned back against the wall.

"I'm no longer sure it's something I ate," Kelsey said with a sigh. "I hope I feel better soon, this is really getting old." She slowly rose to her feet and walked to the sink to wash her face. "Janelle will kill me if I get sick at her wedding."

"I'm sure she'll understand," Patrick said and held the towel out for Kelsey. She dried her face, and he reached into the medicine cabinet for the box he'd bought two days ago. He closed the cabinet as she took the towel off of her face.

"What is that?" she asked as she looked closely at the box he was holding. "A pregnancy test? Are you kidding me?" Giddiness bubbled inside of her but she quickly squashed it. "Patrick, I don't think I'm pregnant."

He tried not to smirk. "But you could be."

She shook her head. It was possible; she'd come off of the pill two months before, and they'd used condoms for only a month after that. They weren't exactly trying to get pregnant. But they weren't exactly trying to prevent it either.

"Sweetheart, just take the test." Patrick held the box out to her. "What's the worst that could happen?"

She could be pregnant.

Or she might not be.

Kelsey wasn't sure which would be worse.

She still wouldn't take the box from him, and he tried not to get frustrated. He hated the fact that her last experience with pregnancy had been such a lonely one, that her ex had been so cruel when she'd found out she was having his child. He hated even more that she might even consider his reaction would be remotely similar.

He set the box on the sink and put his arms around her. "I'm not him," he whispered as he placed a kiss to her hair. "I want so much for you to have my child."

"I don't want to disappoint you," Kelsey said as tears filled her eyes.

Patrick released her and cupped her cheek in his hand. "Regardless of what happens, I won't be disappointed. Just take the test because if you're not, I'll have to take you to the doctor to find out why you're sick every morning."

Kelsey couldn't argue with that. If she wasn't pregnant, then she probably should see a doctor, but even that would have to wait until Monday. It was Saturday morning and Janelle was marrying Nathan this afternoon. She had so much to do today she couldn't take time out of her day to visit the emergency room.

"Okay, I'll do it," she said as she picked the box up. "But don't get your hopes up."

"Of course," Patrick said somberly even though his heart was racing with excitement.

"Now, get out." Kelsey pointed to the door as she took the little plastic stick out of the box and began to unwrap it.

Patrick did as he was ordered and closed the door as he left. He walked to the bed and sat on it as he waited for her to come out. A few moments later, the door opened. She walked toward him and sat down beside him.

"Well?" he asked. She had a serene look on her face that he wasn't sure how to interpret.

"Well what?" She pressed her lips together.

"What did it say?" he questioned.

Kelsey flopped onto her back and threw her arms over her head. "We have to wait two minutes."

Patrick lay back and propped himself up on his elbow beside her. "What should we do while we wait?" he asked as he leaned in to nuzzle her neck. She squealed and tried to roll away, but he pinned her with his arm across her waist.

"Patrick," she said as she laughed, "no."

"If you insist." He lay completely beside her and let his hand drift to her abdomen.

"I'm afraid I must." Kelsey rested her hand over his and began to draw circles on it with her fingers.

She was trying to distract herself with other things. Like Janelle's wedding. Or the house she and Patrick were building on the land behind her current home that had, until six months ago, been wooded and weedy. Patrick had proposed the night they'd found out the manslaughter charges were dropped, then they'd spent the first month of their engagement making sure they could build on the land and getting the permits to do it.

"When do you think the house will be finished?" she asked, and Patrick lifted to his elbow again.

His lips twitched a little at her obvious attempt at diversion. They both knew it would be another three to six months before their new house would be completed. "You know the answer to that," he said as he leaned closer.

She turned her face to his, and her brow came together. "Hopefully only three. Now that Janelle and Nathan are going to be married, I'm sure they'll want this house to themselves."

"So they can work on expanding their family," Patrick said and lightly rubbed Kelsey's stomach.

"I'm not sure they plan on doing that," Kelsey answered with a shrug. "But when they get back from their honeymoon, I doubt they'll want to put up with us for long."

"We're going back to LA when they get back from their honeymoon, so they won't have to," Patrick stated.

Kelsey's lip curled slightly. "Oh, that's right."

"It's your audition." Patrick frowned. "Do you still want to do it?"

Kelsey blew out a long breath. She really wasn't sure anymore. If she got the role, the movie wouldn't start filming for another three months. And if that test on her bathroom sink was positive, she'd be showing by then. She'd always thought she would give up acting if she had kids—she and Patrick had even discussed it. After Zach, she wanted to be the one raising her child. She wasn't sure she liked the idea of a nanny doing it for her. Patrick said he would support her; whatever she decided, he just wanted her to be happy.

"I guess we'll have to see what the test says," she answered softly.

"I'm sure it's been two minutes." Patrick jumped off the bed and held his hand out to Kelsey.

She took it and slowly pulled herself up. "It probably has been." She led the way into the bathroom, keeping her pace smooth and moderate even though she wanted to rush in and pick up the test so she could throw it away before he saw it if it wasn't positive.

They reached the sink, and she picked up the test. She stared at the two blue lines of the test in her hand then looked at herself in the mirror. She gazed into her watery green eyes, brushed a stray lock of hair off her cheek, tucked it behind her ear, and inhaled deeply. Her husband's arm snaked around her shoulders, and she met his grinning gaze in the mirror. A smile slowly stretched her own lips.

Kelsey Lyons was pregnant.

Acknowledgments

There are some parts of this book that were beyond my scope of knowledge and I would like to thank Angie and Judy for your help in expanding my education. Thank you Book Lovers for your encouragement and support. Thank you Stephannie for always enthusiastically reading and being my touchstone. Thank you Michelle for beta reading for me and for the suggestions you offered. Many thanks to Heidi and Ellis, my BQB team, for working with me to make this story ready for publishing.

And, as always, thank you, reader, for buying this book. I hope you enjoyed reading it as much as I enjoyed writing it.